PERFECT ALIBIS

Also by Jane Wenham-Jones

RAISING THE ROOF

and published by Bantam Books

PERFECT ALIBIS

Jane Wenham-Jones

BANTAM BOOKS
LONDON · NEW YORK · TORONTO · SYDNEY · AUCKLAND

PERFECT ALIBIS
A BANTAM BOOK : 0 553 81373 0

First publication in Great Britain

PRINTING HISTORY
Bantam edition published 2003

1 3 5 7 9 10 8 6 4 2

Set in 11/13pt Sabon by
Kestrel Data, Exeter, Devon.

Bantam Books are published by Transworld Publishers,
61–63 Uxbridge Road, London W5 5SA,
a division of The Random House Group Ltd,
in Australia by Random House Australia (Pty) Ltd,
20 Alfred Street, Milsons Point, Sydney, NSW 2061, Australia,
in New Zealand by Random House New Zealand Ltd,
18 Poland Road, Glenfield, Auckland 10, New Zealand
and in South Africa by Random House (Pty)Ltd,
Endulini, 5a Jubilee Road, Parktown 2193, South Africa.

Printed and bound in Great Britain by
Cox & Wyman Ltd, Reading, Berkshire.

For Tim, with love and thanks

In the interests of lasting friendship and the Institute of Marriage, some who helped with this book must remain nameless! But, You-know-who-you-are, thank you xx. My lips are sealed.

Those I can laud publicly include Peter Brookesmith – an inspired four-hour phone-call – and the rest of my family for their love and support. Joanne King – early pearls of wisdom, my step-daughter Sara – a mine of info, Ann Munroe – that reflexology moment, Bill Harris – sage words and cyber support, Lynne Barrett-Lee – bracing emails and therapeutic lunches, Karen Hellier . . . ☺ – thanks, K! Everyone at Transworld of course, especially Sadie Mayne – editing as an endurance sport, and Francesca – always. And finally, with a big hug, my darling son Tom – for not taking a mallet to my computer . . .

Prologue

HOW TO feel happy, strong, uplifted, tingly, light, free and altogether bloody fantastic:

Drink champagne

Eat chocolate

And have three orgasms in the afternoon . . .

Patsy stepped from the shower, deliciously sensual, beads of water bouncing off skin still slippery with oil. She ran light fingers down her belly, wriggling pleasurably at the memory of the hands that had smoothed and massaged, teased and caressed. The set of muscular buttocks she'd admired pumping up and down in the dressing-table mirror, while she'd writhed beneath them.

Mmmmn!

This was sex at its best. The moments when doubts dissolved and she was invincible. She was high and exhilarated, so *fortunate* to have it all . . . Her body gleamed in the huge mirror. She struck a pose, hand on hip, back arched, pouting as she winked appreciatively. Not bad!

Body quite firm, tits still holding up, bottom not sagging. None of that disgusting cellulite stuff to be seen in vast quantities wobbling its way along the side of the pool at the health club. Her face was still damp with steam. Her hair curled in fetching tendrils around her post-orgasmic flush.

She preened. Not bad at all for thirty-eight.

She picked up one of the fluffy towels and wound it around her shoulders, savouring the feeling of elation that hummed beneath her skin. Never mind Prozac! What one needs, girls, is a bit of Afternoon Delight . . .

She rubbed the towel down the length of one smooth golden leg and grinned.

This one was a bit different. He had energy and vitality. He thrust her down onto the bed and he went at it for all he was worth. Bit of a change to feel a hard lean body on top (behind/to the side/any way she damn well wanted it!). The last time she'd had sex with Dave she'd run her hand across the soft layer of jelly over his stomach and she'd actually shuddered. Dave clambered on, grunted a bit and clambered off again. This one, well, this one . . .

Kicking the towel aside, she threw open the bathroom door, one hand cupping a thrusting breast, her thumb circling the already interested nipple in a way that she knew would give him an instant new hard-on.

'It's no good,' she called as she strode into the bedroom beyond. 'You're just going to have to shag me again!'

He was standing – still naked – at the other side of the bed. At the sound of her voice he swung round. She saw the startled panic cross his features.

For a moment they hung there frozen. Both staring stricken at the mobile in his hand. From which was emanating a series of strangled squawks. His wife? How had she found out he was here?

He put a frantic finger to his lips.

Bit late for that now.

Despite his height, there was suddenly something vulnerable and baby-like about his naked body hunched over the phone. His voice had a hoarse note that wasn't usually there. His mouth twitched as he spoke into the receiver.

'I don't know what you're talking about!'

She heard the roar as he jumped.

Christ! Dave!

Patsy clutched at her stomach. He flapped his free hand at her, signalling her not to speak. Goddammit she could barely breathe!

He sounded as if someone had hold of his balls (as soon they might well have). 'Of course your wife's not here. I've told you, you've got the wrong number! Calm down . . .'

She saw his fist clenching and unclenching. She stood, one hand to her mouth, heart thumping.

He was sounding desperate. 'I don't know who you are but I can assure you . . .'

The squawking had stopped. He looked from the phone in his hand back to her. 'He's coming round!'

They stared at each other. Then he dropped the mobile and she made a mad grab for the chocolate wrappers.

Her heart was hammering painfully; adrenalin roared around her body, making her fingertips tingle. She could hear her breath coming in pants as she scurried about the room gathering clothes and belongings.

Knickers! Where are they? 'My bra! What did you do with it?'

'You weren't wearing one.'

'I was!'

They dashed to and fro, fumbling in their panic, screeching recriminations at each other as they scrabbled for clothes, pulled at bed-sheets, swept up wine glasses and tissues.

'Why on earth did you speak?'

'How did I know you were on the phone? Oh Jesus where's *my* mobile?'

'Didn't you hear it ring?'

11

'Of course I didn't. I was in the shower. Shit, there's only one stocking here. Why did you answer it?'

'Why shouldn't I? It's my phone. I thought it was Robbie. He always withholds the number.'

'Robbie? Who the bloody hell's Robbie?'

'It's his house! He told me he'd warn me when he was coming back.'

'You stupid idiot! Where are my shoes?'

'*I'm* stupid? How the hell did your old man get my number? And how does he know where we are?'

'I have no idea!'

'But he's got the address. Couldn't keep your mouth shut.'

'It wasn't me!'

She'd got everything but her footwear in her arms now. He had on a T-shirt and socks. She didn't fancy him at all. 'You'd better get some clothes on,' she said.

He stood dithering in the middle of the room, his palms rubbing against each other. She saw the fear on his face as he howled: '*What are we going to do?*'

'I am going to get the hell out of here,' she snapped, 'and you'd better get downstairs and come up with something bloody good!'

'But how . . .?' he began plaintively. Ignoring him, Patsy carried her clothes into the bathroom and slammed the door.

She leant back against the blue tiles, her fingers barely able to turn her skirt the right way out. Shakily, she picked up her mobile phone and scrolled through for the right number, pressing the send button, holding her breath as she heard ringing at the other end. She felt a rush of relief as it was answered immediately. 'Get M! I need her. It's all gone wrong. I'm here and—'

Patsy threw back her head in frustration as she was interrupted. *What??* Her voice shot up several octaves:

'What do you mean? You know very well what I'm talking about! This is Patsy. Patsy King.'

Christ! These bloody trainees. In her panic she'd forgotten. She took a deep breath and started again, her voice icy.

'Mrs K here. Calling for assistance. Red Alert!'

Operation Caught-with-your-fucking-trousers-down.

At the other end of the phone there was a click and another, more familiar voice spoke quietly and calmly. 'Control. Where are you?'

Right in the shit.

She was breathing more evenly when she came back out. The bed had been straightened, the pillows piled back into the pattern they'd been in when she'd arrived this morning.

Patsy ran along the landing and down the wide stairs. She saw her shoes on the rug in the hall. He was fully dressed again, and pacing up and down. A ring on the doorbell made them both jump. He moved towards her, blocking her path and looking into her face in agitation. 'What are we going to say?'

She stepped past him and pulled fingers through her hair in the hall mirror. 'I'm off. You stay and tell him he's got it wrong.'

'Don't be ridiculous! I can't let him see me!' He grabbed her arm, looking into her face pleadingly.

But Patsy shook him off, shoved her feet into her shoes and swung her bag over her shoulder. The doorbell rang again.

'He heard. He knew it was you!' he said.

'Then tell him he's paranoid.'

The bell jangled one last time. As they heard the outer door open, they ran through the doorway into the dining room. Then someone was thumping loudly on the glass of the inner door.

13

'Let me in!'

Patsy darted across the room, and tugged at the french windows.

Jesus! 'They're locked. Quick!'

She could hear the terror in her own voice now as the beating on the door intensified. In a second he was at her side, twisting at the catch, pulling the door open and propelling her through. Behind them they heard the sharp cracking of fractured glass.

'Open up, you bastard!'

Patsy darted across the immaculate lawn, putting a hand up to check both earrings were still in place.

Keep him away from the back windows. Keep him talking. Her heart was hammering at full power again. She pushed the hair from her sticky forehead as she reached the summerhouse and crouched gratefully behind it. She imagined she could hear faint shouts coming from the house and shuddered as a vision of Dave's fist slamming into her lover's nose filled her head.

He was tall. But Dave was an elephant.

An angry one . . .

She thought about the gravel drive by the side of the house. To reach it she would have to break cover and run across the grass.

OK if Dave were still in the hall or one of the rooms at the front but if he were rampaging around the house searching for her and happened to look out of a window at the back . . .

The tall hedge behind her was too high for her to clamber over. She'd have to get out the front way onto the road. There was a bed of bushes and shrubs over to her left. Maybe she could use them to hide her as she made her way around the side of the house towards the driveway. Cautiously she peered round the little wooden building.

The house looked peaceful and mellow in the afternoon sunshine. There was nobody visible at any of the windows.

Taking a deep breath Patsy ran full-tilt across the grass to the side fence. Dropping to the ground, breathing hard, she crawled behind a lavender bush and eased herself along on her stomach feeling like someone from a Territorial Army poster. God, she was going to be filthy. The bushes here were taller, so she was able to get first onto her hands and knees and then into crouching position to scuttle her way uncomfortably along the hedge towards the drive. Only a couple of small windows here. She held her breath and ducked beneath them. All was quiet.

At last she reached the end of the flowerbed. Just a small ornamental wall to climb over, a couple of yards of gravel to cross and she'd be out of sight. But she had to cross in front of the big kitchen window first.

She squinted through the rhododendrons and jumped.

There was a figure at the curtains.

Patsy shrank back against the hedge and curled into a ball, eyes tightly shut. Had Dave murdered him? (Terrible waste of a marvellous shag but would at least save all that messy business of endings.)

Her scrambled brain couldn't be sure. Perhaps it was panic that had made it look like her husband. Hadn't the figure been taller than that?

Or had *he* found untapped strength and fortitude and done away with Dave? (Convenient from a sexual freedom, inheritance and paying out of life policies point of view but there were the children to think of . . .)

But then surely he'd be out here to see where she was?

She raised her head a fraction of an inch and opened one eye. Heart thumping, she peered through the leaves once more. No-one there. No sign of movement at either of the windows. What the hell *was* going on in there?

She'd have to move now, while she still had the chance.

Patsy took a last look and leapt to her feet. Taking a deep breath, she bounded across the grass, hitched up her skirt and straddled the wall. There was a sharp crunch as her foot hit the gravel and her heel snapped off.

Shit! She did a mad hop-dash down the drive, mercifully hidden now by trees, and tugged open the small side gate, gasping as she reached the grass verge beyond.

Come on! Come on! Her eyes flitted anxiously back to the gates as she brushed earth and mud and twig from her once-lemon T-shirt.

Dave could come tearing out here any minute.

She looked at the stockings hanging in ribbons around her blackened knees as a white BMW drew up beside her. The rear door opened.

The girl driving was new. She nodded as Patsy scrambled into the back. 'OK?'

'Just drive!'

Patsy flung herself down on the back seat as the car pulled away.

The girl spoke over her shoulder: 'I can pull up once we're well away. Start getting your things off.'

The girl's hand came back over the seat, dropping a new pale lemon T-shirt and matching shoes onto the floor of the car.

'Careful!' Patsy jerked her head to avoid being struck by a heel identical to the one she'd just broken.

A packet of stockings landed next to the shoes.

'There's some wet wipes down there too.'

Patsy tugged at her T-shirt, trying to pull it over her head. Not the easiest exercise in the world when trying to lie flat and keep one's head below the window.

The girl was still talking. 'There's two bags of shopping on the floor and an *Evening Standard*. Weather in London's been much the same as here – not cold but grey, overcast.' Her voice was a bored drone: 'The train to Edenhurst left Victoria at 4.17 p.m. You had to stand

16

until Bridgewater South. Ticket cost £9.40 for a cheap day return. We've put it on his card.'

Patsy was scrubbing at her knees. She turned onto her back, lifting a leg into the air to wriggle the fresh stockings into place. 'I'm going to have to sit up in a minute . . .' She pulled her skirt up round her waist, fumbling with the suspenders.

'We're nearly there.' The girl swung the steering wheel as Patsy rose to see the rows of parked cars outside the entrance to Chartwell station. Five minutes down the line from Edenhurst.

As she got out, the girl handed her a carrier bag from Peter Jones and another from Selfridge's. 'DKNY T-shirt, earrings and a scarf and that moisturizer you wanted. And here's your ticket.'

She looked at Patsy critically. 'I should do something with your hair and make-up before you get off.'

Patsy took the bags. 'Yes! Thank you,' she said sharply. 'Tell M I'll call her.'

'Sure!'

The girl got back behind the wheel, started the engine and raised a desultory hand in a wave.

Patsy shook her head. *And when I do, I'll have a word about staff attitudes.*

She walked onto the platform a moment before the train came in, getting into the first carriage that stopped opposite her. She sank into a corner with her shopping, then got out her mirror and stared at her glassy eyes. She looked like a disaster victim. A blanket round her shoulders and she could be an extra on *Casualty*.

There was still a dark mark on her skirt the wet wipes wouldn't shift. Still, trains were filthy places. She pulled a tube of foundation and a comb from her bag. Where was Dave now?

Or were they both dead? She could see it all. Dave

crouched panting over him, viewing the bloody mess of gristle and pulp that was once such a photogenic face while he in a last-ditch heroic struggle, lifted his right hand (in which he was holding the Sabatier carving knife he had grabbed from the work surface when Dave, hand on the other's collar, was pounding his head up and down on the continental tiles) and plunged the blade into Dave's heart . . .

Two funerals, but the distinct possibility that she could come out of the whole thing unscathed – especially if she created a story for the tabloids around a passionate disagreement over a drunken gambling debt. Double sympathy from the community at large – a widow and ex-victim of compulsive addiction.

But as she blended in her make-up with a long, manicured finger, she grimaced at the thought of the least palatable scenario: Her husband forcing the truth from him, throwing her out on some paltry amount of maintenance and the *Daily Detail* writing her up as an incurable old slapper, dredging up her past indiscretions and getting them to give points out of ten for the quality of her blow-jobs . . .

As the train drew in to Edenhurst station, Patsy stood up and moved towards the door, giving her appearance a final check in the window. Her blond hair was back in place, her lipstick freshly applied.

Dave was on the platform, looking breathless and rather red. He rushed up to her, one meaty hand taking her arm, eyes searching her face.

She leant forward and kissed his sweaty cheek. 'Darling! How thoughtful of you to meet me!'

He stopped, chest heaving, as she smiled at him.

She looked at him in concern. 'Are you all right?'

He seemed to be having some sort of emotional struggle. His lips opened and shut as he grasped her elbow again.

'Good day?' he asked at last.

'Oh, you know! Apart from the crowds and the dreadful people.'

She shook her head at the injustices of department store shopping, deftly disentangling her arm and filling his with carrier bags. Taking a surreptitious look at his knuckles as she did so.

'I do hope you haven't parked too far away,' she said over her shoulder as she headed purposefully towards the ticket collector. 'My feet are killing me.'

She looked sideways to check her reflection again in the window of the buffet bar, and gave a tinkling laugh. 'Goodness! I look like I've been dragged through a hedge!'

Chapter 1

Loss of libido is a common problem affecting women of all ages. It may simply be that the two of you have got into a rut and lovemaking has become stale or routine. Work together with your husband to bring the excitement back into your marriage. Set aside time for just the two of you, dress up in sexy underwear, watch an erotic film together, try having sex in a different place, at an unusual time or in a new position . . .

Stephanie slapped down the magazine and moved towards the vegetable rack. What these articles never told you was what to do if you just didn't fancy him any more. What to do if even after three viewings of *Emmanuelle*, when you found yourself squashed into the cupboard under the stairs at five in the afternoon with your legs wrapped round your neck, you still just thought: yuck!

'It's not that I don't feel like it sometimes,' she'd explained to her friend Millie. 'After *Nine and a Half Weeks* was on TV I didn't know what to do with myself. I kept having dreams about Mickey Rourke and waking up all sweaty . . . But I still didn't want to make love with George.'

'Supplements!' Millie had said.

Stephanie selected some potatoes, looking ruefully at the dresser, where a small basket already bulged with pots.

Oil of Evening Primrose stops PMT (in theory).

Selenium ditto.

Ginkgo Biloba improves memory (not always to be recommended), helps reduce cellulite (not seen much evidence yet).

Korean Ginseng (to perk her up).

Resta-Nerve (to calm her down).

St John's Wort (to stop her being a miserable cow).

She crossed to the bin, tossed in a potato that had turned a luminous and no doubt cancer-inducing green, and turned another in her hands, looking it critically in the eyes.

Calcium (so her bones wouldn't crumble).

Multi-vitamins (as general precaution).

Millie had not been deterred. 'Have you tried zinc?'

Zinc!

Millie said she'd gone off it after she'd had Ben and couldn't bear Patrick anywhere near her. Then she'd gone to a homeopath, started taking zinc and wham! Back to normal. She'd said they'd done it four times in one day when they went to Barbados.

Stephanie shuddered.

Millie had tried to be helpful.

'What about a drink first?'

'I just can't. Even with a few drinks.'

Even in fact with a lot of drinks. Even after George had brought home champagne to celebrate his company's latest take-over and she'd drunk the best part of a bottle and a half. And he'd got out the massage oil. Even then . . .

'I end up being sick,' she'd said.

*   *   *

The difference, thought Stephanie now, poking about among the greens, picturing Millie's high cheekbones and wide sensuous mouth, was that Millie was still sexual. She filled the sink, hearing her friend's laughter. Saw her tossing back her glossy hair. She could hear her now: 'Of course I am – thirty-six – I'm at my peak!'

But Millie had always been bursting with it.

On her wedding day, Millie had looked like a gypsy queen, all long dark hair, red lips, nipped-in waist and swelling cleavage. She had stared into Patrick's eyes as if she wanted to eat him. (In Stephanie's bridal pics, she looked as if she needed a lie-down.)

Millie still arrived here some mornings, flushed and glowing. Millie still pushed her breasts out when she entered a room. Millie giggled and made jokes, passed comments laced with innuendo. Millie still liked sex.

Stephanie plunged her hands into the cold water. She herself felt like a withered old prune in that department. *Or she had done.* Not only did the bits no longer work, they curled up in horror and hid under the covers (or would do if that wasn't precisely where the danger lurked.) Until today.

She pulled back outer leaves, sliced through stalks, pausing to look up through her kitchen window at a tiny white plane against the square of bright blue sky. She thought about the passengers undoing their seatbelts, waiting for the drinks to come round, settling with their in-flight magazines, and felt an odd little ripple down the back of her neck.

Coconut oil on warm skin, cold wine on hot terraces, a vibrant splash of bougainvillaea down a white wall . . . She suddenly wanted to be feeling excited, expectant, going somewhere, anywhere.

Did any of those people up there wish that they were safely back in their kitchens doing the sprouts?

Kelly whined outside the back door, scratching at the

wood. Stephanie looked at the clock. Another day gone. In which she'd done nothing but make beds and scrub toilets and arrange flowers and peel sodding potatoes. And pour coffee for—

The ripple shot all over her.

What was it about past loves? Why did exes still have that power to grab you by the solar plexus and bring up feelings that should have been dead and buried long ago?

There should be an operation on the National Health. Attachment amputation. Separation anxiety bypass. So when it's over, it's over. You could see them in the street, trill: *Hi-how-are-you? Fine? Oh Good-that-is-good*, and feel rather less than you did when talking to the milkman (unless it was that relief milkman that came just for the fortnight last Christmas. Mum.)

Stephanie thought she had got to that. Thought she'd dealt with it all.

Obviously not.

'You want to get a life,' she told her rubber gloves.

She pulled the plug from the sink and let the water swirl away. 'You need,' she said to the gritty remains, 'to get a job!'

This had been the master plan when Madeleine and Ken came to dinner. George wanted to invite them. Ken bought all the insurance policies for his car dealership through George's company and George could still thrash him at squash.

Stephanie had said 'What a good idea!' not because she particularly wanted to spend all afternoon with a slab of mad cow oozing blood over her kitchen or take hours over a homemade tiramisu but because Madeleine was a business hot-shot who ran a secretarial agency cum virtual office set-up and even George – who never showed much enthusiasm for any of Stephanie's friends or things female in general – thought she was marvellous.

If Madeleine got her a job, George might stop his discouraging noises. So Stephanie had cooked her heart out and listened to the three of them comparing computer systems she'd never heard of and waited her chance. But when the cue came, George was monopolizing their guest.

'How's business then?' he asked as he poured wine.

'Oh!' Madeleine threw back her head and laughed. Rolled her eyes in mock despair. 'Fine! If I could just get the bloody staff.' She had a low, slightly raspy voice.

George laughed too. 'What a recommendation!' he joked. 'Thought you were a recruitment company.'

Madeleine considered her long, red nails. 'Oh, we're mainly virtual office services these days,' she said. 'That's where the growth is. Companies who can't afford the big office space and the full-time telephonist use us. Or set-ups where a lot of employees work from home. It's very simple – their customers phone a number and we answer in the company name. Then we find out who they want to speak to and transfer that call to wherever the employee is – whether at home, on their mobile or on voice mail.' Madeleine smiled. 'The caller is none the wiser – thinks he's speaking to company headquarters somewhere.'

'Very clever.' George was admiring. Stephanie heard him ask Madeleine about her telephone systems as she brought in the beef.

'Oh look at that!' said Ken, as she placed the platter on the table. 'And what are you up to these days?' he enquired kindly as she sat, positioning the dish of mange-tout in front of him.

Stephanie made herself say it. 'I'm looking for a job.' (I am, George, I am!) But George was helping Madeleine to new potatoes. Only Ken was looking at her. In the early days George and Stephanie used to play the What-do-they-see-in-each-other? game when they met other couples. Sometimes the woman would be the mystery;

sometimes he was. Madeleine was easy – any man would be attracted to her tall, cool sophistication. But Ken always reminded Stephanie of a pig – short and squat with a snout and big fleshy lips. A kind and amiable pig. He smiled at Stephanie. 'What sort of thing are you after?'

She started to explain how graphic design had moved on without her, and anyway there wouldn't be those sort of openings around here and then she took a deep breath and looked straight at Madeleine and said: 'I don't mind what I do. I thought I might take anything that's going, to start with. A job in an office, maybe.'

George made a fuss of moving dishes, picking up Madeleine's wine glass, reaching for the bottle to top it up. Over the top of his arm Madeleine nodded and smiled.

She didn't say: Oh you must give me a call – I'll fix you up! She didn't say anything. She just nodded.

'This looks wonderful,' said Ken, helping himself to another slice of soft red meat.

'Mmmn, marvellous,' murmured Madeleine and the moment was lost.

Suddenly they were all talking about the bar refurbishment at the squash club and what should be done to get funds in and George was pouring more wine and Stephanie sat quite still and swallowed hard. (So hard in fact that two mangetout went down whole, causing Ken to leap to his feet and slap her vigorously on the back. She managed to start breathing again just before he moved in for the full Heimlich manoeuvre but George, staring across the table into her scarlet face, frowned as if she were deliberately making an exhibition of herself.)

Millie wouldn't have let it happen. Millie would have held Madeleine's eyes and said: Got anything good on your books? Filing? Office girl? I make a mean cup of coffee. Millie would have joked and sparkled. Made them

26

laugh till all three were falling over themselves to employ her.

Kelly whined more loudly, thumping her body against the wood of the door. Stephanie dried her hands and opened it.

'You smell revolting,' she said as the dog slunk in.

She tipped the vegetables into a saucepan and banged the lid on. Kelly wagged her tail.

'And you shit all over the garden.' She crashed the pan down onto the ceramic hob. 'And who's the only one who ever picks it up?' Stephanie asked. 'Tell me that!'

She could phone Madeleine, of course. Make one simple phone call. There was time before Millie got here with the kids. She got the red leather address book from the drawer in the hall and looked through for the right number.

She'd be chatty and casual. *Hi, Madeleine! You know I was talking about getting back to work? – That's right, just before I nearly choked to death – well I just wondered if you* . . . But as her hand hovered above the receiver the phone rang, making her jump.

The bloke at the garage was not content with explaining what *had* been causing the car to refuse to start one morning in three and let her down between the traffic lights. He gave a full run-down of all the causes they'd eliminated, parts checked, theories discussed and tests undertaken before informing her that they'd narrowed it down to a double-widget-with-expanding-valve-and-two-way-gauge which was the only bit they didn't keep in stock but he'd get one in tomorrow.

George would have cut straight through this monologue, elicited the delivery time and put the phone down but Stephanie listened and murmured as if she was interested and looked at the clock and wondered if she could really summon up the wherewithal to phone

Madeleine. By the time she had managed to get the receiver back in place, the doorbell rang.

Charlotte and Toby filed past her into the hall with sighs and grunts, dropping lunchboxes and folders as they went. Millie hovered on the doorstep. Stephanie squeezed her arm. 'Thanks so much. Aren't you coming in?' she asked.

'Can't. Got loads to do and I've left Ben in the car.' She was bright and excited. 'But I'll see you later. You *are* coming tonight?'

'Oh, I don't know.'

'Oh Steph, you must. It's just what you need. And Amanda really needs *us*. That bastard Stuart's being as tight as anything since he buggered off with the hairdresser. She's got to make a few bob somehow. Don't know how many she's got coming,' Millie went on, 'but it's always better with a crowd. I asked Jacqui and Sue of course but they can't. Do you know anybody else who'd like to come? You can invite who you like – the more the merrier.'

Charlotte and Toby seemed to have grown again in the eight hours they'd been away. The ceilings shook with the clumping of their great feet. Stephanie looked at the hallway, strewn with shoes and bags and blazers dropped in heaps. Charlotte came back down the stairs and strode past her to the kitchen. At just twelve she was already taller than Stephanie and had her father's dismissive air.

Stephanie followed her. 'I want you to go and clear up after that dog.'

'Ugh, gross.' Her daughter had the fridge open and was pulling out packets and jars, looking at labels and shoving them back in disgust.

'You wanted her. You said you'd look after her.'

'Yeah.' She shut the door and carried the cheese across to the chopping board, pulled open the bread bin and took out a loaf.

'I'm sick of doing everything.'

Charlotte frowned in concentration as she sawed away with the bread knife. 'Where's the piccalilli?'

'I mean it. I'm going to give her away if you don't start pulling your weight.'

'Yeah, right. Like Dad would let you.'

Charlotte – *coup de grâce* successfully delivered – pressed one huge slice on another. 'Come on Kelly. Come with me,' she ordered.

The dog appeared immediately and slavered.

'Not upstairs.'

'Don't keep on, Mum.'

'PAs'

The girl on the other end of the phone had a low, cool voice that immediately made Stephanie stumble. 'Oh, um, Madeleine. Could I talk to Madeleine, please?'

'Who's speaking?'

Toby appeared in front of her with his shirt hanging out. He waved a chocolate miniroll enquiringly under her nose.

'I've had three. Can I have another one?' he intoned in a stage whisper.

Stephanie waved him away as a new voice sounded in her ear. Toby brought his face closer to hers.

'Can I?' he asked urgently, warm chocolatey breath fanning her cheek. She turned her face into the receiver.

'Hello?'

Toby took another one and wandered off.

'Oh Madeleine, it's Stephanie. Yes thank you, I am. And you? Oh that's good. The thing is, Madeleine I was just thinking, I mean I just wondered' – *spit it out for goodness sake* – 'Madeleine!' It came out in a rush. 'Would you like to come to a party?'

*   *   *

29

Stephanie picked up Toby's shoes. Hopeless! Stephanie Walters – Specialized Subject: Communication Skills. She'd failed as dismally as she had on Saturday. Four hours, three courses, half a bottle of port and two layers of chocolate mints and she hadn't managed to get a simple question out.

Toby's bedroom door was half closed, his school uniform scrunched between it and the doorpost. She could hear the high-pitched explosions of a computer game.

Stephanie knocked and pushed the door wide open.

Toby was leaning forward, his eyes only inches from the monitor screen, his fist clenching the joystick.

'Yes!' He let out a hiss of satisfaction.

She waited till the game concluded in a violent limb-ripping crescendo and he fell back into post-battle slump.

'Good day at school?'

'All right.'

Why on earth did she bother? All Charlotte could ever say was: Don't keep on, Mum! Toby's entire repertoire extended to 'All right.'

Children! I cannot stop thinking about a man I used to know . . .

Don't keep on, Mum!

Today I saw him again. He came into our kitchen and drank from one of our mugs and showed more interest in me in a single half-hour than any of you have done for years.

All right.

I kept watching those hands that had once so moved me. As he talked, they turned and shaped, showed me how things could be.

Mum – don't keep on.

All right.

'Toby, could you hang your uniform up?'

'In a minute.' He was already clicking the box for a new game.

'Now, please, Toby!' *Before I scream.*

'All *right*!'

She supposed she should be grateful for small mercies. Pleased that they bothered to speak at all. George often didn't.

'George!' *Your wife here. Remember that one you promised to love and honour?*

George. Tall, dark-suited, still attractive in a greying sort of way. Uncreased as ever, cuffs as immaculately white as they'd always been, he dropped his briefcase into the usual corner of the hall. They came together in the doorway of the sitting-room.

'Mmmn! Who's a beautiful girl then? Who's gorgeous? What have you been doing today my darling? Have you missed me?'

Kelly put both paws on his chest, tongue lolling. Stephanie wrinkled her nose as the unmistakable odour of hot dog (sadly not the sort that came with onions and American-style mustard) rose in her nostrils.

She positioned herself in front of her husband.

'Have you had a good day?'

George rubbed vigorously at the sides of Kelly's neck. Globules of saliva formed at her open jaws, dripping copiously to the carpet. Her tail thwacked back and forth against the end of the pale sofa.

Stephanie looked at the long dark hairs with distaste. 'Dinner's ready. Don't forget I'm going out tonight.'

George looked up in surprise. 'Really? Where?'

'I told you. A friend of Millie's is having an accessories party. Earrings and things, I think.'

'Sounds scintillating.' He grinned at her.

'Just a bit of fun. Millie wants us to support Amanda. Her husband's moved out.'

'You'll come back reeking of fags again.'

And I've invited Madeleine along. I am going to speak

31

to her at last. And go about changing my life. 'Talking of which, that dog smells.'

'I'll bath her with the children at the weekend.' George fondled the top of the dog's head. 'Poor Kelly.'

Madeleine put an exasperated hand to her forehead.

'Come on, Samantha! You're traumatized! Your husband's disappeared. Your mother's on a ventilator. Your sixteen-year-old daughter's pregnant. Your son's in a remand home. You're *upset*, for God's sake . . .'

The girl pouted.

'Let's try it again.' Madeleine snapped her fingers. 'From the top.'

She picked up the phone in front of her and assumed a deep voice: 'Can I speak to Doreen, please?'

Samantha fiddled with her headphones. 'Oh yes! Um. Hold on a minute. I'm not sure where she is . . .' She stopped and sniffed.

Madeleine rolled her eyes. 'For God's sake.'

Samantha looked pained. 'What?'

'What are your hands doing?'

The girl looked at her pink pearly nails.

'Exactly!' Madeleine got up and began walking about the room. 'They should be on the keyboard already,' she rapped out impatiently. 'Calling up Doreen's details, finding her contact number . . .' She stopped and looked pointedly at Samantha. 'While you keep talking.'

Madeleine sat down in a chair in front of the bank of monitors and put a set of headphones on.

'Doreen?' she said vaguely. 'Oh yes. She's been so good . . .' A little sob caught in her throat. 'I don't know what I'd have done without her.' She paused, gulped and composed herself. 'I think she's in the bathroom.' She took the headphones off and banged them down in front of the row of gleaming switches. 'Then you put him on hold! Yes?' She looked up as Jo's dark head poked around the door.

'Mrs K's here.'

Madeleine shut her office door and drew deeply on the butt of her cigarette.

'Absolutely useless. I thought she'd been to RADA!'

She opened a cupboard and pulled out a bottle, tipping it invitingly in Patsy's direction.

Patsy, lying back in one of the big leather chairs, shook her head. 'It was something like that. Monica said it cost a fortune anyway.'

'Well they didn't teach her anything. She hasn't got a clue.'

'She'll pick it up.'

'She'd better,' said Madeleine grimly. 'I know she's Monica's god-daughter . . .'

'Fifteen per cent of the turnover.'

'But it isn't enough. She's wet.'

'She's led a sheltered life. That's why Monica's educating her. At least she'll keep her mouth shut. Anyway,' Patsy pulled a face, 'the others are no great shakes! The one who drove me . . .'

Madeleine looked irritated. '*Her* shift had finished. She needn't have come at all.' She tipped a capful of whisky into her own cup. 'I'm the one who has the headaches with recruitment. Apart from Miss Hopeless out there, I don't see you here helping to vet people.'

'I'm a sleeping partner.'

'Sleeping *around* partner. You're more of a liability than the damn clients.'

She sat down as Patsy got up and walked over to pluck a cigarette from Madeleine's open packet. 'All right, all right!'

Madeleine held out the lighter. 'Thought you'd given up.'

'I have.'

Patsy perched on the edge of the desk, pausing to admire the sheer perfection of her stockinged legs as she inhaled.

'It wasn't my fault,' she said plaintively. 'How was I supposed to know Dave would go rooting through my things! Bloody man's got such a suspicious mind.' She blew the smoke out on a long sigh.

Madeleine raised her eyebrows. 'I don't believe you sometimes,' she said. 'What on earth were you doing keeping the bit of paper anyway?'

Patsy shrugged. 'I didn't mean to. He gave me his number and this address for me to meet him at. I'd written it down with his name and "Wednesday" on it. Then he called the next morning and said he'd pick me up at the station. So his number was in my phone and I just forgot about the note.'

'Where was it?'

'Don't know. In one of my handbags, I suppose.'

Madeleine looked at her. 'You're hopeless. I spend all day saying don't keep anything written down anywhere and what do you do? What did you tell Dave?'

'Just said I'd written it down for you. Somebody wanting a secretary.'

'Well if he's been in your bag, he obviously thinks you're at it again so you'd better be careful.'

Patsy waved a hand dismissively. 'He's got no idea, really. He's just being funny because of the Club drinks thing. He says I was groping the barman!' Her shiny plum lips curled in indignation. 'Can you imagine?'

'You've almost convinced yourself. I was there, remember.'

'I was just messing around. And Dave can talk! He had his hands all over that tarty little builder's wife.'

'He'll see that as quite irrelevant,' Madeleine said calmly as Patsy's voice began to rise. 'Forget it now. Crisis averted. Just learn from it this time.' Madeleine

34

pressed the intercom. 'Jo! Tell Samantha to go home and make sure she's in on the dot of eight tomorrow. Then bring us some more coffee.'

She turned back to Patsy. 'Fancy a night out? Something new to play with? Stephanie's got a friend who's got a friend – some lame duck by the sound of it – having a girls' party. She says it's lingerie and accessories. You know what she's like – probably thinks toys are something you buy for the kids.'

Patsy pulled a small gold mirror from her handbag and stared into it. 'I look dreadful!'

'She wants me to go along. I said I'd ask you too.'

'Can't. I've got to go home and shag Dave.' Patsy yawned. 'He needs settling down. Don't want him cutting up my cards again.'

Madeleine picked up the phone and began to dial. She shook her head as Patsy put on her jacket.

'You'd better watch your back. This time you're really pushing it.'

Patsy laughed. 'That's what you always say!'

Stephanie heard the cab hoot as she stood in the doorway. George was on one sofa, Kelly at his feet. Charlotte lay the full length of the other. Toby sat cross-legged on the floor about three feet from the television, his ears stuck out in silhouette against the glare of the screen.

'Bye, then!'

'See you.' George looked up briefly and waved a hand.

Anne Robinson filled the screen in full magnificent Armani as a small middle-aged man shrivelled on his podium. Both childen appeared engrossed. Stephanie blew them kisses. Neither moved.

'Good night then,' she called from the hall as she opened the front door.

'You are the Weakest Link,' Charlotte called back gaily as she closed it. 'Goodbye!'

Chapter 2

Millie had a glass of wine in one hand and a huge black penis in the other. She grinned as Stephanie followed Amanda into the room.

'All right, Steph?'

Stephanie looked at the plastic veins and tuft of synthetic pubic hair and decided she probably wasn't.

She cringed as Millie, ignoring her blushes, switched it on, holding it to the tip of her nose like a connoisseur. 'Ooh dear! Not nearly enough buzz for me!'

The others burst into raucous laughter. Stephanie took a larger swallow than she had intended of the wine Amanda had pressed into her hand.

Millie was waving the thing in the air. 'You're gonna have to get some better batteries in here if you want to make a sale, Amanda,' she said.

Amanda was thinner, her hair bleached almost white, her dark-berry lips making her face appear even paler. Stephanie had tried to be sympathetic at the front door but had shrunk from the expression on the other woman's face.

'Better off without him,' Amanda had replied coldly and Stephanie had said no more. Now she watched Amanda toss a small white cylinder across the arm of the sofa.

'Here, try this one. Handbag size, carry it with you in case of emergency.'

Millie shrieked. 'Already do. Ever-ready that's me!'

The short fat girl on the rug gave an appreciative cackle. 'Got your own charger yet, Mills?' she asked.

They all laughed again. Stephanie sank into a chair in the corner. Oh God! She'd invited Madeleine to this. She wondered how soon they could decently be able to leave and go home.

She wondered why George was always right.

Stephanie looked around the room at the coffee table piled high with God-knows-what and the assortment of women who were watching Millie appreciatively. Millie enjoyed being the centre of attention. She looked relaxed in her Calvin Klein jeans and tight, tight top. She had her cleavage on show whatever the season.

Now she had discarded her shoes and was wriggling her red-painted toenails in amusement as Amanda held up what looked like two huge marbles on a piece of cord. 'Well, I'll give anything a try once, Amanda. But I've heard they clank together when you walk.'

The fat girl was scarlet with mirth. 'I'd be worried about getting them out again. Enough to make your eyes water just thinking about it.'

It was making Stephanie light-headed. Gulping her wine, she turned her face away as Amanda prepared to elaborate on a peculiar-looking contraption that had already quite put Stephanie off her peanuts.

There was only one other woman who looked equally uncomfortable. She was sitting in the opposite corner, wearing a navy skirt, her eyes downcast, her straight hair flopping lankly across her forehead. She looked up straight-faced and Stephanie smiled at her. The woman looked down again.

'Well, I'm not sure which bit goes in where,' Amanda

was saying, 'but it does say you're promised a completely unique experience.'

Millie held up an even bigger vibrator. 'Hey – this is more like it! Can I take this one for a test-drive?' She held the thing out in front of her and blew it a kiss. 'Won't fall asleep, won't fart . . .'

They all laughed and the woman on the sofa next to her nudged at her encouragingly: 'Always makes sure you come first!'

'If you want to try anything on,' said Amanda as a couple of girls started to rummage through the rack of silky garments in front of the fireplace.

'I fancy this!' The fat girl held a transparent négligé up against her. 'Think my Kevin will, too. Anyone else coming?'

A redhead followed her across the room with an armful of black lace. 'Nice rubber corset there, Millie!'

Millie grinned. 'Later. Come on, Amanda, talk us through the rest of the toys.'

Amanda reached into a box next to her and pulled out something huge and pink and rubbery. Stephanie jumped up gratefully as the doorbell rang. She looked from one to the other of them. 'Shall I?'

Millie, stuffing a handful of tortilla chips into her mouth, nodded.

Stephanie opened the front door to find Madeleine immaculate in a black suit. She kissed Stephanie on both cheeks. Stephanie put a hand on her arm. 'Madeleine! It's not quite what I thought . . .'

Madeleine shrugged. 'It's been a crap day at the office, Ken's away. Don't much care what it is as long as I get a drink.'

Stephanie smiled. 'Oh there's plenty of that.'

She led Madeleine to the kitchen. 'No Patsy, then?'

'Had a bit of a tiff with Dave – thought she'd better stay in and smooth things over.'

Amanda came in and picked up a bottle. Stephanie moved forward and introduced them.

'Hi! Come through,' Amanda said.

Back in the living room, Millie was perched on the arm of the sofa like a pixie.

'This is my friend—'

Millie looked up smiling. 'Oh!'

Stephanie, seeing the recognition cross her face, looked back at Madeleine, but Madeleine was holding out her hand again.

'Pleased to meet you.'

Stephanie looked from one to the other. 'Have you . . . ?'

'No! I just thought – ' Millie poured out a drink and handed it to Madeleine, laughing – 'I thought for a minute you were somebody else.'

Madeleine nodded, settling herself in a chair. 'What have we got here, then?'

Millie picked up a scarlet bustier and held it against herself, sticking out hip and lips. She looked at Stephanie.

'Very nice,' Stephanie said faintly, frowning at her.

Millie picked up a handful of red satin. 'Look at the bottoms!' She held them up for the room to see, stretching the elastic between two painted nails, her thumbs reaching down to demonstrate the split crotch to a chorus of shrieks and giggles. 'Go on!' she said. 'Give George a treat!'

Stephanie felt her face slowly heat to the same colour as the lingerie.

Millie winked at her. 'I think I'll have these myself, then.' She lifted her forearm in an imitation of building-site lust. 'Yeaaahhhh!'

'I wish you wouldn't do that to me,' Stephanie hissed when they met in the kitchen for refills. 'You know I can't do it any more.'

'I was only joking.'

'You just don't understand what a problem it is.'

Millie poured herself another drink and smiled understandingly. 'We all feel like that sometimes.'

Stephanie held out her own glass even though she knew she'd regret it in the morning. 'I've gone off it altogether,' she said.

'No you haven't. You've just got out of the habit. When did you last have an orgasm?'

Stephanie looked at her blankly.

'There you go!' Millie said triumphantly. 'I read it in a magazine. If your body keeps getting aroused but left unfulfilled it gradually shuts down and you think you don't like sex.'

'But it hasn't kept getting aroused. It hasn't been aroused for years.' *Liar! What about in the kitchen today? He* hadn't had to do anything at all. He'd just looked her up and down and she'd felt it at once. That warmth, that jolt, that *thrill* . . .

Millie was looking at her quizzically. 'Perhaps it's your hormones.'

Stephanie groaned. 'You sound like George. Any excuse not to take me seriously.'

'I am taking you seriously. I know just what you need. Let's go and have another look at those vibrators.'

'No!'

'Come on, Steph! Live dangerously. I can kit you out.'

'Ugh no!'

'There are loads of different colours. How about a really small one?'

'I just couldn't.'

'You don't know until you try.'

Millie was performing again. She held up a black lace bra and demonstrated its missing bits. 'I can just see me in this, well, out of it . . .'

'We'll all be up for it tonight!' one of the girls joked, holding up a pair of black and red suspenders. Stephanie examined the bowl of cheese puffs. She couldn't remember the last time she'd been 'up for' anything with George.

It seemed a normal part of all of their lives.

'My Kevin will go barmy when he sees what I've got.'

'We never even got upstairs last time – it was right up against the dishwasher . . .'

'Too right we have a bolt on the bedroom door. Andy likes his Sunday morning session – don't want the kids wandering in just when I've tied him up . . .'

Stephanie looked around her. Why should she be the odd bod? Most of these women were of a similar age, with children and years of marriage under their belts. Yet they were giggling over the underwear they were planning to take home. They still had something she'd lost.

Presumably when their husbands reached out for them in bed tonight, they reached back. Grew warm and aroused like she used to.

I did, didn't I? She could hardly remember. She could recall George coming to the flat all those years ago and her looking at him – so tall and attractive and confident – and thinking: how will he want me? She'd longed to make him hers then. Had willed him to stay the night, had sat at her desk all the next morning, watching the phone till he rang. She had felt fortunate, lucky, blessed that he had chosen her. Craved to be in those same arms she now avoided.

Why did she? What had happened to George, her hero and protector? Fixer of problems, bringer of order to her chaos. Once everything had been so right. When she lay in his arms she was safe and sure. Once upon a time. Until . . .

Today when *he* was in her kitchen that was the feeling

that had startled her. She had desperately wanted him to put his arms around her. She wanted . . .

A burst of laughter brought her abruptly back to the present. She'd missed the last thing Millie said but everyone was giggling again. Except the serious woman in the corner who suddenly spoke, making everyone's heads swing round in surprise: She looked directly at Millie. 'Well, I'm sure your husband will be pleased.'

Millie affected a prim expression. 'It's even more important to make an effort when you've got a husband – ' She held the bra over her own top, smoothing the fabric against her breasts and poking two jiggling fingers through the peep-holes. She grinned. ' – otherwise he's all you'll ever have.'

The room erupted into fresh shrieks. Only the woman did not laugh. She picked up her handbag and left the room, speaking over her shoulder as she went. 'You should be ashamed.'

The room fell silent as they heard the front door open and shut.

Millie dropped the bra, took a swig from her glass, opened her cigarette packet, flicked at her gold lighter without looking up. She held out the packet to Amanda. 'What's her problem?'

'Margaret? Her husband's left her. Gone off with someone else.'

'Don't blame him.'

'You're awful!' Stephanie said to Millie when everyone was talking again.

'I'm honest.'

'Poor thing – she must feel dreadful.'

'She's dreary. Draggy Maggie! She wants to get a bit of lipstick on, get that grey out of her hair, liven up a bit. Course he's going to screw his secretary, looking at that every night.' Millie tossed back her own freshly blackened hair and pursed her glossy lips. Next to her, Madeleine gave a smile. 'She's always been a misery,' Millie said.

Stephanie felt her chest fill. 'I expect,' she replied tightly, 'she's been very unhappy.'

'No, she's just a humourless cow. You're too kind, Steph. Always thinking the best of everyone.'

'Ken would give anything to have a wife like you,' Madeleine said. She laughed. 'He'd love to be looked after the way you look after George.'

Stephanie knocked back the rest of her glass. 'George doesn't love it,' she said, hearing her voice quiver. 'George doesn't even notice it. George pays more attention to the bloody dog . . .'

She stood in the bathroom breathing deeply, mortified by the hot tears that had sprung to her eyes. 'I don't want to be kind,' she told herself in the mirror. 'I don't want to look after people any more.'

She watched her lips as they spoke. Her face was flushed. She knew she was drunk. She couldn't take it like Millie could.

The strip light over the mirror was not kind at all. Her face looked saggy and tired. She fumbled in her handbag for lipstick and comb, widening her eyes, shaking her head as if that could clear her mind. Sod George and his outdated ideas. She was going down to find Madeleine right now.

Downstairs, Amanda was packing up her boxes of tricks. The women were beginning to leave, handing in their order forms with smatterings of self-conscious laughter. Amanda passed one of the catalogues to Stephanie.

'Just write your choices in the boxes and seal it up. Nobody knows what anyone else has ordered,' she said, not looking at her. 'All tastes catered for,' she added with a chilly smile.

Stephanie felt she had to pretend to look but she marvelled as she skimmed through the glossy pages in her lap. The leather and handcuffs ensembles never had struck a chord but now even the lingerie left her feeling strange and detached. Imagine dressing up like this, she thought, looking uncomfortably at the models draped across chairs in their suspenders. The image of herself prancing about for George in next to nothing seemed as unlikely and ludicrous as going shopping in a bikini.

But all of a sudden, she remembered how *he* had surprised her with tiny scraps of black silk. His face as she'd slid shyly round the door. His long, slow outward breath of appreciation. His hands reaching out . . .

She closed the catalogue abruptly, shaking her head. *Don't think about that! Think about Madeleine.* She and Millie seemed to be getting on well. Sitting on the sofa together – smoking each other's cigarettes, laughing and joking. She had to ask Madeleine tonight.

'What are you doing skulking in here?' Millie poked her head round the kitchen door as Stephanie filled a tumbler with water. Her eyes searched Stephanie's face. 'What's the matter?'

'Nothing. I just need to speak to Madeleine. I'm going to ask her about a job.'

Millie looked surprised. 'Really?' She pulled a bottle of wine towards her and refilled Stephanie's glass. 'I thought George didn't want you to work.'

'Well of course he doesn't want me to work! Who'd get the lamb chops on the table? Though if the bloody dog could cook he'd probably be quite happy never to see me again.'

She hesitated as the tiny sober person inside her jumped up and down with a placard marked UNFAIR. Steph took a large mouthful of wine and drowned her.

'He's always been the same . . .'

Millie raised her eyebrows. 'But I thought you—'

'But if I do it through Madeleine,' Stephanie interrupted. 'Has she told you? She's got a sort of recruitment business. George thinks she's wonderful. Said Ken only set her up in it as a tax loss – now she turns over almost as much as he does!'

Millie frowned. 'Well, Recruitment wouldn't really be for you, would it?' she said, looking into her glass.

'Why not?'

'Well, you're not . . .'

'What?' Stephanie felt her face grow hot again. 'I suppose you think I'm useless too!'

'No, I don't. Where is this place of Madeleine's?'

'She's got offices in that new complex on the other side of the park. Why?'

Millie said nothing.

'Well?' demanded Stephanie. She felt unusually bolshie. She picked up the wine bottle and topped up her glass again. 'She said she needed more staff and I'm sick of being at home all day.'

She stopped as Madeleine appeared in the doorway an empty glass in her hand. Stephanie felt Millie's eyes on her. 'We were just talking about you,' she said to Madeleine boldly. 'I was just saying I want to go back to work.'

Madeleine nodded.

Stephanie rushed on. 'And you said you needed someone else in the office. I used to type, answer the phone . . .'

Madeleine put her glass down. 'It's not exactly that kind of work.'

'Filing. I can do filing.'

'It's not filing.'

Millie turned the corkscrew into a new bottle of red. 'It's a lot of computer work, isn't it, Madeleine?'

Stephanie looked at her, hurt. 'How do you know?'

She caught Madeleine's frown in the corner of her eye and swung round. 'You both think I'm useless, don't you? Like George and the kids. Boring old Stephanie!

45

Dumb Mum!' Her eyes were pricking and she heard her voice get high. 'I could learn about computers. I can learn things. My children can do it. Why can't I?' She looked pleadingly from Madeleine to Millie.

She saw them exchange glances and her eyes humiliatingly filled with tears. She turned away, staring into the sink, biting her lip, trying to get a bloody grip before she made a complete fool of herself.

Madeleine leant out and touched Stephanie's arm. 'It's not that at all, sweetie. It's just not your sort of . . .' She looked across at Millie. Millie shrugged. '. . . business. Not your type of thing at all.'

Stephanie turned back, looked from one to the other. 'What are you talking about?'

Madeleine's voice was soothing. 'Look, I'll ask around, see if anybody else . . .'

Stephanie couldn't seem to stop herself now. 'Why can't I come and work for you?'

'I don't have any vacancies.'

'That's not what you said on Saturday!'

Madeleine shook her head. 'You don't understand . . .'

'I understand all right!' Stephanie felt the tears run down her face. 'I'm not good enough. I'm bottom of the heap. Nobody takes me seriously. George . . .' She stopped, her voice catching.

Madeleine stepped over and put a hand on her shoulder. 'Are you and George having problems?'

Millie's house was in darkness when she got back. She waved at Steph and the departing taxi as she felt about for keys. Then she took the copy of her party order form from her pocket and stuffed it deep into her handbag as she crept up the stairs.

Their bedroom door was open. Patrick was asleep. Snoring noisily, mouth open, head tipped back off the pillow.

46

Millie looked at the dark mound of him in their bed and walked softly into Ben's room, her heart turning as always at the sight of his small form, arms flung outwards, duvet in a scrunched heap. She picked teddy up from the floor and tucked him back under the covers. Ben stirred, muttering, and shifted in the bed.

'I don't want to,' he murmured plaintively, his eyes still shut.

Neither do I, she thought. She kissed his cheek, looking at the dark lashes feathered on his soft white face.

'Love you,' she whispered, feeling that warm gush of sentiment from too much wine. But despite her own intake she could still smell the fumes rising from Patrick as she tiptoed past to the bathroom. She shook her head as his breathing stopped for several seconds before his lips reverberated in a rubbery explosion. Once it used to frighten her – she'd shake him anxiously, fearing he'd gasped his last. But now she knew the big stuff only happened to those who didn't want it – it was always the tragic young widows married barely three weeks whose brave young husbands were crushed to death by a passing bus while horrible old bastards whose wives prayed daily for their demise headed relentlessly towards their telegram from the Queen.

Millie pulled off her clothes, looked at her face in the mirror, at the row of costly creams and potions on the bathroom shelf. She saw her mother walking about, picking things up. *Aren't you lucky, Millie? That lovely home. Patrick such a good provider. Darling little Ben bless-his-heart . . .*

Lucky Millie.

She rested her hot forehead on the cold glass. 'Stop it! It's just the drink.'

She wanted to phone Alex. Tell him she would leave after all. Whisper how much she needed him and adored him. Beg him to—

She squeezed her eyes shut. The tears still trickled out.

She could go downstairs – use the phone in Patrick's study. He'd never hear. She'd unplug the phone next to the bed first. Just in case he woke up and heard that tell-tale ping as she made the connection downstairs. She'd whisper.

But of course *She* might hear. Might want to know who was calling his mobile so late at night.

And it was clearly stated in the handbook: *Beware the recklessness alcohol induces.*

She'd feel different tomorrow. Millie picked up a ball of cotton wool and began to methodically strip her streaky face of its make-up. Colours joined together – smoky eyeshadow, pink blusher, ruby lipstick – to form a purple-grey smudge on the white cotton.

She emerged, face shiny, eyes bare, looking – young? Naked! The signs of her thirty-six years were evident but they were still easily camouflaged with tubes and palettes and brushes. Even like this she knew she was still attractive. Knew men desired and wanted her. And she needed to know that. Needed a damn sight more approval than she got here.

Slowly Millie cleaned her teeth. Most people would condemn. Wouldn't understand how you could have so much and still want more.

But Madeleine knew how it was. It was Madeleine who'd told her to grab a little joy while she could.

Joy! Millie was crying again.

Behind her, in the bedroom, Patrick stirred and farted.

George had already gone to bed too.

Stephanie looked in the bathroom mirror and pulled the hair back from her face, inspecting a couple of strands above the ears, remembering Millie's blistering words earlier.

Grey hairs – yep.

Dreary expression – yep.

She giggled.

Lipstick – sucked off hours ago.

Lively? Hardly.

She took a zinc tablet.

George shagging his secretary? No such bloody luck.

She knew she didn't mean it. George uncharacteristically slapping on the aftershave, whistling in the mornings and buying new shirts? ('How To Tell if He's At It' – another invaluable article from *Things To Worry About Monthly*.) It was bad enough him flirting with the dog.

No, what she needed was for her own sex drive to perk up or George's to dwindle away altogether.

No wonder some of these wives greeted Viagra with horror. Imagine looking forward to years of bedding down with three layers of winceyette and your knitting only to find the old man jumping all over you again. It would be rather handy if George were impotent. Family unity, a father for the children – God help her during the teenage years – and dollops of George's love and respect for being so understanding, while very neatly getting her off the hook.

The hook rose to greet her as she slid beneath the sheets. Since she'd gone off it, he was like a man possessed. Hot breath on her ear, immediate hand to her breast. Thigh already sliding over hers.

'Hummn.'

He wasn't even fully awake.

But *it* was.

She wriggled away from him, yawning loudly.

He wriggled after her.

'Good time?' he murmured.

'It was OK.'

'Buy anything?'

'No.'

49

She turned over onto her front and pulled her arms close in against her sides. His hand snaked beneath her stomach. 'Love you.'

He always did when he had an erection.

'I love you too.'

But she did not want to have sex with him. She couldn't stir her body to be fussed with all that thrusting and breathing and general effort. The heat and closeness. The *intimacy*.

'I'm tired, George.'

He was properly awake now. He sighed loudly and rolled over, turning his back to her.

'You're always tired.'

Half a mile in the other direction, Millie got into bed. Patrick was snoring again. She thought of Stephanie's face in the kitchen. For a heart-jerking moment she'd thought Madeleine would tell her. She imagined Steph's wide, startled eyes if she knew.

Stephanie lay on her back looking up through the darkness. George had fallen back to sleep.

She wondered how much longer before he got angry. Before he realized how she had changed. He'd tried to suggest it was some medical problem. Millie thought it was lack of practice and not enough vitamins. She herself had blamed boredom with her small domestic life. But another truth was knocking uncomfortably at her door.

Just suppose the reason she couldn't make love with George was because of Troy.

Chapter 3

She'd only been looking for Situations Vacant.

But the name leapt from the page.

Bartholomew. Cora. Died peacefully on Sunday, 14 March. Sadly missed. Details about cremation and flowers. And four words near the beginning that hit Stephanie in the stomach.

Beloved mother of Troy.

Troy.

Golden haired, guitar strumming, inner peace advocating. Heart breaking, trust destroying, overdraft creating . . .

His mother dead.

Picture painting, music playing, candle lighting . . .

Poor Cora. Tiny, bony like an old cat, with her mass of rings and long dark menthol cigarettes. Her hoarse voice and bright scarves.

All gone now.

Slow, slow lovemaking.

Stephanie's heart was thumping.

She knew she'd see him. Her mind was a rapid picture show of funerals, house clearance. Him popping up where she least expected him. Like the last time.

It was in Woolworth's. Five years ago, maybe. He was

buying Cora light bulbs. Stephanie came round the corner of the aisle, looking for potting compost – or was it that liquid plant food you put on tomatoes? – and there he was. She felt that great jolt of adrenalin that seemed to come right up into her throat – half panic, half excitement – and in the same instant she saw his look of startled recognition.

Real shock and pleasure registered on his face in a split-second flash before the easy smile came on.

'Hi!' The word was a long, lazy drawl, his eyes half closed as if he was lying in a deep bath. 'What a surprise!'

She didn't know why it should have been. He knew she'd married George and moved back to Edenhurst. She knew his mother still lived here. It was a small town with just the one medium-sized Woolie's. They were bound to meet sooner or later if his mother's 40-watters failed in the same week that George's geraniums were under par.

It was a strange, stiff exchange. For her. He of course was his usual chilled-out, so-laid-back-he-was-almost-horizontal-ha-bloody-ha self.

'How's life treating you?' Looking her up and down, asking questions, smiling his brilliant smile, while she could feel her lips pursing up, her face tight. Her stilted voice coming out with a comprehensive résumé of George's promotion, their new house (blush, blush, God! She'd be telling him how their son sang like an angel next!). She found herself talking money and possessions in the way that only a guy who leaves you with fourteen unpaid bills and an overdraft can make you.

As his expression turned to knowing disappointment she cringed and then filled with frustrated outrage. He was seeing her as 'establishment' now. Materialistic and soulless. Was it this injustice that made her wait while he shone the same smile on the checkout girl and paid for his light bulbs? That led her to fall into step beside him as they walked up the High Street, turn into the park, sit together on a park bench as if they were old friends.

Yesterday she'd known it was going to happen again. She had that same funny feeling in her stomach she used to get as a child. The one that came upon her suddenly when something was about to happen. Like when she was walking down the alleyway to the sweet shop and she just knew that round the corner would be ferret-faced June with her fat brother, ready to kick Steph's shins if she didn't hand over her money.

George would laugh and pooh-pooh her psychic feelings – they could be hit and miss – but that morning she'd been very sure. All the time she was filling Toby's lunchbox with things he'd bring home again and driving Toby and Charlotte to school and exchanging flippancies with Millie at the gates she knew that today was the day.

She parked, walked twenty paces behind while Charlotte sauntered up to her friends, remembered to kiss Toby outside rather than in the playground so his friend Charlie wouldn't think him uncool and got back into her car and sat there while it drove her round to the part of town where Cora's house was. She didn't let it actually take her right there of course but as it turned the corner and drove up the hill, there he was, coming down.

Troy was riding a bike, shoulders hunched forward, hair swept back from his face, feet still on the pedals as the wheels spun round, chin down against the wind. But he saw her. That same shock lit his features; and then he'd passed. She'd stopped the car before she knew it. She waited while he turned around and pedalled slowly back up. He arrived by her open window, breathing heavily.

'I hoped,' he said. 'I hoped and hoped I'd see you.'

He was older of course but oddly unchanged. His hair was thinner, starting further back on his forehead, there were lines around his eyes but his was the same face she'd been sucked towards all those years ago. His eyes still had that brightness, that permanent invitation.

'I thought we might bump into each other,' she said feebly. Energy came off him like static. Already she wanted to touch him.

He had got off his bike and was crouching down by the car door, one hand on the crossbar to steady the bike as it leant against him, one arm along the window opening. She could feel his hot breath.

'Not as fit as I was!' he said. And smiled.

She felt her face heat. God, was it just her or was he too thinking of days when he was very fit indeed? She had a tantalizing image of his face glistening with sweat, looking down at her as he thrust into her again and again . . .

'How are you?' Yes, he knew. He was doing it deliberately. Looking at her with that concentrated crinkly-deep pleasurable smile reserved for the very special in his life (almost anyone). His voice slow and suggestive, his eyes teasing her. The five years had folded up into nothing.

'I'm fine, thank you. How are you?' She sounded ridiculously formal. 'Oh, I'm sorry!' she looked away, flustered, 'I'm sorry about Cora. I read it in the paper.'

'Yeah.' The smile went. 'It's hard. I mean I knew it was coming but it's still hard. Brings you up short. Makes you think about things.'

'Yes.' She knew what his mother had meant to him.

She made herself look back at him. He was watching her closely. 'I'd lost so much already,' he said.

That didn't take long. 'Oh, Troy, don't do this again.'

'What do you mean?'

Last time he'd tried it too – the regret, the wishing things had been different, sitting too close to her on the park bench, making all sorts of outrageous suggestions when his wife had just had their baby. Stephanie had got up and walked away in disgust. The same old Troy.

'You know very well what. Start all that stuff – about how we used to be. I'm married to George now. You know that.'

'Steph!' He looked startled and hurt. 'I wouldn't dream . . . You have no idea how I am these days. I've done a lot of thinking and growing since you last saw me. A lot of things have happened. When Mum—' He stopped and looked away, turning back to her, watery-eyed. 'When Mum got ill it changed everything.'

'OK, I'm sorry.' She felt embarrassed now. 'Really,' she added, as he blew his nose, feeling guilty at her lack of sensitivity.

'Look,' he straightened up. 'Can we go for a coffee or something? Just to talk.' He looked at her pleadingly. 'I really wouldn't . . .'

She drove home fast, let herself into the house and crossed the hall to switch off the alarm. She felt jittery and nervous.

She rushed to the mirror.

Thank you! It lied, as all good mirrors should. The one in the hall was always the best. Whatever the time of year, the hall was dim, darkened by the oak panelling and the heavy front door. It was the only thing she'd had her doubts about when they moved in. Now she thanked God for it. In this mirror her skin took on a velvety texture, her eyes glowed above a pleasing jut of cheekbone. She was still – if she thrust her chin forward and to the right a little – young and firm.

He'd already seen her early morning school-run face – the saggy one she'd spread with age-defying, luminescent, tinted moisturizer plus concealer. What did that article say? *If possible, delay applying your make-up until you've been up a few hours. Your face needs time to settle* . . . Hers generally took until bedtime. She pulled out lip gloss, ran hands through her hair, hating herself. She shouldn't care whether he found her attractive. Oh, but she did!

When the doorbell rang her heart thudded but she tried hard – and failed – for the casual air as she held the door wide and gestured him in with the smallest incline of her head.

He was smiling. 'Hello again!' Pleased with the invitation. Right up his street. Troy had always prided himself on his enduring friendships with old loves. Had an ex-girlfriend-turned-best-mate in every port. She had disappointed him with her anger and tears. Early on he'd sent her a card suggesting they could meet and talk. She'd sent it straight back.

Now he was holding out his hands, obviously wanting to kiss her cheek. But vibrating from the strangeness of his standing there in her home, alarmed by the way her nerve endings were jumping about, she backed away from him and turned into the kitchen, grabbing a coffee cup.

'Want one?'

'Yeah.' He followed her. Stood in the doorway, as she filled the kettle, pulled the coffee jar from the cupboard, aware she was fussing and bustling like her mother, feeling the sort of person she never thought she'd feel with him. 'Do you still take sugar?'

He smiled, nodding, looking her up and down in the way she'd seen him appraise so many women. 'You look great.'

'A little more wrinkled.'

'Oh well, we're all that.' He didn't bother to contradict her. She spooned and stirred, feeling clumsy and awkward.

'You can sit down.'

He sat at the end of the table. He was thinner than she remembered. But in Toby's place he looked huge. She handed the mug to him and let herself take a look at his tanned features. He always had a tan. He used to tease her about being so white and it would annoy her because she'd been inside working all day while he'd been lounging about in the garden.

But she – who hadn't been to work since Charlotte was born – was still white all these years later and he was still brown. He looked back at her faded face and smiled again. Then he looked around the kitchen. 'Very nice.' He grinned. 'Not very "you" though – a bit too *Homes & Gardens*!'

'How do you know what's me? I love this house.'

'You've done well.' He managed to make it sound like a rather dubious state of affairs. 'I suppose you made a small fortune out of our flat . . .'

She remembered sculptures and pots, walls crowded with curling posters, dusty candles and quirkily shaped bottles, a quilt coming apart in colourful patches.

'It was my flat.'

He smiled again. 'When I saw you last time,' he said, 'I knew I'd been right about what would happen to you. Women often leave me and go on to material success. I'm a launching pad.'

He looked pleased with himself and she felt that old frustration run through her. She laughed scornfully, feeling safer.

'Come off it. You mean you're attracted to women who want to make something of their lives and so, by virtue of that, they eventually get sick of keeping you and move on. You don't have anything to do with what they do next!'

'I don't know.' He shook his head sorrowfully.

'Except of course,' she went on drily, 'that after living with you, one does tend to find anyone who plays a guitar, talks about inner peace and hasn't got a credit card, quite repellent.'

He gave a shout of laughter. The sound struck her hard

in the stomach and desire surged through her all over again. She wanted to knock the grin from his face.

'When you asked for money from the flat, George wanted me to send you an invoice. Five years of clothes and fags and booze and food and bills paid.' Her voice now sounded mean in a way she hadn't intended. 'See how much you owed *me*.'

He stopped smiling. 'George! The man's a philistine. Money mad.'

'It was lucky for me he had a more responsible attitude to it than you did.'

'Is that why you married him? Because he was responsible?'

'I married him because I loved him.'

'Loved? Past tense, eh?'

'No! I do love him. We're very happy.' Christ! Why did he always make her feel so square and old-fashioned?

'Good. Well whatever it is,' he said looking round, 'it's certainly a bit more des. res. than we were used to.'

Bare floorboards and exposed wires. And bitter cold. All at once she remembered the trail of flea bites she'd woken up with the morning after they'd moved in. All across her stomach like a string of blood pearls.

'Ugh, it was horrible.'

'It wasn't all the time.'

Zipped together in a sleeping bag to keep warm, picnics in bed, the strange electrical jolt that flipped through her whenever he touched her . . .

'No it wasn't.' She hadn't meant to say it out loud.

'Where *is* George?'

He looked around him as if genuinely hoping to see her husband.

'At work, of course.' Her tone was intended to remind him that was still what most people did for a living.

'And the children? I'd like to have seen them.'

'School.' She was sharp now, disliking this old-friend-of-the-family routine. 'Did you have a second one?'

'Yeah,' he grinned happily. 'Phoebe's nearly three. And Lara will be six. They're wonderful kids.'

She nodded.

'Only thing that keeps us together really,' he added carelessly.

She turned away to refill the already-full kettle.

'Oh really? That didn't last long, then, did it? Thought she was the love of your life – whatever her name is – your latest.'

'Tanith. And we've been married seven years,' he said mildly. 'It's a long time. Five years was a long time too,' he added. He was watching her carefully and she suddenly wanted to smile.

'Yes,' she said. 'It took me an awfully long time to come to my senses.'

He sat down, putting the mug away from him a little and placing his slender hands flat on the table. The gesture caught at her memory and she found she was quite still, watching his fingers as they rippled gently up and down on the soft gleam of varnished wood.

'I would never have left you, I don't think,' Troy said.

'You did several times.'

'Oh for a day or two. But I always came back. I've never been able to talk to anyone like we used to talk. We did like each other, didn't we – we were always mates.'

The hairs on her arms tingled. She looked back at his face. It was true. They had liked each other very much. She used to tell Rose all the time. 'But he's my best friend,' she would say. 'We're still such very good friends.' She wore the words like a comfort blanket, kept them around her chilled shoulders as she waited through the night for him to come home, as she left for work leaving him to sleep away the mornings.

'You took too much,' she said now, seeing Rose in that

59

far-off cold kitchen, her eyes as she carried Troy's possessions into the street.

Friends don't treat you like that.

'How long are you here for?' she asked grimly.

'I don't know. I need to get some jobs done on the house before I sell it. Mum couldn't manage much in the end – it all needs painting, the windows at the back are rotten, the bathroom needs re-tiling . . .'

Shame you didn't do that while she was alive! The thought leapt uncharitably into Stephanie's mind and she pressed her lips together.

'I kept offering to do it for her before,' he said, as if reading her.

She nodded. Mr Good-intentions. Mr Big-plans-that-never-happen.

'But you know,' he went on, 'she knew she didn't have long. When I came down she just wanted me to sit and talk to her.'

'Have you been down much?'

He didn't look at her. 'A bit. Once I knew . . .'

He turned his mug around on the table. 'It was difficult – with the kids being so small. It's a long drive, they have all these things they do at weekends . . .' He looked up at her. 'Now I wish . . .'

'Yes, I know.' God, who was she to judge. She only saw her own mother once a year. George had to be dragged kicking and screaming to see his. 'Are you still up in Norwich?'

'Yeah,' he shrugged. 'Tanith likes it there. But we might move – once the house is done up.'

She smiled. 'Not finished, then?' There was always something left unfinished.

'It's a very large house.' He grinned at her. 'I would have finished the flat. When we'd got some money.'

She grinned back. 'No you wouldn't.'

He was serious again. 'I would now.'

'Give me a hug.'

Yes – she said it. She started it. And afterwards she couldn't have said why. It came upon her as a great warm urge. A strange rush of hormones or blood to the head. She didn't look or see his expression, only heard the scrape of his chair on the tiles and found herself held against his chest.

Christ! She pressed her cheek into his shirt, feeling the soft fabric of his collar, the stubble of his chin, breathing in what was suddenly a familiar scent.

He held her tightly and for a wild, giddy moment as she felt the heat, she imagined them tugging the clothes from each other and making mad passionate love on the kitchen table. Mmmmmn . . .

Then he put his hands either side of her face to pull it up towards him and reality thumped down hard between them. She pulled back, hot-faced and embarrassed.

'Sorry! Look, I've got to go out. My car has to go to the garage.'

She picked up the cups, put them in the sink, leant up to close the kitchen window.

'OK.' He went back to lean in the doorway again. 'I'll be around for a bit.' It was a question.

'It's not a good idea,' she said.

'It's so ironic really,' he said casually. 'I could look after you now.'

'About time too.'

'Seriously. I've done OK in the last few years. It was me who did all the original groundwork for the Flowerburst Graphics Pro-pack – I mean they ended up in partnership with Microsoft over that and when the dot-com thing took off I was website design for Staychilled.com – they sold that for a packet – and I made sure I negotiated my cut very early on.'

Stephanie raised her eyebrows. 'Goodness!' she said with exaggerated surprise.

'I'm Mr Respectable now.' He grinned. 'I wear a suit and drive a Saab.'

She laughed. 'A Saab?'

'The kids go to private school . . .'

'What??'

He shrugged. 'Montessori. Tanith just felt . . .'

She looked at his denim jacket and thought about the bike outside. 'You keep it well hidden.'

'Ah that's because the best bits of me have stayed the same.' He was looking at her intently. 'And they have for you too I can see.'

'No, I'm very different now.'

'Not to me you're not.'

She wanted to feel his arms again. 'Come on, for God's sake,' she said irritably. 'We've moved on. We've got children. I'm *married*.'

'So am I. I told you. But surely we can be friends? Have a drink together.'

Kick him out!

It was Rose's voice. Loud and clear and contemptuous. So much as always packed into so little. Stephanie's heart pounded. It was a long time since she'd heard her. Troy was looking out of the window.

'I'll be staying at Mum's house if you want me,' he said.

'Right.'

'I could call you before I go back.'

She hesitated. 'OK.'

It's not OK! What are you playing at?

He looked at Stephanie's mobile lying on the work surface. 'Give me your number,' he said.

Won't phone the house then? Won't be upfront about it?

Stephanie nodded at the phone on the hall table. 'You can call that.'

62

'I don't want to speak to George.'

I bet you don't!

'And what's he going to think if my mobile keeps ringing?'

'I'll send you a text.'

'What for?'

'Can I have your number?' He was serious now. 'Steph, you know how special you are to me. I just want to stay in touch. I won't make things awkward with him.'

George – taller, older, greyer, more solid in every way. She looked at the blond hair before her, the strong cyclist's legs, the sensitive artist's hands.

'On yer bike,' she said.

Stephanie stood at the front door, both shaken and stirred. She closed her eyes on Rose, on George, on her children, on the stretch of gravel and shaped hedge that edged their lives.

All she could see was a mattress on floorboards where she and Troy rolled over and over, wanting each other again and again.

He wheeled his bike down the path. Paused at the gate, swung a long leg over his bright pink and green crossbar, lifted a hand to wave. She realized she was gripping the edge of the door.

It meant something when you gave someone your mobile number. It said: you can reach me any time. You and I can have secrets. George had bought her the phone to keep her safe. So she could be reached by the family.

You didn't go giving your number to ex-lovers. When Troy asked for it she shook her head. She imagined Rose nodding approval.

But Rose turned and walked off when Stephanie wrote it down anyway.

Chapter 4

Kelly had sand and slimy bits of green seaweed all over her. She panted across the floor with her great wet tongue flapping and shook herself, spraying droplets around the kitchen. Stephanie wiped a grain of something from her eye. 'Ugh! Does she have to come back like this?'

'She's been on the beach. What do you expect?' George crouched down and gazed adoringly into Kelly's eyes. 'You like it on the beach, don't you my beautiful girl? You like those waves, don't you?'

'Can't she stay outside till she's dry?'

George shook his head in disbelief as if she'd suggested his mother live in the coal bunker and got hold of the dog's collar. 'I'll clean her,' he said heavily.

'It's only sand, Mum.' Charlotte was spreading Marmite thickly over the peanut butter on her third slice of toast, while Toby wrinkled his nose into his Weetabix.

'I know it's *only* sand,' said Stephanie. 'Why don't you *only* clean it up then? And do eat up!' she added to Toby. 'Your father won't wait for you if you're not ready.' She pushed a small box of raisins quickly into his lunchbox while he wasn't looking. 'If I get the car in time I'll collect you. If not, Millie will bring you back, OK?'

Toby looked stricken. 'Oh Mum! I hate raisins.'

Charlotte glared. 'I want to go to Emma's.'

'Not tonight.'

'Why not?'

'I've just told you – I might not be able to come and get you.'

'So? Her mum'll do it.'

'You can't expect other people to spend their lives ferrying you about. You can go to Emma's tomorrow.'

Charlotte stuffed the last corner of toast into her mouth. 'Yuck that's gross,' she said, as she flounced past Toby who had reduced his breakfast to a grey pulp and was stirring it in a desultory fashion with one hand while the other foraged in his left nostril.

'Use a tissue, darling,' said Stephanie absently, still wondering what on earth she was going to wear.

The horn sounded for the second time as Stephanie put Toby's bag into his hand and kissed his freckled cheek.

'What's in my sandwiches?'

'Dairylea and tuna paste.'

He gave her one of his sudden smiles. 'Bye, Mum, love you too.'

Charlotte rushed back through the door. 'Hurry up! Dad's going ballistic!'

'Well where are you going then?' Stephanie screeched as her daughter bounded up the stairs.

'Forgotten something!' Charlotte reappeared with a magazine.

'Don't look at that in lessons,' Stephanie said feebly as Charlotte charged back across the hall. 'Love you,' she added to the open doorway through which both children had now disappeared. 'Love you both.'

Love.

She opened the text message for the seventeenth time.

Good to see u Love n hugs T xxxx

She'd told George she'd met Troy in the street. Which was true. Partly true.

She'd had to tell George something. To make it safe. George wasn't bothered. He pulled a sympathetic face. 'You don't want to waste your time talking to him,' he said. 'He's just a loser.'

Just a loser she'd loved and lost. She hadn't thought about him for a long time and now . . . Good to see u.

When she thought about him holding her, the hairs stood up on her arms.

She hadn't told George about the interview either. She thought she'd wait till it was all sorted. Just in case it wasn't.

'I might have something after all,' Madeleine had said. Stephanie's mind snapped between images of herself behind a huge desk with two telephones and her own assistant, and wondering whether these days she could manage the filing.

She emptied her entire wardrobe onto the bed to search for that elusive something that would convey cool efficiency or entrepreneurial verve and had to face the fact that she didn't own it. The choice was between a rather dated black suit she'd last worn to George's uncle's funeral or a cherry red wool one she'd bought in a sale and couldn't remember wearing ever. There was a nice array of evening floaty black for George's company dos and some ill-advised sequined tops acquired for the squash club knees-ups. Otherwise it was just jeans, jeans and more jeans and every colour of sweatshirt under the sun. One didn't exactly need a full designer wardrobe to do the school run.

I'll have to go shopping if I get the job, she thought, hugging herself at the thought of working again.

'What do you do these days, then?' Troy had asked, leaning against the door and watching her. Even he had assumed she must do *something* over and above the wiping of surfaces and creation of hot drinks he'd witnessed so far.

'Nothing much!' she'd said, laughing as if she didn't mind.

They'd watched a documentary the other night; she and George on their opposite sofas. It was about burn-out. How all these bright young things were so stressed and busy and worked such long hours in the mad, bad bid for success that they had no time to enjoy themselves. George had shaken his head at the scenes of crowded London stations, the tales of traffic jams and pollution. 'Thank God we don't have to do that any more,' he'd said. But Stephanie, looking at the young couples in their suits, felt moved. She remembered herself just out of art college, heaving her portfolio on and off the tube, invigorated by the crowds and noise and dirt. So full of expectancy . . .

She walked there across the park. The daffodils were open, the crocuses a thick purple rug beneath the trees. It was cold but the sun was shining. It would have been lovely if she'd had the right shoes on. The suit didn't make her look at all how she wanted to feel and she half wished she'd come in her jeans and boots after all. Madeleine wouldn't give her a job anyway. After twelve years of nothing more taxing than matching socks? How would she learn new skills, remember names, make decisions . . .

Come on! she imagined Rose snorting at her. *Didn't you use to run that company practically single-handed?*

God, those days of working for Ronnie! He'd never turn a job down even if it meant working all night. She'd fallen asleep over her drawing board more than once. And the times she'd staggered in at 10 p.m. only to have to get up again at six. While Troy slept till midday.

She still hadn't answered the text. She didn't know what to say.

Good 2 C U 2?
And U?
Don't ever darken my doorstep?
For god's sake come and rip my clothes off?

She stopped in front of the low blocks of offices among the trees and carefully planned beds. The rows of polyanthus were flowering in best spring-like fashion but the wind was fresh. She dug in her handbag for a mirror. Her nose was already a fetching shade of red and her eyes were running. Two black streaks of mascara coursed down her cheeks, giving her the air of someone who far from being the super-efficient PA no boss could do without, had just discovered her entire family had been wiped out in an earthquake. She sheltered against a tree to do some repair work with a tissue and more concealer.

Once she'd harboured a dream of working in Paula's Pottery in the High Street. It was one of these places where the kids could paint their own picture on a plate and get it glazed and fired. An activity Charlotte had been particularly fond of when she was small. They'd accrued a huge collection of bright, splodgily decorated pieces of pottery, filling every surface in the house and keeping both grandmas in presents for ever – forcing even George's mother to affect pleasure.

There'd been a girl there who painted flowers and butterflies to customer orders. Stephanie had watched her sitting at the table in the corner in her blue smocked overall, her hair tied back from her face, features rapt in concentration as she traced delicate patterns and leaves on wafer thin china.

Stephanie had wanted to do that.

She was in there one day when she heard the girl was leaving. Paula the owner had shaken her head. 'Don't know how we'll replace Zoë . . .'

Stephanie had gone there again and again, practically pressing her nose against the glass like a poor child outside a toyshop but while she'd dithered about what to say and what to wear and whether to dig out some floral designs she'd done at college, a young man with a ponytail was employed and sat and painted in the corner. Stephanie didn't go past the shop any more.

But this had to be different. This time she had to show a bit of gumption and see it through. Her stomach was jumping as she pushed open the double doors into the carpeted reception area and looked up at the board. PAs. An arrow pointed down a corridor to the left. She had pushed at the second set of doors several times before she noticed the small buzzer on the door frame. She pressed it, feeling thoroughly silly as she gave her name. But the girl sitting at the desk in front of her smiled.

'I'll tell her you're here.' She indicated a low cream sofa. 'She's with someone just at the moment.'

Patsy appeared through a door, pulling on her jacket. She looked surprised, making Stephanie feel even more out of place among the glass-topped tables and glossy magazines. She felt her cheeks glowing and she needed to blow her nose again. Patsy came towards her, cool and pale. 'Hi there! Haven't seen you for ages.'

There was always something effortlessly co-ordinated about Patsy. The soft jacket, the simple black scoop-necked top, the beautifully cut trousers, the matching shoes and handbag. Steph looked at the perfectly judged gold jewellery at Patsy's throat and wrist and knew that her own look was one of Tries-too-hard.

And here we have Stephanie with the look that doesn't quite come off.

The red jacket felt hot and bulky in the warmth of the

office, the shiny black shoes were too high, too tight. Patsy's low heels looked comfortable and stylish; she picked up her witty slip of a handbag as Steph heaved her own Thatcher-sized haversack onto the other shoulder.

'Here to see Madeleine?' Patsy checked her lipstick in a small gold compact.

'Yes.' Steph's voice sounded higher than usual. 'I want to go on the books.'

Patsy clicked the mirror shut, eyebrows raised. 'Really?'

Stephanie felt her heart thump in embarrassment. God, why was her job-hunting such an unbelievable concept? Did even other women think she was fit for nothing but vegetable-peeling?

'Yes. I do. I can't go on like this!' To her horror, her voice now held a slight quaver.

Patsy threw back her head and burst into laughter. 'Well! You dark horse. Does Madeleine know?'

'Well, yes, she said to come and see her . . .'

'She always says she can spot them at ten paces, but she never said a thing about you!'

'Well, I only sort of hinted at it when they came to dinner.'

Patsy was now looking at her in open admiration. 'That was brave.'

'I've been thinking about it for ages. And then when she came to the party the other night I told her . . .'

'Well, this is the place to come!'

'Yes.' Stephanie was still not sure what was so amusing but was feeling better about it anyway. The jacket was unbearably hot now. She took it off and held it over her arm feeling even more frumpy in the cream blouse.

Patsy was still shaking her head. 'I would never have thought it of you, though. Never! Mrs Perfect, eh? I always thought you and George were the devoted couple.'

'Well we are,' Stephanie said uncomfortably, 'but this is just something I have to do.'

'Oh well good for you, sweets! Don't get me wrong. Just didn't think you had it in you that's all. Still, it's always the quiet ones, isn't it? That's what they say. Not that anyone would call me quiet and you know how—'

'I think you will find – ' Stephanie jumped and Patsy's head whipped round as Madeleine's steely tones came from behind her – 'that Stephanie has come here for a job.'

'What I'd be looking for,' Madeleine was saying, 'is for you to keep on top of the paperwork. There are call sheets to be filed, computer records to be maintained. You know,' she said smoothly, 'details of clients, files on those we carry out the telephone services for. I'm afraid the accounts have been allowed to lapse. We've got a lot of receipts and invoices that need entering in the books.'

Stephanie sat with her hands in her lap, attempting to nod intelligently in the right places. Madeleine was talking as if she was going to take Stephanie on, and as Stephanie glanced around the sleek modern office, she started to imagine herself there: Madeleine's calm, unflustered assistant making her business run like clockwork. She was just picturing herself dressed like Patsy, carrying a laptop and drinking mineral water, when Madeleine leant forward. 'But it's not *quite* as simple as that,' she said abruptly. 'There is something else.'

Stephanie's heart dropped. Here came the complicated computer programing or A level in macramé she didn't have. She should have known it wouldn't be that easy. 'The thing you need to know,' Madeleine went on, looking at her intently, 'is that—'

She stopped as the door burst open and a young blond girl rushed into the room, looking stricken.

'They both rang at once – I played the wrong tape. Her

husband's gone mad – wants to know what she's doing at the airport!'

Madeleine threw down her pen, leapt from her chair and shot off along the corridor with the girl scuttling behind her.

'Won't keep you a mo.' Jo, a sleek brunette in her twenties, came briefly to the door and disappeared again. Jo had given Stephanie a tour when she arrived and she'd seen the blond girl through the glass of a door, sitting at a row of computers wearing headphones.

'That's Samantha in the sound room,' Jo had told her.

'That's where you take the virtual office calls?' Stephanie had asked, remembering how impressed George had been when Madeleine explained it. 'Brilliantly simple!' he'd said. 'That's the way forward as companies get out of the cities and more and more people work from home.' Stephanie had never thought about it before but now she looked at a photo on the wall – two smiling girls sitting in front of monitors – and felt proud to be joining the cutting edge.

'Madeleine will tell you about that,' Jo said.

But Madeleine had dashed from the room halfway through the job description and still hadn't come back. Stephanie looked around. The phone on the desk began to ring and Steph wondered whether to answer it. It stopped and she assumed someone in another part of the building had picked it up. Then it rang again. And rang and rang.

She got up and wandered out into the corridor. About twenty minutes had passed. Jo was not at her desk in reception. Stephanie wandered up the corridor and looked into the sound room. She could see Madeleine speaking, gesturing impatiently. In front of her, Samantha was flicking back her hair nervously while Jo stood watching, a pair of headphones now on her head. Stephanie looked at her watch. She would have to leave or the garage would shut. Millie had been very willing to pick up the kids again but she couldn't put upon her too much. The door was ajar. Tentatively she pushed at it and stepped onto the thick carpet within. Nobody looked round.

'I mean it's a bit different, isn't it?' Madeleine sounded irritated. 'She tells her old man she's spending all afternoon in a steam room having her cellulite pummelled and he phones up to hear the last call for a flight to Malaga. How did you suppose we were going to get her out of that?'

'I didn't—'

'No – you never do! Suppose that had been your godmother's cover you'd just blown – what then?'

'I was only . . .'

'Lucky some of us can think on our feet—'

Stephanie stood frozen as Madeleine appeared to sense her and swung round.

'I need to leave now. I've got to pick up the children,' Stephanie faltered.

'Not yet!' Madeleine said sharply. 'Not yet.'

By the time she got the car back from the garage it was getting dark. As she drove away, Stephanie looked at the clock on the dashboard. She should get straight to Millie's and collect the kids. There was homework, tea, baths, clean pyjamas to think of.

But . . . sod em! She grinned into the rear mirror, feeling giggly inside. Charlotte would be in a strop, Toby would start a three-hour debate on what he was going to eat. George . . . God only knew what George would say.

She thought of Madeleine's lowered voice in the office, the expression on Samantha's face as she'd burst in. Stephanie gave a little shiver of excitement.

She swung the car towards the other end of town.

Cora's house already had an empty feel about it. The small front garden – once so bright and ordered – was a mass of sprouting weeds. One of the curtains downstairs was half drawn in the sort of crooked, loping way that Cora would never have lived with. There were no lights on. She wondered where Troy was. Out cycling? In a bar, talking about black holes and the meaning of the universe with some drunk who'd been there all afternoon? Or had he gone already? Abandoned the jobs on the house as he'd abandoned so many things. She wanted to see him before he went.

Her phone made her jump. Him? George? Her heart leapt and fell. Guiltily she started the engine, anxious to get away, feeling that if she spoke to George, he would somehow know where she was.

She pulled up around the corner. The ringing had grown so shrill she could practically see the handbag pulsating. She grabbed at it, struck by a sudden panic. Suppose it was Millie to say Toby had fallen and split his head open and why wasn't Steph answering when she'd been calling from casualty for hours?

Suppose George had had a car crash.

It was Charlotte.

'Where are you?' her daughter said crossly. 'I've been calling and calling.'

Toby had something revolting smeared down the front of his blue school jumper, and his shoes were scuffed to buggery. Apart from that he was all in one piece, quite calm and content and not – after all – bleeding profusely on a hospital trolley about to be snatched into the jaws of ferocious social workers.

'Thank you!' She hugged Millie. Millie squeezed her back.

'No problem. Ben was thrilled to have someone bigger

to play with. Is everything all right? How did you get on?'

Stephanie looked meaningfully towards the two small boys. Their heads were locked together over a Gameboy. They wouldn't have heard her if she'd announced the world was ending, but she pulled a conspiratorial face just the same. She'd better tell George first. She smiled at Millie.

'I'll tell you about it tomorrow.'

George pulled a bottle of red wine from the rack and reached up for glasses from the cupboard. 'Want one?'

'Yes, please. Thank you.'

For a moment their eyes met. George was clearly making an effort so she made hers smile too, hoping last night's undignified and rejecting tussle beneath bed-clothes might be forgotten. There was a beep. Out of the corner of her eye she saw her mobile light up.

George looked round.

Quickly she moved to the work surface where the phone lay next to her keys. Pressing the button, she rapidly scanned the now-familiar number. Heart beating hard, she dropped the mobile back into her handbag. 'Text – PTA stuff,' she said.

George rolled his eyes. 'Where's Charlotte?'

'Having tea at Emma's. They're going to drop her back later.' She paused. 'I've got something to tell you. I went to see Madeleine today about a job.'

'Oh yes?'

She watched while he poured the wine into her glass and passed it to her, touching her hand briefly with his forefinger. Something inside her slumped in relief. Once they used to hug when he came in. Once he used to lean down and kiss her on the lips, cup her cheek in the palm of his hand. But this was OK.

'So how did you get on?'

'She says she's got a few hours for me.'

'Oh, right.' George sipped at his wine.

'She needs someone to keep on top of the paperwork, get the filing up to date, keep records, sort the invoices, that sort of thing . . .'

'Invoices?' George grinned at her.

Stephanie smiled back sweetly, determined not to rise to it. 'It's not actual figures, I don't have to do any accounts or anything – just put them in the right place.'

He was still amused. 'That's lucky!'

'Very funny! Anyway it can all be in school hours. And I need something to do.'

'You've got enough to do already.'

But he said it without resentment. Stephanie held up her glass. 'My new job!'

He leant over and clinked his drink against hers.

'And all who sail in her.'

She looked at the mobile she'd switched off since the last text. He wanted to see her and the thought of an hour of his undivided attention . . .

If only she could have blended them together and made a perfect mate. Called Goy or Trorge. Absolutely gorgeous, faithful and committed, with supersonic earning prowess and built-in sensitivity. Guaranteed to provide 100 per cent fulfilment. Stephanie laughed at herself as she switched on the bathroom light. Who was she kidding?

'Oh.' George was pleased to find her with a toothbrush in her mouth. 'Going to bed already?'

'Yes – thought I'd have an early night.' She needed to make things better. Get rid of the fear.

She wished she knew what was wrong. It wasn't anything George did or didn't do. His hands moved in the same way they had always done. Maybe that was the problem. Nothing in his lips, warm breath, familiar arms had changed. But she had. Even if her skin responded, even as she was dimly aware of small flickers of desire, there was something cold and empty and dead in her that couldn't fan them into life.

Sometimes her life with Troy was a blur. She couldn't always remember what they ate or wore or talked about. But then whole pieces of time would come back to her crystal clear. She'd never forgotten the way her body would jolt with delicious spasms when he touched her. How the first time, that first time, they had both been shuddering with passion as their bodies touched. In her kitchen there had still been that old connection.

As she forced herself to soften in George's arms, she thought of her head against Troy's chest, his hand that had reached to stroke her hair and suddenly the warmth came. George felt it. He tightened his arms around her, pressed his body more deeply into hers. She felt the relief flow between them. For a few dark moments beneath the duvet, everything was all right again.

Later Stephanie turned over restlessly, knowing she wouldn't sleep for a long time. She sat up slowly so as not to wake George and reached for her glass of water. She had a job! She almost hugged herself with delight. All so daring and forbidden. A bit like Troy. She remembered Madeleine's face in the office, the moment when Samantha had burst in.

Now she thought of Madeleine's voice, lowered conspiratorially. 'Even Ken thinks it's recruitment. And a virtual office service. Everyone assumes that PAs must stand for Personal Assistants.'

She'd laughed and blown out a long stream of smoke. 'All except the clients of course.'

'And what is it really?' Stephanie had asked, feeling as if she were caught up in a dangerous but heady adventure.

'PAs,' said Madeleine, mouth curved into a seductive

smile, voice low and slow as syrup, 'is a discreet service for the chronically unfaithful.'

Her smile had widened at the expression on Stephanie's face.

'PAs stands for *Perfect Alibis*.'

Chapter 5

Madeleine still felt a rush of pleasure, breathless as orgasm, every time she slid her key into the office lock. There was something thrilling about the power she held, the difference she made, the lives she saved from ruin.

She touched the metal plate beside the door. PAs. Her creation. Grown beyond her wildest expectations.

Madeleine knew that many people would find what she did unpleasant. Still, she reasoned – with the brittle conviction of a prostitute justifying her career choice – she was providing a service.

She crossed the empty reception and pushed open the door of her office. She hung up her coat and looked around the room. The imposing black desk, the low chrome and glass table, the vase of lilies. All hers. She walked down the carpeted corridor to the sound room, shaking her head at the tangle of wires and jumble of CDs and cassettes that littered the surfaces.

'Can't you girls ever tidy up?' Madeleine frowned at the girl sitting in front of her.

The sleepy blonde looked up smudgy-eyed from the mug of black coffee she was cradling. 'It's been mad here,' she said grumpily. Madeleine raised her eyebrows as the girl continued: 'That Kennedy woman's been phoning the number herself all night – she seems to think it's the helpline! I'll be surprised if her bloke gets any at all. You'll have to tell her.'

'I'll pop on a surcharge,' Madeleine soothed, flicking through index cards with a long red nail. 'Have these all been updated on the system? When Jo comes on, tell her Monica Marchant wants another twelve hours' cover – still the sick aunt story. Monica gone to get a prescription, etcetera.'

'Yeah.' The girl rubbed at her eyes again.

'Bit of Radio Two in the background, maybe.' Madeleine looked at her sharply. 'Come on, Caroline! Monica's our best client.'

They were all women. Women were so much more thorough about affairs, mindful of details, careful with contingencies. Men discarded their trousers with an easy arrogance, expecting to be believed and trusted. It was simply a matter of confidence, of course. Privately, Madeleine thought many of her clients over-anxious, not blessed with the constitution for in-depth deceit; but who was she to complain while she commanded lavish fees from those fretting to maintain their lifestyles.

It was such a simple idea that Madeleine could sometimes hardly believe it had come to her. If it hadn't been for Patsy, well, who knows, it might not have done. But a few simple back-up stories for her had blossomed, and now look at them – providing twenty-four-hour cover, seven days a week, any alibi catered for complete with background noise; corroborating evidence supplied.

'Isn't Samantha supposed to be here by now?'

Caroline yawned again. 'She called to say her bus was cancelled.'

Madeleine sat in her swivel chair and looked through the day's lists. Stephanie would be here at ten, she had a new client coming at eleven and the rather pleasing prospect of the afternoon at a nearby hotel with the husband of one of her more neurotic existing ones.

Madeleine enjoyed dalliances with a string of husbands whose wives she knew to be safely and otherwise engaged. She had once built up sufficient rapport with one wife to admit to the pastime but such open-mindedness was rare. It never failed to amaze Madeleine how many partners, while making a positive career out of infidelity, could not stomach the thought of their spouses doing the same.

She thought of Stephanie's face when she'd told her. She'd controlled it well. She'd never have thought of employing Stephanie a few months ago – she was far too straight. The golden rule had always been only to employ those who were at it. Those who had a vested interest in keeping their mouths shut and something to lose by blowing the whistle. But they needed a proper admin assistant again. Someone who could deal with all the paperwork and be relied upon to be discreet. Easier said than done. Obviously too much money about the place. Nobody in Edenhurst seemed to need to earn a living these days. All the women she knew had more creative ways of filling in the hours while the kids were at school.

Maybe she could train Stephanie up. After all, nobody could be worse than Samantha. God, that girl had some-thing missing. No wonder she'd been unemployable. She shouldn't have let Patsy persuade her to take her on. Monica Marchant might be Patsy's oldest friend and PAs' founder client – but her god-daughter!

No, Stephanie was reliable. Madeleine had felt that adrenalin high from making the right decision. Stephanie could be trusted. Anyway, there was something about her these days . . .

Stephanie felt good. Not only had George been singing at breakfast and the children – for once – had not come to blows over the cereal boxes, but her look had come together in a way that made her feel she might yet be a proper human being again.

Black trousers were always slimming, the top seemed looser than the last time she'd worn it and the flat shoes at least enabled her to walk without hobbling. She'd driven so that she could go straight to school when she left and as she parked and exchanged smiles with another woman in a navy suit and briefcase also locking a car, Stephanie had a sense of belonging that she hadn't felt for a long time.

Madeleine was on the telephone when she got there. She nodded at Stephanie and motioned towards a chair.

'Yes, absolutely. No – the hotel are brilliant. A hundred per cent. No – we'll book you in – one of our own names, yes. Speak to Jo . . .'

She rolled her eyes heavenwards and nodded towards a cardboard box at Stephanie's feet. It was full of bits of paper of various sizes.

'Yes, lovely. You enjoy! Don't worry about a thing.'

Stephanie turned the first one over. It was a blank cab receipt.

'Bye!'

Madeleine opened her cigarette packet. 'New one. They do get anxious at the beginning.'

Stephanie thought about Troy in her kitchen. She had butterflies just thinking about a beginning.

'That lot needs organizing.' Madeleine pointed at the box. 'I think Pauline must have had a breakdown in her last week here – dumped the lover, went back to her husband.' Madeleine pulled an uncomprehending face. 'Left the paperwork in a terrible mess.'

'Right.' Stephanie looked at the bulging box, wondering what exactly she was supposed to do with it.

'Suppose she found God or something. Ah!' Madeleine swung round as Jo came in. 'Be a darling and show

Stephanie where everything is. And rustle up some more coffee.'

She picked up the phone again. 'Jo's marvellous. Knows everything. Come back in here before eleven and you can watch an initiation. Best way to learn the ropes.'

Stephanie obediently followed her to the outer office where Jo dumped the box on the empty desk. 'All yours!' She grinned at Steph. 'Let's hope you last longer than the last one.'

The woman looked doubtful when she saw Stephanie sitting in the corner. 'My assistant,' said Madeleine briskly. 'We're all in the same boat – no worries there.'

Stephanie blinked nervously. She'd never seen the woman before, but she could pop up next week as the mother of a new child in Toby's class, or the wife of George's latest squash crony. She wasn't sure she wanted her thinking she was 'in the same boat' at all. Particularly as it wasn't true. Her hand slid to the bag at her feet. There'd been two more texts this morning. She felt Madeleine's eyes on her and put her hands hurriedly back in her lap.

The woman was about Stephanie's age, nothing remarkable about her: mousy hair, little make-up, slightly frumpy skirt and top. But she was looking at Madeleine as if she held the key to eternal joy.

Madeleine was handing various things to her. 'You get this user guide – full information on a single credit-sized card, easy to slip into wallet or purse. You get a copy of *How To Have an Affair*, my own personal list of Dos and Don'ts based on thirty years of experience – consider it the A–Z of pain-free extra-marital sex, and you sign this . . .' Madeleine pushed a sheet of paper across the desk. 'The Pledge. Think of it as our own form of the Official Secrets Act.' She gave a brief smile. 'If you break it I can and will sue for breach of confidentiality.'

The woman looked startled. 'That would rather let the cat out of the bag, wouldn't it?' She laughed self-consciously.

Madeleine's eyes narrowed.

'We have a responsibility to each other,' she said sternly. 'My clients do get caught occasionally. Through carelessness and complacency but never through this agency. There has never been a chink in our armour and I intend to keep it that way.'

She leant forward. 'If you do get caught you never admit to this agency's part in the deception. You always stick to the authenticity of the alibis provided. We can have no sobbing confessions. It's like the Resistance – you never bring anyone down with you.'

Stephanie saw a look of respect cross the woman's face and she wanted to giggle. Madeleine had a strange faraway light in her eyes. An image of George listening to this fervent war speech arose in Stephanie's mind: he was being caustic and amusing. Once he had made her laugh so much . . .

Abruptly, Madeleine snapped back to her cool businesslike self. 'If you're not prepared to sign there is no need for us to take up any more of each other's time.'

'No, no, I will.' The woman looked anxious as she ran her eyes down the clauses. 'Don't tell our lovers? Why not?'

Madeleine spoke gently now as if explaining to a small child.

'They're men.'

Stephanie wanted to laugh again. The woman looked up as Madeleine continued drily: 'We assume! For the most part, women having affairs with other women do not need alibis.'

She lit a cigarette. 'But men have wives. The only way we can make it completely tight is to keep it a service for women by women that only women know about. If we let

84

men in, if they even get a whiff of how it works, they might tell a friend whose wife may be playing away. Who knows? Your lover's own wife may already be a client.'

The woman laughed again uncertainly. 'Well it wouldn't matter then, would it, if they were both at it?'

Madeleine gave a mirthless snort. 'Ah the innocence!' She inhaled deeply. 'For men it always matters. They care for different reasons. For women it is the awful realization of love and attention going elsewhere. The excruciating image of his hands covering the same trail on another's body, his whispering the same soft words to someone else. She will think – how could he? Sully our precious times, break our trust, our special, unique togetherness. She will grieve for the loss of his love, his commitment, his faithfulness, his *interest*.'

Stephanie felt her face grow hot. The woman was rapt, gazing at Madeleine like a religious convert.

Madeleine sent two thin streams of smoke down flared nostrils. 'But for men it is a base instinct. A horror of being the cuckold. Men's first question will be "Who knows?" Their second: "Did he have a bigger dick than me?" '

The woman's eyes bulged.

'And be very sure,' finished Madeleine, pulling the ashtray towards her, 'however many times he's screwed his secretary, he will never forgive you.'

The woman shook her head. 'I don't think Terry would . . .'

Madeleine smiled. 'They all would, believe me.'

Stephanie was quite sure George wouldn't. She wondered whether Ken did. It was hard to imagine anyone succumbing to those wet lips by choice. But presumably he had something, for Madeleine to marry him in the first place.

Madeleine was going through the finer details now. 'So

you let us know when you want to be away from home and we'll discuss the alibi with you and tell you which number to give him. Then if he does call, we'll field it and either come up with a convincing excuse why you're not there, with appropriate sound effects, or divert the call to your mobile or hotel room if it's safe to do so.'

'I don't think Terry would—' the woman began again.

'It's an insurance policy,' Madeleine interrupted smoothly. 'That's what you're paying for – peace of mind. It's the just-in-case factor that makes all the difference. There's always a first time: one of the children is sick, he can't find where his pink shirt is, your mother-in-law collapses . . .'

'Actually she's—'

'All manner of things can happen.' Madeleine was firm. 'But you will know that we will cater for every eventuality . . .'

The woman nodded.

'Which reminds me,' Madeleine consulted the sheet of paper in her hand. 'Skills. I see you're a chiropodist.'

'Not since I had the children.'

'Anything else you can do? You haven't ever been in the police force, I suppose?' Madeleine asked hopefully. The woman shook her head.

'Shame. Not quite sure where your particular area of expertise would come in but we have to be prepared to help each other in a crisis. We could do with some more nurses. I suppose it's the hours they work,' she mused. 'And the low pay. We've got a gynaecologist . . .'

The woman clutched her knees. 'I hope I'm doing the right thing,' she said suddenly, looking appealingly at Madeleine. Madeleine flashed her a smile. 'Jo will discuss the most discreet form of payment.' She pressed the buzzer on her desk. 'You can cancel at any time,' she reassured her as Jo's shiny head appeared. 'Jo – Mrs H is ready to set up her account now.'

She held out her hand. 'Enjoy yourself,' she said in her low throaty voice. 'Only here once.'

The woman blushed as she followed Jo from the room, throwing Madeleine an adoring look back over her shoulder.

Madeleine leant back in her chair and looked at Stephanie. 'Get the idea?'

'Yes but – ' God it was so, so bizarre – 'Why give their husbands numbers at all? Why not just have a mobile?'

Madeleine shook her head. 'Mobiles let you down. Background noise, people coughing and spluttering at the wrong time. If you're supposed to be having your legs waxed and you're in fact on the train, or comforting your sick second cousin three miles away when you're halfway up the M4, you're going to come unstuck pretty quick. Worse is when there's *supposed* to be train noise. Imagine! He expects you to be on the Gatwick Express and you're tucked up in bed in the Hotel la Ruche.'

'You could always not answer it, I suppose,' said Stephanie, 'or turn it off.'

'Yes – in an emergency. But this way we smooth things over for a delay in calling back if it's necessary. It avoids suspicion, saves the client getting stressed by the old man phoning again and again till she does answer. And chances are he'll get suspicious anyway because he's got a mobile himself and always switches it off when he's getting his own leg over.'

Stephanie felt her own eyes popping like the last woman's. Again, Madeleine spoke as if having sex with someone else was a normal part of married life. She was still talking. 'Of course it's best if you can act the dizzy little woman who half the time forgets to even take her mobile with her, let alone switch it on. But we've got some very high-powered women on our books. When your wife has been a ruthless model of efficiency for the last ten years, that sort of thing *would* raise suspicion.'

87

'Yes I suppose it would,' said Stephanie faintly.

'And we've got one client whose lover's flat has no signal whatsoever. So you can imagine how awkward that is. Suddenly she's out of contact for two hours when a whole lot of people expect her to be available. That needs very careful handling. We have to cover her by providing alibi details for situations where she'd be forced to turn her phone off. On planes, in hospitals, at funerals of important clients and so on.'

Stephanie blinked. 'But how often would she go to them?'

'You'd be surprised,' said Madeleine darkly. 'Anyway it's not just about fielding phone calls. It's all the little details – theatre tickets if you're supposed to have been there, *plus* a proper run-down on the play. Restaurant receipts – even credit card entries appearing on hubbie's statement – right day, right part of the country. Wherever you've been! Long-lost school friends supplied in person, invitations sent through the post . . .'

'It sounds very thorough,' said Stephanie, brain whirling.

Madeleine looked pleased. 'I've made it my business to help others.' Something in Stephanie stirred. A sort of deep discomfort mixed with a throbbing vein of excitement. Could she . . .

'Oh by the way,' said Madeleine, like a mind-reader, 'of course you'll be entitled to full use of the service now you're going to be part of the firm. You just let Jo know any time you want to be covered.'

'Oh I won't,' Stephanie felt a jerk of alarm.

Madeleine continued regardless. 'It can be as simple as working late here or as complex as you like. But,' she went on, 'I always say the simple stories are best. Less to remember. You see, what people forget is—'

'No, really,' Stephanie interrupted her. 'I really won't be needing anything like that.'

Madeleine smiled. 'Well, the offer's there. All part of the package.'

Please come and see me. Need you. The first text had shocked her but since then she couldn't stop thinking about his hands.

'You may need it some time,' Madeleine continued. 'You never know. A well-placed affair can do wonders for a marriage. Breathe a bit of new life into the bedroom.' God, was the woman psychic! A pleasant tingle caught Stephanie by surprise. There was a certain thrill at being actively encouraged to go off and misbehave.

'But don't you ever feel guilty?' she asked curiously.

Madeleine cackled, pulling her Rothmans towards her. Stephanie watched the lipsticked mouth pulling pleasurably on a cigarette. Little fissures around her lips revealed the age Madeleine's vibrancy disguised. She blew out a long stream of smoke and shook her head.

'Guilt? I gave up on that a long time ago. What hurts is not infidelity itself – it's being found out. I provide a service. A much-needed one. The women who come to me have already stepped over the line. They're already doing it and taking risks. What I am doing is preventing pain, not causing it.'

'But isn't it the affair itself that causes the hurt?'

'Well, maybe.' Madeleine was evidently bored by that line of thought. 'But most of my clients look pretty good on it. *Carpe diem* and all that! Anyway, take a copy of all the bumph and have a look through.'

Stephanie looked at the booklets and sheets she'd been handed. The fee structure was on top. 'My goodness!' she said startled. 'Is that how much it costs?'

Madeleine nodded, unperturbed. 'Cheaper than a divorce.'

Chapter 6

Divorce? Where do I sign? And please God – let George get custody of the kids.

Toby was in trauma over the sight of spaghetti – she *knew* he'd gone off it after the last lot was 'slimy', Charlotte was mid-diatribe about her lot in life. Emma was allowed to go to some dubious-sounding disco in the middle of the dodgiest housing estate in the country but she Charlotte, oppressed of Edenhurst, was made to be an object of ridicule to the whole school, the only girl with a brain-dead mother from the Dark Ages.

'It's way unfair,' she finished accusingly.

'And I hate *mince*,' put in Toby.

George answered the phone.

He held out the receiver to Stephanie, his face expressionless.

For a moment her heart stopped. Not calling her home line now . . .

'It's Hettie.'

'Oh!' Heart started again.

Cousin Henrietta. She was Henry when she was in her dungarees phase, Etta for the ethnic earrings and floppy embroidered skirts, Hen when she first married Jack and had high hopes of being an earth mother. Now she was Hettie. Or sometimes Het. Or 'Het-up', as George used to call her when she was Dettoxing the toys, and sniffing about the floor for germs.

'Hello, Hettie. Er yes, I should think so. Yes, that's still fine. Of course we'd love to have you all . . .'

George looked pained. 'Again?'

'She needs to get out of the house. We're her only family.'

'She's got a husband, she's got two parents.'

'She can't stay with them, can she? They're in Australia.'

'It's all right for them, isn't it? Have these nutty daughters and then disappear to the other side of the world.'

'Your sister did it. We're still stuck with your mother.'

They always fell into the old patterns. He'd say Hettie was insufferable, she'd say, 'Look at your bloody mother!' If she wanted to send him purple with rage she might add: 'and that's how you'll end up'.

Now George's mouth tightened. 'You don't have to be stuck with her,' he said stiffly.

'I don't mind! I come with you to support you,' said Stephanie, already regretting her words. 'And you could support me. Hettie's all right. She just needs someone to talk to.'

'Why does it always have to be you?'

'There isn't anyone else.' *Not any more.*

'Does she have to sleep here?' he asked plaintively. 'You know what she's like. Can't even stay put in the guest room – has to barge about everywhere.'

Stephanie smiled. Last time, Hettie had marched into their bedroom without warning, and found George just out of the shower.

'I don't think she'll do that again,' she said now, recalling the shrieks. 'And it's only one night. Just so I can take her to her hospital appointment the next morning.'

'Can't she get a taxi?'

*   *   *

Stephanie defrosted some brown sludge she'd found lurking at the bottom of the freezer and thought was Bolognese, and made Toby a tuna sandwich and chips. Charlotte was still sulking upstairs. They ate in silence. But George had a way of chewing that spoke multitudes.

'What's wrong with her this time?' he said eventually.

Stephanie looked sideways at Toby. 'I'm not sure you want to know.'

'Well I hope she doesn't upset you this time.'

She felt her smile shrivel. 'It's not her.'

'It is her. You know it is. She talks too much. Stirs things up.' George looked at his empty plate. 'It's not the same when it's been frozen, is it?'

Stephanie looked at her own full one. *No George, nothing is.*

Toby looked from one to the other and laid down his fork with a martyred expression. 'This tuna's got black bits in it.'

'Come and walk Kelly with me!' George interrupted round two of the Disco War by appearing with the lead and the dog. Charlotte sighed and flounced into the hall.

George's answer to everything. Nothing that couldn't be solved by a game of squash or a brisk march round the block. He'd probably like to route-march Stephanie too if he had his way. Get her up at six and put her through her paces. Blow away that neurosis. Stem those tears.

It was true she used to get upset when she saw Hettie. Hettie reminded her of what Rose had done, Hettie never let her forget – and George was uncomfortable with crying. OK if there was some tangible cause – you had dropped the iron on your foot, run over next door's cat or the stock market had crashed – but un-structured, uncontrollable tears for vague emotional reasons of sadness and guilt or some indefinable emptiness and he was lost. Stephanie didn't cry in front of him any more.

Troy had been hopeless in many ways but he'd listen. He'd switch off on matters of bills and jobs and fidelity and overdrafts but for the inner workings of her hopes and fears he would always be there. Him and Rose.

Rose was seventeen when Stephanie met her. A trainee SRN at the Charing Cross Hospital while Steph was at college down the road. Rose was bossy and practical, fiercely self-sufficient. Although she'd been to school with Hettie she seemed much older than both of them. She'd had to look after her younger sisters when her mother left, just had to get on with it, and she had no time for Troy's dilettante ways and indulged upbringing. 'You be careful of him,' she used to say.

Troy would laugh. 'Jealous!' he'd respond. 'Can't get a man herself!'

But Stephanie knew Rose was her friend who looked out for her. Who wanted her to be happy. Rose would listen too. Once, Rose would always have been there.

Hettie was bigger than ever. Her breasts appeared through the door first followed by the panting, sighing, rest of her. The grunting and groaning appeared to be caused less by the baby that was dangling from her neck than by her baggage, which piled up in a pyramid in the hall in the most alarming fashion and made Stephanie thankful that George wasn't there to pull faces.

How she'd managed to get it all into the taxi was a mystery. There was a bulging changing bag, a suitcase, three carrier bags, a mouldy-looking threadbare rabbit with glaring eyes, named Poo-chew (and looking as if it had been subjected to quite a lot of both), several magazines, a packet of digestive biscuits that at this moment was spilling a shower of crumbs onto the

Chinese rug, a pillow and a rolled-up duvet in hurt-your-eyes pink featuring Barbie in a variety of painful-looking poses.

'She won't sleep without it,' said Hettie in explanation. (She prefixed lots of her pronouncements on Erica with 'She won't.')

'She bloody well would if she was mine,' George would have growled and Stephanie silently agreed. Soft mother she might be in the eating department, but she was Attila the Hun compared with Hettie.

'Come in! Come in!' Steph said unnecessarily as Hettie pulled Erica towards the kitchen. The child was making soft grizzly noises, a thumb in her mouth, her other arm wound around her mother's leg, so that Hettie had to haul herself along as if she had a limp. Erica took little shuffles as Het dragged her across the hall.

'Oh, Steph!' Hettie seemed to lean her entire weight on Steph's shoulders as she hugged her, pelvis thrust backwards so as not to crush her sleeping infant in the embrace. Stephanie glanced down at Erica. The child was staring back up at her, her small face framed in blond waves, her blue eyes huge with suspicion.

Steph disengaged herself.

'Hello, sweetheart,' she cooed, reflecting that actually Erica was right to look wary as she couldn't stand her. 'Would you like a drink?'

Erica continued to stare. Hettie pulled the thumb out of her mouth. 'Would you like a drink darling?' she asked, then looked back to Steph. 'Very – ' she leant forward – 'T-I-R-E-D!' she enunciated carefully as if Steph needed to lip-read. Erica pulled her arm away and pushed her thumb back between her small pouting lips.

'Coffee?' Stephanie asked Hettie, looking at the clock and seeing there wasn't time to play drinks-waiter for petulant children. 'I've got to go and get the kids in a minute. Will you be all right here for a bit?'

Hettie was rooting in one of the carrier bags. 'I think I might have some sugar-free rosehip.' She straightened up, a small bottle in her hand. 'OK, well, we'll talk when you get back. Joshua should sleep for a while now – he just dropped off in the cab.'

Stephanie looked at the top of Joshua's downy head in the sling. Tiny rumpled face so blissfully asleep. She had a memory of her own son, fresh-born, still bashed-looking, but wide eyes looking up into hers as she cradled him, exhausted. And the nurse saying: 'There's a friend of yours outside.'

She'd taken Rose for granted then.

Stephanie put the coffee on the table, pulled out a chair for Hettie and watched as her cousin lowered herself onto it, adjusting the sling more comfortably in front of her, and felt a deep, sudden wash of loss.

She'd thought she and Rose would be friends for ever.

There was an informal gathering of the Facelift Club in the playground. Stephanie, Millie, Jacqui and Sue. All knocking on forty's door, all spending that windy five minutes stamping their feet in the playground waiting for the kids to stream out, obsessing about lines and sagging bits, podgy upper arms and drooping bottoms.

It had been Jacqui's idea. She said they should all have the facelifts at the same time and club together to rent a cottage in the country for three weeks while the redness died down and the swelling subsided. They'd all fallen on the idea, desperate for their faces to be ironed out and not wanting any more than the next woman to stand there in front of all the other parents with their bruises and stitches on display. Only trouble was, it had to be before everyone was forty (Jacqui had read an article that said facelifts were at their most effective when you were still in your late thirties and should then last you without sagging until you were mid-fifties). And all the others had much further to go than Stephanie. Sue was thirty-five, Millie thirty-six. Jacqui was thirty-seven and Stephanie was pretending she was thirty-seven too. She hadn't really meant to be dishonest. Jacqui had once said 'You're the same age as me, aren't you?' and somehow Stephanie had nodded and now it had stuck. Millie knew she wasn't but Jacqui and Sue believed it completely. Which was gratifying on the one hand but yet another cause for panic on the other as in seven months' time she was going to have to hide the unspeakable from them.

Stephanie sometimes woke in the night in a panic, just picturing the humiliation if George decided to have a personality transplant and took it upon himself to spring a surprise and she rolled up at school to see a huge banner proclaiming: OVER THE HILL STEPHANIE – 40 TODAY! Just when she – in giggly fashion – had handed over a fiver the day before for the cottage fund two years hence.

Sue grabbed at her the moment she appeared. 'You will still be my other guinea pig, won't you?' she said. 'You've got time during the day, haven't you?'

'Clear out your toxins,' said Jacqui, 'give that sluggish circulation a boost . . .'

Sue smiled. 'Be quiet. It's a balancing thing.' She spoke to Stephanie. 'I need to get your case study in before my exams. I give you six sessions and write up notes on them and then you just sign a thing saying what you thought and on the last one we do it in front of my tutor.'

'What do we do?'

'Reflexology! You haven't forgotten!'

'No of course not!' (She had.) 'Sorry, I was thinking about something else.'

Troy wanted her to visit. Madeleine had said she could have an alibi any time she liked. Even suggested it would do her marriage good. She was nearly forty. There weren't going to be many more chances for a little harmless flirtation . . .

'Who's that then?' Millie grinned, cutting into her thoughts.

'I've got my mum for the elderly, you for the middle' (Steph felt her smile grow fixed) 'and now I just need someone obese I can advise on nutrition.'

Millie nudged her. 'Like – eat less you fat cow!'

Sue elbowed her back. 'You're terrible. You will do it, Steph, won't you?'

'Of course I will.' Who wouldn't want to lie back and have someone else rub their feet for six hours?

'She's not very gentle.' Jacqui pulled a face. 'She had to get my adrenal gland going again and she really poked me about!'

Sue shook her head, laughing. 'That isn't true at all.'

Jacqui continued. 'Well, she *said* it was my adrenal gland – but I don't think she knows which bits she's pressing half the time, I had the raging shits all night.'

They all screamed with laughter.

'Don't listen to her,' said Sue. 'I got a distinction for my last assessment.'

'Oh shit! Here we go,' said Millie as a familiar figure bore down on them.

'Good afternoon, ladies!' Deirdre Brunskill descended with the famous clipboard.

'Hi!' Millie beamed.

'Everyone all right for Wednesday week?' She ticked something off her list (presumably a reminder to say: Everyone all right for Wednesday week?) 'Very important meeting, big agenda, lots to get through.' She gave a cracked laugh (tick). 'Summer fairs don't run themselves, unfortunately' (tick).

PTA meetings were from 7 to 9 p.m. But sometimes they overran. An exhilarating possibility opened up like a flower before Stephanie. Deirdre was looking straight at her. She felt herself blush.

'Yes,' she said. Jacqui gave an almost imperceptible snort behind her and she saw Millie's mouth twitch.

'Sorry, dear?'

'Yes I can come.'

'Oh jolly good.' Deirdre peered at her curiously and made a few more ticks while Sue interjected with lengthy explanations about college courses and endless essays to write.

'I'll help on the day, of course,' she added quite unnecessarily, as they all knew Deirdre would think nothing of arriving at her house at dawn and dragging her out by the scruff of her neck if she didn't.

'I'll be a bit late,' said Jacqui – also unnecessarily, because she always was – 'but I'll get there.'

'Lovely,' said Deirdre ticking like a mad thing. 'Super raffle prizes this year. Have you seen what that kind Mr Philpot's given again?'

Jacqui shook her head. Stephanie – conjuring up an image of the neon-pink plastic cow he had donated at Christmas – made a mental note to remind Deirdre on Wednesday that she was on Cakes this time. No more dragging enormous nameless toys about the place and being mobbed by sticky-handed children.

Wednesday evening. She could pop in to see Troy on the way home. Just sit and talk for a while, like he said. Nothing else.

Millie was looking at her. 'You OK?' she mouthed. Stephanie nodded.

'I've got something for you.' Millie pressed a small box into Stephanie's hand. 'A little present.' She winked. 'Small endorphin boost!'

'What?' Stephanie turned the package in her hands. 'Oh God, Millie, what is it?' And then the kids came out.

*   *   *

98

Toby stripped off his blazer and dropped it, book bag, lunchbox, PE kit and a huge expanse of sugar paper covered in green paint at her feet.

'Did you have a good day, darling?' she called as he tore off.

Millie stood beside her, her own arms filled with similar paraphernalia. 'I got it from Amanda,' she said under her breath. 'Gets straight to the spot.'

'You should have come to that party the other night, Jac,' she went on at normal volume. 'She had poppers, bath toys, the lot.'

'Didn't have a sitter. Or I would have. I wanted one of those rabbits.'

Millie laughed. 'I know someone who's on her third – she's worn out the first two. Come to the next one. Amanda reckons she's doing quite well out of it. Plus of course she gets to play with the stock! Needs to, now Stuart's gone. Stephanie really enjoyed herself, didn't you, Steph?'

'I'd rather have a toy anyway than Stuart,' said Jacqui. 'Never could see the attraction there. Still, I wouldn't have thought it of him. Always seemed so straight. But it's always the ones you'd least expect.' Stephanie felt herself grow hot.

'Toby!' she called across the playground.

He ignored her.

'*Toby!*' she shrieked. Why was she the only mother who had to scream like a banshee to get any response from her child? Deirdre just did a Mrs Robinson 'Waiter' type flick of the head for her three to come bounding over and queue up in alphabetical order.

Toby trailed up, scuffing his shoes on the tarmac.

'Where's your sister?'

Toby shrugged.

'I hope she comes out in a minute,' Stephanie said. 'Hettie and Erica are at home.'

'What, at our house again?'

'Yes.'

He gave a long deep sigh, looking like George.

'Can you try and be nice to Erica this time? Please? Darling?'

Toby sighed again. 'I'll try.'

Toby's idea of trying was to give Erica's Barbie a jolly good pasting with his Action Man and then disappear to his bedroom with his Gameboy. Charlotte emptied the fridge into two slices of bread and prepared to stomp off too.

'Have you said hello to Hettie and Erica?' Stephanie demanded shrilly as her daughter made for the stairs.

'Hello,' Charlotte bent her mouth into a grudging smile at Hettie. 'Hello,' she added in bored tones as Erica grizzled her way back into the kitchen.

But just for once Hettie didn't seem to notice. She didn't comment when Erica had whined 'Toby won't play with me' for the sixth time and Stephanie led her to the pile of videos and jammed *Postman Pat Rides Again* into the machine. Normally they'd have been in for a thirty-minute debate on the perils of too much TV. Today she clearly had more pressing issues on her mind.

Stephanie looked at her. 'Are you OK?'

Hettie looked back. 'Not really.'

Stephanie's phone beeped loudly as she made more coffee. She jumped. Hettie's head whipped round as Stephanie grabbed at it. **Message received.** 'Text from Millie,' she said conversationally, moving the phone out of Hettie's line of vision as she opened it.

CANT STOP THINK ABOUT U.

'What's the matter?' She put a mug in front of Hettie. 'Still feeling low?'

Hettie gave a huge long sigh. 'Oh Steph!'

'I mean obviously *this* business – ' Hettie jerked her

head meaningfully towards her crotch – 'isn't helping much.'

Stephanie found herself nodding at it too. 'What's happening about that?'

'I'm seeing a new specialist tomorrow. The other one thought I was exaggerating.' Hettie sighed. 'Though to be honest I don't think Jack's much interested anyway.'

Stephanie felt a stab of sympathy. Maybe a bit of wife-swapping was in order. She and Jack could curl up and go straight to sleep while George and Hettie panted away on top of each other all night. She pictured the look that would cross George's face at the prospect.

'It's not funny!' said Hettie hotly. 'My marriage could fall apart.'

'Oh God, I'm sorry.' Stephanie put her hand to her mouth, contrite. 'I wasn't smiling at that. I was just thinking that—' She stopped as Charlotte wandered into the kitchen.

'I am so starving!' She opened the cupboard where the biscuits were. 'When are we eating?'

'Have you done your homework?'

Charlotte balanced half a dozen chocolate chip cookies on the palm of her hand. 'Yes, Mum!' She rolled her eyes at the intense tedium of life. 'Don't keep on.'

'Erica! Erica!' Hettie leapt from her chair as her daughter fell through the kitchen door, her small sharp teeth firmly clamped round Batman's head. Toby landed on top of her.

'Give it back!' He grasped at the figure and tugged.

Hettie thudded down between them and attempted to prise her daughter's jaws apart. 'Drop it now, darling! Goodness knows where it's been!'

Hettie sat up panting, holding the wet figure between finger and thumb and turned to Stephanie. 'I thought we'd got over all this. It's just her asserting some territory. She's obviously feeling insecure again.' She sighed.

'She's picking up my vibes. I know she is. I am so F-R-U-S-T-R-A-T-E-D.'

Erica looked at her mother with interest. 'Frustrated?' enquired Toby.

At the sound of the key turning in the front door lock there was a small plaintive cry from the other room.

'Oh, the baby's awake!' Hettie rushed across the hall, nearly knocking George over.

George stopped, pulling a face as he met Stephanie's eyes. 'It would be, wouldn't it?'

By the time Erica had sucked the tomato sauce off four pieces of pasta, Toby had had a nervous breakdown over his fish fingers, Charlotte had rowed with George about the last baked potato and Hettie had smashed the salad dressing bottle, Stephanie had rather lost her appetite.

George sighed as she cleared away his chicken bones and mopped at the table. 'Is he going to cry all night?' he asked, martyred.

'Shhhh! He's just hungry, he'll be all right when he's been fed.'

Hettie returned with the whimpering baby in her arms, sat down, and proceeded to rummage inside her shirt.

BEEP!

'Don't you get a lot of texts?' said Hettie, producing a huge pendulous breast and pushing it into Joshua's face.

'Just PTA stuff.' Stephanie glanced nervously at George but he was too busy looking revolted. 'I think I'll go and watch the news,' he said.

'Fine,' said Stephanie, surreptitiously retrieving her phone from behind the bread bin.

2 messages received

Y U NOT REPLY? ILY XX

I DESPERATE 4 U XXXXX

'When can I have a mobile?' Charlotte took the lid off the cake tin.

'When you need one.'

'Everyone else has got one already. Danni got one when she was ten.'

'Well she'll probably have a brain tumour by the time she's sixteen then, won't she?'

Charlotte scowled. 'What about your brain?'

'I hardly ever use mine.' She grinned at her daughter. 'Ha Ha! Or the phone.'

Charlotte remained stony. 'Why can't I have it, then?'

'Why don't you go and read with Toby and Erica so Hettie and I can clear up?'

Charlotte pushed the last of a jam tart into her mouth and rolled her eyes again. 'Bor-ring!' she said. 'Anyway, it's *EastEnders* in a minute.'

Stephanie sat in the quiet of the kitchen with Joshua in her arms. She remembered that expression – little mouth lopsided, punch-drunk on milk. A lot of Toby's first weeks were a blur but bits came back – moments of softness. She could hear the rise and fall of Hettie's voice in the dining room reading to Erica and Toby, the mutterings of the TV where George and Charlotte sat together, and felt peculiarly dislocated.

She'd turned her phone to silent after she'd replied but it sat in the top of her handbag and she kept stealing glances at it, waiting for it to light up once more.

1 message received

MUST CU B4 I GO.

Her heart leapt and fell. Oh God, she wanted to see him too. She couldn't keep away much longer. And he was going soon.

Stephanie opened another bottle of wine as soon as George had gone to bed, relieved to note that he had drunk most of the first one and would be snoring by the time she got up there. He'd left her alone since the other night. Just put an arm around her waist and dropped off. But the next session hung like the penis of Damocles above her head and she wanted it to dangle there a bit longer.

Curiously, she opened up the cardboard tube that Millie had given her. There was a lipstick inside. OH! Millie had been joking! She pulled the lid off and stared at the bright red tip inside. The whole thing was plastic. She frowned, turning it over in her hands. It didn't seem to do anything. She pulled at the base and all at once it burst into life against her palm, sending deep vibrations down to her fingertips. Stephanie jumped, hastily pushing it back into the off position as she heard Het's feet on the stairs.

'Want a drink?' She dropped the lipstick back into her handbag as her cousin eventually appeared from the marathon of putting Erica to bed. 'Lots of iron in red wine.'

'Got to be a bit careful.' Hettie took a mouthful from the glass Stephanie held out. 'You know – feeding.' She took another one. 'Still, at least the weight's coming off.'

Stephanie nodded. *From where?* 'Your skin's looking lovely,' she said. She fingered her own cheeks. 'I'm shrivelling up here.'

Hettie raised her eyebrows.

'You don't look much different to me.'

'I feel it. Suddenly all that time's gone and I didn't appreciate it. I just took it for granted in my twenties.'

Hettie shook her head. 'Twenties aren't anything special. All that insecurity and worrying about getting a man. I've been much happier in my thirties. Having the children, being with Jack . . .' She suddenly looked as if she might burst into tears.

Stephanie glanced across at her phone. No message. 'My twenties were OK. I mean there was Troy . . .'

Hettie made a loud harrumphing noise like an old cart-horse. 'Troy!'

'I've seen him.'

Hettie's eyes widened. 'Where?'

'He came here.'

'Here?' she jerked her head around the kitchen and looked at Stephanie in disbelief. 'He just turned up?'

'Yes. Well, no. I sort of asked him. We bumped into each other. He was a bit upset. His mother's died.'

Hettie settled herself more comfortably on her chair and leant forward, hands cradled around her glass, eyes intently on Steph's.

'So what happened?'

What had happened? Nothing and everything. He'd had a cup of coffee, she'd given him a hug. It was a non-event. She felt like her whole life had been picked up and shaken.

'He just came in for a few minutes.'

'And?' said Hettie impatiently. 'What's he like these days? Which poor unfortunate woman's he scrounging off?'

'He's married and he's working.'

'Alleluia. Doing what?'

'Something in computers.' Stephanie was surprised to find how defensive she sounded and knew Hettie could hear it too.

'Well thank God *you* didn't marry him! Just imagine that. Imagine if you'd had *children*!'

'He's got two.'

'Poor kids.'

Hettie could be such a cow. 'I expect he's quite a good father, actually. Probably makes them all sorts of wonderful carved toys and takes them on nature trails and things.'

'Huh! Wonder what his wife's like.'

So do I.

105

'Leopards don't change their spots,' said Hettie later, considering the wine bottle. Stephanie poured herself another glass and held up the remainder to her cousin.

'No, I'd better not.' Hettie rose and put the kettle on. 'Someone like Troy will always be bad news. Have you got any herbal tea?'

'I think he's settled down now.'

'Men like Troy don't. Remember what Rose used to say. Remember how upset you used to get. What about that time he went to that party and—'

'It's a long time ago now.'

Hettie laughed. 'Rose used to go round and deliberately wake him up when you were at work. She used to tell him he was a lazy bastard who ought to go out and get a job.'

Stephanie smiled, 'Did she really?'

'We used to have some fun, didn't we? The three of us. She could be so funny, Rose.'

Stephanie could see her and Rose holding each other up, crying with laughter, clutching a traffic cone they'd carried halfway across London, both too drunk to get the key in the lock. The cone had sat in Stephanie's bedroom for months . . .

'When she was being OK,' she said, tightly.

There was a single blackcurrant and vanilla teabag at the back of the shelf – a relic from the week when she'd brushed with giving up caffeine. She handed it to Hettie.

'She introduced me to Jack,' Hettie said. 'Remember me and Jack in the beginning? He couldn't keep his hands off me.'

'Here,' Stephanie pulled a tissue from her pocket. 'Don't get upset. You're tired and you've just had a baby. That's all. It will all seem better soon.'

The wine had gone straight to her head. Her words felt slow and soupy.

Hettie blew her nose. 'Well for heaven's sake don't you

go getting mixed up with Troy again. Not after all Rose did to help you get rid of him.'

'Rose just wanted to control me.'

Rose, standing guard as the locks were changed, heaving cardboard boxes out of the front door, Rose, fierce and protective, telling Stephanie she was worth more, taking down Troy's pictures, never taking no for an answer, leaving Stephanie no space, always there.

'She was a good friend to you when you needed her.'

'I know.'

And where was I when she needed me?

Her heart felt huge. 'Why do you have to talk about Rose all the time?'

Hettie's voice seemed louder than ever. 'Because you won't. We've still never really—'

'What's the point? It's finished. She's gone. She chose to go.'

Hettie poured boiling water into the mug and stirred the deep red liquid savagely. 'I've had to live with it too. I mean I was the one—'

Stephanie stood up. 'We should go to bed – it's late.'

Hettie sighed. 'I think you should be talking to someone.'

'There's nothing to say.'

Chapter 7

The thing about crying before you went to bed was, you might wake up with a face like a slug but at least your wrinkles didn't show. Stephanie pulled on her black jeans, reflecting pleasurably on a new looseness about the crotch. Trauma could be very conducive to a diet and beauty plan. Your crow's feet were puffed out of existence and your stomach was in too much of a flap to accept food. She didn't seem to have eaten properly for two days.

Of course it didn't have quite the same effect on everyone. Hettie was equally puffy and blotchy but already at the breadboard, cramming down toast and peanut butter while George pointed a finger behind her back.

'It's no wonder she's so . . .' he hissed at Stephanie in the hall.

'All right!' she interrupted crossly.

'What?' said George at normal volume, as he followed her into the kitchen, 'are we going to do about that paper boy? He gets later and later.'

'What about strawberry jam, poppet?' Erica was sitting sullenly in front of a plate of buttered toast divided into tiny squares. Hettie tried to push one of them into her mouth. George surveyed Hettie's rear with obvious disapproval and frowned back at Stephanie.

'There's no point having a paper delivered if it's not here before eight. I may as well buy one on the way to the office.'

'Ugh,' said Toby feelingly as she plonked the Weetabix packet down on the table.

'Peanut butter, Erica?' asked Hettie, still hovering at the other end of the table. 'You've got to eat, darling.'

'OK,' Stephanie said nicely. 'Rice Krispies or Shreddies?'

'I hate Shreddies,' said Toby.

'You do not hate them. You had them yesterday.'

'They're disgusting.'

Erica, who had been repeatedly kicking her small foot against the leg of the table throughout the breakfast battle, suddenly stopped and smiled.

Hettie was now rummaging in the larder searching for something acceptable to smear on her daughter's bite-sized toast delicacies so Stephanie was able to scowl at the four-year-old long and hard before turning back with rising irritation to Toby.

But George had positioned himself between her and the cereal packets.

'I need the paper here before I leave—'

'It's Rice Krispies then.' She leant round him and grabbed the packet, poured them into the bowl, splashed milk on top, put them in front of Toby and handed him a spoon.

'Yuck.'

Toby dropped his spoon back into the bowl. It fell against the china with a clang. Milk splattered across the pine table. Rage like a hot flush ran through her. Stephanie snatched up the kitchen roll, slammed it down hard on the pine surface, making him jump.

'EAT IT!'

He stared at her, a mass of hurt accusation, and picked up his spoon.

'Looks pretty gross to me,' said Charlotte, striding in

109

with a bulging rucksack swinging from her hand. 'Why's Kelly still shut out in the garden?'

'She's only been out there a little while,' said Stephanie shortly. 'She upsets Erica.'

Charlotte opened the breadbin. 'So?' she muttered.

Out in the hall, George put the receiver down. 'It's a waste of time talking to that shop,' he said. 'They don't have any idea how to run a business. What you have to do,' he said, 'is vote with your feet.'

What a bloody good idea! Stephanie felt her mouth set tight and disagreeable and even when Hettie turned round to face her she couldn't soften it.

'Have you got any lemon curd?'

'No I haven't.'

'What is wrong with her anyway?' asked George, when Hettie had gone to check on Joshua and the children had all disappeared in various directions. 'She doesn't look very ill to me. Hasn't affected her appetite, has it?'

'Well it wouldn't, would it,' Stephanie said, irritated. 'If you must know, her stitches haven't healed properly since she had Joshua. There's a lot of scar tissue.'

'Urrgh,' said George, clearing his throat.

'She thinks,' Stephanie added, enjoying his look of revulsion, 'they sewed her up too tight.'

Stephanie's voice was growing hoarse as she shrieked, 'Teeth! Shoes! Lunchbox!' at Toby for the fifth time and entered round six of the Not-Letting-Your-Twelve-Year-Old-Stay-Out-till-Midnight-is-Tantamount-to-Child-Abuse debate with Charlotte. 'Because I say so!' she screamed eventually, throwing caution and the whole principle of the How-to-cope-with-Stroppy-Pubescents book to the winds. 'You are sad,' muttered Charlotte through gritted teeth as she flounced into her blazer.

'I suppose you've got PMT?' George asked, adding as he shrugged on his suit jacket. '*Again.*'

'God, that makes me so angry,' said Hettie when they'd gone. 'Jack always says that. I've only got to drop a cup or burst into tears and he says: Oh I suppose it's the time of the month. Anyone would think nobody ever got clumsy or upset for any other reason than their hormones. I expect you're tired and stressed with him and the children and your new job, aren't you?'

Stephanie picked up the bits of broken cereal bowl and blinked back the tears that had sprung to her eyes the moment she'd dropped it.

'No, not really.'

'Oh. What's the matter then?'

'I've got PMT.'

At half-past nine Hettie was still locked in battle with Erica over the Weetabix and Joshua was still – as Hettie reminded everyone in a high-pitched voice – not dressed.

'He's three months old,' Stephanie said. 'He's allowed to go out in his nightshirt.'

'It's a baby-gro and it's filthy.' Hettie leant over Erica and tried to insert a plastic spoon between her clamped lips. 'I want you to eat this, darling or Mummy's going to Get Cross!'

Stephanie peered at Joshua's pale green towelling ensemble. She could detect one small spot of what could be dried milk but, knowing Hettie, was probably intelligence-boosting, free-radical-eliminating, baby-pure rub-it-on-the-gums toothpaste. 'He looks fine to me,' she said, 'but I'll change him if you like.'

She could read her texts in peace upstairs. She found herself looking at her mobile all the time, the flat feeling of disappointment when the screen glowed blankly back at her, the sharp tingle of excitement when there was another message.

Negotiating the heaps of clothes and bags in the spare

111

bedroom, she stepped over the Barbie-clad Put-U-Up and laid Joshua on the double bed.

'He can come in with me – they sleep much better with their mother,' Hettie had said – which was just as well for there was nowhere to squeeze a cot in here. But if this was better, then God knows what he normally slept like. Stephanie had been woken by Joshua at two and three, Hettie singing him back to sleep at four and five and George at six, who had roused Stephanie to share with her the fact that it had finally gone quiet.

She laid her phone next to the baby, flicking through the inbox.

Fone me x

Hettie here – cant talk xxxxx

She'd sent that last night but still the texts from him came. It was nearly a week now since she'd seen him and he hadn't let up at all.

Somthg 2 tell u. when can c u??

She was working this afternoon and again tomorrow morning – but she'd be home by one. He could come round before she picked the kids up . . .

What did he want to tell her?

She didn't see it at first. Hettie was deep in debate over where to sit and whether it was safer for Erica in the back or the front. Stephanie unlocked the car door, still bashing the cobwebs off Toby's old car seat.

'What's this?' She said it before she could stop herself. Hettie's head swivelled as Stephanie pulled at the sellotape, lifting off the little foil package that had been taped to the driver's handle.

'What is it?'

'It's a chocolate!' Erica had appeared at her waist.

Hettie's eyes narrowed. 'Where's that come from?'

Stephanie shoved it into her pocket. 'Toby.' She smiled

brightly at Hettie as her heart pounded. 'Bless him!' she added.

Her eyes flitted around as Hettie wedged the three of them into the back, wrapping seatbelts copiously around herself and the car seat. It was an old joke between them and now Troy had boldly walked up her drive in broad daylight and attached this chocolate declaration to her car. Suppose George had been here! But she grinned to herself. She wondered if Hettie remembered how Troy would always produce his last Rolo with a flourish!

Hettie was silent. Stephanie could feel the tension radiating from her cousin and hitting the back of her neck as she joined the main road to the hospital.

'You're really going to have to start driving again,' Stephanie said. 'Make it much easier for you.'

'I can't. I got into the car one weekend and I just froze. Then Erica got all anxious and Jack had to drive.'

'Well do it when Erica's not there. It'll all come back. It's like riding a bike.' Though in fact it probably wasn't at all like that for Hettie. Even before, her driving was always a rather hit and miss affair with lots of gear-crunching and braking.

'I wouldn't get in the car with her to save my life,' George had said once.

Nobody would now.

Stephanie pulled into the hospital car park and stopped. Hettie looked anxiously at her daughter as she got out of the car. 'I don't even know if she'll S-T-A-Y with you!' she said.

Stephanie sighed. 'Of course she will! Don't be ridiculous!' *And stop bloody spelling everything!*

Erica tried an experimental whimper as Hettie walked away then sat, pulling her Barbie about. Stephanie looked at the mobile in her hands, wondering if she dared call him with Erica in earshot. She could be matter of fact. *You can call round tomorrow afternoon – but I won't have long . . .* She fingered the Rolo in her pocket. Her hands were all trembly.

She'd just dialled the number when Erica squealed. Stephanie cancelled the call and swung round to see Erica pointing out of the window, her eyes shining: 'Look – there's an ambulance over there. Can we go and look – there might be blood!'

Stephanie looked at her sensitive second cousin, who was practically licking her small lips. 'What do you want to see that for?'

'I'm going to be a doctor when I grow up. I'm going to do operations.'

'That's nice.'

Erica was animatedly explaining how very sick people had to have their heart and lungs cut out, and Stephanie had just started to tap out a text, when Hettie threw open the car door. Her face was bright red.

'That was quick,' said Stephanie, stuffing the mobile into her handbag.

'Complete waste of time!' Hettie was panting with indignation. 'If I get divorced I'm going to sue them for negligence. I shall see a solicitor,' she added, quite forgetting to spell any of it out in her agitation.

'What's a solicitor?' asked Erica.

'A boring grown-up,' Stephanie said. 'What happened?'

'I walked out!'

'You'd only just bloody well gone in.'

'Bloody well,' said Erica softly.

'Thank you!' screeched Hettie. 'Now she'll be thrown out of nursery school!'

'Another ambulance!' shouted Erica, hanging out of the window.

'Look, calm down,' Stephanie said to Hettie, getting out of the car before Erica could give them the low-down

114

on liver transplants or terminal syphilis. 'Tell me what happened.'

'I told him,' he gasped, 'that it was all very difficult to *you know* . . .' She stopped and glowered meaningfully at the top of her daughter's head: 'and he practically accused me of being a N-Y-M-P-H—'

'Yes, yes,' Stephanie hastily interrupted her as Erica's head emerged again. 'I'm sure the consultant didn't mean that.'

'He did!' protested Hettie heatedly. 'He said: so your main concern is your inability to have I-N-T-E-R-C-O-U-R-S-E.' She looked at Stephanie, her chest heaving. Joshua stirred in the sling and began to whimper.

'Look,' said Stephanie unbuttoning the side of the sling and lifting Joshua out, 'did he examine you?'

Hettie shook her head. 'I just left.'

Stephanie opened the rear door to let Erica get out. 'Let's go back in and explain how upset you are. Let's say you're ready to be examined now. He can't help you till he's actually seen the problem, can he?'

Erica's face broke into a huge beaming smile. 'Can we watch?'

Chapter 8

Stephanie tried to tell herself – as she squirted a bit more perfume behind her knees – that she always made this much effort with her appearance. She looked critically in the bathroom mirror and made a mad dash for the safe one in the hall.

She hadn't really made an effort at all. Just a bit of lipstick and stuff. She always tried to look her best. For her. To reassure herself she was still attractive. She pushed her hair back into a band. Fiddled with it – pulled a few wispy bits around her face. Oh God.

She'd decided to make some bread. It was nothing unusual. She made it quite often. Aside from making the house smell wonderful, it was sort of soothing – all that squashing and pummelling. And she needed to be soothed after Hettie's stress and angst. She'd given her a huge hug when they'd parted, in pure gratitude for the sight of Hettie's bags finally deposited back at her own doorstep instead of Stephanie's. She'd even kissed Erica and meant it.

There was something pleasing about seeing bread rise. It was a warm and sensual thing. The whole experience made her feel like someone else. Someone better, calmer, more domesticated. She felt flushed with anticipation as she poured a little boiling water over the sugar. Making bread was good for the soul. And certainly nothing to do with any sort of wish that he might be struck afresh by her earthy creativity, her pounding of the pliant dough. (No, it was so that she'd have flour all over her hands and wouldn't be able to touch him.)

She scattered the yeast and watched the grains bob and swell into soft explosions of foam. She remembered him walking in, eyes dropping down her body and back up again, that slow grin, the way he'd touched her, lightly on the arm.

She made a well in the flour. She should have ignored the texts, really. Let him clear out Cora's house and go back to his wife and children.

Twinges of excitement ran up her arms.

You could tell at once when the dough was right. It left the sides of the bowl easily, became plump and elastic, full of air and promise. Today she'd misjudged it. Too much liquid. When the doorbell rang, her hands were coated in a glutinous mass.

Holding them carefully before her, she walked into the hall and up to the door she had left – in case of this very eventuality – on the latch.

'It's open!' she called.

And walked back to her mixing bowl.

Troy arrived in the doorway as she was attempting to pick up the bag of flour with only the tips of her caked thumb and forefinger.

'How domestic!' he said.

She flushed, fancying he knew she had created a scene for him. 'I've buggered it up, actually.' She dropped the bag. Her fingers had enough sticky dough on them for half a loaf.

'Can I help?' His voice was low and amused.

'You could pour some flour in for me. It's too wet.'

He crossed the room and picked up the bag, then

117

tipped it into the bowl, hands, arms close to hers but not touching. 'This enough?'

'Thanks.'

She buried her hands in the floor and rubbed together, dropping long sausages of dough back into the bowl.

She wanted him to put his arms around her.

'Shall I make the coffee as you're doing that?'

'What makes you think you're getting any?'

'You're a kind and hospitable person.'

'You haven't always thought that!'

He laughed. 'Where is it? In here?' He went immediately to the right cupboard. Same memory for detail.

She pulled the last clinging strands from her fingers. She didn't look at him. 'What was so crucial that you had to see me again anyway?'

'Wanted to see if you were OK.'

'Of course I'm OK.' He was wearing combat jeans and a tight T-shirt. She tried to imagine George in similar attire and couldn't. 'Why shouldn't I be?'

'You seemed a little agitated.'

'It was an odd situation, seeing you again. When are you going back?'

'When I've done all the things that need doing.'

'You made it sound as if you were going soon.'

'Well I don't know exactly. How was Hettie?'

'Oh, same as ever. She's got two kids now.'

'Does she still spit blood at the mention of my name? Bet you didn't tell her you'd seen me.'

'I did, actually. She asked what you were doing now.'

Troy laughed. 'Did you tell her I was spending my days dreaming of you?'

'Don't be silly!'

'And that you'd been texting me saying you'd see me just the moment she'd gone because you just couldn't wait—'

'I didn't say that!'

118

'That's what you meant!'

'Rubbish!'

She dried her hands, took a fresh handful of flour and began to roll the dough in the bowl, pushing it down with the heel of her hand, massaging it back towards her.

'Mmmm.' He came up behind her. 'Are you trying to make me horny?'

She looked down at her hands, knowing she was blushing.

He slid an arm around her waist and stroked the back of her wrist. 'Do I break into a rendition of "Unchained Melody"?'

She nudged him away. 'Don't be silly!'

'Though you're much sexier than Demi Moore. "Oh, my love, my darling . . ." '

He had both arms round her now as he crooned. His body was warm against her back. Shifting nervously, startled by the jolts that had leapt through her, Stephanie tried to move out of his hold. 'Think I'd rather have the Righteous Brothers somehow,' she laughed self-consciously.

He had his hands in the bowl now with her. 'Here let me have a go.' He grabbed a lump of dough and fashioned it into a very rude shape. He waved it at her, grinning. 'And I'd much rather have you.'

'Give it back.' She grabbed the dough, half embarrassed, half aroused, squashing it flat again while he winced theatrically.

She moulded the contents of the bowl into a demure sphere. 'What's this important thing you've got to tell me?'

'I'm still in love with you.'

Her hand stopped. 'Don't be ridiculous.'

He moved away. Neither of them spoke while he made coffee. Inside, Stephanie was humming with fear and excitement.

He put a cup down next to her. 'I've always thought

about you. Wondered how you were doing. I knew you'd be all right – fall on your feet and all that.'

She didn't rise to it this time. Didn't bother to explain about how much it took to pay off the debts, get the flat sorted.

'You seem a bit tense,' he said. He was standing too close.

She was still turned on. 'Oh you know – having the house full of kids, Hettie here and stuff. All gets a bit fraught.'

'George gets wound up, does he?'

Without thinking, she nodded.

'So you're not so happily married after all.'

She turned on him in frustration. 'I am happy, you jerk! Guests occasionally cause a bit of stress and tension. So what!'

He had to poke and pick. It was his chat-up line. She'd forgotten. Him leaning up against the door frame at parties, listening intently to some drunken girl's ramblings about her boyfriend, asking probing questions about her feelings, watching as she bloomed beneath his concern and discovered all sorts of deep-seated dissatisfactions she never knew she had.

'Calm down,' he said now. 'I didn't mean to upset you.'

But there was an old light in his eye and beneath her irritation her body throbbed. All at once she jumped as Rose cut in.

'REMEMBER!' she said. 'Remember how it used to be . . .'

Fifteen years ago.

Pop! Fizz! Ah! *Anything can happen with a Bethlehem Bath Ball.*

A rich benefactor might burst through the bathroom door begging to pay off her credit cards.

Troy might return home to tell her that after the first job of work he'd done in six months he'd got a taste for it at last.

Mother might telephone with the cheering news that Great Auntie Dot had finally given in to the laws of averages and the heartfelt wishes of the whole family and died, leaving untold wealth nobody knew about.

Or she might just drown herself . . .

Steph watched the bath bomb that had looked so pretty and seductive in the shop begin its effervescent circuit of the bath. From its clouds of fizzing bubbles supposedly rose the aromas of the season. *Immerse yourself in the spicy sexy scents of Santa.*

It seemed to be mainly cloves.

Relax and feel your mind unwind in deep heat. Difficult when the water was tepid because the boiler was on the blink again.

She sunk her chilly shoulders down lower and tried hard to feel both festive and unwound. *Unlock your fantasies . . .*

She closed her eyes and prepared to float away into a land of waged boyfriends and thick carpets and heating that worked. Then she opened them again and her eyes fell on the black mould growing along the rusting window frames and the place where the tiles had risen off the wall and something nasty was sprouting beneath them.

Condensation streamed down the frosted glass and dripped onto the shiny-papered beribboned heap of bath goodies she was already feeling guilty about. They couldn't afford frivolities. In fact they couldn't afford necessities. They couldn't afford anything at all.

And what would she say to Troy? Not that he'd criticize her for spending money on herself. No! Troy would encourage it. Troy would be delighted. He'd see it as a sign of hope. An indication that she'd finally succumbed to his enduring and all-purpose philosophy on life and 'loosened up'.

'You should buy yourself something beautiful,' he'd say. 'Stop worrying about things that are not important.'

Things that were not important included telephone bills, electricity demands, rates and most currently of all: overdrafts. Overdrafts were a particular source of unimportance, being simply a concept generated by unimaginative and creativity-stifling stiffs-in-suits who did not know how to live.

Troy and his friend Jon spent many happy, dope-filled hours planning a whole host of witty and pithy rejoinders they would deliver to these ignorant of what constituted a fruitful existence, on that future golden day when Troy had made it big in the music business or designed the album cover to die for – which would be exhibited in Museums of Trendy Art across the world – and had more money than those blind bureaucrats would know what to do with.

In the meantime, it was *only* money, something that Steph got far too upset about, which was why she was always grumpy and tired, unlike Troy, who was sublime and clear-eyed and whose chakra points were as soft and pliable as hers were tight.

But not today. Troy was going to get paid today. He was going to come home with the fruits of four days of freelance labour illustrating for a design studio run by a friend of Jon's cousin, for which he would be paid six times what Steph got for slogging her guts out week in and week out at her drawing board for Ronnie, and give her a cheque.

She would be able to pay the phone bill, get herself back within her MasterCard credit limit, sort Troy's final demand from the HP company and still have money left for Christmas.

And be able to tell Rose that Troy wasn't a useless wanker after all.

She was shivering now. But she swirled the water – now bubble-less and a rather unappealing grey – about her a bit longer, feeling duty-bound to get her money's worth. She looked from her goose-pimpled white flesh to the flaking ceiling and hugged herself.

She wasn't going to drown in a sea of depression after all. Troy's work would make all the difference and she'd make sure Troy felt so valued and appreciated and admired he couldn't wait to do it again. She'd got a bottle of Chablis, cooked his favourite pasta, and intended to say again and again how admiring he made her feel and how sexy. Yes! Sexy!

Stephanie got out of the bath and pulled a damp towel around her, wincing as the cold air rushed about her ankles. Leaving splodgy wet footprints on the hardboard she crossed the floorboards to her bedroom and the ancient chest Troy was going to restore when he got exactly the right sort of brass handles.

She rummaged in a drawer for the red and black lace underwired very-uncomfortable-goes-right-up-your-bottom-but-men-just-love-it-all-in-one-thing that probably looked very nice on eighteen-year-old-stick people but which was very unforgiving on the wobbly bits of this particular twenty-four-year-old.

Steph picked it up and sighed. Then she thought of Troy and the difference it would make if he actually earned a living and started to cram her thighs through the leg holes . . .

It was quarter to nine. The seafood lasagne had dried right out and she'd drunk most of the wine to quell the tight knot of anxiety she always felt when he didn't come home. She was still cold. The inadequate heating seemed to have packed up altogether now and she sat in the kitchen looking at the bare plaster walls with two sweat-shirts and one of Troy's jumpers over the red and black thing whose straps were cutting her under the arms.

She wondered whether it wouldn't be more practical to wait in bed. He must have gone for a drink with the other guys from the studio. Well, she wouldn't nag or spoil his day. She'd learned her lesson on that one over the business of the new amplifier and the electricity bill.

She looked around at the poking-out wires. It would be a lovely kitchen when it was finished. The whole flat would be beautiful, everyone said so. And they'd been so lucky to have got it, just when prices in the area were rock bottom. Everyone, Troy told her, agreed, this was going to be *the* up and coming area next . . . It was already worth so much more than they'd paid for it. She comforted herself with this thought on her two-buses-and-change-of-tube ride into work each morning and her just-the-same-but-often-took-an-hour-longer journey home each night.

Not to mention every time she opened a bank state-ment and jumped with fresh horror at the size of the mortgage payment. A payment that had been based on one mediocre income from a tiny ad agency and one massive bulging pay packet from one destined to be designer-of-the-year till he fell out with the boss and left after three weeks.

This place will be worth a fortune when I've finished with it, said Troy.

Trouble was, Steph thought, looking at the pile of unpaid bills sitting on the window ledge – would she be finished first?

'Look who I found.' Troy's voice floated down the hall. His head came around the kitchen door, blond curls framing his face like a gold cloud. He was wearing a soft cream shirt she didn't recognize. He smiled, his special, glowing, just-for-her smile, as he put down a clanking carrier bag and kicked off his shoes.

Jon and Lucinda appeared in the doorway behind him. Jon looked stoned already, Lucinda thinner than ever; her bony wrists stuck out from the huge sleeves of an over-sized sheepskin coat.

'Hi!' she drawled as Jon nodded, eyes half closed in a slow smile. Steph tried to look pleased but her insides curled in disappointment. Troy pulled out a bottle of champagne, crinkled his nose at her, eyes shining. He held the bottle up. 'To celebrate', he said. He jerked his head back towards his friends. 'Luci bought us the bubbles.' He swung round to grin at her. 'And Jonny's got some really good gear . . .' He grinned happily. 'Come on, baby!' He crossed the room, winding an arm around Steph's waist, nuzzling her ear. 'What's the matter? I thought you'd be really pleased.'

'I'm cold.'

He let her go. 'Then we'll light a fire!'

He swung round, face lit already. 'Jon, Luce, come and see this beautiful fireplace.'

They all went into the front room. Steph trailed behind hearing them exclaiming over the Victorian grate. 'It was boarded up!' Troy was saying. 'Can you believe some philistines?'

He was scrunching up newspaper, stuffing it into the opening. 'We'll soon warm the place up.'

'We haven't had it swept,' Steph said doubtfully. They all laughed, Troy loudest of all. 'Hey babe, get the glasses, let's party!'

He was standing on the sheets of hardboard she'd bought to finish putting over the rickety floorboards on the landing upstairs, bending them towards him, snapping and cracking them into strips.

He shook his head at her indulgently. 'We can soon get some more,' he said, reading her thoughts. 'Come on, let's have a drink.' Steph went back to the cold kitchen. Lucinda wandered in after her, holding out a fat joint. 'You look like you need to chill out a bit.'

The flames were leaping up high, licking up the chimney. Heat belted out into the room. Steph wriggled back from the hearth a bit, her face glowing though her back was still cold. She looked at Troy in the firelight: he was sitting back, relaxed, happily drawing on the joint Lucinda had given him, swigging from the glass beside him. His hair was a golden halo in the light from the fire and his eyes shone. Jon's eyes were closed, and Lucinda sat chewing the skin around her nails. Steph wished they'd go home but they looked settled in for the night. She was longing to ask Troy how much he'd got. She was tired. She wanted to go to bed and cuddle under the duvet with him. She caught his eye, yawned and looked at her watch.

'Hey babe, come on! Don't go to bed! I've got something really exciting to tell you . . .'

A job! Please let it be a job . . .

'You know Darren? The one I was doing the cover for?'

She nodded eagerly.

'He's such a great guy and he made me this fantastic offer.'

Yes!

'It means I can work from home, earn some real money and keep my creative integrity.'

She breathed out: a whoosh of joy and relief. *At last, two incomes, bills paid, money to do up the flat with.* 'That's wonderful! Tell me about it.'

'It's got everything: sixteen channels, balanced inputs, effects loop, low-noise circuitry and – ' Troy paused for full dramatic effect – 'parametric eq.'

Steph stared at him blankly. Troy grinned. 'Do you realize what that means?'

126

Jon had woken up again and was grinning dopily. With a sick feeling in the pit of her stomach Steph realized she probably did.

'You've bought something?' she asked weakly.

'Steph! I was meant to have it. Chances like this just don't come along . . .'

'How much?'

He leant towards her, hands outstretched in that helpless, appealing gesture she knew so well. 'He's going to throw in, just give me – I mean for nothing – some great speakers and an amp. They've never been used. We can set up in the spare room. It's going to be so fantastic.'

'How much, Troy?'

Lucinda got to her feet and left the room. She threw Steph an odd look as she went.

'Darren says there are guys just queuing up for cheap studio facilities. With a mixing desk, not only can I get my own music off the ground – Darren reckons I could really go places. I can charge these guys £50 an hour to mix theirs.'

'How much?'

He held up two fingers – grinning.

Shit. OK, but there must still be the best part of a thousand left. He said he'd got more than he thought he would. And he'd expected a thousand.

Still, there was no point letting him get away with it entirely. 'Two hundred quid?' she said slowly.

Over Troy's shoulder Lucinda had reappeared, joint in hand. She inhaled, leaning back against the doorpost and watching Troy, eyes narrowed against the smoke that curled upwards. She gave a sudden peculiar laugh.

Scrawny little minx, Rose called her. Rose had no time for any of them. Jon was a dope-head, Lucinda a spoilt madam.

'Two grand,' Lucinda said, triumphantly.

'Two thousand!' She'd screeched it before she could

stop herself. 'I haven't got to pay it all now,' Troy was saying. 'He's letting me pay the rest in instalments . . .'

Steph sat on the edge of their bed trembling. Lucinda and Jon had left. Troy stood before her, hurt. 'I'm going to give up smoking and use all the money I save for the repayments.'

Steph shook her head in disbelief. 'But I pay for your cigarettes!'

Troy looked annoyed. 'You really embarrassed me tonight. You never have any faith in me. And in front of our friends . . .'

'We needed that money, Troy. The phone's going to be cut off. I've got an overdraft already and I'm not paid till the end of next week.'

'I don't know why you have to get so wound up. It'll work itself out. You want to be a bit more like Luci, stay cool—'

'Luci can afford to stay cool,' she exploded. 'Luci has a father who picks up all her bills.'

'She works—'

'She doesn't work. She drapes herself about that ridiculous gallery a couple of days a week. That's not work!' Stephanie was amazed at the hot stream of venom that was suddenly pulsating through her veins and straight up out of her mouth before she could stop it. 'Luci's a spoilt, indulged brat who's childish and irresponsible and boring!'

Troy stepped back as if he'd been slapped.

'We haven't got enough money for the outgoings we have now – let alone a load of bloody new ones. And we won't have until you get a job instead of sitting round here producing this crap!'

She picked up the mystic pyramid he'd spent a week making and hurled it at him. He dived across the room and caught it as it crashed towards the floorboards.

'Steph!'
'You're a bloody waste of space!'

Stephanie looked at him now in her kitchen and wondered how different he really was.

'You were bad news, you know. Rose always said so.'

He walked around the kitchen table, stood too near her again. 'You were beautiful.'

'Thanks for the past tense.'

'You still are.'

'Huh!'

There was a small silence. Her heart was still beating with unusual vigour.

'Actually,' she added softly, 'so were you . . .'

He was one of the best-looking blokes she'd ever seen. He had an almost Pre-Raphaelite beauty, his nose straight and chiselled, an amazingly sculpted chin and huge dark-lashed eyes. Still in front of her now he had that same strange magnetism.

He smiled. 'What happened to Rose, by the way? Do you still see her?'

For a moment she thought about telling him. 'No. No, not any more.'

'What a dragon. She was always trying to drive a wedge between us. Couldn't stand seeing anyone else happy, that was her problem.'

'She wasn't like that! Anyway, we weren't happy. Or I wasn't anyway. How could I be when you left me so anxious and worried? You were never there, we never had any money, and you were always disappearing . . .'

'You loved me though!' He was grinning openly now.

She looked at his chest, the old resentment coming back. Remembered sobbing against it, beating it with her fists. For all the difference it ever made.

'Not really. I was young. I didn't know what it meant.'

'I think you did.'

'Get out!'

'Come on, Steph!'

'I mean it.'

'Steph – you loved me and I loved you. We were special together – it was something so pure. You know how it felt. I was mad to spoil that. We were so right together. I've never stopped wishing it could be different.'

The morning after he'd left, she'd woken suddenly, gripped with anxiety, feeling that sense of something amiss even before she'd properly opened her eyes. The other side of the bed was empty and undisturbed. Steph sat up, the row of the night before coming back to her in full gory detail. Immediately she was washed with the panic she always felt when they'd fallen out. The familiar row started up inside her head as the doormat-guilt-queen wrestled with the tiny sliver of I-deserve-better still left.

– Oh God, now he's not speaking to me. I've upset him and he did work so hard last week . . .

– You work hard every week!

– He's right in a way – it's only money – and at least he's got plans and ambitions – he's trying to make something of himself.

– He's on a hiding to nothing. A makeshift recording studio in the spare room isn't going to pay the water rates.

– I shouldn't have put his cheese plant on the pavement. I shouldn't have done that.

'Yes you should!' An hour later, Rose paced about the room looking for other things to join it. 'It's about time you stood up to him. He's a parasite. What does he ever do for you?' She picked up the wooden heart he'd carved Stephanie for Valentine's day. 'Well?' she demanded.

'He makes me laugh.'

'Yeah!'

'He does the flat up.'

'Does the flat up?' Rose was brandishing a soapstone sculpture of two heads Troy had picked up in the market. 'Does what exactly? You've been in here for almost a year and it's still a dump. Spending three months painting a mural on the bathroom wall isn't doing it up. He'd do better to try filling a few cracks.'

'He's stripped the tiles round the fireplace.'

'Oh marvellous! Never mind that the window frames are all rotten, you've no carpets and the hot water system doesn't work. Troy's stripped the fireplace tiles. Poor little lamb must be exhausted!'

Stephanie sank deeper into the lumpy sofa and wiped her eyes.

'Face it, Steph. He's a wanker. You're better off without him.'

'I love him.'

Rose pressed her lips tightly together.

'And he loves me!'

'So where is he, then?' Rose enquired. 'Climbing out of someone else's bed, I expect.'

Pain struck Steph beneath the ribs. Fresh tears rolled down her face. 'He wouldn't do that.'

'Don't you ever wish that too?' Fifteen years on, Troy's voice was soft. And as sexy as ever.

Stephanie turned away. 'Stop it!'

She turned and leant on the sink, breathing heavily, rage rattling down to her fingertips. He came up behind her and slid a finger beneath a strand of her hair that was caught up in the scrunchy band. At the moment she felt his touch on her neck, the sensation of that tight curl being freed, she was lost. She turned and kissed him.

He already had his mouth open.

Chapter 9

'M's in the sound room,' said Jo as Stephanie came into reception. 'We've got a bit of a rush on.'

Patsy, perched on the edge of Jo's desk, applying lipstick, smiled. 'It's the warmer weather – brings out the rabbit in all of us.'

Samantha appeared with two cups of coffee and a petulant expression. 'It wasn't my fault,' she said sulkily, handing one of the cups to Jo. 'I couldn't hear what she was saying.'

'You should have thrown the bad-signal switch and cut her off. She was calling from her mobile, wasn't she?' Jo took a mouthful of coffee. 'Never mind, M will smooth it.'

'It was only the daughter,' Samantha said. 'She's only about ten.'

Jo raised her eyebrows. 'Kids are very cute these days. You don't want to underestimate them.' Stephanie glanced at her. Jo wasn't that old herself. But confident and assured in a way Stephanie had never been in her twenties. Or now.

'Pain in the bloody arse mine are, far too precocious,' put in Patsy, taking the coffee Samantha was just about to drink. 'You can go and make another one can't you, darling?'

'Well this one just sounded like a little kid,' argued Samantha, looking put out.

'And why was she calling?' rapped out Madeleine, who had appeared without warning among them. 'Because her father had asked her to!'

She shook her head disapprovingly at the idea of any man having the temerity to question his wife's whereabouts and strode in the direction of her office. Stephanie and Samantha looked at each other and followed.

Madeleine gathered up some papers from her desk and slid them into her briefcase. 'You obviously need some more training,' she said coldly to Samantha.

'What are you doing this afternoon?' she asked Patsy, who had now transferred herself to the edge of Madeleine's desk and was flicking through *Hello!*

'Going home to soak my body. I've got a very hot date tonight.' She winked at Stephanie. 'Oh dear, look at this – she looks all droopy since she had a baby.' She held up a picture of a radiant-looking actress. 'Wouldn't mind a go with him, though. I do like my men toned . . .'

'Where are you going?' Madeleine asked. 'Have you cleared it with Jo?'

Patsy didn't look up. 'No need.'

'Just remember what I said.'

She picked up her jacket and headed for the door, addressing Samantha over her shoulder. 'I'll be back about four. Till then, for God's sake just help Stephanie with the filing.'

'I suppose she'll make me work late again now,' Samantha said when Madeleine and Patsy had gone. 'And I'm supposed to be meeting Jed at seven. I never wanted this job anyway.'

'What are you doing it for then?' Stephanie asked kindly, picking up the tray of invoices she was ordering.

'My mother was going on and on. She wanted me to

133

work in an estate agent's!' Samantha pulled a face. 'And then Aunty Monica said this would be more glamorous.' She rolled her eyes to show how ill-informed her godmother had been. 'So she fixed it with Patsy. I hate it. Mum thinks it's just recruitment, of course.'

'What would you like to *do*?' Stephanie glanced sideways at Samantha. She was supposed to be eighteen but she seemed more childlike than Charlotte.

'Be an actress or model or something. Or on a magazine. Someone like Lady Victoria Hervey. Or Normandie. Jed, my boyfriend, he does stuff for all the newspapers in London. He says it's just a matter of knowing the right people. Once he's made it, he'll get me a job on the fashion pages no problem. You just need the right face in the right place, he says. I don't want to be stuck here for ever with all these sad old bags trying to pretend to have a boyfriend like they're still young.'

Wince. Stephanie tucked two theatre tickets into a folder full of restaurant receipts. 'No, well, I expect it's a bit more complicated than that.'

Samantha flicked back the silky blond hair from her perfect, unlined face and curled her lip in distaste. 'Well, I think it's disgusting. What did they get married for if they can't even be faithful?'

Stephanie picked up another cardboard folder. She hadn't done anything yet. A kiss didn't count, did it . . .

Guiltily she pushed down memories of how passionate it had become. She'd forgotten how a kiss could be. That electricity between them, how their bodies had cleaved together. But they'd stopped. She'd stopped. And if she didn't see him again . . .

Samantha was still talking. 'It's like that Andrew and Harriet say on the telly – it's a commitment. You can look at another but you don't do anything about it.'

Stephanie grimaced. What was it with the youth of today? Charlotte was bizarrely fond of the sanctimonious and sickeningly happy Andrew and Harriet with their homilies to the nation each weekday morning and had to be prised away from the TV with threats of no breakfast or she'd never get to school.

'I'd never cheat on Jed,' Samantha said. 'When we get married it will be for ever.'

'That's nice,' said Stephanie, securing a thick wad of hotel bills with a bulldog clip. Yes, well they all started off like that. 'Is the wedding soon?'

Samantha fiddled with her hair. 'Oh, well no, we haven't planned anything. We need some money first, you know.'

Stephanie nodded. Yes, she knew . . .

Money. The root of all the rows she and Troy ever had. Before the mixing desk fiasco – last in a line of back-crushing financial straws – there'd been endless spats over allocation of funds (hers) with Stephanie putting in a fervent bid for the electricity that was about to be cut off and Troy nodding and gaily coming home with a drum kit. Or once – memorably – a telescope he'd bought for an incredible knock-down price from the bloke in the pub where he'd gone to spend the month's water rates. 'We can look at the stars,' he'd said appealingly. 'That whole incredible galaxy out there.' It had been covered with dust at the back of a cupboard when Troy moved out.

She'd shouted, she'd begged, she'd cried. Today, she almost smiled, remembering him rushing from the flat where she sat weeping over her overdraft, returning with a bottle of champagne and a box of chocolates he'd spent her very last £20 on to cheer her up.

Now she marvelled. He had a job and a house and paid school fees . . .

'What shall I do with these?'

Stephanie looked at Samantha blankly. 'Sorry?'

Samantha held out the pile of photographs. 'I don't know where to put these.'

'Oh – I don't know. Sorry, I was miles away there for a moment.' Steph leant over and looked at the pictures Samantha was shuffling. They all seemed to be of men. 'Um, put them in that box – it's all stuff I need to ask Madeleine about. I think she said they needed coding or something.'

'Need shooting by the look of them,' said Samantha. She held a photo up for Stephanie to see. 'Look at this old codger!' Stephanie looked. He was about forty.

'How old's Jed?' she asked.

'Twenty-two,' said Samantha happily.

Troy had been twenty-two when they'd started living together. She was nineteen. She'd stayed over in Troy's bedsit the night he moved in and never went back to her college room.

Her mother had been horrified by the smallness and the damp, by the very idea, but Cora had given them jugs and ornaments, brightly coloured bedding and frayed towels to tide them over. Troy had come to London to make his fortune – make enough fortune for both of them. When Steph finished college she'd only need a job for a while, just till his money came rolling in. From the paintings, the music, the fabulous ideas, the amazing inventions. Troy was going to conquer the world. 'He's *so* talented,' said Cora.

'So what exactly does Jed do?' asked Stephanie. 'He's a journalist, is he?'

'Well he writes articles, and sometimes he takes photographs too.'

'Oh that's interesting,' said Stephanie politely. 'Which papers?'

'Well you know that Eleanor wotsit – the one who was in *EastEnders* as the dentist's mother?'

'Sort of,' said Stephanie, none the wiser.

'Well when her liposuction went wrong he caught her leaving the clinic in bandages and then he got one of the nurses to tell him how many stitches she'd had and everything,' said Samantha proudly. 'He sold it to the *News of the World*.'

'Did he really?' asked Stephanie, feeling sorry for the unfortunate Eleanor whoever-she-was and feeling very glad she wasn't famous enough to warrant a Jed hanging about when she and the Facelift Club went under the knife.

'But most of all he wants to get a permanent job on the *Daily Detail*. That's where the top blokes are, he says. He's done a few bits for them but the editor's a woman – and a real hard-nosed bitch. A real man-hater.'

'Oh dear.' Stephanie sorted the pictures Samantha had handed her into a neat pile.

'He's working on something now,' said Samantha. 'He says it'll be a real exclusive. But he won't tell me what it is. It's something big, though,' she lowered her voice, 'because he keeps staying out ever so late.'

That's what he tells you anyway, said Stephanie silently and immediately recoiled at the thought. What had happened to her? A couple of weeks working here and already she was assuming the worst of everyone.

'Then we're going to get a flat in London,' said Samantha eagerly. 'Get out of this dump.'

Stephanie smiled to herself. It didn't come much more exclusive than Edenhurst with its rapid train link to town. Half the city-working population would dream of a home here with its leafy lanes and stockbroker houses, celebrity homes and ladies that lunch. Or – as it turned out – spent their time in other ways.

The phone on Madeleine's desk rang again and this time continued to ring. 'Shall I?' Stephanie raised her eyebrows at Samantha.

'I shouldn't,' said the girl feelingly. 'Jo said they were all going through to her. Madeleine went mad when I answered it when I wasn't supposed to.'

But Jo came into the room and the phone carried on ringing. She spoke to Stephanie. 'What time did Madeleine say she'd be back?'

'About four, I think.'

Jo looked at her watch. 'Yeah, that's what I thought. Well I hope she hurries up. Not quite sure what to do about this one. Client's turned up' – she nodded in the direction of the reception area. 'She's in a right old state!'

'Can't you call Madeleine on her mobile?'

'Er no – not really.' She looked sideways at Samantha, who was still digging about in one of the filing cabinets. 'Hotel la Ruche,' she mouthed at Stephanie.

'Ah,' said Stephanie, not having a clue what this meant. The phone on Madeleine's desk stopped and then began to ring again. 'I'll take it out there,' Jo said. 'Can you look after Mrs V for a minute?'

Stephanie followed her out to reception where an anxious-looking woman of about thirty-five was sitting on the edge of one of the sofas clutching a mobile phone. She jumped as Stephanie approached. 'Mrs V? Would you like to come and have a coffee?'

'Will Madeleine be back soon?' The woman looked at her beseechingly. 'I don't know what I'm going to do.'

'We're expecting her any minute.'

Stephanie led her to a chair in the office outside Madeleine's. 'I won't be a moment.'

'He just phoned out of the blue.' Mrs V leant up and grabbed at Stephanie's arm as she tried to move away. 'Said he'd found them.'

'Who? Found what?'

'The photographs. A whole heap of them. Gary took them and now Donald's found them. And I haven't got a thing on!'

'Oh God.' Stephanie sat down suddenly beside her.

'What am I going to do?' Mrs V sank back into the chair herself and put her head in her hands. 'He said I've got to go straight home and tell him who he is!'

'What did you say?' asked Stephanie, aghast.

'Nothing! I pretended my battery had run out like Madeleine says.' She held out the mobile to Stephanie like a child. 'Can you do it for me?'

'What?' Stephanie took the phone, bewildered.

'Oh I'll deal with that.' Jo had reappeared. 'We've got a machine,' she explained to Stephanie. 'Discharges them. Makes it all look authentic.' Turning to Mrs V she said, 'I've spoken to Madeleine. She's on her way – and it's all going to be cool.'

'Is it?' The woman looked at Stephanie. 'I thought of telling him I'd had them taken for him – you know, professionally, as a surprise – but they were all Polaroids.'

Stephanie shook her head not knowing what to say. How on earth could Madeleine sort naked photographs? 'I'll um make you a coffee,' she said.

When she came back Mrs V was staring manically into space. 'Will she be here soon? Oh!' She leapt up as Madeleine strode in. 'Oh thank you.'

'Right, don't panic,' said Madeleine.

'He's waiting for me at home. There's about six of them. In one I'm—'

'When's his birthday?'

The woman looked startled. 'January.'

'Right. Wedding anniversary?'

'November.'

Madeleine frowned. 'Hmmm. Still a bit far off, isn't it. What else have you got coming up? Any celebrations, milestones, landmarks?'

'No. Nothing.'

Madeleine tutted impatiently. 'Come on, come on, think! The children done anything special? The dog died?'

139

'No.' The woman shook her head miserably.

'How long have you lived in your house?'

Mrs V looked up, surprised. 'Um – ten years, I think, yes, nearly ten years.'

'When did you move in? What month?'

'End of May I think – yes 27 May!'

'Excellent!' Madeleine said triumphantly. 'And you've been so happy there, haven't you?'

'Well . . .'

'You have been so happy you have organized a very special present for him to mark the occasion of having lived in this lovely home of yours for ten years. Not a boring domestic family present but a special romantic just-for-him present to remind him of how you were all those years ago when he carried you over the threshold . . .'

'I don't think he—' the woman began uncertainly but Madeleine swept on, clearly warming to her theme.

'You wanted something to last for ever the way your love will. And what better than the ageless, timeless gift of an oil painting of you nude!'

The woman gasped. Stephanie felt her own mouth drop open. 'Go home now and tell him they were taken by a female painter. Then cry! Sob how disappointed you are that the surprise has been ruined. Weep with hurt at him thinking the worst of you when you'd put so much effort into his celebration.'

Mrs V gulped.

'Jo, call up YK – she's some sort of artist – get her to rustle up a half-finished oil. Doesn't have to be much good. And you – ' she said, turning to the shocked Mrs V – 'can get round there in the morning, get your kit off and show your face so she can make sure it looks vaguely like you.'

'But the sort of positions I was in . . .'

'No problem,' said Madeleine airily. 'Tell him she's

140

modern. Tell him to think Tracey Emin rather than Holbein. Say she was experimenting to see how the light fell. Then get her to knock you one out with your legs crossed if you're worried what the neighbours will think when it's hung in the dining-room.'

Mrs V paled. 'Well, if you're sure it will work . . .'

'Of course it will. Jo will give you the number to call. He can speak to YK direct if he doesn't believe you. We'll call her Arabella – nice arty name. Then when she turns up in a couple of days with a half-finished canvas, he'll be begging forgiveness. You'll probably get a lavish present yourself.'

'Oh thank you so much, I'm so grateful.' Mrs V took a step towards Madeleine and for a moment Stephanie thought she was going to kiss her. 'But next time,' Madeleine said severely, stopping the woman in her tracks, 'don't leave things like that lying around.'

'I thought they'd be safe. They were in my knicker drawer.'

'In that case,' said Madeleine when Mrs V had gone, 'I think she could find Donald's got a secret or two of his own.'

Stephanie giggled, feeling slightly hysterical. 'Well she won't do that again anyway, will she?'

Madeleine poured a little whisky into the mug of coffee Jo had brought her. 'She certainly won't when she sees the bill.'

Chapter 10

'I'm sorry,' Jed said again. 'But this is big stuff.'

Samantha sat on the edge of her bed and bit her lip. 'It was really hard getting away on time,' she said peevishly. 'Madeleine wanted to keep me there for training. I've rushed home and got ready.'

'I know.' Jed was sounding bored now. 'And I'll make it up to you but this is hot, you know, I've got to go and follow something up.'

'Can't I come with you?' Samantha whined.

Jed laughed. 'Don't be thick. I've got to be discreet. Keep myself out of the way. Can't have two of us.'

'Shall I come over to your place and wait, then?' she asked hopefully.

'No, don't do that.' She heard Jed sigh. 'Look, it could be a long one. I might have to hang about all night. You stay there at your mum's and chill. We'll get our own place in town soon. Be together all the time.'

'Well, when will I—'

'Gotta go now honey.'

Samantha looked crossly at the receiver as the line went dead. She wished Jed wouldn't be so secretive. All he would say was that this was the one that would make the 'dried-up old bitch at the top really sit up'. Davina! He was still smarting over the piece on the Blow-up-doll-found-in-Disgraced-Minister's-prison-cell exposé when he'd done all the snooping about, brought the story to the news desk on a plate and hadn't even got a byline.

'But why not?' Samantha had asked indignantly, seeing her dream of a flat in London with a modelling career hovering out of reach again. Jed shrugged. 'Old witch obviously isn't getting any,' he said.

Patsy was getting plenty. She stretched, rolled over and picked up his Marlboro Lights from the bedside table, lit two and slid one of them between his lips. 'I'll let you have a little rest now,' she said, inhaling.

He looked nervously at the clock. 'Better be getting back soon,' he said.

Patsy ran her nails slowly across his stomach. 'I haven't finished with you,' she said provocatively. 'Not letting you go just yet.'

'You're insatiable.'

'Complaining?' she asked, trailing her fingers lower.

She felt him stir. 'Have to be careful,' he muttered. 'It's getting late.'

'So what? She doesn't really care what you do anyway, does she?' Patsy balanced her cigarette in the ashtray and prepared to climb astride him again.

'No, but it's not her, is it. If it gets out . . .'

'How will it?' Patsy took his cigarette from his fingers and put it with hers.

'I don't know – there was this phone call – asking one of the girls . . .'

'Oh but you're going to get that, aren't you – in your position.' She lowered herself onto him, her tongue playing across his chest. She felt his breath quicken.

'And I've been worried ever since your husband—'

'I can handle Dave. He's fine – completely off the scent.'

She ran her hands over him again, feeling him tense.

'It would be the end of this job. It could ruin my career.'

'Only if we get caught. Mmmn . . .'

'Robbie's back tomorrow – we won't be able to use this place any more.'

'I thought he was your best friend.'

'He is, but . . .'

'Can't he help a mate out? Or in.' She blew into his ear, watching as he shuddered helplessly.

'When he's here,' he struggled, 'he's got his own entertaining to do.'

'OK, well I'll find somewhere else.'

'Well it'll have to be—' he broke off and gasped as Patsy moved abruptly and impaled herself on him. She looked down triumphantly as his eyes rolled in sudden pained ecstasy.

'For fuck's sake,' she said, rotating her hips with malicious pleasure, 'do shut up!'

Jed was getting pissed off. The mild evening had given way to a cold wind and he was shivering in his denim jacket. It had been too dark to see who was in the passenger seat of the navy blue Mercedes that had crunched up the drive four hours ago – for all he knew it was the bloke's wife – and there was no sign of anyone emerging. It was probably one of their stuck-up celebrity dinner parties and they'd all be snorting away till dawn.

Though didn't the bloke have to get up for work? Suppose the lightweight was staying over. Jed could be out here all night for nothing while his prey was tucked up in bed.

Jed rubbed at his arms, trying to warm up. Here he was freezing his arse off and they were sitting inside in the lap of luxury. It was enough to do your head in. Sometimes the waves of hatred that came over Jed shocked even himself. 'Come out, you bastard,' he muttered aloud. He just wanted one good picture. One cast iron shot. Both in the frame at the same time.

He looked at his mobile. After midnight and another naff picture message from Sam. She was just like a kid sometimes. But always very willing! Perhaps he should have told her to wait in his flat after all. He could do with a shag now after all this hanging about. He smiled. He liked to wind Sam up. Poke fun at the exclusive boarding school she'd been to. Her college for 'Young Ladies'. He'd got a certain satisfaction out of introducing her to the real world. 'What would Mummy think?' he'd say, making her go out in her little leather skirt, nothing underneath, watching her sashay across the dance floor for him in the sleaziest club in Streatham. 'What would Mummy think if she knew what her little girl got up to?'

He could see one small light in an upstairs window beyond the tall hedge. No movement anywhere. He took a last look up the driveway to the house, pushed his mobile into his pocket and started to walk towards his car.

He wasn't going to give up. He still had the first lot of photos and he knew there was a story there. And he'd make Davina-bloody-shrivelled-tits take him seriously next time too. It was all jobs for the boys on the *Detail*. Nepotism and smooth-talking graduates who wouldn't know a story if it jumped up and parked the Porsche for them. Jed had done it the hard way. No expensive education for him. He'd been writing copy since he was fifteen, made all his own contacts, no help from anyone. And this was going to be his big break that would show them all. However long it took. He pulled out his car keys, took one last look back at the silhouette of the house in the moonlight and scowled. 'I'll get you, you bastard, you wait.'

Chapter 11

Beep!

need c u again.

Beep!

Where R U? xx

Beep!

RU OK?

Beep!

pls visit tmrrow. v. urg. x

Beep!

dont be like that ily.

He opened the door and his whole face lit up, shining and glowing.

'Hi!' He stretched out, taking her hand, pulling her in, the single syllable stretched into long seconds of warmth and pleasure. 'I hoped and hoped you'd come.' He was taking her jacket off, pushing the front door closed behind her: 'But I didn't know . . .'

'I can't stay long. I told George—'

'Shhh.' He was folding his arms around her, breathing his warm breath against her face, stroking her hair. 'Mmmm, you smell wonderful.'

Warmth spread through her, rapidly followed by something much more dangerous. She flushed and wriggled away from him.

'Troy I can't . . .'

He let her go. Squeezing the tops of her arms briefly then walking away from her down the hall towards the kitchen. 'You know I wouldn't push you into anything.'

He turned back, smiling. 'I'm just so pleased to see you.'

She wanted to curl up in his arms. 'It's nice to see you too,' she said primly.

'Shall I make you a coffee? Or wine? I've got some white here in the fridge or there's probably whisky – you know what Mum was like.'

Apart from her obvious blind spot about Troy, Cora had been nice. Stephanie looked around at the china and little pots and silver thimbles lovingly collected from the antique shops and markets, scattered around the room exactly as they had been when they'd come here years ago. She could see Cora's bright eyes and unconventional clothing as clearly as ever. Could see Troy too, in his velvet trousers and big baggy shirts, carrying his guitar so he could play his mother his latest song when they were all drunk on her gin.

'Hello, lovelies!' she'd cry when they arrived, swooping on them, flinging her arms around their shoulders, pressing large glasses into their hands, while simultaneously lighting one of the long thin dark menthol cigarettes which were never far from her lips.

'You all right, my love?' she'd ask Steph warmly. And Stephanie would nod, not wanting to spoil anything, seeing how happy and proud Cora was that Troy was there. Everything Troy did filled his mother with joy and admiration. Only once when they'd been alone and Stephanie had tried to raise the subject of work and money – why Troy never stuck at it or earned any – did Cora's eyes cloud over . . .

'I hate whisky,' she said now.

Troy looked at her in surprise. 'Do you? I'd forgotten.'

'Why should you remember? It's years ago.'

He made her coffee in the small kitchen while she wandered about looking at the rooms that were in some ways so familiar, in others forgotten, already with that air of the strange and empty and bizarre the way rooms and possessions became when their owner had gone.

'What are you going to do with it?' she asked, indicating the house, the dozens of things.

He picked up a china figurine. 'Don't know where to start, really.'

She saw the pain in his face. 'Isn't your wife going to come down and help you?'

'Oh, you know, she's got the kids.' He gestured around the room – at the delicate porcelain, coloured glass, brass candlesticks. 'Imagine the pair of them in here!'

Stephanie nodded. 'There are some reputable house clearers about – some who'll give you a proper price.'

'Oh I know, but,' he put the figurine down, picked up a patterned bowl filled with dusty pot-pourri, 'I've got to decide what I want first.'

She smiled. Of course – most of it would go home with Troy. She wondered how his wife coped with his hoarding and squirrelling. All at once she remembered him staggering in at 2 a.m. with a huge battered chimney pot he'd found in a skip. Recalled paying some bloke a small fortune to collect a heap of railway sleepers Troy was going to make into a bench. George had paid a similar amount two years later to have them taken away again.

'Still like to collect things, then?' she said wryly.

'Not like I used to.' He turned an ebony elephant in his hands. 'Just this – you know – a few bits – to remind me of Mum . . .'

'Yeah.'

'If you want anything . . .'

'No!' Suddenly it felt all wrong to be there. She put her coffee cup down and looked around for her jacket. 'Thank you.'

Stephanie remembered George looking in disbelief at all the things still piled high in the spare room of the flat. 'Looks like Steptoe's yard,' he'd said, shaking his head at the lumps of wood saved for carving, the pots for painting, the black sack of egg boxes that would make up the sound-proofing once Troy's recording studio was up and running, the battered easel he'd promised to mend so Steph could start painting again.

'Shall I chuck it with the other stuff?' George had asked, standing in the doorway. 'That's probably full of worm,' he'd added as she hesitated. 'I'll buy you a proper one.'

Troy came rapidly across the room and put his hand on her shoulder.

'Hey don't go yet – you've only just got here.'

'I told you I couldn't stay long.'

'I wanted to talk to you.'

'We have talked. What more is there to say?'

'Lots!'

She folded her arms, put her head on one side in mock concentration. 'Go on then – talk!'

'Well it's just that I'm sorry it didn't work out and stuff.'

'It worked out fine. I got shot of you!' She grinned at him.

He pulled a face. 'Very funny! But . . .' He sidled up to her, voice low and persuasive: 'Didn't you miss me?'

'Yeah but I'll get you next time.'

'I want to make love to you.'

OH! It went through her like a spasm. She swallowed. Troy was smiling at her knowingly.

'Don't be silly.' She was trying to sound brisk but it came out strangled. 'I'm happy, you're happy, we've got new partners, we've got kids. I've got to go, Troy. I hope you get all this sorted out and can go home.' *Back to Tanith and your bits of wood waiting to be shaped.*

'Why did you come, then?' He was holding both her shoulders now, looking intently into her face, still smiling. 'You feel what's still between us too, I know you do. When you kissed me . . .'

Mmmm yes. Again. Again . . .

'I'm sorry about that!' She could feel herself blushing. 'That was just . . . a rush of hormones.' *And they're in another mad dash now.*

'I'm glad *you* said that!' He laughed. 'There was a time when if I'd dared to suggest . . . dear me there'd be hell to pay.'

'Hell to pay!' she said mockingly. 'You always loved to talk as if I was the dominant one, the ogress who called the shots.'

'You were!' He was grinning. 'I was terrified of you. Especially when the bills arrived.'

'Shame you weren't terrified enough to go and earn some money to pay them.' His face was inches from hers. She held his gaze, her body still throbbing.

He shook his head. 'You never let up, do you? Always the money.'

'It wasn't really the money, Troy, you know that.' She felt the old frustration rise in her. 'It was the stress and worry. The constant anxiety that I had to handle all on my own. The way you had so many talents but you wouldn't use any of them to make things better for me. You were the one who controlled our relationship. You had all the power. It was how you behaved that would make or break my day.'

Her voice had risen too. All those old feelings she'd thought were gone.

'Why didn't you kick me out, then? Five years, Steph.' He let go of her and stepped back. 'If it was that awful why didn't you get shot of me sooner?'

'Why didn't I? You lied, you lay in bed all day, got stoned all night . . .' She began to pace the floor. 'God, it seems incredible now.'

'How could you stand it?' George had said, piling rubbish sack upon sack into the skip he'd hired, pulling at rotten skirting boards, frowning over credit card statements. 'He didn't deserve you,' he said and Stephanie had felt grateful to be worth that much to someone at last.

'You loved me,' said Troy softly, voice gentle again. 'And I loved you. We were twin souls.'

Stephanie blew out her cheeks, shook her head at him. 'You still sound like some old hippie.'

'We had something special,' he went on, ignoring her. 'I remember once when we were in the bedsit. We were down to our last couple of pounds. Waiting for Mum to come up with a food parcel at the weekend.' He stopped, looking misty-eyed. 'She was good, Mum, wasn't she?'

Stephanie silently nodded.

'We spent it on a bottle of cider and chips – we went out in the rain to get them. And we got so wet. We were laughing at how soaked we were – we didn't care – all your hair was streaming, stuck to your head and your make-up had spread into great black circles, like a panda. And we went home and took our clothes off and sat in front of that Calor gas heater we had and the wet clothes we'd hung up made the windows steamy and we sat there with nothing on, eating chips and drinking cider . . .'

'Blackthorn.' Stephanie's heart was beating harder; there was an odd feeling in the pit of her stomach as she watched him.

'And we made plans,' said Troy, 'for all the things

we were going to do when we had money. Do you remember?'

She nodded. She felt trembly inside.

'Whatever did you see in him?' George had laughed when the last of Troy's things had gone, when they stood looking at bare sanded floorboards and bright white walls, just before they handed the key to the estate agent who was going to sell it for three times what Stephanie had paid. 'Lucky escape, eh?'

'We were going to get a place in the country, somewhere where the water table was high and I could dig out a natural lake. We were going to make it a beautiful retreat. With ducks and water-lilies. You were going to paint and do pottery. I was going to have a studio in one of the outbuildings and write my music. You wanted to bake bread and have loads of children . . .'

Stephanie tried to fathom his expression. Suddenly she couldn't tell if he was laughing at their young selves or genuinely feeling wistful.

'However did we think we were going to manage all that?' she said lightly.

'We never even tried,' he said. 'We could have done anything if we'd wanted it enough.'

'No,' she shook her head, 'it doesn't work like that. Not in real life. We would still have had to pay for it all. You can't get things just by wishing.'

'Sometimes you can.'

'Not usually. Usually it needs a bit more than that.'

He gave a dreamy, faraway smile. 'I was always the positive thinker, wasn't I?' he said, and she wanted to slap him.

She put on her jacket, glad the mood had been broken for her.

'I'm going.' She walked away into the hall.

'Do you still paint?' The question rang out like a challenge.

'I haven't done any lately,' she said, not looking back.

Not for more than ten years in fact. The last time she'd got her paints out Charlotte was tiny. She'd covered the dining-room table with newspapers, laid out pots of brightly coloured poster paints, put a soft wide brush in the little round fist. And she herself had set up her small easel in the corner, got out her watercolour palette, sat and mixed smudgy blues and greys and pinks into some rain-drenched mythical landscape while her daughter laughed and made colourful splodges and runny wet splats across thick white paper.

In those days George kissed her when he came in. He planted his lips on the side of her head, sweeping the little girl up into his arms. 'Painting, eh?' he'd chortled. 'Which one did the baby do?'

'You did amazing stuff at college,' said Troy. 'You should have kept it up. You're a very creative person.'

She stopped, turning back to him, smiling gratefully.

He put his hands on her shoulders. 'We'd do it all so differently now, wouldn't we, Steph. I'm not the same as I was then. I've learned. I've learned what you meant to me – what you still mean.'

What did you see in him?

All those years ago, Steph had turned to George – strong, capable, knowledgeable George who was such a sweet *relief* after Troy – and put her arms around him. 'I don't know,' she'd said shaking her head. 'I don't know.'

But now she looked into Troy's eyes – fervent, passionate, full of life and possibilities – and, wishing she hadn't come, and so glad she had, she remembered what she had seen in him all too clearly.

He lifted her up. He showed her dreams. *He made my heart sing.*

Chapter 12

'Let me go!'

She'd screamed and struggled and thrashed about but there was no hope of freeing herself. He was far stronger than that. He'd worked quickly and deftly, unmoved by her frantic cries. The thick, soft rope bound her tightly at wrist and ankle, rendering her spread-eagled across the buttercup-printed duvet, skirt around her waist as he slowly and deliberately spread a little more Greek yoghurt up the inside of her thighs . . .

'You must let me go!' she gasped again. 'My husband . . .'

She'd already heard him come in. Very soon there would be a heavy footfall on the stairs. She pulled against the thick rope that bound her so tightly to the bedposts. Discovery was a shocking, heart-stopping few seconds away. *He* appeared not to notice any noises off; he was intent on the job in hand. 'You are mine,' he'd said as he first unrolled the cords. 'And I will never ever let you go.' He'd begun by licking her ankles. Now as he moved slowly upwards, despite all her fears, she heard herself moan . . .

Briefly she forgot the looming threat of discovery. For a split second she grew warm and soft, letting herself float away on the rhythms he was creating. Felt the hard throbbing core of them send intoxicating tendrils down to her toes and fingertips. For a single moment she was lost and then the footsteps came. Faster and faster, they pounded up the stairs, along the landing, slithering to an abrupt halt outside the locked door. She heard the thud of a body against the wood, shrank from the imperious rapping upon the panels. Her heart thumped and pounded but – thank the God of Orgasms for the potency of fear – the rush of adrenalin did the trick. Beneath the roaring of the blood in her ears, came the first wicked wave of abandon . . .

Yes, yes, yes! Mmm mmmm mmmmn . . .

'Let me in!'

The hammering on the door had intensified.

She fell back, shuddering as the last ripple of pleasure tingled its delicious way up her guilty spine.

Breathing heavily, she tried to sit up. *He* had scarpered.

'What do you want?' She knew her voice was high and strange.

Toby's was aggrieved. 'Daddy says the chicken nuggets are burning!'

The 'lipstick' safely back in her handbag and clothing adjusted she appeared in the kitchen doorway.

'What were you *doing* up there?' George looked up irritably and held out a smoking baking tray.

'Can't I even go to the loo in peace?'

How to Have an Affair © PA Publishing:
Chapter 3: 'Modern Technology: the Scourge of the Philanderer'

A Word about Phones
Mobile phones are of course an essential tool for the infidel and a crucial means of communication. The agency requires its clients to possess one and to keep

them turned on at all times during proceedings (they may be switched to silent or vibrate!).

Use of home phone and land lines should be avoided except in dire emergency, (see Troubleshooting, page 152) and if used certain safety precautions should be observed:

1. Do not imagine that you have invented the **single-ring-of-the-phone** signal. Every couple ever involved in the extra-marital has used this. It can mean different things to different pairs: He's gone to work, she's out at her embroidery class. Thinking of you, phone me back, I'm wearing those crotchless knickers you bought me . . .

   Whatever, it will raise suspicion in a very short space of time, as will –

2. **Wrong numbers.** The law of averages suggests that everyone will experience a wrong number some time in the space of two years. When they occur more frequently – like two Thursday nights running when your husband is meant to have left for his car maintenance course or apron-dancing session at the lodge but happens to be tardy in getting his shoes on – this is bound to ring bells.

   We suggest you have an imaginary friend – let us call her Janet – whom you utilize in any awkward situation. Thus if the phone should ring at an inopportune moment, you might answer like this:

   'Oh Janet! You poor dear. Of course I want to hear about what the doctor said about your haemorrhoids but I must just kiss Brian goodbye – he's just off to his class. Ring you back?'

   Delivered calmly this will be far more effective than shrill renditions of 'You've got the wrong number' and blushing. At all costs avoid the rapid repetition of 'Hello? *Hello?* Is there anybody there?'

156

which never sounds convincing. Remind callers to use 141 at all times.

Text messages can be useful. Not only can they be received silently (see your mobile phone handbook) but they are discreet, particularly if you develop a code. For safety's sake we recommend this should be either

1. for the career woman – associated with the individual's employment,
    e.g. 'My next case begins at 10 a.m. tomorrow'
    'I have a patient with gynaecological complications'
    'Stocks are falling'
    or
2. connected with your IF (imaginary friend – please see page 32 for development tips)
    e.g. 'Bill is being beastly again. Can you phone?'
    'Haven't heard from Dick for ages – please advise.'

Itemized bills are a particular—

'What are you reading?' George was looming over her. She hadn't even heard him come in the room. Stephanie snapped it shut. 'Some boring manual Madeleine gave me about office procedures.' She blinked at the readiness of the lie.

'Hmm. I've got a game with Ken at six so don't worry about food.'

'Oh, right.' She hadn't given it a thought. 'I'll just feed the kids then.'

George picked up the paper and studied the headlines. 'How are you getting on there with Madeleine? Enjoying it?'

'Yes, yes, I am.'

He turned the pages, clearing his throat.

'That's good. You look happier.'

She was certainly something! Apart from having re-discovered the restorative powers of the DIY orgasm ('all those endorphins – bound to cheer you up': Millie) and walking around in a permanent state of sexual arousal, the job was so bizarre it was hysterical, this undercover office front for the vow-breaking of any number of respectable women. Stephanie sitting at her desk, or bending over the filing cabinets in the outer office, tried to keep her head down and her face turned away as various elegant women were shown past to Madeleine's inner sanctum. But one couldn't help but glimpse the swish of the odd skirt, the back of a glossy head that looked strangely familiar. She was sure she'd spotted the children's dentist. Once she looked up straight into the face of an actress she'd seen on *The Bill* only the week before.

'You'd be amazed by our A List,' said Madeleine smugly.

And they looked so glowing. Patsy had come in yesterday, eyes huge and bright, her very being humming with energy. Stephanie – in with Madeleine, handing over the newly indexed account sheets – had slipped out as she'd swept in. But she'd heard Patsy breathe out rapturously as Steph quietly closed the door.

'I thought Leonardo was good but this one is something else! No-one but *no-one* has ever come close to him. The other afternoon just blew me away . . .'

And Madeleine's steely response: 'Don't get blown too far. You're really asking for it this time.'

Stephanie wondered why Madeleine always seemed so disapproving of Patsy when she was only doing what the whole agency was set up for. Perhaps it was because she broke the rules. Samantha had heard Madeleine telling Patsy she was a loose bloody cannon and one day she wouldn't be able to get her out of the holes she dug.

But personally Stephanie thought Madeleine could get anyone out of pretty much anything. Her powers of quick thinking were awesome.

One afternoon Jo had appeared in the office waving urgently at Madeleine to come off the phone.

'Mrs H is on the line! Terrible state!'

It turned out Mr H had gone away for the night, and her seven-year-old had crept out of bed and looked through the crack in the sitting-room door. Now he wanted to know why a strange man was giving Mummy a cuddle on the sofa. Jo threw up her hands.

'What shall we do? She's terrified the kid will spill the beans when her old man gets home tomorrow.'

Madeleine barely hesitated. 'Bad back! Tell him she had to call out a chiropractor to do an emergency home visit with full manipulation. You know what they're like – lie on top of you all the time. Sort her out an invoice and look through the books and see what we've got. Isn't JG a physiotherapist or something? Get her to do a follow-up visit when the old man's there – wrap her legs round the girl's neck, crack a few joints, make sure she mentions her colleague popping round a couple of nights before . . .'

Madeleine lit a cigarette, shook her head and sighed. 'Crept out of bed indeed! Don't they listen to a word we tell them?'

Stephanie had listened with her usual fascination. The risks they took! Imagine taking a lover into your own house. It was nerve-racking enough going to bed with a lipstick!

The thought of Toby finding her in a clinch on the sofa was ridiculous. And these women went out all the time – on evenings, overnight, all weekend. They had nerves of steel. She felt guilty when Troy simply phoned her. And much too jumpy to go on any secret assignations.

However persuasive he was.

'Can't you just say you need to pop out and do something?'

'They'd all want to know what.'

'See a friend?'

'Suppose the friend rang up while I was out?'

'Walk the dog?'

'I hate the dog.'

'Well, say you want to stop hating the dog. Say you realize that a lot of the problems you're having with George are to do with your dislike of the dog and that you'd like to start taking it for walks to do some doggie bonding and strengthen your marriage.'

You should get a job with Madeleine!

'You are such a smooth liar, aren't you? Is this how you carry on all the time? Do you lie to your wife like this? Did you used to—'

'Please come and see me tonight.'

'I can't!'

Kelly shot off down the road the moment Stephanie turned out of the gate, almost tugging the lead from her hand. Scurrying after her, Stephanie giggled, imagining herself looking like the wife in the classic John Smith's advert where the dog dragged her off to the pub. She had a sudden absurd image of being towed straight to some sleazy drinking den or – more likely – being tugged at top speed through the doors of the squash club and deposited at the bar.

But Kelly was clearly heading for the beach. 'Hold on!' Steph hauled the dog to a stop at the top of the road that led to the sea. 'We're going this way . . .'

Troy opened the door and pulled her into his arms,

kissing her long and deeply before she could stop him, holding her as if he hadn't seen her for months. Then he bent down and rubbed the dog's head. 'Hello, girl!'

Kelly's tail thrashed against the hall wall. Stephanie took off her lead.

'It's taken for ever to get her here. She'll probably knock me over in her haste to get back.'

Troy laughed when she told him about being dragged to the squash club. 'Or to the house of the barmaid George has been secretly visiting for years,' he grinned.

She smiled and shook her head. But at the thought of George, amusement gave way to a hot flush of guilt. He had been so amazed and delighted when she said she'd take Kelly out. 'I need some air,' she'd said feebly, shamed by his pleasure. 'Been sat in front of the computer all day. I've got a bit of a headache.' And suddenly his face fell again. *Another one . . .*

'I'm not staying long,' she said now.

'You always say that. But you've got time for a drink. I got you some gin. And I remembered the lemon!'

She sat on a stool in the kitchen while Troy emptied ice-cubes into two tall glasses. He was wearing a green silk shirt, loose over faded jeans. She looked at his hands and bare feet, his hair . . .

'There!' He speared a piece of lemon and dropped it into her glass. 'Cheers! Here's to us!'

They clinked and he stood in front of her watching as she sipped. His eyes looked very green above the shirt, his teeth white in his tanned face. She wondered if he would suggest making love again. She squirmed on the stool.

Troy put her drink back on the work surface and took both her hands. 'I wanted to see you because I'm going home tomorrow.'

'*Oh!*' Something inside her jerked with disappointment.

'Just for a few days.'

More internal leapings.

'Then I'm coming back.'

He looked around the room, at the laden shelves and dresser crammed with assorted china and knick-knacks. 'I haven't got as far with this as I thought I would.'

She looked too. It seeemed exactly the same as it had last time. As far as she could see he hadn't got anywhere.

'I've told Tanith we may as well really do it up properly and get a good price. I'm going to get my computer – so I can keep up with a bit of work while I'm here.' He leant out and stroked her hair. 'It could all take some weeks.'

She frowned 'Doesn't Tanith mind?' Delicious little shivers ran down her spine.

'Mmm?' He pulled her close to him and began to nibble at her ear. 'I'd forgotten what perfect little lobes you have . . .' His hand trailed across her back. She felt the heat pour through her.

'Just stop it. Tanith – does she . . .' She should leave, really. It would look odd if she was out much longer but she felt her body strain towards him.

'She's fine about it.' Troy's mouth moved down her neck. His words were punctuated by soft kisses. She was falling apart inside. 'Understands that – you know . . . now . . . after Mum . . . I need a bit of space . . .'

She stiffened and raised her eyebrows. 'That used to be code for you wanting to sniff round someone else.'

'No, it—'

'It did!' She stood back and poked at his chest. 'What about that *meditation* weekend you went on with Jon when you needed *space*? "Just something I've got to do, Steph." And wasn't that when you met that bloody Angela, who kept phoning up?'

Troy looked perplexed as if struggling to remember. 'Oh you mean Angel?'

'Angel! Knew it was something stupid.' She looked at him sideways. 'And I bet you slept with her, didn't you?

Your idea of showing your *sensitive, female side* was to try and screw one!'

'I didn't!' Troy put on a hurt expression. 'She just got a thing about me. I couldn't help it.'

'Huh. Women were always doing that, weren't they?'

'That wasn't my fault, was it?' He stretched out his hands, leant forward and kissed the end of her nose. 'She just worked there. Jon told you I hadn't—'

'Jon would have said you'd spent the weekend abseiling down the Eiffel Tower with a rose in your teeth if you'd told him to. What about that letter I found?'

He looked at her innocently. 'I can't remember.' His lips gently brushed hers. 'You are so sexy . . .'

'You're dreadful. I could never trust you.'

'You are utterly gorgeous.' His fingers trailed across her throat and down to the buttons of her shirt. 'It's years ago. What's the big deal now?'

Stephanie's nipples had leapt to attention. She kept talking valiantly. 'That brings it all back. What's the big deal, chill out, don't worry, life's too short . . . The big deal, you bastard,' she nudged at him, 'is that I know what you're really like. The big deal is that I'm married and you're my ex-boyfriend and I shouldn't be here.'

'But you are!' His hands slid inside her top.

Little shocks danced across her skin. 'I hope to God nobody saw me coming in. You know what this town's like – people will talk.'

He laughed mockingly. 'People will talk? What's happened to you, Steph? What's George done to the girl I loved?'

'Helped her to grow up.' She moved out of his hold. 'Right! I have to leave or he'll be out looking for me.' Pining for Kelly, she thought, doing her top button up. 'And we mustn't do this again. What about your wife? How would she feel?'

She marched into the hall, where Kelly was stretched out panting.

'Steph! Steph!' He rushed after her and grabbed her arm. 'Don't go like that, sweetheart.' *Sweetheart*. The top of her head tingled. He used to call her that when she was nineteen.

He hugged her. 'It was all different then. I was young and stupid.' He looked into her face with the kind, concerned, repentant eyes that always lured her back long ago. 'Let's not spoil what we've got now.'

'We haven't got anything. I've got to go.'

But he had his arms tightly around her now. 'Steph, we're friends. Soul mates. Whatever you say. I'm going to be here for you now – make it all up to you. I won't force you into bed or anything . . .'

Why not? Her body was electrified. She wanted to slap herself.

He kissed her forehead. 'I'll see you when I get back.'

George greeted Kelly as if she'd been in quarantine for six months.

'Did you have a good time, did you?' He rubbed at the dog's face, his own a couple of inches from her lolling tongue and hot breath. Stephanie handed him the lead.

Eventually he looked up. 'Are you OK? You look flushed.'

'It's windy out there – made my eyes water.'

'Did you go along by the beach?'

'No.'

'She likes it down there.'

'I noticed.'

He put a hand on her arm. 'Thanks for taking her out. Is your head better?'

'Yes, yes it is. I was just a bit tired, I think.'

George nodded. 'Shall we have an early night?' he asked hopefully.

She was a seething mass of nerve endings. Desperation battled with the last of her moral propriety and won hands down.

'Good idea.'

He rang the next morning. 'You're looking very beautiful today.'

Stephanie swung round. She couldn't spot anyone amongst the splatter of morning shoppers.

'Where are you?' she said into the mobile.

'Over the road, I've been watching you for ages. You still move so wonderfully.'

She searched the row of High Street shops. 'I can't see you.'

'Boots!'

The phone went dead and she saw him bounding out of the chemist's and over the pedestrian crossing.

She stood still as he strode up to her. 'How did you know I was here?'

'I followed you.'

'You were waiting outside my house? I didn't see—'

'No, well, you women drivers, no powers of observation at all.' He laughed, as she pushed at him. 'I was well concealed. I did tracking in the Scouts.'

'You were never in the Scouts.'

'I lost you for a moment when I had to park but then I spotted you coming out of the bank.' He grinned at her, pleased with himself. 'Come on, I want to give you something.'

He took her arm and began to lead her along the road.

'What are you doing?' She looked anxiously about her. 'Someone might see—'

'We're not doing anything! Can't two old friends have a chat these days? I just wanted to give you a hug before

I start the long cold journey down the motorway away from you. Before I go back to that barren half-life without you.'

'Don't be dopey!' But she giggled. His arm was still through hers. It felt warm and exciting.

He stopped outside the florist's and the raft of flowers banked up on the pavement in the spring sunshine. 'What would you like?' His foot nudged at a bucket crammed with tulips.

'Troy I don't need—'

'But I want to.'

She looked at the array of lilies and narcissi, the deep purple irises against the yellow splash of the daffodils, delicate pastel freesias in the glisten of cellophane.

'These!' He picked up two slender bunches. 'You always said they smelt so good. And . . .' He picked up a huge bouquet of deep red rosebuds, packed together in paper. 'You must have these.'

'No, Troy . . .'

He grinned at her. 'You can look at them and think of me.'

He swung into the shop. She stood dithering then grabbed at another bucket and followed him.

'Can I have these instead?' she said breathlessly as she saw him lay the roses on the counter and the woman began to roll back the paper.

He looked round, amused. 'Of course you can, you can have both if you want.'

'No, just these.'

The woman put the red blooms to one side and took the bunch of creamy white roses Stephanie proffered.

'She doesn't want to take red ones home,' said Troy conversationally, winking at Stephanie. 'Or her husband will know they're from her lover.'

Stephanie gave a strangled snort of embarrassment, but the woman smiled widely at Troy, clearly under his charm.

166

'Ah,' she said knowingly, 'but it's white that's for true love. Red is just for lust.'

They both laughed as Stephanie felt her face turn the same colour.

'You are dreadful,' she said outside, the roses nestling against the freesias. 'And I am not your lover!'

He bent forwards and kissed her lightly on the lips, causing her stomach to flip over and a delectable spasm to run the length of each thigh.

'You will be soon . . .'

Chapter 13

Deirdre was in overdrive.

A small thin man called Alan, who was a new PTA member press-ganged from the reception class, had held proceedings up not only by declining to agree the Minutes of the Last Meeting but by actually producing a Matter-Arising as well. This had never happened before in the whole history of the St Mary's Primary School Parent-Teacher-Association which Deirdre had run with a hand of steel since time immemorial and she was beginning to look rather red and flustered.

'I do not wish to be pedantic,' said Alan for the sixth time, squinting at Deirdre through his little metal-framed glasses. 'I'm not one to split hairs . . .'

Deirdre glowered at him while Stephanie studied the rest of the agenda and tried not to catch Millie's eye.

'Well don't then, eh!' Jacqui smiled brightly across the table. 'Some of us want to go home tonight. And by the look of this lot . . .'

'Item three!' Deirdre rapped her biro smartly on the table and took a deep breath. 'Summer Fair – Allocating Stalls!' She looked around the table, pen poised while everyone shuffled their agendas. 'Now we still need one more person for face painting, two on the barbecue and someone for Name the Donkey.'

'Surely,' put in Alan, 'you mean Pin the Tail on the Donkey?'

'I know very well what I mean,' said Deirdre huffily. 'We have been given a lovely soft toy by Mr Philpot and the children will guess its name.'

'It said "Name the Teddy" on the list you gave me,' insisted Alan.

Deirdre ignored him. 'What about you, Stephanie dear?'

Stephanie jumped. 'Sorry?' She'd been miles away, mind still churning over the text Troy had sent her. **Awful without u. miss u so much. Ly xxx**

Millie nudged her arm. 'Name the Donkey,' she said meaningfully.

'I'm Cakes!' said Stephanie feeling panic set in, visions of last summer dancing before her eyes. 'You said I could be,' she pleaded. 'At the last meeting,' she added. Jacqui snorted with laughter.

'Oh yes.' Deirdre made a series of ticking motions on her sheet and spoke frostily to Alan. 'How about you, Mr Brown?'

'Always willing to help out.' Alan noted something on his own piece of paper. 'Will there be a list of names or shall I assume responsibility?'

Deirdre frowned as she considered this.

'Dobbin!' said Jacqui helpfully.

'Ned,' suggested Millie.

'Eeyore,' grunted Mrs Murphy from the corner, making everyone swing round in surprise because she never usually spoke.

'Thank you!' said Deirdre briskly, looking equally startled as Mrs Murphy resettled her enormous bulk in the biggest staffroom armchair and sank back into a stupor. 'Mr Brown to do names.' (Tick.) 'Got that, Gillian?' (Tick.)

Gillian looked up anxiously from her minutes pad.

'Is that with two Bs?' she asked, frantically scribbling.

Alan looked perplexed. 'Of course not,' he said pushing his glasses back up his nose. 'B-R-O-W-N. Like the colour.'

Gillian turned pink. 'I was still writing down the names,' she explained nervously. 'What came after Dobbin?'

'God!' said Millie, stretching out her legs on the pub seat. 'I thought that was never ever going to end.'

'Tell me about it!' Jacqui yawned. 'I only offered to sort through all those damn toys just to bring it to a close. So you lot – ' she looked sternly around the table, 'can damn well help!'

'Not me!' Sue jumped up. 'I've got my last exam in three weeks' time. Steph – you OK again same time Thursday?'

Stephanie hesitated, counting off in her head how many days Troy had said he'd be away. 'I think so,' she said slowly. 'I'm working now – just part-time – but it should be OK.'

'I'll ring you,' she added as Sue closed her bag and prepared to leave. It had been lovely, sitting back on the sofa while Sue rubbed oils into her feet, pressed her fingers all over them in a strangely soothing rhythm. It had been uncannily accurate too. Bit of water retention, Sue had picked up, the fact that she was probably pre-menstrual, the stiffness in her neck since she'd slept awkwardly and . . . 'You seem a bit stressed,' Sue had said.

That was one way of putting it! Lucky you couldn't pick up secrets, lies and disturbing flush-inducing sexual fantasies from the soles of your feet too.

'You haven't told us much about this new job of yours,' Jacqui said, as she stood up as well.

'Oh it's just some office stuff, you know. For a recruitment agency.'

170

'That's great!' Jacqui said, doing up her coat. 'You'll have to find me something new. The old tits at the council are driving me mad. Got anything mornings only?'

'I don't know. I'm new – haven't been involved with the jobs really.' Stephanie was aware of Millie beside her, saying nothing, head down looking into her glass, turning the beer mat in long slow circles with her finger.

'You two staying?' Jacqui picked up her glass and drained the final half-centimetre of lager. 'Old drunks! See you in the playground!'

Sue touched Stephanie's shoulder. 'Call me about Thursday, yes?'

Stephanie smiled. 'Sure.'

Millie was waving a hand to Jacqui as she disappeared through the door. When she turned back, she looked oddly ill at ease. 'Another drink?' She got up from the table.

Stephanie nodded.

Millie fished at the piece of lemon in her glass, made a fuss of squeezing it against the side, sucked at the rind. 'Are you enjoying it at Madeleine's?' she asked eventually.

'Yes, yes I am.'

'What exactly are you doing?'

'Just filing, book-keeping, that sort of thing.'

Millie smiled wryly. 'No telephone work?'

'No telephone.'

'I used them once.'

'What, to look for a job?'

Millie looked in her glass again and gave a short laugh. 'It's OK – I know all about it. Madeleine phoned me after she'd found out we were friends. Said she'd destroyed all my records. That I shouldn't worry because you'd never find out about me.'

'I guessed. After I started work, I remembered the evening at Amanda's.'

'What did you guess?'

'That you'd met before, been unfaithful. It sort of made sense – fitting in with all the jokes and stuff. It doesn't matter to me. I wouldn't tell anyone.'

'No, I know.'

Neither spoke. Then Millie turned and looked directly into her eyes. 'Steph, are you?'

'What?'

'You know what. Having an affair.'

'No.' Her heart thumped. *Not yet*. 'Why?'

'Just wondered – as Madeleine gave you the job.'

'I think she was desperate.'

'Yes, well. Staffing's bound to be a problem.' Millie fell silent.

Stephanie asked, 'When was it?'

Millie screwed up her face. 'Four or five years ago. I couldn't keep that up for long. Too expensive for a start.'

'I think I'd find it too nerve-racking. Have you seen him since?'

'I meant using PAs, not having an affair.'

'What do you mean?'

'The affair's still going on.'

Millie ran her hands through her hair. 'I don't know what will happen. He can't leave unless I do. That's the thing. He'd have to leave her in the house, only fair to the kids. And most of his salary would go to keeping them all. He could only leave if he could come to live with me. I can't expect him to sit around waiting in some bedsit. Which means I have to separate from Patrick.'

'And you don't want to.'

'I don't know.'

'Do you still love him?'

'When he's sober.'

They left the pub. 'Come home with me,' Millie said. 'I want to get back and check on Ben. Then we can talk.'

'What about Patrick?'

'He'll be in bed.'

The lights in the kitchen were low. Millie had gone upstairs to look at Ben. Stephanie sat at the table. She felt oddly nervous. Uncomfortable that she had kept back her own guilty secret. But nothing had really happened yet. Her ex-boyfriend was back in town and they'd kissed. Had a cup of coffee together. A bit of a grope. Nothing had been broken. She hadn't really been *unfaithful*.

Millie came back into the room, kicked off her shoes, flicked on the kettle and settled herself on a tall stool against the breakfast bar. 'Dead to the world,' she said. 'He's so good. Sleeps through everything.' She shook her head. 'Just as bloody well sometimes.'

Stephanie watched as Millie made the coffee. 'But I always thought . . . well, you and Patrick. He seems so . . .'

'What? Normal?' Millie handed Stephanie a mug. She pulled her cigarettes towards her. 'Dependent drinkers aren't all down-and-outs swigging meths on a park bench, you know. Just because Patrick holds down a job and pays the bills, doesn't mean he hasn't got a problem.' She lit up.

'Why do you think I do everything on my own these days? We never go out as a couple any more. He gets home and heads for the Scotch bottle. By 9 p.m. he's legless, by ten he's asleep. If I'm lucky. If I'm not he starts crashing round the house telling me what a bitch I am.'

Stephanie stared. She'd held this picture of Millie and Patrick in her head for so long. A party years ago in someone's garden. Toby was a few months old. It was hot. Stephanie felt fat and frumpy in a flowered tent while Millie was slim and golden, wearing a yellow backless dress. Patrick stood beside her, his hand gently stroking the smooth brown skin of her spine all the time as she spoke. Stephanie had watched wonderingly.

When George had come up beside her and touched her arm she'd hurried away to check on the sleeping baby, peaceful in his little carry-seat in the shade beneath the trees. She'd stood looking at him, grateful for the excuse to get away from the others, unable to cope with it all, longing to go home . . .

Millie's voice was flat. 'I've had to face it. He's an alcoholic. It's the price I pay for this.' She gestured a hand round the enviable kitchen.

Stephanie shook her head. 'You shouldn't have to pay a price.'

'Yes I should!' Millie was suddenly savage. 'That's how it works. He pays a price too.'

She sucked again on her cigarette. 'It would be so easy, wouldn't it?' She laughed sourly. 'You see, my husband had a drink problem. We were all under such terrible strain. I just needed someone . . . someone to hold me. Someone I could rely on. Someone who wouldn't get pissed every night and call me a cow.' Millie looked directly into Stephanie's eyes. 'But the truth is, Steph, I can't remember what came first. I want to think his drinking drove me away. That's what Alex says. That I was lonely and neglected and desperate to be loved. But I'm not sure. I'm not sure it wasn't the other way round – that I made *him* lonely. Patrick. That I started this by wanting something more than I had. By never being satisfied . . .'

'But you didn't make him an alcoholic,' said Stephanie. 'He's got to be responsible for that.' She sounded like Rose. 'What about Ben?'

'Ben's OK. He doesn't realize yet. At the moment he just thinks Daddy gets tired because he works so hard. He hasn't worked out yet that the reason that Daddy gets grumpy on Saturday mornings but cheers up once he's

174

had lunch is anything to do with the bottle of claret he had with it! He probably thinks all fathers spend half the weekend passed out on the sofa.'

She drank some coffee. 'And pissed fathers can have their advantages,' she said flatly. 'Catch him in the right mood and it's new trainers or the latest video game for Ben, flowers and chocolates for me. Trouble is, getting the timing right.' She pursed her lips. 'Some weeks when he leaves early in the mornings I only see him sober for a couple of hours from one weekend to the next. And there's no point talking to him if he isn't. Not if you know what's good for you.'

Stephanie frowned, shocked. 'He's not violent to you?' She thought of George, who suddenly seemed so safe and reliable, back at home in his little routines, turning off the lights in the same order he turned them off every night.

Millie shook her head. 'No, not physically. He shouts a bit. Makes nasty comments. Threw a plate at me once. Doesn't usually remember it in the morning.' She bent her cigarette end into the ashtray. 'Or says he doesn't.'

She got up and pulled the blind down over the dark window behind the sink. 'But sometimes,' she said quietly, 'he does remember and he says sorry. He tells me he loves me and he doesn't know why I put up with him. He tells me how things get on top of him and he doesn't know how he'd ever survive without me. Once,' she turned and looked at Stephanie, her own eyes filling, 'once he cried and said please don't ever take Ben from me.' Millie pulled a piece of kitchen roll from the holder on the wall and pressed it to her face. 'I promised him I wouldn't.'

Stephanie got up from her chair and put a hand on Millie's arm. 'And what about Alex?'

'I don't know. He's there. He's always been there for me. Sometimes I can't bear it. I can't bear to be involved with him. I can't bear for him to be involved with anyone else. At times I think I don't have enough faith in us to throw all this up to be with him and yet at others I love him so much and just know life would be so much simpler if we were together.'

'It might not be.' Stephanie's voice sounded disapproving in a way she hadn't intended. She knew she was talking to herself as much as Millie. 'I mean, what about Ben? And didn't you say Alex has got children?'

'Two.'

'And his wife? I mean are they unhappy or what?'

'Oh, she's awful. Apparently she moans on all the time about how little money they've got but won't get off her arse to do anything about it herself.'

Millie – who had not worked for years – shifted her own perfectly proportioned buttocks back onto the stool and gazed appealingly at Stephanie. Then she laughed. 'I know!' she said, blowing her nose. 'I'll have to find a job if we split. I have been meaning to since Ben went to school. But I'll give Patrick one thing: he's never mean about money – chucks it at me. Makes him feel better and then gives him a chance, once he's got a skinful, to be abusive about how I spend it!'

'Alex and I fit together.' Millie was talking softly now. 'When he holds me my head fits into his shoulder. I feel safe. He looks after me, you know. Makes me eat properly, buttons up my coat when it's cold, cuddles me when I cry, tells me off when I'm a bitch.' Millie smiled. 'I need that, Steph. I want to be cherished sometimes. I know it's stupid.'

'No it's not.'

She had a sudden flashback. Early on with George. They'd stayed a night in Bristol where George had clients. The next morning they'd gone down to the docks to see the SS *Great Britain* and she'd slipped on the wooden floor, twisting her heel, the sharp pain making her gasp as she almost fell. He'd shot out a hand to save her, pulled her towards him, putting an arm around her shoulders. 'Don't hurt yourself,' he'd said. 'You're too precious for that.'

She blinked, finding it difficult to imagine, unable to reconcile that George with how they were now.

Rose used to look after her too. She stayed for three weeks when Troy had gone. Swept up the bits of broken china, went out and bought coal for the fire. On Saturday mornings they'd be in the double bed together, drinking coffee, reading the papers, listening to the radio, talking, sometimes even giggling though Stephanie's heart was broken.

It was in bed that they made the lists.

Rose had jumped out for a notepad and pen and numbered things in order of priority.

Things Stephanie Must Do
1. Ask for a pay rise
2. Find herself a new bloke

Things the bloke mustn't have:
1. Mystic pyramid
2. A cheeseplant
3. A guitar
4. Any ideas that involve inner peace and the insignificance of man against the mind-blowing infinity of the universe
5. Another girlfriend
6. A mother

'I think that last one's going to narrow things down a bit,' Rose said drily.

'You know what I mean!' Stephanie said. 'A mother like Troy's who thinks everything he's ever done is absolutely fucking wonderful and anyone who worries about the bills is just a moany old dragon who doesn't appreciate his talents.'

'Let's concentrate on what he should have,' said Rose. 'Like a job.'

'And a Gold card,' Stephanie added.

'That's no guarantee of anything,' said Rose. 'You should know that!'

Things a bloke should have
1. A job
2. A bank account with money in it
3. A credit card with credit left
4. Only eyes for me

They'd fallen across the bed in hysterics though it wasn't really funny. Seemed pretty ironic now . . .

'Alex puts me first,' Millie was saying. 'He really thinks about how I feel. He's caring. He's strong.'

'I used to envy you and Patrick. You always seemed so, so . . .' Stephanie broke off, almost embarrassed, unable to find the words '. . . physical.'

'Yeah we used to shag a lot,' Millie said matter-of-factly, 'but once that had gone well, there wasn't anything else. Alex is my friend, my confidant, he listens to me. Patrick only cares about himself. And where his next drink's coming from.'

'I don't really know what George cares about these days,' said Stephanie, 'except that blasted dog. Do you know, he bought her a birthday present? When it was my birthday, he said: "Get yourself whatever you like." Kelly's big day and it's a new bowl and a packet of choccie logs – *wrapped up*, would you believe!'

Millie smiled. 'That's rather sweet.'

'It's totally nauseating. I'm surprised he didn't invite all the other dogs in the street and play party games. Blind dog's buff. Pass the choccie-log parcel . . .'

'Are you still having problems with sex?' Millie asked sympathetically. 'Maybe you should go to the doctor's, you know, Steph, find out if there's any medical reason why you've gone off it.'

'I haven't gone off it.'

It was such a relief to talk about Troy. Stephanie felt the tight knot in her stomach loosen as the words fell from her mouth.

'And I feel so awful,' she finished, 'because actually it's improved things with George. I mean I still don't initiate anything but if he does, well I just, well I mean, if I just think about Troy . . .' She broke off guiltily.

'Millions of wives do that,' Millie said. 'How do you think all the fat, bald, toothless ones ever get any?'

'It's so strong,' Stephanie said. 'The pull of him. It's so powerful.'

'And you say he's changed?' Millie asked.

Stephanie nodded, knowing how it sounded. 'I really think he has. He seems to finally be everything I ever wanted him to be . . .'

TWADDLE!

That's what Rose had said. She'd sat frowning over a piece of paper while Stephanie snivelled into a heap of soggy tissues. Then she grinned and threw the pen onto the table. 'Got it!'

She pushed her scribbles towards Stephanie. 'TWADDLE,' she said.

'What?' Stephanie sniffed.

'That's what you say – out loud – every time you think you want him back. TWADDLE.' Rose ticked the letters off on her fingers. 'Troy Was A Dirty Devious Little Egocentric.' She smiled. 'I wanted to say "wanker" ' she added, 'but it didn't quite work.'

'He wasn't dirty,' Stephanie protested weakly.

Rose was still for a moment, thinking. 'Hah! This is even better.' She picked up the pen. 'Tosspot!' she cried triumphantly.

'Troy Out, Selfish Sponger, Piss Off Troy.'

She rolled about the sofa, clutching herself, laughing, 'Tosspot, tosspot.'

And somehow Stephanie had started to giggle too.

The trouble was, it hadn't been a proper ending. In a way they'd never really said goodbye. He'd moved out and Rose had stepped in. Stephanie would have let him come back – to 'talk it through' – but there was Rose and later George both speaking of clean breaks and new beginnings. 'Waster!' said Rose. 'Loser,' echoed George.

And now Troy was back. No-one had ever inspired such rage and frustration and disappointment nor taken her to such heights. For every time he let her down he also opened up a dozen shimmering possibilities. The past was past and you could never tell what would happen in the future – Rose at least had taught her that – but Troy was here now. And what did Madeleine always say . . .

Millie looked back at her. 'It will start to hurt.'

They were both silent.

'Someone told me,' she went on eventually, 'to stop while it was just sex and excitement. Get out before your feelings are really involved, they said. I didn't listen.' She shook her head. 'Perhaps I should have stopped while I still only fancied Alex. While I still could.' She gave a wry smile. 'Madeleine used to say it's only being found out that causes the pain. But it's not true.'

She put her hand on Stephanie's arm and shook it softly. 'Be careful, Steph. Think about it – before you start loving him again.'

Stephanie nodded. And thanked her for the advice.

But it was too late for that.

Chapter 14

She felt excited, strung out, little ripples of expectation trembling up her spine. She wasn't sure quite when it had happened, what exactly had made her decide on wild abandon, but it felt good. She looked at herself in her rearview mirror. Just for once, amazingly, her reflection shone kindly back: her lips looked glossy and pouting, cheeks smooth, her blond highlights shone. Her eyes glittered.

And her heart thumped as she locked the car and swung her handbag over her shoulder. She almost smiled as she strode away from it, amused at the whole ludicrous scenario, her keys dangling from a manicured finger, black leather boots tap-tapping along the pavement, expensive jacket swinging.

Bloody hell! She suddenly felt as though she looked like the woman she'd always wanted to be and of course she wanted to smile. Outside she looked like the well-heeled, middle-class executive wife she was. Mother, committee member, pillar of the community . . .

Her. Steph. Who'd have thought it.

She turned up his path. Inside . . . inside she was a nineteen-year-old virgin.

He opened the door. And she stepped in.

Or a thirty-nine-year-old slapper.

She had to do it straight away. On the crest of a wave of adrenalin. Before she could rush home and hide in a cupboard. There was a look of shock on his face as she dropped her bag and cast off her jacket. Part of her was outside, looking on, amazed at the one fluid movement. She saw the way she wrapped her arms around him, pressed her lips up to meet his, pushing him gently backwards towards the stairs. For a moment he was still, almost rigid: she felt his disbelief and might have stopped. But then he pulled her to him, tight, tighter, throwing back his head, his lips parting on a long sigh.

It was that noise that did it. That gasp of want, that long outward breath of desire. It was passion. George only had erections.

There was a split second when she was suddenly apart, looking on, seeing them feverishly tugging at each other's clothes. There was the tiniest space – rapid as a heart-beat – as he peeled off her jeans, ran his hands across her stomach, his eyes moving hungrily up and down her body, when she nearly stopped again. Almost panicked thinking: oh God, we're really going to do this! She hadn't thought beyond her opening gambit, her playing at seductress, wanting to find out. But it was too late and she was shocked by the strangeness of him and then as startled by the old familiarity.

As he gathered her to him, it all came back. She watched his face, so intent and absorbed. He covered her with kisses, gasped over her, wrapped her legs around his shoulders, licked her, held her, stroked her, squeezed her. And it took over. That old power that had lain between them, that had never gone away, that had always kept her wanting and would always – now – keep her coming back for more.

*　　　*　　　*

He came into the room, naked, carrying two mugs. He set them down on the side table and sat on the bed beside her.

'You looked as if you wanted to eat me.'

Stephanie felt the heat flood her face. She hid in her hands.

He pulled them away, pulling the rest of her to him, holding her in warm arms. 'No, no, it was lovely. It was so special . . .'

But she was crying.

'Oh God, what have I done?'

'You wanted to do it.'

'I know. But now I have, I can't believe it.'

'Do you wish you hadn't?'

'I don't know.'

'Oh Steph, I'm so glad you did. It felt so right. It crystallized everything I've been thinking about us, cemented all my feelings.' He held her face in his hands, seeming overcome with emotion. 'I love you.'

She pulled the quilt up around her shoulders, huddling under it wordlessly.

'It was beautiful,' he said. 'You are beautiful. Here!' He handed her a mug of black coffee. Alcohol rose in the steam and hit her nostrils, making her blink.

'What've you put in it?'

'Brandy. You looked like you needed it!'

She sipped at the scalding liquid, gasped and spluttered.

'God! How much is in here?'

He laughed, slid under the duvet with her, wrapping his limbs around her again, pulling her head against his chest. 'It's for the shock!'

For the shock.

Shock to her skin and senses. Those forgotten, delicious, tendrils of ecstasy. That feeling of being all at once high and powerful and helpless and utterly empty. She could feel his heart beating.

'We belong together,' said Troy. 'We always did. Inside you never stopped loving me, did you? I never stopped loving you.'

They lay quietly, their bodies moulded together in the warmth, his fingers trailing gently down her arm. He spoke softly, soothingly. 'That was just a release of emotion. You've been keyed up, wanting me. I've felt like that too.'

His arm tightened around her and he sighed with pleasure. 'This feels like coming home.'

She felt her body relax, and was filled with a deep peace. Suddenly it all seemed to make sense. It *was* right. He felt warm and safe. 'What are we going to do?' she asked.

He stroked her hair. 'We're going to keep on loving each other and never let go.'

They lay in silence.

'What are you thinking?' He nuzzled her ear.

'I'm hungry.'

He laughed. 'You always were. Good sex always made you starving. I remember all the times you kicked me out of bed and demanded toast and peanut butter—'

'Liar! I always had to make it!'

'You used to eat it. The bed was always gritty – full of crumbs from your little post-coital snacks.'

She giggled. 'You can talk! Who used to stay in bed *all* day sometimes, eating God knows what . . .'

'Rubbish.'

'Got any now?'

'What?'

'Peanut butter.'

He came in with a tray. 'Don't think Mum was into peanuts. There's lots of Bovril.'

'Ugh!'

'But I've got you biscuits.'

184

He held up a packet of chocolate digestives and proffered a plate of cheese on toast decorated with twiglets.

Stephanie smiled. 'You still eat those?'

'Mmmm, not half.' His cheeks were already bulging.

She took a square of toast, crunched into the hot, salty cheesiness. It tasted fantastic. 'Yummy. There's something about food made by somebody else.'

He reached across her and took a piece. 'There's something about food in bed.'

He ran a hand across her stomach and she felt the warmth shoot through her again.

'What was the first food I ever made you?' he asked.

'Sausage sandwich.'

He laughed. 'With brown sauce. Served to you in bed and you said you'd never had one before.'

'Was I talking about the sandwich?'

'You used to make that wonderful curry, do you remember?'

'I used to grind up my own spices. God, I was keen.'

'You were a wonderful grinder. And a great cook.'

'When you turned up to eat it.'

'I wasn't that bad. I was always on time to eat you.' His tongue was warm and wet in her ear. His teeth gently found her lobe. 'I could eat you now . . .'

'I'd better go back soon,' she said, wriggling against him, not looking at the clock.

'Come here again first,' he replied softly, reaching out with one hand and lowering the tray to the floor, the other pulling her back down beneath the duvet.

The last of the coffee was tepid now but she swallowed it down, enjoying the glow of the brandy in her throat. The bed was warm. She felt heavy and soft. Troy lay close beside her. For a short while time could stand still.

'Don't let me fall asleep,' she murmured, closing her eyes anyway. 'I mustn't stay too long.'

Troy tucked the quilt around her shoulders and she buried her cheek in a pile of pillow. He leant over and kissed her eyelids. 'I want you to stay for ever. I want to hold you and cherish you and take care of you, Steph. I want to put it all right for you.'

She took his hand.

'You have.'

Chapter 15

Samantha wandered into the living-room of Jed's flat in one of his T-shirts. Her long blond hair flopped across her face as she rubbed her eyes. 'How long have you been up?' she asked.

He was sitting on the floor in front of the low square coffee table, his laptop in front of him. She squatted down, draped her arms around his neck, rubbed her face up against his stubble. He didn't move, just went on clicking through photo after photo on the screen.

'What are you doing?' she asked, looking at a shot of a dark blue car parked outside a large house. 'Come back to bed.'

'In a minute.'

His fingers continued to tap and the car grew huge on the screen and faded away again. Samantha yawned. Then she saw the next picture flash up and sat back, surprised.

'*Oh!* Why've you got one of Patsy?'

He swung round. 'You know her?'

'Well, yeah – she's a friend of my godmother.'

'She's not?' Jed looked at her in disbelief then banged his fist down on the table in triumph. 'Fuck me!' He grinned at Samantha. 'Got her!'

Samantha looked at Patsy's smiling profile. 'Like older

women then, do you?' She'd meant it to sound joky, but it came out wrong.

Jed shook his head impatiently. 'Tell me everything about her, Sam. It's important.'

'Why? Where did you get her picture from?'

'Just tell me!'

'What is there to tell? She's an old friend of Monica's – they went to school together, I think. I'd never met her until she got me this job. Why do you want to know?'

'What's her other name?'

'King.'

'Married?' He leant forward and studied the picture more closely. Patsy had a mobile phone held to her ear. He fiddled with the mouse pad, zooming in on her hand. 'It looks like she's got a wedding ring on there.'

'Tell me why you want to know, Jed.'

'Has she got children?' He was pacing about the room now, his brows knitted with concentration and suppressed excitement.

'Yes, she said she had.'

'Brilliant!'

'What's this all about?'

'And this job she's got you? What's her involvement there?' He walked out into the kitchen and returned with a bottle of beer. 'I don't even know what you do – it's a recruitment agency or something, isn't it?'

'Yes,' said Samantha, nervous now. 'And a virtual office.'

'And this Patsy works there?'

'No. Well, not really. She comes in quite a bit. She's a partner.'

'Who's her boyfriend?'

'What?' Samantha tried to look surprised. 'I told you, she's married.'

Jed looked at her hard. 'Don't act thick,' he said disparagingly. 'Where does she live?'

Samantha didn't answer. She looked uneasily at the picture on the screen. 'I'll lose my job,' she said at last.

'For telling me where someone lives? Come on – this could be big for me.'

Samantha was uncomfortable. 'I don't know exactly.'

'I can find out.' Jed had cleared the picture and was tapping away at the keyboard.

'But why, Jed? You've got to tell me why.'

'There might be a big story in it.'

Samantha looked even more nervous. 'What sort of story?'

'Sam – this could make my whole career. Just think – we can get that flat in London. Get you some modelling work, launch you properly. You'll meet all the right people, go to the big glitzy parties.' He ran a hand along the length of her leg. 'You've got it all – you could be another Kate or Naomi.'

She moved closer to him, put her arms back round him. 'I just want us to be together – be, you know, a proper couple.'

'And I want that too.' He knelt before her, looking earnest. 'We'll get married and we'll be terrific. Me big in Fleet Street – ' he laughed – 'or Wapping anyway, you on all the fashion pages.' He ran a hand around her neck, stroked her cheek. 'But I need a break, honey. You know what it's like.'

Samantha snuggled up to him sympathetically.

'You know that ponce James Kirkby?' Jed shook his head. 'He's got his own column now! Can barely wipe his own arse and they give him a column. Why? Cos his old man used to be editor of the *Guardian* and he went to Cambridge.'

Jed glowered. 'If I can break a really big story it'll set me up. Job on the *Detail* or at least some regular slots. I'm sick of coming up with all the leads and getting fuck-all for it. I've got to do the whole thing this time.'

He pulled her close again. 'You've got to help me, Sam. I need you to tell me all about Patsy. Everything she does and everywhere she goes. I need to follow her.'

He was kissing her neck now, his tongue moving up, gently licking her delicate ears. Samantha felt herself melting. 'What's she done?' she asked. 'Tell me what she's done.'

Patsy got out of the car and leant back through the open window, making sure he got a good view of cleavage. 'Tomorrow?' she asked.

The man at the wheel put out a hand and stroked her arm. 'Don't know yet. There might be something on with her in the evening.' She said nothing, just watched him in the darkness, her tongue flicking slowly across her lips; she knew her eyes would be shining as his were, caught in the dull yellow of a single street light. She saw his expression change. 'If I can get away could you manage lunchtime?'

She smiled. 'No problem.'

She crossed the dark narrow side-street and unlocked her own car, blowing him a kiss, ripples of pleasure revisiting her body at the thought of the evening that had just gone, of the many more still to come.

He was delighted by her. By her boldness, her adventure, her free spirit. The way she was high on the risk.

'But aren't you worried about your husband?' he'd asked again. 'Afraid you'll really get caught one day?'

And she had shaken her head and smiled in the slow wicked way she knew turned his stomach to jelly. 'I'm careful,' she'd told him. 'Since I can't be good.' She knew he was the one who was afraid. Aware of how much he had to lose.

'Where are you supposed to be tonight?' he'd asked her, nervously she thought, as she'd sat on the bed, brushing her hair, reapplying lip gloss.

She'd shrugged. 'It doesn't matter where,' she'd replied. 'I have an alibi – that's the main thing.' And she'd kissed him again, feeling his breathing quicken.

'An alibi?' he'd murmured into her hair, already undoing buttons again. 'Is it unshakeable?'

She'd pushed him back across the bed, sliding across him, feeling the thrill run through her at his obvious excitement. His hands gripped her, but she raised her head for a moment to answer.

'It's perfect.'

Chapter 16

'Surely you haven't forgotten?' Madeleine looked up from her desk and laughed.

'Well no, no, of course not,' Stephanie said awkwardly. 'I mean I knew it was George's birthday, I just hadn't thought about it being the day after the do.'

'But Ken says he's fifty!'

'We don't really make a fuss about birthdays.'

George didn't. On her twenty-first Troy had woken her up with vintage champagne and smoked salmon on toast. The flat was a mass of shiny helium-filled balloons that bobbed against every spare inch of peeling ceiling. He'd been up since 4 a.m. inflating them, he told her proudly. They could barely afford to eat for the rest of the month.

'Yes but the big five O!'

'I did ask him what he wanted to do,' Stephanie said defensively. 'He said lunch with the kids or something. No fuss. Of course he's really looking forward to the Saturday night.'

George had looked at the invite and sighed. 'A Sixties Night!' he'd said. 'Do I have to get dressed up in a lot of silly clothes? Suppose we'll have to. Ken's on the committee.'

'It might be fun,' Stephanie had said. 'I thought I might see if Millie wants to come.'

'Perhaps she could go instead of me?' George had asked hopefully.

'Well, Ken thinks we ought to make a bit of an occasion of it,' said Madeleine. 'Get some banners up, bring a cake out at the end, that kind of thing. Let them play, eh?'

'Play what?' Patsy came in and dropped her handbag on Madeleine's desk. 'Jo's in a bit of a flap,' she said. 'Monica's got to have double cover – needs the lover fed a line too. Nipping off to Madrid with a restaurateur she met last night, by all accounts.'

Madeleine rose to her feet. 'That woman! She's like a dog on heat.'

'Think of the turnover, darling!' Patsy called after Madeleine's retreating back. She laughed gleefully and lit a cigarette. 'If we had ten Monicas we'd be rolling in it!' She exhaled and looked at Stephanie. 'So what are you and M plotting?'

'Just talking about the squash club thing next month. It's George's birthday the next day. Madeleine and Ken want to do something for him.'

'Oh, right.' Patsy clearly had scant interest in that. 'I've got my own little plan for that night. Dave's away so I can come on my own. Do a spot of circulating, make sure everyone sees me, then – ' she winked at Stephanie – 'slide off for an hour or two. That's what I call a perfect alibi.'

'You be careful!' Madeleine's voice was sharp as she reappeared in the doorway. 'You're taking enough risks already.'

She looked pointedly at Stephanie, who hurriedly gathered up her files and went back to the outer office.

She heard Patsy's unrepentant laughter as she closed the door. 'Surely, he's the one who's doing that . . .'

*　　*　　*

'You're doing a lot for that school at the moment, aren't you?' George put his knife and fork together. 'Thanks, that was good.'

Guiltily Stephanie picked up his plate and put it in the dishwasher. 'There are all these toys to sort out,' she said vaguely. 'For the fair . . .'

'Can I come?' Toby said.

'No, you can't. You'll be in bed. Go and get your reading.'

'Shall I do it with him?' George got up from the table.

'Oh! Yes, thank you.' Stephanie smiled awkwardly as he walked past her and touched her lightly on the arm. 'Can't do everything, can you?' he said.

Stephanie was gripped with anxiety as she cleaned her teeth. She didn't know if George was suddenly being warmer and nicer or if she was just noticing his good points in a way she'd forgotten. For a moment she wanted to text Troy and tell him she couldn't come after all. She wanted to put the children to bed and sit on the sofa opposite George and watch something mindless on television.

But as she brushed her hair, carefully lipsticked her mouth, pressed her lips together, her body was already stirring at the thought of *his* hands, *his* eyes, *his* passion.

She stood in the doorway, watching. George had his arm around Toby, both profiles intent on the book.

'I'm going now,' she said softly. Toby looked up. 'Night, Mum.'

She crossed the room and dropped a light kiss on his cheek and then George's. 'Good night!'

George looked up and gave a brief smile. 'How long will you be?'

'I'm not sure, depends how long it takes.'

'I'll leave a light on.'

'Thanks.'

194

She heard him as she reached the front door, calling after her: 'Love you.'

She walked quickly away down the path. Millie lived only a few streets away. She wouldn't normally take the car – especially if they were going to have a glass of wine while they worked. She looked at her watch. It would take at least twenty minutes to walk to Troy's, maybe longer. God, suppose Jacqui telephoned. Or Sue to confirm the next reflexology session. And George said she was at Millie's sorting toys and they said . . .

Suppose Millie herself called? She knew what Stephanie was doing tonight – Stephanie had reminded her several times – but suppose she forgot?

Maybe she should have asked Madeleine for an alibi! It was free, after all. How did these other women afford it, for God's sake? How did they cope with the worry? Was it only her in this turbulent sea of doubt? Patsy didn't seem to care. Patsy skipped in and out of the office these days looking so young and free and *happy*.

She'd come into the loo later that morning, skin glowing. 'Do you know?' she'd said to Stephanie, 'there was a bit in the paper on Sunday saying they've done a survey and extra-marital affairs can make you ill! It's the stress, apparently. If you're feeling guilty more than five times a week you're three times more likely to get heart disease or HIV.' She'd thrown back her head and laughed. 'I would have thought that had more to do with putting it about without a condom, wouldn't you?' Stephanie had forced a smile.

'It doesn't make me feel ill, I can tell you!' Patsy continued. 'I feel utterly fantastic all the time. Sometimes things just feel right, don't they.' She winked. 'Can recommend it!'

Stephanie, peering in the mirror at the crease of anxiety between her eyes, feeling the churning of her stomach at the thought of the lies she would tell tonight, hadn't been at all sure she could. But still she walked towards Troy.

Jed poured the last of the champagne into Samantha's glass. 'You all right?'

'Yes.' She smiled as he put the heavy bottle back on the table. 'This is nice.'

She'd been surprised to find Jed waiting for her outside the office. He said he'd been there for some time. Said he just couldn't wait to see her – wanted them to have a really long evening together to make up for all the times he'd had to work lately, to make it really special.

Since then he'd been so sweet. There'd been champagne and olives and little spicy crackers. Quite honestly she could have done with some more food – the champagne had gone straight to her head – but it wasn't like Jed to be so romantic and she didn't want to spoil it by asking for something more substantial.

He reached over to his jacket and pulled a small paper packet from one of the pockets. 'Give us your mirror.'

Samantha sat up and fumbled in her handbag.

'Want to do a line?'

'No.' She shook her head as usual. 'No, it's OK.'

She watched as he tipped the white powder onto the glass surface. 'Going to have to get used to it when we hit the scene in town.' He laughed. 'All the models do it – how do you think they keep their figures?' He produced a credit card. 'Gives them that confidence, that extra sparkle.'

Samantha looked at his head bent over the small mirror, his hair flopping across his forehead, brows knitted in concentration as the card moved across the powder. She just wanted to be with him for ever.

'What does it feel like?' She watched as he produced a £10 note and rolled it tight. He always said it was just a bit of fun, but she was nervous.

'Just makes you feel good, honey. Warm and bright and sexy.' He ran a hand up her thigh.

'I mean, I don't want to get hooked.'

He laughed again. 'You won't get hooked, honey. Am I hooked? It's like drinking champagne. Champagne and Charlie. Special treats.'

He held it to his face and snorted. 'You're special.' He reached out and touched her face. 'And I want us to have a very special night together.'

Samantha was beginning to feel light-headed. At lunchtime Madeleine had only let her disappear long enough to grab a bottle of water and a Crunchie from the newsagent's on the corner. She tried to sit up.

'I feel a bit woozy, Jed.'

'That Madeleine's working you too hard.' He pushed her gently back onto the sofa and stroked her cheek. 'You were busy today, weren't you? Lots of people coming in and out.' He stopped and sipped at his champagne, continuing in a bright voice. 'And you know, funny thing, I thought I saw Janice Sanderson from the *Sun* going into your place. What did she want?'

'I don't know.'

'Well, was she sniffing about?'

Samantha shook her head. 'I don't know who you mean. Lots of people come to see Madeleine.'

'Well, can you find out? Ask a few questions?'

Samantha looked alarmed. 'Madeleine hates me. She wouldn't tell me anything.'

'Well, one of the others then. What about that secretary? Wouldn't she know?'

'Stephanie? I'm not sure.'

'There must be a reason for Janice to be hanging about.'

'Well she probably just . . .'

'What?' Jed's eyes glinted.

'She's probably a friend of Madeleine's or something.'

'Or she's on to something too!'

'What do you mean?' Samantha stifled a yawn.

'Hey!' He put his arm around her. 'You're not going to crash out on me, are you? I want us to make plans – I'm really close this time. We're going to be able to move soon. Get our flat in Soho. It'll be all-night partying then. No falling asleep before the night's begun.'

He jumped up, crossed the room to the stereo and took a new CD from the rack. 'I was tired earlier but I'm all bright now!' He grinned at her as he slotted the disc into the machine. 'I feel *fantastic* and I'm ready to play. Can't wait till I get that job on the *Detail*, mixing with the A List, all those supermodels . . .'

He tapped the side of his nose.

Samantha sat up straighter. 'I could just try a little bit . . .'

It didn't seem to do anything at all. Just made her nose tingle and her eyes water.

'Have a bit more a bit later.' Jed was lying on the sofa with her now. He'd opened another bottle of champagne and was kissing the palm of her hand, running gentle fingers up her arm. She loved him when he was like this.

She wished he'd stop asking her about Patsy, though.

'So what was she up to there today?'

'I didn't really see her, she was with Madeleine.'

'But she mixes with the rich and famous, does she?'

'I don't know.'

'The thing is,' said Jed, still stroking her, 'that I saw someone else arrive today. Gabriella Gordon. Now what's a celebrity like her doing in a recruitment agency?'

'She must know Madeleine.'

'Or Patsy? Seems to me there's quite a number of important people going in and out. I've been watching a lot lately.'

'Have you?' She cuddled up to him.

'Have you met anyone famous there?' Jed nuzzled her ear.

Samantha shook her head. 'I don't remember.'

He picked up the bottle once more. 'Have a few more bubbles.'

Troy had bought cider. 'For old times' sake.' He grinned at Stephanie, took her bag from her hands and wrapped his arms around her. 'Thought we might go for chips later.'

'I can't stay late.'

'Shhh.' His breath was warm against her face. 'You've only just got here.'

'You look happy,' he said when he'd led her upstairs. 'You look young.'

'Hettie says: "You're thirty-nine. Just accept it." It's her way of telling me I look my age.'

'Bollocks to Hettie!'

Troy licked at her shoulders, eased her bra straps down her arms and deftly undid the fastening. 'You are gorgeous. Bet you look a damn sight younger than she does.'

'I am.'

'Only a bit, mmm.' He was kissing his way down her spine, sending delicious tremors down further. 'Bet you look years and years younger. Bet she looks like your grandmother.'

'She doesn't!' Stephanie laughed.

'And you look even younger when you smile,' he said. 'Which reminds me, I've bought you something.' He handed her a soft flat package of dark blue tissue. 'I remembered,' he said.

She peeled back the paper and pulled out the black and red lace, holding it in her hands, feeling suddenly shy.

'Put it on.'

'I'm a bit old for this sort of thing now.'

'You look like you did when you were nineteen.'

She twisted round and pulled him down to kiss her. 'What would I do without you?' she said.

Later as they lay back on the rumpled bed, Stephanie's head on Troy's chest, she said: 'That was twenty years ago.'

'I know.'

'But imagine. Wouldn't you have been amazed if that first night someone had told you you'd be doing this to me in twenty years' time?'

'No, I knew then you were the one. I recognized that light about you. You really were my soul mate.'

'I bet you've said that to every woman you've ever slept with.'

'I have not!' He made a face of mock indignation, then smiled, and touched her cheek. 'You are beautiful,' he said seriously.

'I'm middle-aged. I've got crow's feet and thinning lips.'

'You're lovely. You've always had this . . . serenity. This inner calm.'

'You should have seen me screaming at the kids this morning.'

'It's the way you hold yourself. Your straight back. When I first saw you walk towards me, with your chin up like a dancer, I wanted you.'

'I've got cellulite and sagging breasts and the beginnings of a varicose vein . . .'

He sat up, reaching for his glass, suddenly sounding irritated: 'What's wrong with you? Why can't you accept my compliments? Why do you always have to ruin it?'

'Because you're not being real. I didn't have any "inner calm" – you used to say I was neurotic!'

'You worried, yeah.'

'I had reason to worry.'

'It was only money.'

'Only money and flirting with other women and staying out half the night and leaving me frantic . . .'

He shrugged, raising his hands in that old gesture of helplessness. 'Sorry.'

'Why did you do it?' The cider made her reckless. 'Why did you think it was OK to treat me like that? To sit around while I went out to work, to go off to parties while I was getting up at dawn, to chat up anyone you liked?' An old, dull rage felt like a stone in her chest.

She waited for the denials but he looked thoughtful. 'Think it was Mum,' he said. 'She always told me I was different – special in some way. She said . . .' he stopped, struggling with some emotion, then went on: 'that I only had to believe in myself. I only had to reach out and I could have anything I wanted . . .'

Half of her wanted to say something contemptuous, the rest was deeply touched by the tears in his eyes. She took his hand. 'And now?'

He squeezed her fingers and smiled his shining smile again. 'I'm still reaching, Steph. Reaching for you. Just hoping it will still work.'

A ripple moved through her.

'But when did you change?' she wanted to know. 'When you met Tanith? When you had the children? You know,' she said lightly, 'get responsible? The grown-up job, your own home etc.'

'Well, Tanith's old man helped us with the house and . . .'

'Oh, right.' Disappointment as something inside dropped into place. Of course.

'But I've completely paid him back now.'

Jed ran his tongue lightly across Samantha's stomach. 'You have such a perfect body,' he breathed. 'You could

201

do anything. Not just modelling, you could be an actress. I could really see you breaking into films . . .

'Come and get into bed.' He pulled her up from the sofa and led her into the other room. 'You lie there.' He rolled back the duvet. 'And I'll come in and look after you.' He unbuttoned his shirt as she slid under the covers. 'You look fabulous . . .'

'I really love you, Jed.' Samantha felt more awake now.

'I know, honey and I love you too.' His fingers still trailed across her. 'You're irresistible. I want you all over again.'

'My mum will go on if I don't come home.'

'You can phone her.' Jed picked up the champagne bottle. There was about an inch left in the bottom.

'Oh who cares, she'll soon be OK when we're engaged.'

He poured it into Samantha's glass.

'We are still going to get married, aren't we, Jed?'

'Of course we are, you know that.' He traced a finger across her lips. 'Got to get you a better job first, though. Got to get you launched on your career.'

'Do you really think I could be a model?' she asked.

'You could do anything. With me behind you, anything.'

He was kissing her again. She felt herself melt inside. Wonderful Jed, who was going to marry her and love her and take her away from Madeleine's constant complaints. She felt suddenly bright and confident.

'I can't wait to leave that job,' she told him. 'She really takes me for granted, that Madeleine, really puts upon me. She says I can't act but when we get to London things are going to be a bit different, aren't they? I'll be modelling and—'

'How does she know if you can act or not?'

'Oh! I don't know. But when we go to London . . .'

'I need my big break first,' Jed was saying, his tongue hot in her ear, 'then we'll be able to move. Then we'll go and get you a ring.'

Samantha sighed happily and pressed her body closer to his. 'That's what I want, Jed, that's what I want more than anything.'

'But you'll have to help me,' he murmured.

'I will,' she breathed. She wound her legs around him. 'I'll do anything. I can do anything. What do you want me to do?'

He moved inside her, thrusting deeply as she gasped.

'This office of yours,' he asked in a low voice. 'And your Patsy. What's really going on?'

Stephanie put the phone back down and reached for her shoes. She felt slightly unsteady. 'No taxis for forty-five minutes.'

Troy put his arms around her again. 'Oh well.'

'Troy, I must go home.' She just wanted to curl up and go to sleep. 'George will wonder.'

'Say you were sitting around talking and you didn't realize the time. He'll believe that.'

'I know but . . . No, I'll have to walk.'

'I'll take you.'

'It's OK. I can go on my own.'

'Are you kidding? I'm not letting go of you a second earlier than I have to. Not now we're so close again. We'll have a snog in the car.'

She looked at the empty cider bottles. 'You've had too much to drive.'

He stopped and considered them as he reached for his shirt. 'Have I? You're probably right. OK, I'll walk you.'

'Come on, then.' She was anxious. 'Hurry!'

'I know!' Troy leapt up, his face alight with childish enthusiasm. 'I'll take you on my bike.'

She watched as he wheeled it down the side of the house and looked down at her long floaty skirt. How the hell did he think she was going to get on that?

'Come and sit on the crossbar.'

'Who do you think you are? The Sundance Kid?'

'It was Butch Cassidy.'

'It looks bloody uncomfortable.'

'Just get on.'

'How?' She perched on it sideways, suddenly giggling as the bike nearly fell over. He laughed too as they weaved across the road, Troy somehow managing to pedal while keeping one arm around her as she balanced precariously on the metal bar. 'See, you're enjoying it! This is what you need, Steph – a bit of fun! With me!'

She grinned, anxieties already fading. The cider had gone straight to her head in the night air.

'Are you hungry?' Troy's voice came softly in her ear as they neared the small row of shops three streets away.

'Starving!'

'Knew you would be.'

He left her under a street lamp, holding the bike, as he darted across the road. 'I've got to go home,' she protested half-heartedly but inside she felt bold and daring again. George would be asleep by now anyway. She shrugged to herself. Millie would back her up.

'Here – ' he thrust a warm damp parcel in her arms. 'Get back on.'

They giggled hysterically as they wobbled off again, Stephanie clutching at him with one hand. 'I'm going to slide off.'

'No, you're not.' He had slowed down. 'Hold on tight.'

He put his feet on the ground as he steered the bike through a gap in the hedge into the recreation ground.

'Where are you going?'

'Short cut.'

'It's pitch black!' cried Stephanie, squealing as they bumped across the grass.

'All adds to the excitement.'

It did. As she clung to him, afraid she'd fall, as they

careered across the uneven surface in the darkness, she felt the surge of adrenalin. She was high and giggly as he brought the bike to a jerky halt by a park bench.

'I told him loads of vinegar and salt.' As she unwrapped the layers of paper, he pulled the small rucksack from his back. 'Always be prepared!' He produced another bottle of cider and two plastic cups.

She shook her head, laughing. 'I can't drink any more.'

'Rubbish.' He picked up a chip and slid it into her mouth. 'Me, cider and chips. What more could you want?'

They tasted wonderful – fat and floury, seeped in vinegar making the cider seem sweet and heady. She realized she was ravenous. 'Mmm, they're great,' she said, with her mouth full.

'You're great.' He was sliding his hands up her thighs, taking her skirt with him. 'Ever made love on a bench at midnight?'

'Stop it!'

'I can't – I have got to have you. You are too gorgeous . . .'

She could feel her own breath coming more quickly too.

'Can anyone see us?'

'Probably.'

They emerged onto the street at the other end and as they swung down and bumped off the pavement the breeze took Stephanie's skirt and blew it up into a balloon. She smoothed it down, feeling her hair blowing across her face and all of a sudden she was wildly, wonderfully, fantastically happy. She felt light and bright and beautiful. Troy leant forward and kissed her and she was deeply certain that Madeleine had been right. *Carpe diem*. You had to grab a little joy while it was around.

Chapter 17

Madeleine was beginning to fidget. The woman in front of her was showing no signs of coming to an end.

'I mean once we went walking and listened to music and gave each other flowers. I used to write him really long letters, telling him every little thing that popped into my head. I lived and breathed him, I really did . . .'

Jo was making faces through the glass of the office door.

'But now it's just sex. And it really is *sex*. Not long, lingering lovemaking like it was in the beginning. It's a quick fix. I just want to hurry him through to get back home . . .'

'What?' Madeleine mouthed crossly. The woman across the desk was fumbling for her tissues.

'The other day I found myself counting, you know to pass the time, willing him to come before I got to fifty . . .'

Madeleine looked at her watch. A bit of counselling was part of the package but the woman wasn't even renewing, for God's sake.

'. . . I mean I can do that at home with Henry.'

Madeleine got to her feet. 'Well I'm sure you've made the right decision!' she said briskly. 'Thank you so much. Jo will see you out.'

206

Jo came through the door mid-sentence.

'Someone to see you,' she hissed, jerking her head to the reception area beyond and rolling her eyes. 'Just turned up!'

'Two minutes!' Madeleine dived into her handbag for mirror and lipstick, looking critically at the cracks around her eyes. Today was one of those days when she felt she was fast approaching a time when the dreaded phrase 'well-preserved' might hover on malicious lips. She slapped on a bit more of everything. Then she pushed the intercom on her desk. 'OK.'

She rose to greet the woman with some surprise. Experience had taught her that infidels came in all shapes and sizes but this one very definitely was not the type. It was nothing to do with how she looked. Madeleine had seen enough of those pearl-decked cardigan gets-ups to know they guaranteed nothing. No, it was more the aura that was missing. Women embarking on the illicit exuded something – like the elusive scent that pulls a tom-cat. Madeleine could sense it at ten paces: spot them in bank queues and standing at bus stops. This woman was not at it. She held out her hand and took the cool, firm one that was offered, with a small ripple of unease.

Madeleine looked at the form Jo had handed her. Helen Markwell. Claimed to be here through personal recommendation. As they usually were. Early forties probably, but lovely skin, neat middle-class bob. Square framed glasses, sensible shoes. Something of the vicar's wife about her. It didn't quite add up.

'Perhaps you could tell me something about how it works.' The voice was low and cultured. Madeleine looked at her. 'And you were recommended by?'

'I don't think she gave me her real name.' Helen Markwell returned her gaze. 'We met at a health farm. swapped confidences. She just said I should come to you.'

Madeleine's eyes narrowed. 'What have you been told already?'

Helen Markwell smiled. 'Alibis?' she asked.

She was sitting quite still, hands folded in lap, head bent slightly as if listening intently, as Madeleine began her patter. At last the clear grey eyes met hers. 'That's perfect,' Helen said quietly. 'Just what I was hoping for.'

Madeleine nodded. 'Well then, it's simply a matter of settling the fees and then letting us know when you'll be needing cover and where you're supposed to be. Leave your husband the number we give you. Let us know if you want any extras – train or parking tickets, résumé of a film or play, souvenir from a day out, you know. Oh,' she added almost forgetting, 'we ask for a photograph of your husband – just in case he appears where he's not supposed to.'

She gave a small laugh, slightly uncomfortable under the scrutiny of the unsmiling gaze, thinking fondly of her latest source of amusement carefully picked from a vast array of such photographs which had never been needed for any other purpose. It was almost time to get ready. 'Jo will see to the paperwork with you.' She began to get up but stopped as Helen Markwell remained quite still.

'I haven't quite explained,' she said softly. 'It's my husband who is having the affair.'

Madeleine sat back down, irritated at the wasted time. Now it all became clear. These misunderstandings did occur from time to time but not usually with someone of Helen Markwell's apparent intelligence.

'I'm sorry, we can't help you. We're not a detective agency,' she said briskly. 'I can, however, recommend—' She opened the drawer of her desk.

'No!' Helen's voice stilled her hand. 'I understand perfectly what you do. And I want you to do it for Malcolm. Provide him with perfect alibis every time he sees her so that I never find out.'

Madeleine felt herself slump slightly in her chair. She passed a hand across her forehead and looked at the woman sitting opposite. She'd seemed sane but was quite clearly barking.

'I'm not quite with you,' she said carefully. 'You clearly *have* found out already.'

Helen gave a small, patient smile.

'Indeed I have. But he does not know that. For some time he has not extended me the courtesy of being careful to avoid my detection. He does not appear to feel I warrant that respect.' Her voice had taken on a silky quality that made Madeleine shiver.

'But this time it is something more. He is becoming quite desperate for me to find out. He believes he is in love.' She said it sorrowfully, sympathy tinged with distaste as if speaking of some unfortunate infection.

'Ah,' Madeleine sat forwards. 'And you are pretending you don't know.'

'I have no intention of making it easy for him. I want him to tell me himself. And I am quite prepared to pay you to make sure he has to.'

Madeleine was only too willing to take anybody's money but this one was beyond her. 'And how exactly would that work?' she asked wearily.

Madeleine lay on the hotel bed and stared at the ceiling as her latest showered. It hadn't been so good this afternoon. She'd found it difficult to concentrate. His thrustings had been tedious and she hadn't been able to get the level gaze of Helen Markwell out of her mind.

'And what will you do when he does tell you?' Madeleine had asked with a smile. 'Stick the bread knife in him?'

Helen had said quite seriously: 'Oh no, I wouldn't kill him. I would never have another chance to punish him then. It is far better to let him live. To spend the rest of his days wishing fervently that he had been killed. So that he could be free of my revenge.'

And she had smiled back, gently like a Sunday School teacher. For the first time in as long as she could remember, Madeleine had felt afraid.

She saw her again as she left the foyer. She was standing near the desk, looking at a brochure, demure in navy blue coat and hat. Madeleine wondered if she were keeping watch for her husband. Did she know the hotel to be a favourite haunt of philanderers? Madeleine – fresh out of bed with one of them – felt her skin crawl with an unfamiliar discomfort.

Helen Markwell was obviously mad.

But still something didn't quite add up.

Jed punched the air. 'Ye-ee-sss!'

He paced up and down the living-room of the small flat. 'You mustn't say a word to anyone. This is mine and it's going to be massive. If I can get a full client list out of Sam . . .'

He stopped and sighed. 'Still think you should have signed up properly – you could have really got in there.'

Helen Markham – staff writer on the *Daily Detail* – put down her coffee mug. 'Oh yeah, and who was going to pay for it? You've seen how much the subscription was. I had to make her think I was bonkers and get rid of me. But I can go back. I can hang about outside looking disturbed . . .'

'I need names.'

'You're the one with the girlfriend in there.'

'And pictures. If I can get a shot of my man being a naughty boy . . .' Jed sighed pleasurably at the magnitude of the possibilities. 'Fuck me, this is big!'

'Talking of which . . .' Helen lit a cigarette and surveyed him coolly. 'Got time before you go?' She'd taken off her glasses and applied a slash of red lipstick.

She watched him as she inhaled, stretching out her stockinged feet on the sofa.

Jed gave a slow smile. 'I should think so.'

He sat down beside her and cupped a hand around her breasts, flicking at the string of pearls dangling in her cleavage. 'There's something about you in a twin-set . . .'

Chapter 18

'Charlotte!!! Come away from that television. Turn it off!'

Stephanie sighed with exasperation as her daughter remained unmoved, her eyes glued to the screen where Andrew and Harriet were sitting on their red leather sofa either side of a woman sobbing for Britain.

'What's the matter with her?' Stephanie asked in spite of herself.

'Ssshhhhh!' Charlotte flapped a hand in annoyance.

Across the screen in a matching squashy armchair a man sat stony-faced as Harriet thrust a mike and her cleavage towards him. 'So you're adamant the marriage is over, Brian?' she yelled as the sobs hit a crescendo. 'In spite of Maureen saying how sorry she is.'

'She was in bed with him from the wood yard,' Brian intoned robotically. 'That's that, that is.'

Harriet turned to camera and lowered her voice. 'Maureen and Brian have been married for nineteen years and have three children,' she said mawkishly. 'All are very distressed by their mother being ejected to the shed . . .'

Stephanie crossed to the TV set.

'No! Don't!' wailed Charlotte, twisting her head round her mother for a glimpse of Andrew Carlisle's white teeth.

He flashed a great mouthful of them. 'Like many happily married couples, Harriet and I are no strangers to the attraction of temptation,' he said, oozing sincerity. 'But we also know . . .' Stephanie was momentarily stopped in her tracks as Andrew and his wife leant across and clasped hands over the top of the woman's heaving form, 'that the secret of happiness is total fidelity.' Stephanie snapped off the power and Andrew mercifully vanished.

'Mum!' Charlotte screeched, hurling the remote control at the sofa. 'I hadn't finished watching that.'

'It's time to go to school!'

'You are well unfair.'

'And Dad's going to be well late if he doesn't leave in a minute. Now go and get ready.'

'Why can't you take us, then?' Charlotte said belligerently, staying exactly where she was.

'I've got Sue coming at nine to do reflexology before I go to work.'

'Yes it's always about you, isn't it?'

'What?' said Stephanie, taken aback. 'What are you talking about?'

'Nobody cares about me in this house!' Charlotte flung herself onto the sofa too. 'I'm not allowed to go out or have any fun . . .'

'That is not true . . .'

'It is true! You switch off the television when I'm watching it. You keep me in here, you're always going on, you won't let me do anything.'

'What do you mean? You do lots of things!'

'You wouldn't let me go to Sean's party!'

'He's eighteen. It was in a pub!'

'Emma's mum let her go.'

Stephanie raised her eyebrows. 'You're telling me that Emma went to a pub on a Saturday night? I shouldn't think they'd let a twelve-year-old in.'

'I didn't say she *went*,' said Charlotte, screwing up her face and fixing her mother with a look of pure disdain. 'I said she was *allowed* to go. Her mum would have let her but Emma didn't want to go without me.'

'Oh right!' said Stephanie. 'Well next time I'll phone Emma's mum, shall I?'

Charlotte glowered. 'And you didn't let me go to that disco' – she adopted a dreary whine that was supposed to be an imitation of her mother's tones – '*because it's a school night*.'

'Well that's perfectly reasonable,' said Stephanie crossly. 'You don't do your homework half the time as it is.'

'It's abuse!'

Stephanie fought the urge to slap her.

'Don't be so ridiculous! We'll talk about this later,' she added hearing George's feet coming down the stairs. 'You've got to go to school.'

'Yes,' screamed Charlotte, now scraping the barrel for fresh proof of her victimization. 'I get sent to school while you sit here gossiping with your friends.'

'I'm helping her with her college course!' Stephanie said, wondering how she had come to be defending her movements to a stroppy pre-teen.

'You said it was lovely and relaxing and you really enjoyed it!' Charlotte spat accusingly.

'Well that's OK, isn't it?' Stephanie felt her temper rising. 'Aren't I allowed to enjoy myself?'

Charlotte blew out her cheeks, her voice sneering. 'What would you know about enjoyment? You are just so *sad*.'

'What's going on?' George appeared in the doorway and adopted his best children-should-be-seen expression. 'Don't be so rude to your mother, and get a move on!'

Charlotte flounced past him muttering darkly about ChildLine.

'Don't let her upset you,' he said to Stephanie. 'Probably just her hormones.'

She nodded gratefully as he gave a sudden and surprising grin.

'Can't think where she gets that from.'

Her own hormones were in bloody uproar, Stephanie decided. Ever since she'd arrived at work Troy had sent a series of texts ranging from the mildly suggestive to the downright pornographic till she'd barely been able to concentrate.

And she was supposed to be getting the hang of the helpline. 'We need to train someone else up to do this,' Madeleine had said casually. 'I'll put the phone on speaker – have a listen in – see what you think.' Stephanie thought it was terrifying. Women phoned up in varying states of panic and desperation while Madeleine dispensed advice. Stephanie wouldn't have known where to start. She could just about have cobbled together excuses for how to explain one's car parked in the wrong place all night or being seen leaving a restaurant with a man when you're supposed to be out with your sister but she'd have been at a complete loss when Mrs BR came on the phone.

The woman's voice was frantic. 'He's read all of it!' she shrieked. 'What am I going to do?'

'Take some deep breaths,' said Madeleine briskly. 'Now, what's happened?'

BR's voice rang out round the room. 'He was supposed to be away till tomorrow,' she wailed. 'But he came back early and the letter was still on the kitchen table.'

Madeleine shook her head in disapproval. 'And what does it say?' she asked.

'Everything – how good it was to spend the night with me and how he hoped John would go away again soon.' Stephanie bit her lip. God, even Madeleine wouldn't be able to talk her way out of that one. But Madeleine was firing off questions. 'Typed or handwritten? Sent through the post? Addressed to you personally? Hmmm.' She frowned while Stephanie found herself twisting her own hands anxiously as she listened to the woman's rapid breath on the other end of the line.

'I just ran out of the house,' she was saying. 'I came in and saw him standing there holding it and I didn't know what to do . . .'

'Hmmm.' Madeleine sat quite still, apparently deep in thought. 'What's your job?' she asked.

'Oh!' BR sounded surprised. 'I work part time at the doctor's.' Madeleine sat up straighter. 'Ah. Doing what?'

'Receptionist.'

'Good.' She nodded at Stephanie. 'And tell me, how did he sign the letter?'

'All my love D.'

'Just the initial?'

'Yes.'

'Right. Got it! This is what you say . . .'

'Yes?' the woman's voice was filled with hope.

'You say,' said Madeleine slowly, 'that D stands for Daphne . . .'

What? Stephanie looked at Madeleine in surprise. Even if he were daft enough to believe it, it was still sex with someone else!

BR clearly shared her doubts. 'Oh no, I couldn't.' The woman's voice rose. 'He talks in the letter about Saturday night – how he bent me over the—'

'Never mind that,' interrupted Madeleine. 'We don't need the details. You say it was written by Daphne who is a patient at the surgery and who has developed an unhealthy obsession with you.' There was silence at the end of the phone. 'You say she suffers from a delusional disorder known as Erotomania and she believes that you and she are engaged in an affair.'

'But—'

216

'You tell him that she overheard you telling another receptionist that your husband was going to be away and her fevered imagination ran riot. That she has convinced herself you've been lovers. You throw yourself into John's arms and say how frightened you've been without him there to protect you – how you wonder where it will all end. You talk of the phone calls she's made that you didn't want to worry him about and now this letter . . .' Madeleine went on, now fully into her stride.

'He won't believe me.' BR still sounded uneasy.

'He *will* believe you.' Madeleine was firm. 'Because tonight Daphne is going to appear at your gate, clutching a bunch of flowers and gazing adoringly up at your bedroom window until your husband in manful fashion goes outside and moves her on.' Stephanie put a hand over her mouth.

'Daphne will declare her passion for you, referring to her letter and telling your husband she spent the previous night in your bed – describing your room in such inaccurate detail that he is totally convinced she is not only completely unhinged but has never been near the place.'

'Oh.' BR seemed lost for words.

'He will give her a flea in her ear and she will scurry away never to return and you can be eternally grateful for his macho intervention.'

'Suppose he wants to talk to her doctor?' said BR, suddenly recovering.

'Hippocratic Oath,' said Madeleine immediately. 'Doctors can't discuss patients. And you will say that this sort of thing is an occupational hazard and you don't want anyone thinking you can't cope. I'll get Jo to sort a "Daphne" right away.'

The woman appeared to be weeping with relief. 'Thank you! thank you!'

'And remember,' finished Madeleine sternly: 'What's the golden rule about paper?'

'I don't . . .'

'You never write on it and you don't keep it!'

She put the receiver down over a further gush of thanks and turned to Stephanie, who was still open-mouthed. 'They never listen. Tell Jo to get hold of RG – she calls herself an actress though I've never known her appear in anything – and get her round there tonight in a headscarf and a pair of ankle socks, looking deranged. I'm really going to slap on the expenses for this one. Imagine leaving it on the table,' Madeleine raised her eyebrows. 'A bit of sex and they lose all reason.'

Indeed. Stephanie rushed from the office on the dot, ignoring Madeleine's knowing looks, driving straight home and diving into the shower. Somebody saner might have made it a cold one but Stephanie, buzzing with recklessness and nerve, had a long, hot, steamy one. Smothering herself in body-smoothing lotion and dabbing on perfume, she sent Troy a text instructing him to come round immediately.

She looked at her watch as she heard his footsteps on the path outside the open front door. Forty-five minutes left before the kids came out of school. She was trembling. Her shirt was undone just an inch or two below normal, her hair still damp, tousled in the abandoned way he'd told her he loved. Underneath the shirt, another new shove-them-up-and-out red lace bra was cutting into her ribs but it would be worth it for the look on his face when he started undoing her buttons . . .

She felt wicked, wanton, daring – free!

The morning after the last time she'd been in a blind panic. She'd woken with palpitations, convinced someone would tell George his wife had been spotted clutching a strange man on a bike or doing obscene things on a park bench. Troy had hugged her when she told him.

'No-one's going to find out, babe,' he said affectionately. 'That was just your hangover.'

'But what's real?' she'd asked, agitated. 'My feelings change all the time. When I've been with you I'm high. A couple of drinks and I'm carried away, confident. Then I believe in us, that we can't help this.'

He'd nodded as he held her: 'That's right, babe, that's right.'

'But other times, I know what we are doing is wrong, I feel guilty and ashamed. Selfish! And supposing George—'

'He won't.'

'This is the real you,' he'd said, rubbing her hair. 'That bright, bold, precious free spirit you used to be – just taking a little happiness. Life's short, Steph. I won't be here for ever.'

No. It would be over soon. It had to be, didn't it? She'd be off this emotional roller-coaster and back to reality. This was a mad interlude before she accepted age and things past – a last, final taste of Troy.

'Darling!' She bobbed into the hall to greet him.

Jesus! Her heart jumped so alarmingly she thought for a moment she was in the throes of a coronary.

George!

'You made me jump!' she said feebly, the best excuse she could manage to explain her popping eyes and the beads of sweat that had sprung out on her forehead. Her hand went guiltily to her buttons.

'Had a meeting cancelled,' George said. 'Thought I may as well come home. See how you were,' he added.

'I'm just off to school. Collect the children,' she gabbled, fumbling with her shirt. 'Got to see Millie on the way. I'll just get my shoes on . . .'

Her hands were shaking as she forced her heels in. What was she going to say if Troy walked in before she managed to get out?

George would recognize him, of course he would. Stephanie remembered them facing each other years ago, across the threshold of the empty flat. 'I have no interest in you,' George had said when Troy tried to explain. And Troy had smiled. That you-have-no-grasp-of-the-power-of-the-universe and I-feel-sorry-for-you-because-you-are-a-poor-Unenlightened-Capitalist smile. He'd tried to include Stephanie in it – tried to say with his eyes 'What are you doing with *him*?' She had turned away, embarrassed.

George was talking but she hadn't heard a word he said.

'Is that OK?' He had taken his suit jacket off and stood before her in his shirt, looking perplexed.

'Yes. Sorry, what?' The front door still gaped open. Troy could appear in the hall at any moment.

'I've got a game at seven. So I'll eat later.'

'Right.' She grabbed at her handbag, nervous fingers shuffling at the pot on the hall table for keys.

'Are you all right?'

'Just in a rush. Told Millie . . .' She hurried towards the door, hearing him sigh behind her. 'See you.'

There was no sign of him outside. Cautiously she pulled out of the drive, looking both ways up the road, wondering what to do. What would Madeleine do?

Suppose she drove off and he turned up in a minute and rang the doorbell. Should she pull round the corner and keep watch? Whatever had possessed her? She should have gone to his house. She scrabbled in her handbag for her phone, hands still trembling. There was a text message already waiting. Oh thank God.

SAW G CAR AM UP ROAD X

She slumped in relief. Of course – the car.

Troy was laughing when he answered the phone. 'I wondered if you'd be panicking.'

'Well for God's sake, of course I was! Imagine if you'd come face to face.'

'But we didn't.'

She could picture the indulgent smile on Troy's face. It was all a game to him.

'You haven't really got the temperament for this, have you, sweetheart? Far too jumpy.'

Jumpy? She was still on the verge of a heart attack.

No I bloody well haven't.

Chapter 19

'Do we have to?' Charlotte yawned. 'Grandma's is like so boring.'

Stephanie frowned. 'We haven't seen her for ages and she wants to give Daddy his birthday present.'

Charlotte rolled her eyes. 'Another skanky jumper.'

'And you know she loves to see you both,' Stephanie continued, picturing her mother-in-law's expression of disapproval whenever her eyes fell on her grandchildren, 'and that's what families are all about – keeping in touch.' *God save us.*

'Daddy doesn't even like her.'

'Don't be so silly.' *Nobody likes her!* 'She's his mother.'

'So?'

Toby had already packed. He heaved his bulging rucksack into the hall and looked plaintively at Stephanie. 'We've only got beef crisps left.' He wrinkled his nose. 'I've gone right off them.'

'No eating in the car!' George clipped the lead onto Kelly's collar and picked up his keys.

Toby's mouth dropped. '*Mum!*'

'Don't want crunching and crumbs. Or that thing making a silly noise all the way up the motorway.'

'Dad! That's my Digivice. I have to—' But George had

banged the front door. Toby looked mutinous. 'Dad is *so* unfair.'

'What am I going to eat?' Charlotte came down the stairs. 'What's all this lot?' She tipped Toby's rucksack over with her foot and watched as the contents spilled onto the carpet.

'Stop it! Leave his things alone.' Stephanie glared at Charlotte, who rolled her eyes.

Stephanie watched Toby re-packing. He frowned in concentration as he fitted various flashing, buzzing, beeping gadgets and extra-terrestrial weapons back into place. 'There!' He pushed a Thunderbirds pencil sharpener into the last square centimetre of space.

'Have you got any clothes in there, Toby?' she asked.

Toby looked surprised. 'No.'

Charlotte had a T-shirt, some stick-on tattoos and a bottle of glittery nail varnish in a carrier bag. 'Clean knickers?' enquired Stephanie.

'I've put them in your case,' her daughter replied sweetly. Charlotte added another dollop of mayonnaise to the three inches of ham she'd piled on the end of a loaf. Stephanie looked at Charlotte's ever-lengthening legs and sent up a short prayer for her daughter's metabolism. Let it remain in overdrive. Anyone else would weigh fifteen stone by now.

She went upstairs. Charlotte had indeed added her underwear to the case on the bed. And two pairs of jeans, a very short black skirt, two more T-shirts, a sweatshirt, pair of glittery sandals, her new trainers and half a dozen CDs. Stephanie shook her head. 'We're only going for one night!' she yelled.

One night too long. George would be uptight all the way there and would barely speak once they arrived. Certainly Agatha was difficult – hyper-critical and contrary – but she wished George could be a little more relaxed and accepting. He always got in a foul mood before their occasional visits, was monosyllabic through-out the stay and would never talk about it afterwards.

'Come on,' she urged the children. 'Dad wants to leave as soon as he gets back.'

'I don't know why Kelly can't come with us,' said Charlotte.

'Because Grandma won't want her in the house and she doesn't want to be cooped up in the car for hours.' *And I'd have to listen to her ridiculous panting and smell her horrible doggy breath*. 'She'll be much happier round at Sheila's.'

One lot of canine noises was enough, she thought as George marched about barking at the children, who were putting on shoes with impossible slowness, stopping intermittently to thump each other and send George's blood pressure soaring. At last they were all in the car – Toby engrossed in electronic warfare, Charlotte sulking and Stephanie's nerves in shreds.

The silence was laden. As George pulled onto a garage forecourt and got out, Charlotte breathed out noisily. 'God! Is Dad moody or what!'

'Shh!' Stephanie looked out of the window at George's dark profile at the petrol pump. She got out of the car and caught up with him as he stalked off to pay. She pointed at the bright buckets lined up outside the shop.

'Shall we get her some flowers?'

George didn't stop. 'What's the point? They'll only be the wrong ones.'

Agatha had left the front door open for them as usual. As they came into the living-room, calling, she made a fuss of getting up from her chair.

'Ah there you are,' she said flatly.

'Hello Grandma!' Charlotte strode in and plonked herself on the sofa.

'You've got very tall again,' Agatha said accusingly.

224

'How are you?' Stephanie kissed the papery cheek, which blenched as it always did. George grunted.

'Isn't that boy going to say hello?' Agatha ignored her son and nodded at Toby, who slid his Digivice back into his pocket.

'What shall we have? Tea?' Agatha lowered herself back into her chair. George looked out of the window.

'I do wish,' said Stephanie when he eventually came into the kitchen, 'that you wouldn't make an atmosphere the moment we arrive.'

George picked up the tea. 'It's not me who does it,' he said firmly. He gave Steph a small nudge with his elbow. 'How long today before she mentions Teri?' he asked.

She smiled and for a brief moment their eyes met in conspiracy then George turned and carried the tray back into the other room.

'Had a lovely long letter from Teresa,' Agatha said as she dropped another sugar lump into her cup. 'Daniel's vice-president now, you know. Such a land of opportunity.' She pointed at the mantelpiece. 'Get that, please.'

Charlotte obediently rose and handed her an envelope. 'Lovely pictures of Edward and Sophie. She says they're doing ever so well at school. Mind you, their schools are better than ours.'

'Of course they're not,' said George. 'Why do you think they all stay there till they're twenty-five?'

'Nothing wrong with education,' said Agatha, fingering the photographs.

'It's all right if you don't have to go out and earn a living,' said George.

'Of course Daniel's got a brilliant mind.' Agatha's beady eyes were fixed on her son. 'And with Teresa being so clever, of course the children have a head start . . .'

'The garden looks lovely.' Stephanie crossed the room to the french windows. 'What beautiful fuchsias.'

'It's not what it was.' Agatha put the pictures down. 'I

225

can't bend any more and that gardener chap you got me, George, is hopeless. Well, he's not a gardener. Doesn't know one plant from the next.'

'It looks very pretty to me.' Stephanie made herself smile at her mother-in-law.

'You should see next door. Now her garden really is something.' Agatha picked up her tea and stirred it loudly. 'But then her son comes to do hers. Every Sunday!'

'She chose that gardener,' said George crossly as they took the bags upstairs. 'She said she wanted the same one as Mrs Harbottle. All I did was walk down the road and get the damn man's number.'

'Don't take any notice.' Stephanie unzipped the case and lifted the children's clothes out. 'You just rub each other up the wrong way. Here, take these,' she said as Charlotte came into the room.

But Charlotte had something much more pressing to report. 'Mum! Guess what!' She stuck two fingers into her mouth and mimed throwing up. 'She's made steak and kidney pie. Gross!'

The hard line of George's mouth softened slightly. 'Well that's something, I suppose,' he said.

'I like to see a girl eat potatoes,' said Agatha approvingly as Charlotte took her ninth. 'Though what will happen to that boy I don't know.'

'He'll be OK,' said Stephanie.

'Not much goodness in toast,' said Agatha. 'He should have had an egg.'

Toby wrinkled his nose. 'I don't like eggs. They're all slimy.'

'Not if they're cooked properly!' said Agatha triumphantly. 'Your Aunt Teresa always had eggs. Helps the brain to function.'

226

'That's why yours doesn't,' Charlotte told her brother. He pulled a face at her.

'That's why Teresa did so well at school,' said Agatha. 'That's why she went to university.'

Stephanie glanced at George. One Christmas when Charlotte was small, George had banged the table and shouted. 'And much good it did her!' But today he appeared to be absorbed in his cabbage.

'So,' said Agatha, when everyone except Toby had waded through chewy apple crumble and custard. 'Going to be fifty.'

'Looks like it,' said George.

'Dangerous age. Let's hope you've got plenty of genes from my side. We all go on and on. Not like your poor father.'

'Oh George is in great shape,' said Stephanie brightly. 'It's all that squash and walking the dog – his last medical said he was very fit.'

She glanced at George. She was surprised by the expression on his face. He looked touched, *grateful* even.

Agatha was unmoved. 'That's what they said about William. Never had a day's illness in his life. Then bang – over he went. Just like that. On the way to the bathroom.'

'Well that won't be happening to George,' said Stephanie, annoyed as she saw the anxiety cross Toby's face. 'The doctor said he'll live to a hundred,' she added, smiling at the little boy and fixing Agatha with a warning look.

'Hmm.' Agatha pursed her mouth but said nothing more. 'There's some chocolate in that cupboard,' she told Charlotte a moment later. 'Get it out and share it with your brother and we'll have a nice game of cards.'

Charlotte stood up.

'And you two may as well go for a walk,' Agatha continued, addressing a point somewhere to the left of

Stephanie's ear. 'You don't want to be stuck in here with me all evening.'

'Oh don't be silly. Of course—' Stephanie began but George interrupted. 'Good idea!' he said briskly. 'Help your grandmother clear up, Charlotte.' He looked at Stephanie. 'Get your shoes on.'

'My father died of desperation,' he said as he strode rapidly off down the road with Stephanie scuttling along in his wake. 'And why do you think Teri buggered off to the States the minute she could? Everyone wanted to get away from her. God!' he said vehemently, 'I hated it in that house.'

Stephanie put her hand on his arm. 'Slow down,' she said. 'It's a lovely evening.' For a moment his arm stiffened under her touch. Then he slowed. It was one of those warm mellow nights, the sky a soft pink. They had reached the end of Agatha's street of tidy 1930s semis and George turned towards the town. 'Let's go for a drink.'

The High Street had changed even since the last time she'd been here. They passed Italian restaurants, coffee bars and small expensive boutiques selling candles and sculptures. 'It was so dreary here when we were growing up,' said George. 'No wonder she's always moaning about it now – wouldn't want people to enjoy themselves too much, would she!'

All at once an image of Cora flashed into Stephanie's mind. Cora, who would get drunk and stand up in the middle of a pub and give an impromptu rendition of her favourite songs while Troy accompanied her on piano or guitar. Who would dance and flirt like a teenager.

'Mum knows how to enjoy herself,' Troy once told her accusingly. 'She knows what's important.' The reproach was clear. Cora would not nag and have a miserable face just because of a few money worries.

As if on cue, a young couple wandered towards them, arms wrapped around each other. As they approached, he squeezed her tighter into the bend of his arm, rubbing his cheek against her hair. The girl looked up at him smiling, eyes closing, squeezing him back.

Stephanie felt her heart doing the same.

'This looks OK.' George steered her through a green door into the cool wooden interior of a wine bar. 'Happy with red?' He picked up a wine list. 'Go and sit down.'

Stephanie chose a table in the window. As she waited for George, she looked at her hands. She used to despair of them when she lived with Troy. They always seemed short and stubby and scarred from her DIY efforts, nails bitten or broken, fingers covered in cheap silver rings. Then she'd look at other women's hands and wonder at their long shapeliness and manicured finesse. Now hers were the same, her nails rounded and polished, diamonds glinting against the gold of her wedding ring, skin smooth and creamed.

What would she have thought if she could have had a glimpse of these hands then? Known how she would end up. Manicured meant grown-up, rich, settled, *happy* . . .

A pretty girl in jeans and white cropped T-shirt came over and smiled, placed a dish of olives and peanuts in front of them. Stephanie looked at the strip of brown midriff as she lit the candle in the centre of the table. There was a small silver ring in the girl's navel and the sight of it made Stephanie feel old.

George too seemed aged and weary tonight. She felt the distance between them and wondered at how it had happened. She looked at his hands as he placed the wine and glasses on the table. Once they had felt so comforting in hers. Then one day, without warning, she realized they didn't hold hands any more.

They were in Bath, watching a busker. He was playing a keyboard. Just some young guy with long brown hair and a faded T-shirt. She couldn't remember his face, just his hands. She'd been mesmerized, fumbling in her bag for coins, unable to take her eyes from his fingers as they rippled across the keys. George was impatient, wanting to move on, but she stood watching, unable to let go. She had this image in her mind, strange and powerful, of a dried sponge expanding in water. She wanted to cry, wanted to be touched by those hands. It was the sensuality she was hooked by. Or perhaps it was just desire . . .

George sat down. 'You're miles away.'

She jumped. 'I was remembering when we went to Bath that weekend without the children.'

'Oh yes.' George poured two glasses. 'We should do that again.' He didn't meet her eyes and she was grateful.

'Yes, we should,' she said, pushing down the apprehension she felt at the thought. She took a sip of her wine. 'This is nice.'

George gulped at his own glass. 'I certainly need it!'

Stephanie longed to know what was really going on inside him. 'Did Agatha love your father?' she asked cautiously.

'She doesn't know what love is.'

'Well, was she upset when he died?'

'I don't know. Teri was heart-broken. She was in tears all through the funeral but I never saw Mother cry.'

'Did you?' Stephanie held her breath.

'I don't remember.'

George had gone to the bar for another bottle. Stephanie picked up the match that had been left by the candle and ran it up the side, catching the soft trickle of wax against the wood. They'd been there an hour and she worried that they should go back, but George was adamant.

'She'll tell them when to go to bed. They'll be fine.' He was probably right. Charlotte appeared to get on with her grandmother strangely well when they were left to their own devices. Toby would be in a world of his own.

'My father would have liked you,' George said unexpectedly as he sat back down.

'I'm sure I'd have liked him,' she answered, uncertain what to say.

'It was a pity really.' George was matter-of-fact as he poured more wine. 'He didn't live long enough to see what I did with my life.'

'Yes.' Stephanie waited.

'I wasn't quite the failure they both predicted.'

'I'm sure it wasn't like that really.'

'Oh, he never said anything – that wasn't his way. Just looked at me sadly. Still, he had Teri. She was the golden girl.'

'I expect he was proud of you too.'

'What for? For failing all my exams and leaving school at sixteen.'

'You've made up for it since. Not bad. From selling insurance to running a big company.'

George looked at her and she saw the hurt in his eyes. 'Too late. Mother made sure I knew how "disappointed" he was.'

'Well you can't believe everything she says.'

'It was constant. Reminders all the time that I had squandered all my opportunities. She's never stopped.'

Stephanie fiddled with the candle. It was the deepest conversation they'd had for years.

'I don't remember her ever helping me with anything,' George was saying, 'or showing any interest. When I see you on the sofa all cuddled up with Toby . . .'

She pulled off a soft finger of curling wax and held it in the flame, her heart beating hard . . .

'I can't ever recall her reading with me. Or holding me. Not once. Imagine that . . .'

231

Something had happened to his voice and she looked up. His face was slipping.

'Oh George!' She felt tears spring to her own eyes but instinctively knew she must keep them back. She took his hand. He squeezed it tightly back.

'Why didn't she like me?' His voice was thick now, bewildered, like a child's.

'She just couldn't show it.' Stephanie's throat hurt. 'She loves you, really – she just can't do affection.'

George shook his head. 'She never wanted a son.'

She saw a tear drip from his jaw. Around them the bar had filled up. She became aware of the chatter and laughter. It was dark now and she was glad for him that the lights were low. 'That was what was so lovely about you,' he said, so quietly she had to lean towards him to hear. 'You were so warm. Always hugging me and holding my hand and – ' He stopped and drained his glass, letting go of her as he refilled it.

She looked down. His use of the past tense twisted her heart. How must he feel? Guilt sat sickly in her stomach.

'I do love you, you know,' he said. She couldn't tell if it was emotion or he was slurring slightly. He'd drunk most of the wine himself. 'I know I haven't always been—'

'I love you too.' She spoke quickly, afraid of what he might say. 'Shall we start to walk back?'

He shook his head. 'Not yet.' He poured the rest of the bottle into his glass. 'We never cuddle now, do we?' He took a long swig, almost emptying it.

She looked at her watch. 'I hope Toby's asleep. I hope he was OK being there without us.'

'Toby.' George was definitely slurring now. 'That's when it started, isn't it? I was only trying to look after you. I was worried—'

'I know.' She stood up. 'Come on, George.' Her heart was hammering.

Agatha and Charlotte were already in the kitchen when Stephanie came down in the morning. Agatha was cooking sausages. Charlotte was sitting on a stool eating toast and looking pleased with herself. She licked her lips as Stephanie filled the kettle. 'I'm getting a fry-up,' she said.

'Sets you up for the whole day,' said Agatha. 'Don't know what that boy wants. He's somewhere in the garden.'

'OK,' said Stephanie tightly, 'I'll see to him. Are you making some for George?'

Agatha didn't turn round. 'If he can get himself down the stairs.'

Stephanie poked a tongue at her back. George rose early nearly every day of his life. He'd gone straight upstairs when they got in last night and by the time she'd exchanged pleasantries with Agatha and received a thinly veiled critique of her parenting, he was out cold. She'd found a paracetamol for him in the bottom of her handbag this morning.

Stephanie had crept into bed, reflecting on the irony of the fact that the one night she actually wanted to wrap herself around him, she was in a lumpy twin bed three feet away.

She found Toby sitting under a tree deep in concentration over his Gameboy. 'Would you like some toast?' she asked, squatting down beside him.

'Nah,' he said cheerfully without looking up. 'I'm on the fifth level now.'

George's face was impassive as he opened up his jumper.

'Very nice,' he said, folding the yellow and navy diamonds back into the paper.

'I was going to buy you something special,' said Agatha, 'but you've got everything you need already.'

And George – amazingly – had crossed the room and

233

put an arm across Stephanie's shoulders, had reached out and ruffled Toby's hair.

'I have,' he said levelly, looking straight at his mother. 'I'm very lucky.'

'Hmmm.' She sniffed, and made a fuss of rooting in the cupboard.

'Because I'm happy,' said George.

Agatha handed two packets of wine gums to Charlotte. 'For the journey,' she said. Then she looked across the room at George and threw a glance at Stephanie before turning away. She muttered it but they all heard her. 'Ignorance is bliss.'

'What did she say that for?' Charlotte frowned as she got into the car.

'Old ladies say ridiculous things,' said George, slamming the boot. Stephanie sat silently. She realized her hands were shaking. There was something about the way Agatha's eyes had cut into her just before she said it.

'Ignore her,' George had murmured as they carried the bags up the path, leaving the children to bid farewell. Stephanie had tried to make light of it, tried to tell herself she was being paranoid and ridiculous but guilt throbbed away at her.

It was as if Agatha *knew* . . .

Chapter 20

'I don't believe this.' Troy was pacing the room looking anguished. 'George has a bit of a cry and suddenly you think the whole thing's your fault.'

'It *is* my fault. We should have communicated more.'

'Well that's down to him too.'

'I know but . . .' She paused. 'There are things that have happened between us that I should have . . .' She stopped again. 'I feel I've let him down and now I feel so guilty that . . .' She took a deep breath, trying to keep calm, 'I've got involved with you again.'

'You haven't got involved with me, you've fallen back in love with me, you know you have. You said yourself you never really stopped.'

'I was just getting carried away. I am fond of you, of course I am, but this has been madness.'

'Fond! You're not just *fond* of me. I can't just carry on without you now. I can't just live with Tanith as if nothing's happened.'

'You're going to have to.'

'I can't!' His voice rose. 'She's coming down at the weekend, bringing the kids. And I'm dreading it.' He grabbed at Stephanie's hands. 'It's been hard for a long time. Now it's going to be impossible.'

He pulled her towards him, looked into her eyes, his

face soulful and pleading. 'Sometimes, Steph, things are just meant. All these years we've been fighting it, but we were supposed to be together. You're not meant to be in that house with George. We should be living somewhere rugged and beautiful. You're a free spirit like me. A poet, an artist . . .'

'And what about my children?' she shouted, suddenly furious. 'Do I just uproot them? I'm sure they'll be thrilled to be landed in the middle of somewhere *rugged and beautiful*. What will they live on? Where will they go to school while we're busy communing with nature and writing poetry and prancing round the mystic stone?' She pulled her hands away. 'This is all just a fantasy!'

'I'm in love with you.'

'You're in love with being in love.'

She sat down and looked at him, exasperated. 'Think about it, Troy. What on earth are we doing?'

He knelt down in front of her. 'Steph, be honest. You're in love with me too, aren't you?'

'I don't know. I go to sleep thinking about you, I wake with you still in my mind. But it's not always a nice feeling. It's deep in the pit of my stomach. It feels like an exam I haven't revised for. An interview I'm going to fail.' She gave a small smile. 'Like some horrible dental treatment I've got to go through.'

'Great. That makes me feel really good.'

She shook her head and added, hesitantly, 'George never made me feel like that.'

What had he made her feel? She kept trying to re-member, but the harder she tried to recall their early years the further they slipped away. She knew she'd so wanted to marry him. But she couldn't get the feeling back to look at it again.

Troy stood up. 'That's because you weren't passionate about him.'

'It's because I was happy.'

236

She picked up her bag. 'I said I'd only be half an hour. I'm supposed to be dropping some school stuff at Millie's.'

'When will I see you again?'

'You won't. We've got to stop this, Troy. I'm going home to my family where I should be. You go back to yours where you should be too.'

He looked dejected. 'I don't think I can.'

Guilt was replaced with irritation. 'Well sometimes we just have to make ourselves. What about your children? Don't you miss them?'

'Yes of course,' he looked wounded. 'Why do you think they're coming down?'

'Well, take them home with you on Monday. Finish sorting this bloody house and sell it and just go. You'll have forgotten about me in no time.'

He picked up a small rose-patterned jug and held it out accusingly. 'It's Mum's house.'

'Yes, I know, sorry.' She looked at the door, desperate to get out now. While she felt strong. Before he got to her again. 'Troy, I'm going.'

There was a song he used to sing, about a man recalling the last time he saw the girl he loved. Seeing the back of her dress as she slipped through the door. It was about knowing she was the love of his life and nobody else would ever match that. Troy had said it was for her. But as she'd sat in this very house, a single candle illuminating Troy's face as he sang it to her, Stephanie had wept silently. Hidden in a pool of darkness, she'd been touched with loss even then.

'Look, take this.' He reached over to the old oak sideboard and picked up a bracelet. 'I've been keeping it for you.'

She shook her head. 'I can't.'

'I want you to have it,' Troy said, catching her hand, fastening the heavy band around her wrist. 'Mum would have wanted it too.'

It was a solid circle of flattened rose-gold, patterned with flowers, dented in places, fastened with a delicate safety chain. She touched the bracelet with her forefinger, a lump in her throat.

'It's beautiful,' she said, 'but I can't take it.' She undid the clasp and slid it back over her hand. 'Give it to your wife.'

'She doesn't feel like my wife.' He held her arms. 'Steph, I live in a dead marriage in a dead life. We don't talk deeply or share special things or make love. We just exist together for the children. Seeing you again has taught me how very special *we* were. Perhaps I didn't truly realize it at the time. I was young and ignorant. But I know now. And I am not going to let you go.'

He began to kiss her neck, releasing one of her arms, his hand gently stroking her hair, her ears, her throat, fingers moving down her spine . . .

She was silent, her solar plexus a tight ball of need. She wanted him to let her go. She wanted him to hold her for ever.

'Does George make you feel like this?'

She was growing warm. Her handbag dropped back at her feet. 'Get off,' she said unconvincingly, allowing him to push her slowly back towards the sofa. 'Just leave me alone . . .'

He was kissing her now, holding her tightly to him as he lowered her down on the cushions.

'Not going to . . .'

'Troy please . . . Oh . . . Troy!'

'You are a manipulative bastard.' She began to pick up her clothes from the floor.

He laughed. 'And you look all flushed, sweetheart. Must have been all that fighting me off.'

She threw her shoe at him in mock outrage. 'Don't push it.'

He ducked and put his arms around her. 'Oh, why not . . .' He put his head over her shoulder and kissed her cheek. 'Do you feel good now?'

'Mmmn,' she said grudgingly.

'See. You need me! Nothing has to stop, darling. Tanith isn't interested in me now. I could spend half the week down here.' He gestured around him. 'I'll keep this house. We can see each other here, keep our love going until the children are older . . .'

'Suppose George finds out?'

'He won't. We'll be careful. And if he does we'll deal with it. When you feel ready, when the kids are grown a bit we'll be together all the time. Please take the bracelet. Wear it as a symbol of us.'

She smiled. 'With this bracelet I do pledge . . .'

'I will honour thee, love thee, comfort and obey thee . . .'

'Obey me? That'll be the day.'

'With my body I thee . . .'

'To the exclusion of all others?'

She'd suddenly stopped laughing. He took her face in his hands.

'You are all I want, Steph. All I'll ever want.' He looked at her seriously. 'I'll be true to you for ever.'

'And you'll get the chips?'

'I mean it, Steph.'

'You've got to mean it.' She looked deep into his green eyes. 'I can't ever go through what I went through with you before.'

He pressed the bracelet back towards her. 'Wear this. Mum always liked you,' he said. 'And I've never stopped loving you.'

'And you always will?'

'Always.'

'No disappearing acts?'

'None.'

239

'No chasing other women.'

'Never.'

'What will I do about George. He'll still want to . . .'

'Shhhh . . .' He kissed her. 'We'll work something out. Suggest separate rooms or something.'

'It'll just be you and me?'

'You and me.' He fastened the bracelet around her wrist and held her. They stood in the darkening hall and she felt him shiver.

'Don't leave me again, Steph.' His voice was muffled against her hair.

She put her arms tightly around him, tears in her eyes, feeling an overwhelming warmth and relief and certainty.

'I won't. Not ever.'

Chapter 21

'You'll have to scout about for Blu-Tack!' Deirdre handed Stephanie a piece of card and two sheets of paper. 'Mr Brown's mother had a complication, so set it up anywhere for now.'

'What?'

'The donkey, dear, the donkey!'

'What? I'm Cakes.'

Deirdre stared in horror across the school field. 'For Pete's sake,' she shrieked, breaking into a run, 'who's moved the barbecue?'

'Menopausal old bat,' said Millie, wandering up with a can of Coke in her hand.

'She said I could do the cake stall,' Stephanie complained, looking at the huge expanse of white card. 'I don't know what she wants me to do.'

'Jac!' Millie bellowed. Jacqui came over the grass carrying a box of psychedelic plastic earrings. 'What's Steph supposed to be doing with the donkey?'

'Think of some names. Alan was supposed to but his mum's about to croak and God knows where Debbie is. Same as last year!'

Stephanie peered for the thirtieth time into her handbag. There must be a text soon. But the word ORANGE glowed up at her emptily.

'Here.' Millie laid the card on an empty trestle table, scrawling across it in thick black curly lettering. *Guess my name and take me home! 50p a go!* 'Right, let's have some names.'

'I'm not very good at names.'

'Any old crap will do.'

'Eeyore,' said Stephanie, remembering the meeting. 'Dobbin . . .'

Millie wrote. 'God knows what donkeys are really called,' she said.

'King, Ned, Billy, Dolly, Veronica . . .' said Jacqui, returning with her arms full of tablecloths. 'Come and help me with these,' she said to Millie, 'before I crown Deirdre.'

Stephanie, left alone, looked in her handbag again and then back to the sheet.

Victor, Donald, Long-ears. God, she was hopeless at this.

She hadn't heard a word from him since Tanith arrived. She'd lain awake for what felt like most of the night, constantly looking at the phone secreted in her bedside drawer.

Benjamin, Carrot-top, Stanley. Troy. Shit! She'd written it down. Her fingers were trembling as she tried to change it with the thick black pen.

'What does that say?' Jacqui's head was over her shoulder, jabbing a finger at the splodge of black ink halfway down the page.

'Trojan.'

'Wasn't he a horse?'

Deirdre had changed into a lime and orange frock and was making an incomprehensible welcome speech into the ailing PA system. Stephanie stood tensely behind the table on which Trojan was now slumped, his woolly ears drooping in the heat. It was only two o'clock but it felt like midnight. Her stomach was a ball of anxiety. Still no text.

She forced a smile as George and Toby came across the field towards her. Over in the far corner Charlotte was already in a huddle with Emma.

'Hello, darling. Have you got some money?' She made her voice bright for Toby. He nodded and opened his fist to reveal pound coins.

'What do we do, then?' George had Kelly on a lead.

'Just wander round and have a go on everything.'

'Can I do the bouncy castle first?' Toby prodded the donkey.

'Of course.'

'Can you look after this?'

She looked at her phone again as she slid the Gameboy into her handbag. Nothing. A stream of parents and children were coming through the school gates. Across the field on the tombola, Millie waved.

Trojan had glassy eyes, a lolling red tongue and a blue felt bridle. He was a cross between a donkey and a huge rabid mongrel and the stuff nightmares were made of. But the children all seemed strangely enamoured.

'Ten goes,' said a flashy, fleshy father with sunglasses and a thick gold chain round his neck. 'Go on, princess, you choose!'

His daughter sucked precociously at the blue biro provided and considered her options.

'Do you have any change?' asked Stephanie, looking at the £20 note being proffered.

'No darlin', I don't.'

Deirdre bustled up with a bag of coins and a nasty-looking beaker of tea.

No text.

'I don't know who did the tombola numbers,' she said severely. 'But there were three tickets saying 555 and only one prize. And that was pickles.' She stared hard at

Stephanie as if it might be her doing. 'It doesn't give a good impression.'

'Splat-the-Rat needs adjusting,' Jacqui said, appearing with a money belt and half a lager. 'Gillian's in a right flap – all the prizes have gone already.'

Deirdre sniffed loudly, looked pointedly at the beer glass and shot off. Jacqui took a swig. 'All the kids are knocking seven shades out of that rat with one hand.' She held up her drink. 'Want one?'

Stephanie shook her head. 'Better not, I'll fall over. Where'd you get it anyway?'

'Brought a cool box.' Jacqui grinned. 'Can't get through this sober. We should have a beer tent. I told her that last year.'

It was funny how quickly you recognized people. Even before she'd put together the outline of the blond hippie hair and the red T-shirt, the lope of the blue-jeaned leg, the oversized Nike trainer, all her nerve endings were jangling.

'You all right, Steph?' Jacqui was peering at her.

'Yes.' She felt sick. 'Just a bit hot.'

'I'll go and get you some water.'

Not here. Not on her school field where just across the grass her son was trying to knock a coconut from a metal perch and missing by miles, where her husband was watching. Please not here.

Her heart was banging and she was suddenly self-conscious in a most peculiar way. The floral print of her skirt, the navy blue of her vest top, the sweat running between her breasts. She felt all at once old and fat and tired and terribly young and afraid. And angry.

She was with him.

What had she expected Tanith to look like? In that half-formed ethereal way you picture people, she'd probably seen her as a sort of cross between the skinny Lucinda of years ago – all nail-bitten black-eyelinered

244

chic – and a kind of tanned, swaying hippie earth mother, with bare feet and long mauve embroidered dresses, long fingers, hundreds of bangles . . .

She was sort of like *her*. Stephanie. Sort of average and wearing white cotton trousers with a biggish bum and reasonably hefty thighs, quite ordinary brown hair pushed back in a scrunchy band. She had a small child on her hip – must be Phoebe – fair curls, patterned dress. They walked a little ahead of him. He held Lara's hand. She was just as Stephanie had imagined her. Long white-blond hair tossed over her shoulder, pink clips in her hair.

Tanith stopped. Put the child down on the grass, turned, said something to Troy. He nodded, let go of Lara's hand for a moment, pointed across the field to the bouncy castle, and touched his wife's arm.

'Can I have two goes?'

'What?'

The small boy in front of her held out a 50p coin. 'Can I guess two names?'

Did Troy realize this was her school? Did he know this was the same summer fête she'd told him she was coming to? Of course he must do. Why had he done this? To flaunt Tanith?

'Can I?'

She didn't like red-haired, freckled children – always too full of themselves. 'You haven't got enough.'

'I haven't got any more.'

'Go and ask your parents.'

'I don't know where they are.'

'OK then.' She was barely concentrating.

'So I can choose two?'

'*Yes!*'

They were coming towards her now. Troy was grinning at her, eyes crinkling, mouth pursed into a mischievous, secretive kiss as he came up to the table.

245

'Hello!' It was the bright, surprised greeting of a chance meeting in the supermarket. 'How are you?' He spoke with all the warmth he could muster for this dearly respected and long-lost acquaintance he'd happened upon amongst the baked beans.

Stephanie was smiling back before she could stop herself; oddly at Tanith as much as any of them. Tanith smiled vaguely then bent to put Phoebe down. Stephanie dragged her eyes away and felt her smile fall manically on the girl. Phoebe looked at her, wide-eyed.

'OK?' Troy was still speaking in the same jolly tones.

She felt her face grow hot and looked down in panic. 'Yes, yes fine thank you. And you?'

He nodded. 'Shall we have a go, darling?' He was looking at Tanith. She smiled back at him, pulling a face of mock horror at the huge toy. Troy laughed, a hand caressing his daughter's head. He winked at his wife as though they shared a special joke. 'Go on!'

She opened her purse and produced a pound coin, nudging Troy playfully with her elbow. 'You'll have to carry it!' She turned towards Stephanie. 'Two please, thank you.'

The coin slid from Stephanie's fingers and clattered loudly into the pot. For a moment their eyes met. Stephanie couldn't fathom Tanith's expression. Was she looking searchingly at Stephanie? Then she turned to the children. 'Come on Lara – choose a name.'

Stephanie's heart was thumping. Tanith would see the blot of ink and what she had written first.

'I'll – text – you!' Troy mouthed the words as Tanith bent over the sheet.

Stephanie frowned. Any moment now Tanith would turn and catch him gazing at her. Would look back at the splodge on the paper. But Tanith was putting down the pen, straightening up again, moving off without a backward glance. 'Come on, girls.' Stephanie looked back at Troy. He winked. *Bastard*.

'Here!' Jacqui was back at her side proffering a glass of water. 'Who's that? Never seen him in the playground. Wouldn't say no to meeting him in a dark alley, though.'

Stephanie shrugged. Troy and Tanith were walking away, side by side, almost touching. She saw them stop to make way for a mother pushing a buggy. As Tanith stepped aside, Troy's hand ran casually down her hip, patting her bum as his other hand reached for their daughter. Stephanie was still shaking. 'What time is it?' she asked Jacqui. *Not much longer surely?*

'Three o'clock.'

'God – is that all?'

Still another hour to go. She felt like she'd been there for ever. She scanned the list. Tanith had written Phoebe's name against 'Ruby'. Lara had written her own name in spindly childish letters. She'd chosen 'Pippin'.

'Bit of a sales drive?' Deirdre was sweating. 'You walk around, dear. I'll jump on the microphone.'

Stephanie looked around the crowded field. She didn't want to parade around in this heat with the hairy, unappealing Trojan. Quite aside from the nightmare visions of last summer when a small boy had upended his ice-cream on the head of the over-sized Dalmatian that was that year's delight, plaguing her with killer wasps for the rest of the afternoon, she couldn't cope with coming face to face with Troy and his entourage again.

'Perhaps it's better if I stay here,' she ventured, as Deirdre fanned herself with the list of names. 'Then everyone will know where I am.'

Whatever Deirdre said was a mystery. The mike coughed and spluttered and people looked at each other blankly but gradually parents and children wandered

over and the names were taken, till only a few were left –
including Trojan – and the hands of Jacqui's watch crept
around to four.

'Thank God,' said Millie. 'Thought there was going to
be a punch-up over that tombola. No-one cared much
about the mushroom soup but it was a different story
when it came to the Asti Spumante, I can tell you.'

George appeared at her side with Toby and a panting
Kelly. 'I'll take the kids home, shall I?'

'Oh yes, right.' Stephanie realized she hadn't even seen
Charlotte. 'I'll be a while – I'll have to help with the
clearing up.'

'She does a lot, doesn't she?' George turned on Deirdre,
who had sprung up with her clipboard. 'She's worked
very hard for this fête, all the hours she's put in.'

Stephanie's stomach gave a flip of alarm as she saw the
wide-eyed surprise on Deirdre's face, saw her mouth
begin to limber up. Then Millie was there, smiling at
George, patting Toby's shoulder.

'Yeah, Steph's been marvellous, we're all so grateful . . .'

The phone beeped as she pushed the last of the bunting
into a cardboard box. She made herself walk calmly the
few steps to her handbag. Message received: **You looked
gorgeous.**

She jabbed at the erase button, filled with rage, tears at
the back of her throat.

That was not what she wanted to hear. She wanted to
know why he'd turned up with *her* in tow. What had
been happening between them.

What the fuck he thought he was playing at.

She lowered herself into the bath. Everything ached.
She poured in a great globule of rose-and-geranium-
rebalance-your-body bath elixir and sighed. If only there

were a bath foam to rebalance the mind. She lay back beneath the bubbles and closed her eyes.

Somebody was shuffling outside. Then there was a tap. 'Who is it?'

It was George. Balancing a wine glass and a dish of peanuts. Putting them down on the edge of the bath, carefully.

'I brought you these.'

'Oh! Thank you.'

He looked down at her anxiously. 'Would you rather have had gin and tonic?'

'No, no that's fine. Thank you.'

'Are you all right?'

'Just tired.'

He left, pulling the door behind him, speaking awkwardly over his shoulder: 'I love you.'

'Love you too.' She said it automatically but it was true. She did love George.

But she still wanted Troy.

Why was he doing it to her? He must have looked at his phone by now, seen her message begging for contact, known that she was in pain. How long did it take to send back a X, an ILY – a *something*? If only Tanith wasn't there, if only she could press the two buttons that would dial his number. Just to hear his voice.

He might be watching a film. One of the kids could be throwing up. She didn't want to think about early nights. About him being in bed with her . . .

Stephanie sat in the empty kitchen, her phone in her hand, and loathed herself. Her stomach had been hurting for hours, a deep twisting pain that brought waves of nausea. Her head was throbbing now too. No text.

The rest of the house was dark. George had been snoring the last time she crept upstairs. That was her safe for tonight, then. If she got in very, very quietly and didn't adjust the duvet till he was in a rhythm again.

11.35 p.m. Still no text.

It brought it all back. The hours she'd once spent, face against the window waiting for him to come home. Lying in bed, watching the ceiling, body straining to hear the sound of his key in the lock. Fearing she'd finally pushed him away with her tears and recriminations.

'I wouldn't just stop loving you overnight,' he used to say.

'I've never stopped loving you.' He said it again just the other day. But he might stop. She'd just remembered that was exactly what Troy did. He was all sweet light and empathy, soul mate and confidant, friend and saviour – until the demands became real, then he stepped back. Then he drifted away, smiling, shrugging. Chill out, Steph. Life's too short, Steph. It's not worth it, Steph.

Troy, Troy, why ever did you do this to me?

You started it. It sounded like Rose but it could have been Hettie.

Let him go!

She couldn't. She couldn't let him go. They were meant to be together – that's what he'd said. They were going to love each other for ever.

11.45 p.m. Tired. Sick. Give it to midnight? No, she'd wait till 11.50. Then she'd make a decision. Decide whether to wait till midnight.

Midnight. Switch off the phone.

Switch it back on. Put it on silent. Slide it in drawer. In case she needed it. Just in case.

Quietly, gently, slither into bed, lift the corner of the duvet, holding her breath.

Please don't wake up, George. Not tonight. Tonight I could not make love with you for my life.

Chapter 22

Troy held out his hands. 'I couldn't, Steph! No chance to get to the phone.'

'I was worried.'

'There was nothing to worry about. She never said a thing.'

'I didn't know what was happening.'

'I sent you a text after we saw you.'

'Three words. For all I knew you'd made everything all right with her and I was never going to see you again.'

'Don't be silly! You know how much I love you, Steph. There's no way . . .'

But he didn't meet her eyes. And she knew. 'Did you have sex with her?'

'What?' Troy looked startled. Then wary.

'Did you make love to your wife? Your wife you have such a bad relationship with? That you hardly ever have any sexual contact with any more. Did you have sex with her?'

Her heart felt swollen. She couldn't bear the idea of their bodies entwined, of his hands – hands that belonged to Stephanie – running their way over *her* body. Stephanie touched her stomach. It still physically hurt.

This was what being with Troy had always been about. Deep, biting jealousy that shrivelled all your good, generous parts until you were dry and bitter and empty. She felt in a flash every old pain she'd ever had. The fear of never being enough, having to watch other women blossoming in his light. Most of all she couldn't bear that. Another woman thinking – knowing – Troy wanted her.

'Steph, I had to!' Troy's voice was appealing. 'Do you realize how odd it looks if a bloke refuses sex?' Stephanie stood quite still.

'It was the last thing I was expecting. I mean she's never interested. But she went and had a bath and I thought: Good! She'll go to bed, and I was just about to text you and then she appeared down here all dressed up and . . .'

He stopped and looked uncomfortable at the same time as the words hammered home.

'Dressed up? What do you mean dressed up?'

He was shaking his head, not looking at Stephanie. 'She had this teddy thing on.'

'Jesus Christ! First you say you hardly ever have sex, then it transpires that in fact you do it at the first available opportunity, now you tell me you have fucking dressing-up sessions.'

'It's not like that. I think she does it for herself. She says she wants to feel sexy sometimes.'

And when she did, his eyes would come alight. 'Mmmm!' he'd say, 'this is nice,' cross the room, stroke a finger down between her breasts, let his hands trail softly across the lace . . . The pain was exquisite.

'Where did it come from?'

'What?'

'This teddy thing.' She spat the word out.

He shrugged. 'A shop?'

'Don't be bloody clever! Did you buy it for her?'

He looked sullen now. He put his head in his hands, a gesture of weariness, and sighed.

'Was it like mine? Was it black and red? Was it the same style? Was it?' Stephanie was shrieking, hurt and rage rattling in her throat. She wanted to kill him. Kill her. Kill herself.

'When did you buy it? Since you've been down here pretending to be in love with me?'

And then he looked up and she saw his expression.

'Oh no. It was mine, wasn't it? You let your wife put on my underwear that you bought me, and then you made love to her in it.'

He jumped up, tried to take her hands. 'Steph, she found it – I had to say I'd bought it for her. I *had* to.'

Stephanie pulled away from him. 'Didn't she think that a bit odd? That you'd bought her sexy lingerie when you never ever have sex?'

'I said—'

'What did you say, Troy? Oh Christ, you are so disgusting!'

He shook his head sorrowfully. 'I'd have rather made love to you. I wanted it to be you – I kept thinking . . .'

'Is that supposed to make me feel better?'

She let him make her tea. He brought it to her as she sat woodenly in Cora's big chair, then he settled himself at her feet, put his arms around her knees and rested his head on her lap. She felt frozen and detached.

'Look,' he said. 'We agreed to keep the status quo for the moment. You said – no big announcements. Don't upset the children. We keep things going at home until we're ready. That's what we *agreed*. Steph? Listen to me. I was just keeping the peace.'

'Would you have told me if I hadn't asked?'

'I didn't want to hurt you.'

'Were you sleeping with Lucinda?'

'What?' His head shot up. 'That was fifteen years ago!'

'Did you? I need to know, Troy. I need you to tell me the whole truth.'

He shrugged. 'Only a couple of times.'

'You bloody bastard.'

He gave a forced laugh. 'Oh come on, Steph. I can understand you feeling jealous of Tanith but why do you care about Luci now?'

'I don't.' She did. All these years later she hated the idea of him on top of Lucinda's bony body. The girl's smug pride in the knowledge that she could tempt Troy to be unfaithful.

'Rose always said I should watch you two.'

He exhaled a long sigh of disdain. 'Rose would.'

'Well she was right, wasn't she!'

'Oh it was nothing. We were drunk or stoned or something. She never came close to you. Nobody,' he sat on the arm of the chair and tried to hug her, 'has ever come close to you.'

She stood up, knocking the teacup out of its saucer.

'I must have been mad to think you'd changed,' she said, her voice tight with pain. 'I couldn't trust you then and I can't now.'

She started for the front door but he wrapped his arms around her. 'I love you, Steph. I love you so much. Please don't cry.'

Please don't cry. He said it over and over again.

As if he thought she might be able to stop.

She called in sick. George took the children to school. 'Go back to bed,' he said. 'Get some sleep.'

He'd been kind the night before too. She'd told him – truthfully – that she had terrible stomach pains and needed to lie down and he'd gone for fish and chips, stood over Charlotte while she did her homework, read with Toby.

Now, lying beneath the duvet, huddled in her dressing gown, she felt dirty and ashamed. She'd heard George's voice floating up the stairs when he was on the phone to the dairy, complaining about over-filled bottles and the inconvenience of milk spilt down trousers at 8 a.m. and something deep inside her had smiled in spite of it all. She needed George. She couldn't ever lose him. She would miss him marching about, being in charge, getting things done.

While Troy would let endless chaos wash over him and befall her, sleep through an emergency, be in the wrong bed when she needed him most. George had always looked after her, protected her.

Protected her. She would never forget that phone call. Her looking at George appealingly. 'I have to go . . .'

'No,' he'd said. 'You should be here. Looking after us. Looking after your family.' And he'd pointed to Toby. Curled with his tiny red thumb deep in his mouth.

'I was trying to protect you,' he'd said later. When she fell asleep she dreamt of Rose . . .

She awoke suddenly and looked at the clock in fright. For a moment she thought she'd slept too long to collect the children. But it was only half-past one. Kelly was barking downstairs.

She got out of bed and walked slowly downstairs. She felt as though she'd been in an accident or undergone some huge ordeal. It all seemed deeply unreal now. Troy had always represented pain – he'd caused her enough to last a lifetime and yet she'd walked straight back into it for some more.

Kelly was making a racket at the front door. Stephanie tightened the front of her robe as she went towards it. She glanced in the mirror. She looked deranged.

'Steph! Aren't you well?' Sue stood on the doorstep looking concerned.

'Oh Sue!' She'd forgotten about the reflexology session completely. 'Sorry, come in.'

Sue was wearing her white coat, her hair tied back, carrying her folder and smiling. She waited while Stephanie settled herself on the sofa and positioned herself on a chair opposite. 'How have you been?'

'Just an upset stomach, that's all.'

'Did you feel any after-effects from last time?'

'No.'

'No drowsiness? Increased need to pass water? Did you sleep well?'

'I can't remember.'

'OK.' Her pen hovered over the page. 'We'll see what we find today. Are you sure you're OK, Steph?'

'Yeah, really. Just a few things on my mind.' *Like the affair I've been having. Nothing much.*

'Right.'

Sue's hands began to move over her feet, massaging, loosening, warming. Stephanie relaxed a little. She still felt drowsy.

Sometimes things happened and you thought life would never be normal again. Like when Troy had finally moved out, when Rose had gone. When George came home with Kelly and she chewed everything . . .

'Ouch! Which bit's that?'

Sue fingered Stephanie's big toe. 'Head and neck – bit of tension there maybe.' She smiled. 'Or you've been thinking too much.'

She'd feel better when he'd gone. And surely he'd go soon now. Tanith would want him home.

'Is this tender?' Sue's fingers circled the centre of the sole of her foot. Stephanie nodded, suddenly close to tears.

'What does that mean, then?' she said, forcing herself to speak.

'It's the solar plexus – centre of emotions.' Sue's voice was soft and soothing. 'It doesn't always follow, but perhaps you've been worrying about something, holding some feelings in . . .'

It was funny who you revealed things to. Millie used to say that friends were horses for courses, that the one you spilled the beans to about your drunken encounter with the Scout master was never the one you went to when you had piles.

Stephanie, tears now falling, was finding the people you tell the unexpected to could be very unexpected indeed.

She liked Sue. Sue was lovely. But she was the sort of round, warm girl you made quips with in the playground about eating too much and wondering what it would be like to be married to Jeremy Partridge, father of Kieran in year six. She was the sort of friend who you only ever saw at PTA dos or children's book parties. She was not the sort of friend you'd imagine being there while you cracked apart.

Stephanie couldn't stop it happening. Chin shuddering, shoulders heaving, the tears just kept coming. Words tumbled out of her mouth. She could hear them but she couldn't stem them. She was talking about Rose and Troy and George, on and on like a crazed woman, telling Sue who knew nothing of any of it about the voices and the pains and dark hours in the middle of the night when she knew she was heading for some black place she couldn't go . . .

'I'm going mad,' she sobbed, horrified by her lack of control. 'I'm going mad.'

'It's all right.'

Sue had let go of Stephanie's feet and wrapped her arms around her shoulders. She felt solid and warm and dependable and Stephanie cried even harder. She could hear her own sobs in the distance as if they belonged to

257

someone else. And above them, dimly, she heard Sue's voice.

'I don't know much about this, Steph,' she was saying as she held her tight. 'But it doesn't sound like madness to me. It sounds like grief.'

Chapter 23

'Why aren't you going to this sixties thing yourself?'
Millie smiled brightly at Hettie as Stephanie poured out
coffee.

'I'm staying to look after the children.' Hettie gestured
vaguely around the kitchen. 'Someone's got to.'

'I have been trying to find another sitter,' Stephanie
said. 'But my usual girl is away at college now. I'd ask
Mrs Becket from over the road but she's getting on a bit.
Charlotte is staying over with Emma but there's still
Toby. Three is quite a handful for anyone else but
Hettie.' She winked at Millie.

Millie stirred her coffee. 'I'll do it!'

Steph looked at her. 'I thought you were coming with
us.'

Millie shook her head. 'I'm not bothered about going
and it would be nice for you to have a night out, Hettie. I
can bring Ben over and I'll look after all of them.'

'But what about . . .' Hettie looked anxiously at Joshua
asleep in his rocker.

Millie laughed. 'Ben was that age once, you know! I
can still remember how to change a nappy.'

'And Erica's a bit funny with people she doesn't know.'

'We've just met!' Erica had taken one look and buried
her head under a cushion.

'Well if you're sure . . .' Hettie said doubtfully.

'We can't let you do that. You don't want four kids all evening.'

'They'll be in bed, won't they?' Millie looked meaningfully back at Stephanie. 'I'd like to. Really.'

'Fine.' Stephanie nodded, her face neutral. 'There you are, Hettie – you can come!'

She closed her mind to the expression on George's face.

'And there's a spare packet of baby wipes on the dressing table in my room.' Hettie hovered at the front door pulling anxiously at her electric blue caftan. Millie smiled. 'Everything will be fine, Hettie. I'll have them all in bed in a moment.'

'Well, Erica might—'

'Are we going?' George jiggled the car keys. 'We've been standing here for ten minutes.'

'It's just you know how sensitive Erica is.' Hettie allowed herself to be led along the path to the car. 'It takes nothing to give her nightmares.'

'She'll be fine,' Stephanie said again soothingly.

'But if Millie reads her an extra story . . .'

'I'm sure she will,' Stephanie said, knowing Millie's main agenda would be to get them all out cold double quick before Alex turned up. She checked her mobile was in her bag. She had to alert Millie as soon as she knew they were leaving the club. Part of her wanted to warn Millie generally. Wanted to shout: Don't do it! But she tried to remind herself that her friend's situation was more complicated. That she really needed Alex.

'I've just got to see him,' Millie said with feeling, when Hettie was out of earshot. 'I've had no chance all week.'

'Well for goodness sake make sure they're all asleep,' said Stephanie, picturing Hettie's face if Erica spilled the beans.

Millie laughed. 'I will. Even if I have to take a mallet to

them. It will be such a relief to be out of the house. Things have been pretty grim with Patrick.'

Stephanie had squeezed her arm sympathetically, grateful that she herself was feeling very much better. She still felt embarrassed at how badly she'd fallen apart in front of Sue but there was no doubt it had been a turning point. Afterwards she'd felt cleansed, empty, new somehow. As though the whole Troy thing could be put behind her.

He was still texting and her heart still twisted every time but she'd had a narrow escape. 'He showed me what it would have been like,' she said to Millie. 'I got out just in time.'

George might be grumpy about having to don purple cords and a psychedelic shirt but she knew where she was with him. He was her husband and she loved him. They were going to enjoy tonight, get Hettie packed off home early in the morning, go to his favourite restaurant for his birthday lunch tomorrow. She knew she was lucky.

The car park at the squash club was nearly full. 'And half of these will still be here in the morning,' said George reversing into one of the last spaces. 'We'll get a cab home too, shall we?' he asked Stephanie. He grinned suddenly and reached out to squeeze her fingers. 'Don't think I can cope with this on orange juice.'

'Of course not,' she squeezed back. 'Though you know what the wine's usually like.'

'And the food.' George pulled a face at her as he opened the back door for Hettie. 'Mrs P's spread . . .'

Stephanie giggled.

The food looked as bad as it always did. Mrs P's idea of catering hadn't wavered in ten years. Sausage rolls, Scotch egg cut in half, a whole dried-up looking salmon decorated with hundreds of flaccid cucumber circles, and for that money-no-object look dozens of enormous head-on king prawns dangled over the edge of practically every dish. Whatever plate you approached there was a pair of manic black eyes above a set of pink whiskers. Even over the pine-nut pâté – the one concession to those who wouldn't eat 'proper food'.

Stephanie picked tentatively at a breaded mushroom which turned out to be a rubbery piece of chicken. Ken wandered past in a pair of silver flares.

'Are you all right?' he asked as she buried the offending article in somebody else's leftovers.

'Yes, thank you!' The wine was something indeterminate from a carton yet already she seemed to have drunk several glasses. The beads wrapped around her forehead kept slipping down over her nose.

'Good do, eh?' Ken nodded towards the crowd of cheesecloth-clad would-be hippies guffawing around the bar. She could see George in the middle waving a pint about and Hettie deep in conversation with another bra-less earth mother.

'Where's Madeleine?' she asked Ken, not sure what else to say. 'She's here,' he said jovially. 'Not wearing much of a skirt!'

Not much of one at all but you had to hand it to her – she looked terrific. Most women of her age wouldn't have dared go out in a tiny leather mini, scoop-necked top and long black boots – Stephanie shuddered at the thought of her own legs on such display – but Madeleine stalked about looking a million dollars and all the male heads at the bar swivelled.

'Having a good time?' she asked Stephanie. She looked at her searchingly.

Stephanie nodded. 'Sorry about missing work last week. I'll be back on Monday.'

'Not a problem – you've done a good job getting me up to date again. Got on top of it.' She lit a cigarette. 'Caroline's got some bloody bug and I've had to give Jo the night off so I've left Samantha on her own.' She inhaled deeply. 'I've told her to keep me informed. Lucky it's a really quiet night. Saturdays often are – all out where they should be for once, I guess.'

'Didn't bother dressing up, then?' she said sharply, as Patsy came up to them.

'I don't intend staying long.' Patsy ran a hand down the hips of the plunging, clinging sheer dress that must have cost a fortune.

'You look very nice,' said Stephanie, feeling ridiculous in her own long beaded creation. One of her false eyelashes was already coming loose. She put a hand to her eye. 'Just popping to the ladies.'

Patsy joined her a few minutes later. She stood at the next basin, carefully blending in her lipstick as Stephanie wrestled with the little tube of glue.

'Isn't it all stupid?' said Patsy. 'I'd like to leave right now.' She pouted into the mirror. 'I can't be bothered to circulate. I almost don't care whether Dave thinks I've been here all night or not. Just want to go and have a shag, frankly!'

Stephanie smiled. If George didn't drink too much and Hettie didn't spend the entire night pacing the landing singing 'Five Little Piggies' she might even be in the market for one herself. She'd looked at him as they got changed that evening. He was still attractive. Once their lovemaking had been good. She was going to try.

'All going well?' she asked lightly. 'With your . . . er . . . friend?'

'Mmmm.' Patsy licked her lips. 'It's all rather special, actually. You know I think I might finally be getting monogamy.'

Stephanie nearly choked. 'But—'

Patsy laughed. 'Well not with Dave, obviously!' She put her lipstick down and perched on the edge of the basin next to Stephanie.

'Normally I'd have had enough by now and be telling

myself I'd never do it again,' she said unexpectedly. 'You know when the excitement goes and you start to worry that your home will be lost and the children upset? I've always got to the point where I think it's not worth it any more.'

'Well it often isn't,' said Stephanie with feeling. Her eyelash fell off again and lay in the sink like a sat-on spider.

Patsy pulled a packet of Marlboro from her tiny jewelled bag. 'But then it happens again – that buzz, the anticipation, the thrill of strange skin against mine . . .' She looked thoughtful and quite un-Patsy like. 'That's what it's about. I'm addicted to the newness of things.'

I'm not, thought Stephanie. It was familiarity that had drawn her back to Troy – the warmth and comfort of things forgotten. It was the way Troy would hug her so she was lost in him, the way he watched her intently while she spoke, put his head slightly to one side to properly consider her words. She felt a stabbing in her stomach – part loss, part anger at her own stupidity.

George seldom met her eyes when she was upset. But then they'd so rarely spoken about feelings these last few years. She could not imagine telling him the kind of thoughts she'd so frequently spilled out to Troy. George baring his own soul was unheard of. Or it had been until Agatha's. Maybe they could start talking after all.

Patsy flicked her lighter and lit up. 'But I really think it's different this time,' she said. 'For the first time I feel like I've found the one who would be enough. It's always just been good sex before – and that high of someone different, the excitement of all those first little secret meetings.' She blew the smoke out in a long stream. 'But very soon it all wears thin. They're all the bloody same underneath. That's why I'd never thought about leaving Dave. I mean what for? Another Dave. A bit of a different shape with a different name, a different line in snoring, farting and falling asleep in front of the telly . . .'

'How many have you had?' The question was out of Stephanie's mouth before she could stop herself. Too much to drink on three prawns. She giggled. 'Sorry.'

Patsy was unabashed. 'Oh Christ knows. Lots!' She laughed. 'Not as many as Monica Marchant! Mind you, you'd have to go some to beat that woman,' she added admiringly. 'I've known her have two different ones either side of breakfast!'

'But this time . . .' she stopped laughing. 'This time I've got it bad. I'm walking around talking to him in my head all day long. I'm not even thinking about the sex – though Jesus, that is *fantastic*.' Her face lit up again. 'It's just him – his voice, his hands . . . Oh Steph, what am I going to do? I think I might be in love.'

'Well, that's—' began Stephanie and then Madeleine walked in.

Patsy snapped open a compact and was back to her usual self. 'That's the best I can do,' she said, dabbing bronze powder on her cheekbones. 'Quick hello to all the old farts and I'm off!'

'You be careful,' Madeleine said as Patsy's red dress retreated through the door. 'I've got a bad feeling about this.'

Stephanie looked round in surprise. 'Even with twenty-four-hour cover?' she asked with a smile.

Madeleine did not smile back. 'Do you know who he is? He's the one who needs an alibi.'

Hettie pulled Stephanie into the corner, caftan flapping. 'I need to tell you something.' Her tone was even more censorious than usual.

'What is it?' Stephanie asked. Hettie's mouth was turned down in disapproval. 'Has something happened?' Her imagination leapt into overdrive.

Had Hettie phoned home checking on the children and heard Alex in the background? Or – worse – had Alex actually picked up the phone?

'I don't know,' Hettie said shortly.

For God's sake, what was Millie thinking of? How had she explained it? Old friend? Second cousin miraculously returned from the outback? Passing Jehovah's Witness invited in for a drop of Horlicks and a spot of lively debate on the afterlife?

Then she saw her mobile in Hettie's hand.

Oh bloody hell.

'I couldn't hear a thing in here,' Hettie was saying. 'I just wanted to call to see if Erica had had her strawberry milk.' Her eyes were boring into Stephanie's. 'So I went out to the car park and was about to dial your number . . .'

Another text from him must have come through. And bloody Hettie must have bloody read it.

'Obviously,' Steph would say to Hettie when she got a word in edgeways, 'it must be a mistake – intended for someone else entirely.'

Unless it mentioned George. Or – *oh God* – something rude about Hettie herself.

She found herself gibbering. 'Trouble getting through? I get so many wrong numbers these days! Texts I don't understand! Crossed lines too. Think I'm talking to Millie and someone else answers altogether.'

Hettie frowned. 'What?' She looked at the phone in her hand. 'Oh no – I haven't called Millie yet.'

Jack must have called. Hettie had just found out he was a lying, cheating philanderer and her heart was about to break.

Stephanie put her hand on Hettie's arm and spoke gently. 'It may not be as bad as you think . . .'

Hettie stared hard at her. 'I do hope you're right,' she said coldly. 'Troy's outside.'

*   *   *

He was leaning against the wall, wearing a patchwork suede jacket that wouldn't have looked out of place inside. He started forward as Stephanie approached. 'Oh babe! I really need to see you.'

'George is in there!' She jerked her head back at the club.

'I know. I won't stay.' He tried to take her hands. 'I've been calling and calling and it just goes to voice mail, you haven't answered my texts . . .'

'There's no signal in there.'

'But you didn't answer them yesterday. I can't lose you, Steph. Not again.'

Stephanie looked nervously round. 'I have to go back in.'

'Steph!' He pulled her towards him, eyes searching hers, and she realized he was drunk. 'Steph, we have to be together.'

'No, Troy. I have to be with George and my children and you have to get yourself and your family back to Norwich as soon as you can. I want my life back to normal. I want this over.'

'Tanith wants to move here.'

'What?'

'She says it's quiet and clean and she likes being nearer the sea. Thinks we should move into Mum's until we find somewhere bigger.' He was slurring slightly. 'It's a chance for us to move up the property ladder and it's a good place to bring up children.'

Stephanie's stomach had gone into a tight knot. 'She can't . . .'

'We'd be able to see each other all the time . . .'

'No!'

Troy looked hurt. 'I thought that's what we both wanted. Really, deep down.'

'I'm not having an affair with you.'

267

'What do you think we're doing now?'

'We're not. It's finished.'

It was frightening and bizarre. He thought he could just sleep with both of them. She wanted to be back inside with George. She wanted Troy far away.

'Steph!' He was trying to hug her, his breath smelt of whisky. 'I love you, Steph.'

'We'll talk about it tomorrow.' She pulled back. 'Go home.'

'I want to talk about it now!' He was beginning to shout.

Hettie was standing in the doorway as Stephanie tried to walk back into the building. Her face was stony. 'What's going on?'

'He's drunk, that's all. He's been a bit emotional since his mother died.'

'Does George know?'

'There isn't anything *to* know.'

'Troy told me he loves you.'

Tell me you love me . . .

'Let me tell you something,' he said, slowly licking Patsy's stomach. 'You are the most amazing woman . . .'

His hands moved over her thighs. Her body stirred again, despite the fact that they'd been at it like rabbits for the last two hours. She was aware for the first time in her life she wanted more.

For once the slow movement of his fingers and tongue was not her main priority. She wanted him to move up next to her, hold her in his arms, pull her head into his shoulder, wanted them both to sink into the pillows, under the quilt, to be safe and warm, protected from the world.

Last night they'd sat in his car in the dark, under the trees near the PAs office. He was telling her about his morning. She watched the movement of his jaw as he spoke, the shine of his dark eyes, his hand carelessly running through his hair as he laughed and she had longed for something she couldn't quite name. It was a warm, soft night. 'We could walk,' she'd said, wanting to wander along with him holding hands, like a couple.

'Better not!' He'd given a small nervous smile, hand patting her thigh. 'Not here.'

Not here. Not here where he was so well known. Where anyone might spot him. Not in London either where any other illicit couple could sink into anonymity. It had to be in this carefully chosen hotel, or in a dark street away from prying eyes.

And soon he might begin to balk at that too. Already he said he was worried about being followed. Patsy had laughed. 'By who?' But he'd looked troubled. 'I'm not sure. Just a feeling I've had.'

'Come here!' She sat up now, holding out her arms. But he winced as he shifted position.

'Still don't feel right, a sort of pain . . .' His hand went to his ribcage.

'You've just had too much lunch.' Patsy imagined how he would react if she offered to leave Dave. He'd be horrified. Would pull back in alarm – as she had done so many times before when ardent lovers had wanted too much. There was so much for him to lose. Whole career in one move! She slid a leg over his. 'All that rich food. You need a bit of exercise . . .'

Ken was jigging away to the strains of 'A Hard Day's Night', his hands firmly clamped to Stephanie's shoulders. She tried to jig with him.

'This brings it all back,' he shouted in her ear.

She smiled. She wanted to go but they were stuck here till the end. George seemed to be enjoying himself, Hettie was tucking in at the food table, but Stephanie couldn't relax. She was terrified that Troy would come back and she just longed to be home in bed, safe from him, away from Hettie's probing.

'You must have encouraged him,' she'd said accusingly as she loaded her plate. Stephanie had walked away.

Patsy came out of the bathroom and up behind him as he stood by the window looking down into the street. 'More champagne?'

He shook his head. 'No, I still feel . . . keep back!!' He dived onto the bed in the centre of the room, pulling her with him.

'What?' she asked, startled.

'Over there – it's the same young chap I saw earlier. He's trailing me.'

'Are you sure?' Patsy looked doubtful.

'Yes, he was there when I arrived. He probably got a picture of you coming in as well. Oh my chest! Burning . . .'

'Well, he won't know what I was doing here,' she said calmly, though a *frisson* of alarm had run through her.

'I think I saw him the other day too. He might have seen you getting out of my car.'

They were lying down now; she kept her eyes on the ceiling. 'And if he did?' she said carefully.

'Well, they'll splash it everywhere, won't they. Me! Mr Fidelity screwing a married woman. Your husband will probably kick you out. We'd be forced to . . .'

'What?'

He gave a grunt.

'Would it be so terrible?' she asked lightly. 'You might find that new opportunities came along.'

He didn't reply, just made another peculiar noise. She sat up and turned to look at him, afraid she had said too much. His skin was grey – sweat lightly beaded across his forehead and upper lip. He was holding his chest, his eyes crumpled in pain.

270

'What's the matter?' Patsy leant over him as he gave a small groan. 'Oh Christ, what is it?'

He rolled onto his side, arms crossed over his front and shook his head soundlessly. Then he let out a low, strangled cry and clutched at himself. His face had turned from grey to red.

'My – heart . . .' he gasped.

Patsy stared at him aghast. Heart attack! Her own was pumping so hard she felt she might be next. She looked wildly around the room, trying to remember diagrams she'd seen of the recovery position. He was writhing on the bed. Should she give mouth to mouth?

'I'll call an ambulance!' He was doubled up, his hands grasping his body, his breath rasping in and out. He seemed to be shaking his head. Thinking of his job? If he got found in a hotel room with another woman . . .

She looked at his naked body. Imagined the ambulance crew's faces. For a moment she dithered, then his eyes closed.

She grabbed at the telephone.

Samantha sat alone in the sound room drinking Coke. The answering machine in Jed's flat was still switched on and his mobile switched off. He hadn't told her he was going out. But perhaps something had come up. She'd call him again in an hour. She curled into the chair with her magazine and waited for time to pass.

Phone five rang, making her jump. She scanned the cards in front of her, flicking the switch for seventies music and a jumble of middle-aged voices to flood the room.

'Who?' she shouted convincingly above the noise. 'Hold on!' She waved the receiver towards the speakers.

'Anyone seen Barbara?' she yelled in her deepest voice. She laid the receiver down making it clatter as she waited a moment. Then she picked it up again: 'Sorry love, she's here somewhere, Elaine was just talking to her she says. Expect she's in the loo. Shall I get her to call you? Yes we're having a great time. Nearly all the girls managed to get here . . .'

Samantha's fingers moved rapidly across the keypad, calling up Barbara's mobile. There was an anxious squawking at the other end as it was answered. Samantha spoke soothingly to the older woman. 'Just phone him back, say you've had to go into the garden because the noise is so loud. If it gets awkward tell him your battery's running low. Give it a minute and cut him off. He sounded OK as soon as I said you were there.'

She sat back feeling pleased with herself. She did have acting skills. She could cope. But she wished she hadn't told Jed about what went on here. She'd felt ill in the morning as well and he'd been a bit distant since. It wasn't such a bad job after all, she thought uncomfortably, imagining Madeleine's wrath if she knew what Samantha had revealed.

The second phone rang almost immediately. What was that? Oh – tricky one. Calls to her mobile diverted here to be dealt with. Samantha grabbed it, almost forgetting to turn the train noise on.

'Hello?' The male voice at the other end sounded irritated. 'Jean, is that you?' Samantha reached for the little device that generated conversation-stopping crackles on the line and then slammed down the receiver as phone line four burst into life. Samantha felt herself grow hot. Madeleine had said it would be quiet. What was this one? Fund-raising committee? Just a voices tape then. 'Hello?' she said at her plummiest.

But the number flashing up on the computer screen wasn't listed for today.

'Hello?' she repeated cautiously.

'Get Madeleine!' Patsy's voice was shrill. 'For fuck's sake get her now!'

Chapter 24

Stephanie followed Madeleine outside. She wanted to make sure Troy had gone. She wanted some reassuring advice on what to do if he hadn't. She was relieved to find Madeleine alone, smoking a cigarette.

'Hot in there.' She shook the phone in her hand. 'And this bloody thing won't work either. Is yours any good?'

'No.'

'They must have a mast down or something. I'll have to use the club one – better check on that silly girl.'

'OK.' Stephanie would need to phone too. She had to tip Millie off before they left. There'd probably be a signal up the road but Hettie still had her mobile. (She wouldn't own one herself, citing the dangers of radiation and the expense, but was quite happy to commandeer anyone else's on the rare occasions she was separated from her children for more than three minutes.)

'I'll see you later then.' Madeleine disappeared inside.

Stephanie looked at her watch. She could use the club phone and order a taxi for later. The shock of seeing Troy had sobered her up, but she'd still drunk too much to drive. Shame Hettie couldn't get herself back behind the wheel – she'd been on orange juice all night. Then she saw the figure running across the car park and her stomach jolted all over again.

'Oh Stephanie,' Samantha was gasping for breath. 'Where's Madeleine?'

'She's just—' Stephanie half turned but Madeleine, with her usual radar, had reappeared beside them.

'What the hell are you doing here? Who's covering the phones?'

'I had to come – the club was engaged and your mobile's switched off.'

'Of course it isn't. It's the bloody signals. It must have taken you ages to walk here. Go back now!'

'No, I can't.' Samantha looked as if she might cry. 'It's Patsy – she's got a big problem.'

Madeleine marched her away from the open doors of the squash club into the darkness of the car park. 'What?'

Stephanie saw Samantha's chin tremble. 'It's her boy-friend.'

'Yes?' Madeleine gave the girl a small shake. 'What's important enough for you to have left the office and abandoned our clients? To come bursting in here and risk our security. Hey? Tell me!'

Samantha gave a small sob. 'I think he might be dead.'

Stephanie clapped a hand to her mouth.

Madeleine was quite still. 'What?' she said icily.

'She phoned from the hotel and—'

'Not the La Ruche!'

Samantha nodded.

'Shit!' Madeleine's jaw was set.

Samantha's voice broke. 'She said he was having a heart attack.'

'What did you say?'

'I called an ambulance.'

'*What??*'

Stephanie had never seen Madeleine lose her cool before.

'You did what?' She dropped Samantha and began to

run across the car park. 'You silly little idiot. Come on!' She turned back to Stephanie 'You too!'

'But George . . .'

'I need you.'

Back in the office, Madeleine's eyes bore into Samantha as she sat sniffing. 'Luckily for you the hotel assumed it was a hoax. At least you didn't give the bloody room number.'

Samantha blew her nose. 'I didn't know it.'

Stephanie watched the hard line of Madeleine's face and kept remembering the softness of Patsy's when she said she was in love. This was just a problem to Madeleine. Another cock-up to be solved.

'But why couldn't he just go in the ambulance?' she asked her. 'Why are you doing all this?'

Madeleine pulled out another cigarette. 'Because our man is that dickhead Andrew Carlisle, that's why! You know,' she said tartly, 'Andrew of Andrew and we-have-always-been-totally-faithful Harriet on that nauseating programme. Can you imagine the field day the tabloids will have if they find him on top of Patsy!!' She lit up.

Stephanie felt her mouth open.

'I'm pretty sure they're on to them already as it is. What about that joke of a vicar's wife character we had round here the other day? Do they think I'm bloody stupid?'

Stephanie stared at her. She had never seen Madeleine so agitated. She'd driven here like a maniac. Madeleine picked up the phone and stabbed at the keys. 'God knows how long they've had wind of this. God knows what Patsy's told him. She seems to have lost every last brain cell she ever had.'

She slammed the receiver down and pulled the ashtray towards her. 'Bloody engaged now! And it's going to completely screw up relations with the La Ruche – you would not believe who uses that place. If they think PAs is behind a security breach then I'll lose it as a venue and we make a lot of money there.'

Stephanie was shocked. 'Suppose he dies?'

'As long as he doesn't drop this whole operation in the shit I don't much care.' She dialled again.

'That's a dreadful thing . . .' Stephanie was silenced by the curt wave of Madeleine's hand.

'Hannah? Got a medical for you at La Ruche. Might be a coronary.' Madeleine's voice hardened. 'I don't care if you are on call. That's the deal. And if this place gets blown apart we won't be here for you next time you're off duty.'

Stephanie looked at her watch again. It was twenty to twelve. She'd tried to phone George at the squash club but the line was constantly engaged. His mobile would be in weekend mode – switched off and at home.

'What are they all going to think?' she'd asked Madeleine in exasperation, hoping she would be dismissed, but Madeleine was still talking rapidly into the phone, issuing instructions. Whoever Hannah was, she had to revive Patsy's bloke and get him the hell out of the hotel. The whole process appeared to involve a string of other people too. Every now and again Madeleine would bark a name at Stephanie for her to find on the database. As she typed the elaborate code next to the names into another program, phone numbers came up that she had to relay to Madeleine. She was doing it as fast as she could but all stages were password protected and it wasn't quick.

'Come on!' Madeleine's red nails clattered on the desk top. She whipped round as Jo appeared at the door. 'Have we still got an undertaker on the books?'

Jo frowned. 'Think she got divorced.'

'Well, find a nurse. Or that matron of the old people's home – she must know what to do with stiffs.'

Madeleine looked coldly at Stephanie, who had gasped. 'Just in case! We'll try and save him first. And let Jo get on the computer now, she knows what she's doing. Go and make some coffee or something.' Stephanie got up, wondering how you became the sort of person to say 'make it your bloody self'.

'I need to get home.' The club phone was still busy. Her own mobile went straight to divert. Still in Hettie's handbag, no doubt.

'You won't get a cab at this time. I'll drive you in a minute.' The office phone rang again and Madeleine grabbed it. An odd expression crossed her face.

'It's OK. I've got a doctor – she'll be there any minute.'

She listened for a few more seconds, looking troubled as she replaced the receiver. She turned to Jo in disbelief. 'Patsy's crying,' she said.

It was almost 1 a.m. when Madeleine dropped Stephanie off. She seemed tired and dispirited. 'I've never known Patsy like this before,' she said. 'And there wasn't even anything wrong with him. Hannah said it was indigestion and a bloody panic attack!' Madeleine snorted with derision. 'She says it happens all the time – these blokes get a bit of heartburn, convince themselves they're dying and hyperventilate till they pass out. And to think I dragged Hannah out of Intensive Care for that. Looks like Patsy panicked herself.' Madeleine made it sound like something to be deeply ashamed of.

'What am I going to tell George?' Stephanie asked for the third time. The answerphone had been on each time she'd called home. For once, Madeleine seemed to have no ready solution. As far as Stephanie knew, she'd made no attempt to contact Ken. 'Tell him we had a problem at the office,' she said vaguely.

'At night?' Stephanie asked. 'What sort of problem?'

Madeleine stared out through the windscreen. 'I suppose I'm going to have Monica on the phone ranting about her precious god-daughter being out of a job.'

'You were a bit hard on her,' Stephanie said. Madeleine had piled Samantha's bag and jacket into her arms and propelled her out through the door.

'She deserved it!' Madeleine sat up straight, her voice snappy and decisive once more. 'Tell George you're sorry there was no time to let him know but our top client's system crashed. Say we hold back-up files of their data-base and we had to access it for them urgently. Say I'm branching out into disaster recovery – twenty-four-hour.' She laughed. 'Bloody good term for it, eh!'

Stephanie opened the car door and looked at Madeleine. 'I don't think I can work for you any more.'

One of the kitchen lights had been left on. Stephanie's handbag was in the middle of the table, her mobile phone beside it. She grabbed it in alarm but there were no missed calls. One text from Millie. **Hope u ok. Call me.**

She crept up the stairs. The spare room door was shut and then she saw that so was her own. A sense of dread came over her. They never closed the door. Even when there were people staying – even with Hettie and the kids in the house – George would only push it to. Stephanie turned the handle, knowing.

George was lying on his back with his eyes open, staring at the ceiling. He didn't turn his head as she came in.

'Hello.' She sat down on the edge of the bed. 'Did you get my message on the answerphone?' George did not move.

'One of Madeleine's clients – one of the big ones – it was a computer crash or something, we had to get all their info off our computer – you know, back-ups.' She stopped, frightened by his silence. Her stomach was hurting again.

'I know where you've been.' He was still looking at the ceiling.

'I've been with Madeleine – she's just dropped me off.'

George shook his head, his expression one of contempt.

'George, really! I've just got out of her car. Ask her!' she added desperately.

He sat up, looking at her now, seeming almost embarrassed for her. 'He rang,' he said.

'Who?' She didn't know what to say. Nothing had prepared her for this.

'Troy, of course.' George's voice was even, reasonable. 'Your boyfriend.'

'He's not . . .' She was trembling all over, her stomach filled with stabbing pains of anxiety.

George rolled over onto his side, away from her.

'Just go away.'

'How could you?' Moments later, Hettie in her dressing gown filled the kitchen doorway. 'They brought out a beautiful cake for George at midnight, lit candles, sang Happy Birthday and everything.'

Ken had shown her the cake. Courtesy of Mrs P it was a fondant cream creation sporting a lopsided squash racket and ball in lime-green icing with five candles. Mercifully she'd stopped short of a giant prawn peering round one of them.

'George doesn't care about things like that,' Stephanie said, cradling her teacup, sick with shame. She imagined his controlled features as the DJ bellowed his name, as they all burst into song and waited for him to blow out the candles.

God, it was his birthday now. The kids would be getting up in a few hours, bringing him presents and cards.

'It'll be your big one next,' said Hettie spitefully. 'The

Big Four-O. How would you feel if George disappeared off with another woman when you were celebrating?'

'I did not disappear off with anyone,' Stephanie said furiously. 'Except Madeleine. We had a crisis in the office.'

'That's not what Troy's wife thought.'

'What?'

'After your phone kept ringing and there was no-one there when George answered, he phoned the number back. And *she* answered. She'd got his mobile by then. Said Troy had been out for hours and then come in drunk.'

'He wasn't with me.'

'George won't believe that. She knew all about you. Troy had told her everything. Just before he passed out.'

Stephanie put her head in her hands. Christ. Typical! How well she remembered those drunken, remorseful confessionals. 'What did Troy tell her?' *And what did Tanith tell George?*

'I don't know.' Hettie filled the kettle. 'He just went upstairs.'

'Oh God.' Stephanie covered her face with her hands. Tears trickled down her palms. She felt utterly empty.

Hettie was crashing about as usual. Opening cupboards, chinking spoons. 'Life's supposed to begin at forty – looks like you've just finished yours,' she said.

'You don't need to remind me,' said Stephanie tightly. Why was Hettie being so awful? 'I remember that every time I look in the mirror and see my skin.'

'There's nothing wrong with your skin. It's good skin. It's good thirty-nine-year-old skin! Why are you always moaning about your age?'

'Because thirty-nine is nearly forty and forty feels like over-the-hill. I can't handle it. I suppose I could if everything else was right, but it isn't. Remember Clara? She threw that huge lavish party, wore that badge:

Pleased to be Forty. And why wouldn't she be – successful career, a man who adored her and thought she was beautiful . . .'

'For Christ's sake!' The words exploded out of Hettie. 'It seems you've got *two* men who love you and think you're beautiful! What else do you damn well want? Is this what it's all about? Your age?'

'I don't know.'

Maybe it was. Or maybe she just wanted someone to *tell* her they thought her beautiful. Someone to show it. Or perhaps she'd just been chasing her past self. Wanting upstanding breasts and a high-cheeked bottom.

Stephanie felt the tears prickle at the back of her eyes again. 'I suppose – yes – I wanted to be young again.'

Hettie banged her empty coffee mug down on the kitchen tiles. 'Well you can't be!' she said.

Stephanie closed the bedroom door behind her. She hadn't even tried to sleep. George had his eyes closed but she knew he was awake.

'Happy Birthday!' she said quietly.

George gave a bitter sigh.

'I'm going to take Hettie and the children home,' she said. 'And collect Charlotte. Then they'll want to give you your presents.'

He didn't reply.

'Then later can we talk? I need to explain.'

His eyes snapped open and he sat up. 'I've had it all explained,' he said, pushing back the duvet, crossing the room, putting on his dressing gown. 'I've had it all explained to me perfectly.' He swung round, speaking in a high, whining artificial voice. 'How could I ever give you up, Troy? You make my heart sing!'

Christ! She couldn't even remember saying that. How could he have repeated it? God, what else did he say? Her stomach went into a spasm of fear. George was a George she had never seen before, sneering, pointing, voice laced with the worst sort of contempt.

'It's touching, isn't it? Is that what he does for you? Makes your heart sing?'

It seemed – despite George's jabbing finger, the malice in his eyes – a moment for honesty.

'He did,' she confessed, 'but not any more.' Stephanie swallowed. 'It was just a moment of madness. I just wanted – ' she said, her voice breaking, ' – to feel – ' she stopped. She'd been going to repeat 'young again' but it wasn't really that, whatever she'd said downstairs. Suddenly it seemed crucial that George should understand. 'I just wanted to still be me. The me I used to be.'

George slammed his fist against the wardrobe. 'I suppose you've been seeing him for years, haven't you? Got the bills paid, the nice house, the kids, had that useless hippie on the side. Bet you've both been laughing at me, haven't you? Stupid, trusting George. No wonder you don't want to sleep with me. No wonder you're tired. Too busy screwing him all day when I'm at work.'

'No, no.' She was shaking her head. She felt dizzy, sick. 'He just turned up a few weeks ago – his mother died. Troy was upset . . .'

George strode across the room, stopping inches from her face. For a horrible moment she thought he was going to hit her.

'I don't want to hear about his sodding mother,' he spat. 'Or how you comforted him. Go and live with him. Get out of here.'

She was shaking badly. She held onto the edge of the door.

'The children . . .'

'Just get out.'

When Stephanie came onto the landing Charlotte was standing in her bedroom doorway crying.

'Charlotte! What's happened? How did you get back?'

Charlotte looked at her mother in anguish. 'I hate you. Why have you done this? Poor Daddy. It's disgusting.'

'I haven't done anything – it's all a misunderstanding.'

'You've got a boyfriend!' Charlotte's voice rose to a wail. 'I heard you. I heard you both.' She burst into noisy sobs. Stephanie led her back into the room and sat down on the bed beside her, wrapping her arms around her in a way Charlotte hadn't allowed for a long time.

'He's not my boyfriend,' she said, stroking her daughter's hair, filled with a hot shame. 'He's an old friend and it's all got a bit complicated. I'll explain to Daddy when he's calmed down. There's nothing to worry about.' Charlotte still had her head on her shoulder. Her voice was muffled.

'Are you going to get a divorce?' she asked.

'No!' Stephanie squeezed her tighter. 'Of course not. I love Dad, you know I do.' She was trying not to cry herself now. How could she have done this to them? To George who had always looked after her. To her children. 'Where's Toby?' she asked.

'Downstairs watching a video.'

'Did he hear anything?'

'I don't think so.'

'Don't tell him. I don't want him upset too.'

'OK.' Charlotte sniffed. 'I won't. And Mum,' she raised her face as Stephanie kissed the top of her head. 'You won't really go, will you?'

Hettie's bags were in the hall. She was sitting on the sofa, Joshua on her lap, Erica and Toby on the floor at her feet, gazing at the TV screen.

Stephanie bent and kissed Toby's cheek. 'I'll be back soon, darling. Daddy and Charlotte are upstairs.'

He stood up. 'I want to come with you.'

Hettie was silent as they all got into the car. Stephanie

helped strap the children into place, letting Toby sit in the front. He grinned at this breach of the rules. Hettie sniffed.

Nobody spoke much. Hettie had a rather forced exchange with Erica about why Daddy wouldn't be home – lots of emphasis on how hard he worked and how lucky they all were as a result – and flashed eyes at Stephanie in the rearview mirror. There followed a rather desultory game of I-Spy which Erica insisted on winning even though she didn't guess anything right and which Toby studiously ignored. The fifteen-mile journey seemed to take for ever.

When they arrived, Hettie sent Erica indoors. 'Go and show Toby your new Tweenies video.'

Toby did the predicted nose-wrinkle. 'I don't like Tweenies,' he said, 'they're babyish.'

'Just go anyway,' said Hettie testily.

'Please, darling,' Stephanie touched his arm.

'O - K.' He sighed and disappeared down the hall. Hettie heaved Joshua onto her other shoulder and walked back down the path a little way.

'You want to hold on to George.' Hettie's voice was trembling. 'He's a good man.'

Stephanie swallowed. 'Don't you think I realize, Hettie? Don't you think I feel absolutely dreadful? I never meant any of this to happen.'

'That's what they always say,' said Hettie heatedly. 'But that doesn't help those left behind hurting, does it? Doesn't make it any easier to know you're second best – that your partner would rather jump into bed with someone else – anyone else other than you.' She wiped her eyes with the back of her hand. 'Have you any idea how that feels, Steph?'

'Yes, sort of. I can imagine.'

'Well you should do with Troy! He slept with enough other women when he was supposed to be with you!'

284

'He didn't . . .'

'He did. I knew it. Rose knew it.'

'Lucinda a couple of times. He told me.'

'Not just Lucinda. There were others.' Hettie spoke scornfully. 'Why do you think Rose wanted you to throw him out? Just because you had an overdraft? She went round there and found him at it while you were at work. Some girl he'd picked up at a party.' Hettie's voice was shrill now. 'Think about it, Steph – in your bed . . .'

'Stop it!' Steph covered her face with her hands.

'Well you're just as bad as Troy ever was. You, Troy, Jack – selfish all of you.'

'What's Jack done?' Stephanie looked up at Hettie's face which was working in pain.

'Can't you guess? He didn't mean it either. Just a girl at a conference. Too much to drink, not *his* fault, of course.'

Stephanie handed her a tissue. Hettie looked up at the sky, swallowing. 'It just happened, he said. How can something just happen? Things don't just happen – people make them happen. Nothing ever just happens between me and Jack at home.'

Her face streamed with tears and Joshua woke and began to wail. Stephanie gently took the baby from her, rocking him against her while she patted Hettie's arm. 'I'm sorry, I'm so sorry.'

'What's the matter with you?' Toby was suddenly at her side, looking up into her face and she turned it away, afraid to lean down and hug him in case she gave way altogether. She rubbed his hair instead. 'Everything's fine. We're all tired, that's all.'

She walked back up the path when she'd got Toby in the car.

Joshua was still crying. 'He's hungry,' said Hettie.

'What did you do?' Stephanie asked.

'Do? What was there to do? I've got two children. He's my husband. I love him. He's promised it will never

285

happen again. I have to believe that. But . . .' Her eyes were boring into Stephanie's and she felt her face colour. 'However much you mend it, you don't forget.'

Stephanie put an arm around her. For a moment Hettie resisted then leant forward in an awkward embrace. 'What are *you* going to do?'

'I don't know.'

Chapter 25

'Just don't do anything,' Millie said. She put a mug of coffee in front of Stephanie. 'Just sit tight and wait for George to come round. He will. He loves you. He's not going to want to break up the marriage any more than you do.' She indicated the whisky bottle on the kitchen worktop. 'Do you need something stronger?'

'No – I can't think straight as it is.' Stephanie put her hand on her abdomen. 'I feel so ill. I was sick twice this morning.'

'It's the stress.' Millie sat down opposite her. 'Unless, oh my goodness . . .'

Stephanie shuddered. 'No. We only did it a couple of times. Really. I've come on since. Oh God, Millie, I don't know what possessed me.'

'It happens. You don't plan it. I should know.'

Stephanie looked up stricken. 'Millie, I'm so sorry. Hettie still had my mobile and Madeleine was going frantic in the office. I just clean forgot to ring you. What happened when they came in?'

Millie gave a short laugh. 'Luckily we had our clothes back on. Though Alex looked a bit dishevelled and I definitely had a just-been-had air about me! Hettie went straight into Disgusted-of-Bromley mode – said she hadn't realized I was going to be having "visitors" and

George walked straight past. I knew something had happened from his face. He barely looked at us. So what went on?'

'Troy had been leaving messages all night. My phone rang with them as soon as George and Hettie left the club. George took the phone and listened cos he thought it would be from me.' Stephanie bit her lip. 'He erased most of them – still don't know what they said. The only one I heard, Troy sounded really drunk, kept saying he loved me and needed to see me. But God knows what he said in the others.'

'They were probably all like that. What have you told George?'

'Nothing, really. He won't let me speak. His birthday was awful. We went out to lunch but no-one ate anything – not even Charlotte. Now he just walks out of the room when I come in. That's why I wanted to bring Toby with me today – so George would know I wasn't going to see Troy.'

'Have you seen him?'

Stephanie shook her head. 'Sent him a text. Said I needed to be left alone. Told him George was very upset.' She looked at Millie. 'I'm sorry I let you down. Hettie's been pretty upset with me but I'm sure she won't tell anyone about you.'

'It's different for me,' Millie said. 'Patrick and I have gone past the point of no return. When you really fall out of love, I don't think you can get it back.'

'But I want George back. I never thought I'd feel so afraid of losing him. Last night I dreamt we made love. And when I woke for a moment I thought we had and I was so relieved and then I realized the bed was still empty.' Stephanie's voice broke and she leant forward clutching herself. 'God, my stomach is agony.'

Millie squeezed her arm. 'That's because you never stopped loving George deep down. I can't bear Patrick.

Can't bear to look at him, touch him, be touched by him. He's lost all my respect. When that goes . . .' She shook her head. 'I've just got to get my head around doing something about it.'

'Is Alex going to leave his wife?'

'I don't want that responsibility. I still don't know whether we would work. Alex has always been my safety net but I've got to do this without him, to be sure.' Millie lit a cigarette. 'Madeleine said to me a long time ago: never leave your marriage because you're having an affair. Only leave because the marriage wasn't working anyway.'

'Madeleine!' Stephanie put down her mug. 'I don't think she understands a thing about love and need and emotion. How can a marriage work if you're involved with someone else? I should have talked to George – tried to get some of the love back. Not gone running to Troy.'

'I gave it my best shot,' said Millie. 'I did really try.'

'Oh God, I know.' Stephanie took her hand. 'I was talking about myself. But are you really sure it's over?'

'Last night,' said Millie in a low voice, 'last night he—'

She swung round as Ben and Toby appeared in the doorway. 'Can we have some crisps, Mum?' Ben waved his Gameboy at Millie. 'Toby's shown me how to get a really cool TM move. Will you buy *me* Silver Version?'

Millie opened a cupboard, pulled out two packets of cheese and onion. 'Get yourselves a drink too,' she said, distracted.

'My pokémon evolved.' Toby shoved his own game under Stephanie's nose. 'Quilava evolved into Typhlosion and I got the gym badge.'

'What are they talking about?' Millie looked at Stephanie as the two boys disappeared with Cokes.

'What happened last night?'

'Oh it doesn't matter.'

They sat in silence for a moment. Then Millie unbuttoned her shirt. Across the top of her left breast was an angry red patch, already turning blue with bruising.

'I wasn't sure,' said Millie. 'But I am now.'

Chapter 26

The doorbell rang again. Kelly had bounded downstairs and was still barking. Stephanie couldn't get out of bed to look but she knew who it was. He'd sent text after text this morning wanting her to go round when she'd dropped the kids off at school.

It was all she could do to drive home – her stomach was in constant spasm. She'd just made it to the bathroom then collapsed into bed. Kelly had padded after her, lying down on the carpet beside her. Stephanie heard her breathing as she dropped off to sleep.

He'd gone now. Kelly came back into the room, tail swishing, and returned to her sentry position by the bed. Stephanie felt oddly touched. She put down a hand and briefly stroked the dog's head. 'Can you go and collect the children for me?' she asked. Kelly licked her arm.

Millie picked them up. She stood in the bedroom doorway looking worried. 'You look dreadful, Steph.'

'I've got a stomach upset. I feel dreadful.'

'I knew you must be in a pretty bad way,' she said. 'Not like you to have the dog upstairs.'

Stephanie smiled weakly. 'She's been here all day,' she said. 'And I need all the friends I can get at the moment.'

Millie crossed the room and opened a window.

'Things no better?'

'No.' She closed her eyes again.

Rose was sitting on the edge of the bed. She was shaking her head. 'I told you,' she was saying. 'I told you and told you.'

Her words were a spiral. Stephanie lay back, her mind revolving through a swirling mist of pain.

'I've come to see you,' said Rose. She leant over Stephanie. 'You've got to look at me.'

Stephanie opened her eyes. Toby had his face very close to hers. 'When are you getting up, Mum?'

She struggled to see the clock. 'Oh God, sorry – I'll come and do some tea.'

'I think Dad's doing it.' Toby wrinkled his nose apprehensively. 'Are you better yet?'

'I'll be OK in just a minute.' But there was a deep dull aching band around her middle. Her limbs felt heavy. And all the time this sick place deep inside her that wanted normality again. She had to sort this out. Make George listen to her, be calm and cheerful and reassuring for the children. But as she got out of bed she felt her insides go into spasm again and lurched towards the bathroom.

She heard Toby's feet thundering down the stairs. 'Bucket, Dad! Mum's being sick again!'

George stood in the doorway. She was still huddled on the bath mat. 'You'd better go back to bed,' he said heavily.

'What about dinner?'

'I think I can manage to feed the children.'

Stephanie held her stomach, willing herself not to throw up again. 'I don't know what Toby will have. Maybe you could make him beans on toast . . .'

But George was already turning away. 'I'll cope,' he said. 'I'd better get used to it, hadn't I?'

* * *

She dreamt that Toby was crying. He was in a room with smoked glass walls and nobody would let her in to comfort him. 'You must go and find the key,' she said to Charlotte. 'Ask Daddy to find the key.'

But Charlotte kept shaking her head. 'He says you've got it . . .'

She woke with a start. 'I've dropped it somewhere!' she cried out. 'I need to get to Toby!'

'Shhh.' George was standing by the window. 'You were shouting,' he said flatly. All at once the pain swirled back, an intense, drawing pain that made her cry out. 'What's the matter with you?' he asked in the same strange lifeless voice.

'I don't know,' she was crying, holding her stomach. She forced herself into a sitting position. 'I don't know, George.' She got one leg over the side of the bed. She felt that if she stood her insides would fall out of her. The room dissolved into an array of black and white spots and her stomach turned over. 'I'm going to be sick,' she said. And passed out.

It was a doctor she'd never seen before. He pushed a thermometer beneath her tongue and fired questions at George. Charlotte stood in the doorway in her dressing gown. She looked very young and frightened. Stephanie tried to smile at her. The doctor looked tired. George crossed the room, put an arm around Charlotte's shoulders and led her away as the doctor lifted Stephanie's T-shirt, ran fingers across her stomach. 'Is it tender here?' She couldn't tell where it was tender. The pain was everywhere now. 'Here?'

'Aggghhhh!'

'Diarrhoea? Sickness?'

Yes to everything. Both ends. Endlessly. How long? God knows. For ever. Feels like a lifetime ago when I was well and married and normal and had a husband . . .

293

Hospital. The doctor is patting her arm. Need to take a look. Discussions with George on the landing about an ambulance.

'I'll follow when I've woken Toby.' George stands close to her, but still not meeting her eyes.

'Don't wake him,' she says. 'See me in the morning.'

As they lift her onto the stretcher, George touches her arm. 'You'll be all right,' he says.

It's getting light in the street. George and Charlotte watch as the doors close. The pain's an odd thing now. It stretches its deep fingers through her whole body but she almost feels she's floating above it.

You'll be all right, George says. But she doesn't know what he means.

She was lying on something hard. Something heavy on her chest, coming up out of somewhere deep and empty. Her mouth was dry. As she opened her eyes, a face looked down at her.

'Ah, you're awake now.' Face smiling into hers. 'You're in the recovery room. I'm Sukie. I'm here to look after you.'

She'd done something terrible. Forgotten them. Left them there at home for days maybe. 'My children!' Stephanie sat up, panicking, heart pounding. 'My children are all alone . . .'

But even as the nurse was soothing her, telling her she'd been dreaming, she remembered the truth. Knew what had happened. Her hand went to her stomach.

'It was your appendix. All out now.'

A dull ache as she shifted painfully on the narrow trolley. All at once a huge surge of loss and self-pity.

'Not a very big scar. It will fade, you'll hardly notice it.'

Eyes burning. Tears running down her face.

I couldn't care less about the scar. Cut me from one end to the other. I just want my husband back.

294

*   *   *

'Your brother's here!' Sukie smiled at Stephanie as she showed Troy into the room. 'There! Someone to cheer you up a bit.'

Stephanie sat up in alarm. 'What are you doing here? Suppose George . . .' She looked wildly at the door. 'You've got to go.'

He sat on the edge of the bed and her legs shrank back beneath the covers. 'I drove past your house. George's car's still in the drive.'

'He might have left as soon as you'd gone past.'

'I won't stay long.'

She looked at him. His face didn't look soft and sensitive any more. It was as weak and selfish as it had always been.

'I've been going frantic,' he said. 'I went up to the school in the end, asked everyone I saw. One of your friends told me you were in hospital.'

Terrific. Now they all knew.

'I just wanted to say sorry,' he said. 'See if you were OK.'

'No, I'm not OK. George wants a divorce. The children are upset. I feel absolutely terrible. I should never have got involved with you again. You hurt everyone you touch.'

His head snapped back in shock. 'That's not fair, Steph. I love you. You know I love you.'

'Only because you can't have me. Only because it's a challenge. How long before you got bored? How long before you looked for someone new?'

'I wouldn't with you. We're right together. That's why I told Tanith. I knew I had to. When you're out of here we'll—'

'We won't do anything!' Her voice was hoarse. 'Just get back to Norwich and put this whole bloody nightmare behind you. You've got to leave.' She was sobbing

295

now. 'You've got to sell that house and promise me you'll never ever come back. I cannot bear it if you do. I can't live here. The children will have to change schools.'

'We'll talk when you're better . . .'

'No! Leave me alone. Leave me alone.' She thrashed away from him in the bed, chest heaving.

'You heard her!'

George was in the doorway, his mouth a thin line. Stephanie buried her face in her hands. The whole thing was deeply unreal. Where were Charlotte and Toby? George's voice was low with fury: 'Get out and leave my wife in peace.'

She heard Troy leave the room. And knew she had to meet George's eyes. What should she say? Thank you? Sorry? Please, please forgive me?

But when she looked up, he had gone.

Charlotte and Toby looked uncertain as they came slowly into the room. Toby was carrying a card he'd made. Stephanie held out her arms.

'Look!' he showed her, 'here's the doctor with a syringe and there's you being sick on the floor.'

Charlotte nudged him with her foot. 'You're the one who's sick. You should have painted flowers.'

'It's lovely,' Stephanie said, pulling him towards her. 'Come and give me a hug.'

'I was going to get some chocolates,' said Charlotte. 'But Dad said you wouldn't want them.'

Stephanie kissed her and smiled. 'No, I don't think I could manage them yet. Where is Dad?'

'He stayed in the car,' said Toby.

'He's gone to see the doctor,' said Charlotte. She looked at her fingernails. 'I could have eaten them, couldn't I?' She smiled awkwardly.

'You've got your own bathroom.' Toby pulled open the door. 'What's this red button for?'

'Don't touch it! That's in case I need the nurse suddenly.'

'Funny bath. Where are all the other sick people?'

Mercifully not in here to see her crying every five minutes. She'd heard the doctor on the landing talking to George. 'Have you got medical insurance?'

'Of course.'

Of course. Even their insurance had insurance. Once she joked about it. Now she was so glad, so grateful for the quiet and solitude. 'They're in other rooms,' she told Toby. 'Or on the wards,' she added with a twinge of guilt.

'This is private,' Charlotte told him loftily. 'Dad fixed it.'

'How are you getting on?' Stephanie asked. 'Are you doing your homework?'

Charlotte rolled her eyes. 'Yes, Mum!'

'What have you been eating, Toby?'

Toby frowned, thinking. 'Can't remember.'

'Kelly keeps whining,' said Charlotte. 'Dad says she's missing you.'

Stephanie felt a sudden lump in her throat. *Wish Dad was.*

George gave the children money to go to the hospital shop. 'Don't spend it on rubbish,' he said as Toby gleefully pocketed the coins. 'They've been very good,' he said gruffly when they'd disappeared.

'Charlotte says Kelly's been a bit funny.' She sounded stiff and self-conscious.

'Yes, odd isn't it? You can't stand her and she's pining for you.'

Stephanie swallowed. 'It's not her, really. It's not Kelly as an animal I mind. It's just that . . .' She had to say it. If they had any chance at all, it all had to be said. 'I suppose I've been jealous. You give her so much love and affection and interest.' It sounded pathetic.

George looked at her. 'And why do you think that is?' He turned and looked out of the window. 'Who else have I had? You stopped giving me any affection after you'd had Toby.'

'That's not true.'

'It is true, Stephanie. I thought at first it was just because it was a difficult birth and then you were tired because he never slept and – all the other stuff. But it went on and on. You weren't interested in me. And it was lonely. I had nearly five years of that. So yes when Charlotte wanted a dog I was glad. At least Kelly's pleased to see me when I get home. At least I've got a friend.'

'I had a friend once,' said Stephanie, her voice trembling. ' "All the other stuff", you call it. You won't even say it. You never let me talk about it. It happened and it was brushed under the carpet and all the time . . .' her chest was bursting as she tried desperately to stay in control, 'if only I'd done something . . .'

George slammed the flat of his hand down on the windowsill. 'You were always doing things for her,' he shouted. 'You had a small child and a baby and you were exhausted and all you ever did was run round Rose.'

'I didn't . . .'

'You did! She was always in the house, telling you what to do, carrying on about herself. And Hettie too – in and out all the bloody time, bleating on about whether Jack was ever going to marry her. Poor sod should have got out when he could.'

'Rose needed me that day. If I'd gone to see her when she rang . . .'

'If, if, if!' George's voice had risen again. He brought his face close to hers. 'It would have happened anyway. Maybe not that afternoon but sooner or later. You can't always make things better.'

'I could have done if I'd gone myself. If only I hadn't left it to Hettie.'

'It was an accident, damn it. A bloody accident. Hettie can't drive to save her life, you know that.'

He stopped, realizing what he'd said.

'No,' said Stephanie flatly. 'And she couldn't save Rose's either.'

The silence had stretched into minutes.

'So you're still blaming me, are you?' George asked eventually.

Stephanie shifted carefully in the bed. She still felt as though she'd been kicked in the stomach. 'I just wish we'd talked about it. Perhaps then we wouldn't have got so far apart.'

'That wasn't just me. Hettie's tried to talk to you about it lots of times, she told me.'

'I wanted to talk about Rose to *you*.'

'Well you didn't try very hard, did you?'

'You're not very easy to get through to sometimes, George.' Her voice rose in frustration.

'Neither are you!' he snapped back. 'Though I suppose the hippie managed OK.'

At the mention of Troy her anger deflated and gave way to shame. 'This has got nothing to do with him.'

'Hasn't it?'

She watched his unforgiving back as he stalked away.

'Oh dear!' said Sukie half an hour later. 'You are in the wars. But look at these beauties.' She carried a vase crammed with carnations, roses, freesias and small pale lilies. A huge extravagant bunch trailing with tasteful greenery – the sort of flowers Stephanie would once have fallen on with pleasure. Once.

'I don't want them.' Now she scrubbed her face with the hundredth damp ball of tissue. 'Take them away.'

Sukie looked at her reproachfully.

'Whatever for, my love?'

'I don't get on with my brother,' Stephanie sniffed.

Sukie placed the glass vase on the top of the locker. 'You are silly.' She took the flowers in her hands, lovingly plumping them up, adjusting a trailing piece of fern. 'They're not from your brother, sweetheart. They're from your husband.'

Chapter 27

Davina Stacy-Clarke was on the phone when Jed was shown into the enormous office. She did not look up. 'Well fucking sort it then!' she said succinctly and banged the phone down. 'Hi!' she said, looking up at Jed with the gimlet eyes that had frozen out anyone who had ever tried to stand in the way of the editor of the country's biggest-selling and sleaziest tabloid. 'So what have you got?'

Jed swallowed. It had taken him days to get in front of her. He'd phoned and faxed and emailed endlessly, determined to get to the very top with this one and not be fobbed off with someone on the news desk who'd swipe all the glory.

'Andrew Carlisle. He's been having an affair.'

Davina shrugged. 'He's always at it. Can't keep his dick in his trousers for more than five minutes, but he's never been caught. Got any shots of him sucking her feet?'

'Well no, but . . .'

'Anyone claiming he's giving her one?'

'Not . . .'

'Nothing doing then. Unless you got the pictures or some little tart ready to spill the beans, no-one here's gonna give a fuck.'

'But that's just the start,' Jed said hurriedly as Davina appeared to be getting up. 'There's a lot more.' He held a cardboard folder in front of him as reverently as if it were a baby. 'This is something absolutely incredible.'

Davina sat back down. 'Well?'

'This is such a big story – you're not going to believe this operation. Some of the names in here . . .'

Davina lit a cigarette. 'Spit it out,' she said flatly. 'I've got a meeting in five.'

'It's an undercover agency.' Jed could barely contain his excitement. 'Its front is recruitment. But really it's alibis for women having affairs. Quite prominent women.' He looked at her meaningfully. 'It's expensive, so there's going to be some big names here.'

'Have you got any names?' Davina asked sharply.

'They're in code at the moment, my contact inside got fired before she could get the master list, but I'm sure we could—'

'We can't run a story that's not been substantiated.'

'But I know where to look now. If we could just get into the office . . .'

Davina glared. 'Get into the office? I hope you're not suggesting this paper gets involved in anything illegal.'

'If we could get a full list of clients it would be such a story. All those women at it – all being given slick, unshakeable alibis – their husbands not having a clue what's going on.'

'Yes! Thank you.' Davina's hand shot across the desk and took the file. 'I'll look into it.'

'But I'll get the credit,' Jed stammered. 'I'll get the chance to write it up. I've been working on it for weeks. I brought it straight to you as you're the best—'

'Very wise.' She opened the drawer of her desk and dropped the file inside, deftly locking it. 'I'll be in touch.'

Jed stared across the desk. Everything was in that file: the lists, the notes, the photos of Patsy . . .

'This is my story,' he said, as firmly as he could manage. 'I want to be in on it.'

'Yes,' said Davina. 'You will be. If we're able to run it.'

She waited for the door to close on Jed's dejected shoulders before pressing the intercom on her desk. 'Get in here, Suze!'

A tall redhead appeared seconds later. Davina opened her drawer. 'Something for confidential waste. And get Madeleine on the phone. Tell her crisis over and in future, I'll expect my fees waived . . .'

Andrew Carlisle – TV personality of the year, devoted husband and recognized authority on the sanctity of marriage – fiddled uneasily with his gearstick.

'You're one hell of a woman,' he said to Patsy. 'I mean you're just great. It's been really great.'

Patsy turned in the passenger seat to look at him.

'Is that it then?' she asked lightly. 'All over?' She made herself smile brightly. 'You don't want to see me any more?'

'Oh I do, you know I do.' He put a hand on her knee. 'But you know, that business in the hotel – think we'd better let things calm down a little.'

'Thing *have* calmed down. Madeleine dealt with everything. No-one's got a whiff. And anyway, you know what they say about "Any publicity . . ." If the tabloids made a splash, the offers would pour in.'

He looked horrified. 'I couldn't be seen to break up a family,' he said incredulously. 'I'm Mr Fidelity. Harriet and I are a national symbol of commitment.'

'Are she and the producer still . . . ?'

'Oh yes.'

'We'll just have to be very discreet.' Patsy could hear the slightly pleading note that had crept into her voice. 'We'll find another hotel till I get a place of my own.'

'But you've got *children*.'

'They're no trouble,' said Patsy desperately, ignoring his shudder. 'We'd still have lots of fun.' She ran a last-ditch hand up his thigh.

She heard his breath quicken. 'Look,' he said, checking the pavement was clear in his rearview mirror. 'I'll call you Wednesday . . .'

'I don't know what we're going to do about the paperwork now Stephanie's gone.' Madeleine lit a cigarette and looked at Jo. 'Don't know why these admin assistants are all so lily-livered.'

Jo shrugged. 'And we need someone else for the phones.'

'Well we'll just have to manage. Or Patsy can shift her butt for a change – take her mind off love's young dream. I'm not taking on just anyone – not after that Samantha fiasco. Telling her boyfriend indeed! Little cow!'

'Oh, meant to tell you. Monica's booked up for the whole of next week.'

'Good.'

'Says she needs double cover twenty-four seven. I think she's trying to make it up to you.'

'Even better.'

'And she's got a new one on the go.'

Madeleine smiled. 'Excellent.'

'You take it easy!' Sukie watched as Stephanie stepped gingerly into the back of the cab. 'No lifting now!'

Stephanie smiled. 'I won't. Thank you for being so kind.'

'Don't know why you can't wait for your other half.' Sukie shook her head. 'You should be in for another day as it is.'

'I need to go home now.' Stephanie pulled the cab door shut. 'Thank you again.'

She had to go home and find out what was happening.

The thought of yet another day in limbo not knowing if she had a marriage left was too much to bear. Since the flowers she had only seen George with the children. He had been distant and polite – not hostile but not exactly encouraging either. He had stood in the room while Charlotte and Toby chatted, rarely meeting her eyes, and when she'd tried to get the children to disappear by saying 'Why don't you go to the shop while I talk to Daddy?' he'd simply shaken his head and said: 'Leave it till you come home.'

So now she was coming home, unannounced and unexpected at six o'clock, an hour before they thought they were coming to visit. As the taxi wound through the streets, she looked at the people wandering home from offices and shops, bags and briefcases in hand, and she wondered where she would sleep tonight. Had George gone back into the marital bed since she'd been away? Would she be expected to stay in the spare room?

'Can you manage, love?' The driver swung her bag out from the boot. 'I'd better take that for you or I'll have that nurse after me!'

Stephanie smiled as she walked behind him up the path, aware of how bashed-up she still felt. She pressed the money into the driver's hand, her heart in her mouth. As she opened the door she could hear them talking in the kitchen, the chink of cutlery. Toby saw her first.

'Mummy!' He was out of his chair, throwing his arms around her, pressing his head against her middle. She hugged him, trying not to wince.

'Be careful of Mum's stitches.' George looked at her briefly and then back to Toby. 'Sit down now – you haven't finished.'

Charlotte, mouth bulging, mumbled hello and half smiled as Stephanie looked in wonder at the plates on the table. They all contained sausage, mash, gravy and vegetables – even Toby's. She waited expectantly for him to wail his protests but he sat obediently down and loaded his fork.

She sat down herself, rather weakly, on a stool at the breakfast bar. She looked at George who had resumed eating, then back at her son. George met her eyes and raised his eyebrows quizzically. She was never sure afterwards if he gave her an almost imperceptible wink. She still didn't know what would happen but she knew things would never be quite the same again. Nothing was as she knew it. She'd just seen Toby eat peas.

'Dad says do you want a glass of wine?' Charlotte's head poked around the sitting-room door. George was being very solicitous, if from a distance. He'd suggested she rest on the sofa and all evening there had been a stream of offers – via the children – of food and drink, blankets and things to read, plus electronic war games to look at (Toby), the last week of *EastEnders* on tape (Charlotte) and wet tongues to have plastered all over her hand (Kelly).

George himself had stayed in the kitchen; the dog, she noticed, after an initial effusive greeting had stayed with him.

When Charlotte came in to say good night, Stephanie felt apprehensive as she kissed her. Soon they would be alone. She was tired. Some time she would have to broach the subject of where she would be sleeping.

George was at the kitchen table reading the paper. He looked up expressionlessly. 'You should be resting,' he said.

'Are you going to come and sit with me?'

'Do you want me to?'

He brought a bottle of Beaujolais and two glasses. She waited while he poured it then took a deep breath. 'Shall we talk?'

'If you want.'

'I think I need to explain.'

'I don't want to know what happened,' he said. 'I just want to know it won't happen again.'

'Nothing happened,' she said. 'Nothing important.'

She saw the relief on his face and knew she had to keep it that way.

'It was all just a fantasy. We both got . . .'

He took a mouthful of wine. 'Don't give me details – it will only come back and haunt me for ever.'

'OK. But it wasn't really about him at all. It was just lost stuff – you know, old hopes and dreams. It was wanting to feel that, that . . .' she broke off, struggling for the right words. 'How I felt when I was a student – that feeling that everything was full of possibility. I'd lost that. My life was full of the children and the house and being here all day and you stopped me getting a job . . .'

'I never stopped you.'

'Yes you did – you know you did. All that talk about tax and how it wasn't worth it the little I'd earn.'

'I was trying to make you feel better. Trying to say you didn't have to work – I could look after you. You always said that loser never supported you – you always had to do everything. I wanted to be different and when you first talked about work you were so tired already. Toby was a baby, you couldn't cope.'

'I was just low! Like lots of women when they've had a baby. I wanted to be able to cope. I wanted to feel I was the sort of person who could! You reinforced all my negative feelings.'

'I didn't mean to.'

'And now you don't believe in me at all.'

'You've got a job, haven't you?'

'Not any more.'

*　　*　　*

'Seeing Troy again,' she said when George had refilled her glass, 'raked up so much stuff. When I lived with Troy I was in tears all the time.'

'I'm not surprised,' he said drily.

'I kept thinking about Rose. Remembering the sort of things she'd say and do. Hearing her voice in my head. Telling me what I should and shouldn't be doing.'

'She was good at that.'

'If she thought she had some influence over my life it made her feel more in control of her own. She was deeply unhappy, George. When Jason left her that was the last straw. She wanted a husband and children – all the things that I had.'

'But that wasn't your fault.'

'No, but she did a lot for me. Kept me strong till you came along. I think she felt displaced by you.'

'Maybe. But that wasn't healthy – living her life through you.'

'She had depression.'

'OK, but Hettie was her friend too. Is she still beating herself up?'

'She's never driven a car since.'

George crossed the room. Poured more wine into her still almost-full glass.

'Rose wasn't your responsibility,' he said, suddenly sounding venomous. 'You couldn't just drop everything the minute she called.'

Hettie said she'd go. Hettie said that Rose was being dramatic, that she probably wouldn't really do anything. Just a cry for help. But she'd drive over anyway. Except she went too quickly round a corner, too busy worrying about Jack, crashed her car into a wall and wrote it off. And didn't arrive.

When Rose wouldn't answer her phone, George said even if she had taken something they'd soon pump her stomach out. Hettie would be able to deal with it when she got there.

Stephanie never remembered how she ended up on the floor but there she was, the wine glass on its side, the ruby liquid a dark gash seeping into the green carpet. She was beating the floor with her fists, sobbing with rage.

Rose was a nurse. She knew what to do. She put cotton wool soaked in chloroform in a plastic bag and tied it over her head. She'd been dead for hours when they found her.

And then George was beside her with his arms wrapped tightly around her, rocking her back and forth against the rug, stroking her hair and saying over and over again: 'I'm sorry, Steph, I'm so, so sorry. I love you. I love you. *I love you . . .*'

Chapter 28

'All right?' George asked.

Stephanie smiled. 'I'll survive.'

'We'll be off then.' He kissed her as Charlotte heaved an enormous rucksack over her shoulder and waggled her fingers in farewell.

Stephanie looked at the clock.

'Got to be in early,' said Charlotte. She was taller than Stephanie now and looked frighteningly grown-up in her uniform now she was at Holyoake High. 'Need to get a book from the library and finish my homework.'

'See you tonight,' said George. 'Don't work too hard!'

'Just going in to finish that order of buttercup jugs then I'm coming home.'

She saw Millie first. Though she should have guessed from the fact that Toby was giggling beside her.

There they were – the facelift club welcome committee standing in front of the school gate beneath a banner made from what – Stephanie noticed – was clearly one of her old sheets, crumpled from what must have been its journey in Charlotte's rucksack but emblazoned with red gloss for all the world to see.

'I'm glad I'd already admitted it,' said Stephanie wryly

looking at the foot-high 'FORTY' against her name. 'No secrets from you lot.'

Millie winked at her. 'Talking of which . . .' she murmured.

Stephanie bent to kiss Toby, who was still laughing. 'Have a lovely day, see you later.'

'What are you doing tonight?' Jacqui said, thrusting a card into Stephanie's hands as Toby ran off. 'Where's he taking you?'

'Tonight,' said Stephanie, 'we're all eating at home – George is cooking – but tomorrow we're dropping the children at his mother's and going away for the weekend.'

'Four-poster and champagne in bed?' Jacqui grinned.

'Sounds wonderful,' said Sue.

'You want to get down to Amanda's new shop,' said Millie. She ran her hands down her sides and wiggled her hips. 'She's got some very sexy little numbers in there, I can tell you.'

Stephanie smiled.

'Bought something for Alex there for his birthday. I opened the front door wearing it . . .' Millie gave a peal of laughter.

'Haven't you let that poor bloke move in yet?' Jacqui asked. Millie shook her head. 'Happy as I am,' she said. 'I like living on my own with Ben. Much better to have a drop-in lover.' She winked again. 'More flexible.'

'You sound like Patsy,' said Stephanie.

'I've got something to tell you about her.' Millie put a finger to her lips.

'Doesn't Alex's wife wonder where he's disappearing to all the time?' Jacqui persisted.

'Oh I'm pretty sure she knows. Think it suits her. She's taken up bird-watching. Some funny bloke in an anorak keeps calling for her to go and watch the lesser-spotted dick-head or something. It's quite obvious what he's got

311

his sights on but Alex says all he'll get is the feathered variety because Marion went off sex years ago.' She laughed. 'You know what men are!'

'Look out!' said Sue, suddenly.

'Oh save us.' Jacqui wrapped her scarf more tightly round her throat. 'I'm off – gotta get to work.'

'Have you just got a minute, ladies?' Deirdre thrust the clipboard into Jacqui's path. 'Only a week to go till our festive extravaganza!'

'Can't wait,' said Millie, glowing with sincerity.

'Now,' Deirdre consulted her list. 'We have the most beautiful giraffe . . .'

'No!' said Stephanie, so firmly that Sue jumped. 'I am not doing the name thing.'

Deirdre frowned. 'Of course you're not, dear. You're plate-painting with the children. Can't have all that talent go to waste.' She put a tick on her sheet.

'Mrs Cartwright will look after Rodney, I'm sure.' She fixed Millie with her most piercing stare.

'Rodney?' enquired Millie, straight-faced.

'Well obviously the head will pick out the final name,' said Deirdre confidentially, 'but he looks like a Rodney to me.'

'So,' said Millie, putting her arm through Stephanie's when they'd escaped Deirdre and the others had said goodbye, 'got time for a coffee and a birthday doughnut?'

Stephanie looked at her watch. 'Later on? Told Paula I'd get a batch of cream jugs finished. Special order.'

'I bought my mum a set of your daisy teacups. She loved them. You should go out on your own.'

Stephanie smiled. 'That's what George says but it's not really me, being the big businesswoman. I'm not Madeleine.'

312

'That's what I was going to tell you.' Millie lowered her voice as they walked back along the pavement. 'She's shut up the office.'

'No!'

'Yep! And you'll never guess why. Ken's gone off with someone else and Madeleine is devastated.'

'You're joking!'

'I'm not. *And* – ' said Millie, clearly enjoying herself, 'you will never guess in a million years who he has gone off with.'

Stephanie shook her head.

'Do you remember that Margaret who was at Amanda's first party. Draggy Maggie. The one who stomped out in a huff and said I should be ashamed?'

Stephanie frowned. 'Yeah, vaguely.'

'Well it's her. Apparently she got a job at Ken's car place – doing the invoices or something – and Madeleine turned up there unexpectedly one day and found them in a clinch across his desk. Ken admitted everything – said he'd been in love with her for months and wanted to marry her!'

'My God!' said Stephanie, agog.

'And apparently she still looks just as dreary and it turns out Ken likes her that way and he never could stand how much make-up Madeleine plastered all over her face!'

'How do you know all this?'

'Patsy told me. She's furious because Madeleine's sitting at home crying and won't do anything with PAs. I think Patsy needs the money since Dave's being so difficult about the divorce.'

'But Andrew Carlisle must be loaded.'

'He is but he won't commit to her, will he? Keeps saying his career will be in ruins. Still, she seems to think his shagging prowess is worth it.'

'God,' said Stephanie again, her imagination still

313

struggling to provide a picture of Madeleine in tears. 'George said he hadn't seen Ken at the club for a while.'

'Well now you know why!' They had reached Stephanie's car. 'Come round later, yes?' Millie hugged her. 'Happy Birthday, Steph!'

Stephanie pulled out her keys. Kelly's head immediately shot out of the back window, tongue flapping. Her breath steamed in the cold air. 'Come on, then,' Steph said. 'Very, very quick walk.'

She parked at the end of the street. Clipped Kelly's lead on and wandered along the row of houses until she got to Cora's. She would always think of it as hers, whoever lived there.

The front door was painted dark green and already a holly wreath hung above the new brass knocker. They'd put up different curtains too. She'd always kept away but today it seemed right to come and see – to lay some ghosts before her Life Began. She smiled to herself. Forty wasn't so horrific. She hadn't woken to find her wrinkles deepened tenfold or her breasts and bottom hitting the floor. She'd spent so long dreading it, the reality could never be as dire as she'd feared.

She hoped someone would come out. Just so she could look and feel . . . what would she feel? It all seemed like a dream now. She walked on past, hoping to get a glimpse of something that would tell her. She turned by the postbox, walking slowly back up towards the house, willing someone to appear as they passed. Still her heart jerked painfully as the door suddenly opened. For a moment she pulled at Kelly and hurried away across the road. Then she stopped on the pavement, took a deep breath and looked back.

The man was young. He was carefully manoeuvring a buggy up the narrow path, leaning over it to open the wrought iron gate, squeezing through carefully, checking the wheels either side. On the pavement, he crouched down, adjusted the blue woolly hat on the head of the toddler. 'Come on then, mate,' she heard him say and then he straightened, turned the buggy around and began to push it away in the opposite direction. She watched him go.

'Come on!' She walked on herself, Kelly trotting beside her. 'Back to the car.'

So he'd gone. Was back in Norwich or somewhere else. With Tanith and the children – or someone else. Stephanie breathed deeply. The air was so cold it made her chest tingle. She knew in that instant that this time she really would never see Troy again.

And then her phone beeped. She pulled it from her pocket, feeling shaky. Of course he would remember it was her birthday. Know it was a big one. Today would be the day he'd get back in touch, express some last sorrow, regret, apology.

Message received.

And wouldn't it just be the way – that he'd send a text just as she was thinking about him. That old telepathy they'd always seemed to have, at work still . . .

She pulled off her gloves and pressed the keys, heart thumping.

Have gd day. will always love U. always did x

She smiled, opened the car door to let Kelly back in. What had Troy always said – it was meant to be? That they were brought back together for a reason?

The cold bit at her fingertips as she started to press out her answer but she could feel the heat of Kelly's breath coming through the open door. After the first three words she stopped. What could she say that would express it?

That sense of things lost and rediscovered. How true, deep feelings do endure however much they may get blurred or blunted along the way. So much to be said. But in a text message?

Kelly gave a whine and suddenly she decided. Sometimes it was what you didn't say. Sometimes it was best to keep it simple. Avoid confusion.

I love u 2 x

She got in the car and pressed the send button. Winging the message away into the ether – and back to George.

THE END

RAISING THE ROOF
by Jane Wenham-Jones

Cari's jobless and has an overdraft the size of the national debt. She'll be homeless too if she can't come up with some cash to buy out Martin, her ex-husband – he who cut up her Barclaycard before he moved in with another woman. No wonder she's desperate enough to fall for dodgy entrepreneur Nigel's get-rich-quick scheme, buying the worst house in town to convert into flats. All she has to do – he tells her – is get a bank loan and the money will roll in! But it doesn't work out quite like that . . .

Cari's lumbered with a bank manager on the warpath, a sister on the verge of a nervous breakdown, a friend who's permanently pregnant, a friend who may be pregnant – but not by the right man – and a tenant who won't pay the rent. It's not long before there are bailiffs at the front door and Cari finds herself in the back of a police van. And Nigel's mysteriously disappeared. There *is* a knight in shining armour on the horizon, but naturally he's married to someone else.

Whatever happened to Cari's wish list? Make some money, lose some weight, find someone to have a grand passion with, and become so rich and successful that Martin is consumed with jealousy. Will any of them ever come true?

'Thoroughly enjoyable, moving and full of deft, sparky humour'
Jill Mansell

A Bantam Paperback
0 553 81372 2

JULIA GETS A LIFE
by Lynne Barrett-Lee

Forget all that stuff about finding the inner child; it's sexual healing Julia Potter is after when husband Richard strays from the marital bed. The one he's been playing in belongs to Rhiannon (North Cardiff single mum, siren and witch). He's sorry, or so reads his Post-it apology, but, as he says, 'It's so hard being a man . . .'

But Julia's not ready to forgive or take up handicrafts quite yet. Re-styled, re-vamped and re-acquainted with hair gel, her new mission statement is 'Up'. Unfortunate, then, that where sex is concerned, the only 'up' she can manage is up the wrong tree.

But at least Julia's photographic career is back in focus. And it isn't long before she's swapping her Teletubbies and tripod at Cardiff's Time of Your Life Photo Studio for the slinkier lines of a low-slung black Pentax – the better to zoom in on the more mature torsos of Kite, Britain's megastar number one band. But while Julia's finding out who put the 'Mmmm . . .' into mega, has her marriage to Richard gone into freefall?

'A fantastic book that gets you hooked from the first page'
New Woman

'I absolutely loved it – hurray for Julia! This is funny, original, well-written and unguessable – I had no idea how it would end. It also has the very best closing paragraph I've read in years. Completely wonderful, dazzlingly entertaining, unputdownable'
Jill Mansell

A Bantam Paperback
0 553 81304 8

BACK AFTER THE BREAK
by Anita Notaro

Ever had your heart blown to smithereens? Ever wondered if happy ever after wasn't the greatest cliché of them all?

Lindsay Davidson is not your usual angst-ridden thirty-something. She's struggled and has finally learned how to fly. Her life is sussed. She's just about to marry Paul Hayes – think Johnny Depp meets Colin Firth – when a phone call rips her life apart. Cue bucketloads of tears and self-doubt, giving Lindsay very little to smile about until she lands her dream job.

Her new life in television is nothing if not exciting, with as much drama off-screen. Lindsay makes some famous friends and a few enemies in a world where sex and champagne go hand in hand with scandal and rumour. Meanwhile, Paul has realized his mistake and makes a play to get her back . . .

'Fresh, bubbly and hugely entertaining'
Patricia Scanlan

A Bantam Paperback
0 553 81477 X

A SELECTED LIST OF FINE NOVELS
AVAILABLE FROM BANTAM BOOKS

81305 6	VIRTUAL STRANGERS	Lynne Barrett-Lee	£5.99
81304 8	JULIA GETS A LIFE	Lynne Barrett-Lee	£5.99
50630 7	DARK ANGEL	Sally Beauman	£6.99
50631 5	DESTINY	Sally Beauman	£6.99
50326 X	SEXTET	Sally Beauman	£6.99
81276 9	SUMMERTIME	Charlotte Bingham	£5.99
81387 0	DISTANT MUSIC	Charlotte Bingham	£5.99
81277 7	THE CHESTNUT TREE	Charlotte Bingham	£5.99
40614 0	THE DAFFODIL SEA	Emma Blair	£5.99
40372 9	THE WATER MEADOWS	Emma Blair	£5.99
81256 4	THE MAGDALEN	Marita Conlon-McKenna	£5.99
81331 5	PROMISED LAND	Marita Conlon-McKenna	£5.99
81394 3	MIRACLE WOMAN	Marita Conlon-McKenna	£5.99
81261 0	DANNY BOY	Jo-Ann Godwin	£6.99
81333 1	FAR FROM THE TREE	Deberry Grant	£5.99
50556 4	TRYIN' TO SLEEP IN THE BED YOU MADE	Deberry Grant	£5.99
81219 X	ON MYSTIC LAKE	Kristin Hannah	£5.99
81396 X	SUMMER ISLAND	Kristin Hannah	£5.99
50486 X	MIRAGE	Soheir Khashoggi	£6.99
81186 X	NADIIA'S SONG	Soheir Khashoggi	£6.99
40730 9	LOVERS	Judith Krantz	£5.99
17505 X	SCRUPLES TWO	Judith Krantz	£5.99
40732 5	THE JEWELS OF TESSA KENT	Judith Krantz	£6.99
81337 4	THE ICE CHILD	Elizabeth McGregor	£5.99
81477 X	BACK AFTER THE BREAK	Anita Notaro	£5.99
40941 7	MIRROR, MIRROR	Patricia Scanlan	£5.99
40943 3	CITY GIRL	Patricia Scanlan	£6.99
81292 0	FRANCESCA'S PARTY	Patricia Scanlan	£5.99
81299 8	GOING DOWN	Kate Thompson	£5.99
81298 X	THE BLUE HOUR	Kate Thompson	£5.99
81431 1	STRIKING POSES	Kate Thompson	£5.99
81372 2	RAISING THE ROOF	Jane Wenham-Jones	£6.99